# MURDER AT SUNRISE LAKE

## THE CARPATHIAN NOVELS

## ANTHOLOGIES

## SPECIALS

# MURDER AT SUNRISE LAKE

###### CHRISTINE FEEHAN

BERKLEY
New York

MYS
FEE

BERKLEY
An imprint of Penguin Random House LLC
penguinrandomhouse.com

Copyright © 2021 by Christine Feehan
Penguin Random House supports copyright. Copyright fuels creativity,
encourages diverse voices, promotes free speech, and creates a vibrant
culture. Thank you for buying an authorized edition of this book and for
complying with copyright laws by not reproducing, scanning, or
distributing any part of it in any form without permission. You are
supporting writers and allowing Penguin Random House to continue to
publish books for every reader.

BERKLEY and the BERKLEY & B colophon are registered trademarks
of Penguin Random House LLC.

Library of Congress Cataloging-in-Publication Data

Names: Feehan, Christine, author.
Title: Murder at Sunrise Lake / Christine Feehan.
Description: New York : Berkley, [2021]
Identifiers: LCCN 2021006574 (print) | LCCN 2021006575 (ebook) |
ISBN 9780593333143 (hardcover) | ISBN 9780593333167 (ebook)
Subjects: GSAFD: Mystery fiction. | Suspense fiction.
Classification: LCC PS3606.E36 M85 2021 (print) |
LCC PS3606.E36 (ebook) | DDC 813/.6—dc23
LC record available at https://lccn.loc.gov/2021006574
LC ebook record available at https://lccn.loc.gov/2021006575

Printed in the United States of America
1st Printing

*For Abbie Thomason,*

*a true inspiration for this story.*

*Happy Birthday!*

# FOR MY READERS

Be sure to go to christinefeehan.com/members/ to sign up for my PRIVATE book announcement list and download the free ebook of *Dark Desserts*, a collection of yummy desserts. Join my community and get firsthand news, enter the book discussions, ask your questions and chat with me. Please feel free to email me at Christine@christinefeehan.com. I would love to hear from you.

# ACKNOWLEDGMENTS

As with any book, there are so many people to thank. Brian, for competing with me during power hours. Domini, for always editing, no matter how many times I ask her to go over the same book before we send it for additional editing. Thank you to Mehriban (Mary) Schulz for your help, invaluable information and inspiration in this story as well. Denise, for staying up nights and letting me write while she does the brunt of the business I never want to do. Thanks to Denise and Abbie for all the additional information I needed for the locations, and the sheriff and deputies who were willing to talk to me about various crimes scenes. I can't thank all of you enough.

I combined real and fictional locations in this book. There is no town of Knightly or Twin Devils to climb. I also need to thank Mr. Knightly, the courageous rooster who guards his ladies night and day from all predators, for the inspiration for the name of my town.

I have a great love of the Eastern Sierras. It's a beautiful place unlike any other.

# MURDER AT SUNRISE LAKE

# CHAPTER ONE

*Mommy, Daddy's doing the bad thing again.*

The child's voice very clearly said the words she'd said to her mother when she was four years old. When she was five. When she was seven.

Stella Harrison knew she was dreaming, but she still couldn't fight her way to the surface. This was the fifth night in a row she'd had the dream, and the camera had widened the lens just a little more, as it had every night, so she saw additional pieces of the hideous nightmare she couldn't stop. The man fishing. He wore denim bibbed overalls tucked into high olive-colored waders. A blue cap was pulled low over his eyes so she couldn't see his face. There were boulders among the heavy reeds and plants that grew thick along the shore, creeping out into the lake. He'd made his way through the boulders to get out from under the shade of several trees.

She tried to warn him. Yelling. Calling out. *Don't cast. Don't do it.* Every night she saw his line go into the same spot. That little darker area that rippled in rings like a little round pool, so inviting. The fisherman always did the same exact thing, like a programmed robot. Stepping forward, casting, the lure hitting perfectly, sinking into the middle of that inky spot, dropping beneath the water into the depths below.

The camera switched then and she could see beneath the water. It should have been tranquil. Peaceful. Fish swimming. Not the man in the wet suit, waiting for that hook, waiting to tug and enter into some kind of terrible game with the fisherman above the surface. The fight for the fish became a real life-and-death battle, with the fisherman lured farther and farther from the safety of the shore and into the reeds and rocks—closer to the threat that lurked beneath the water.

The mythical fish appeared to be fighting. He seemed big, and well worth the exhausting battle. The fisherman paid less and less attention to his surroundings as he reeled the fish nearer to him and realized he was close to winning his prize.

Without warning, the killer beneath the water rose up right in front of the unsuspecting fisherman, slamming him backward so that his waders couldn't find traction on the muddy floor of the lake. The fisherman hit his head hard on the boulder behind him and went down. Immediately the killer caught his legs and yanked hard, dragging him under the water and holding him there while the fisherman thrashed and fought, weak from the vicious blow to his head from the boulder.

Stella could only watch, horrified, as the killer calmly finished the scene by dragging the body to the surface for just a few moments so he could pull the bottom of the wader along a boulder. The killer then pulled the fisherman back into the water and tangled him in his own fishing line just below the waterline in the reeds and plants close to the shore. The killer calmly swam off as if nothing had happened.

The lens of the camera snapped shut and everything went black.

———————

STELLA WOKE FIGHTING a tangle of sheets, sweat dripping, hair damp. She sat up abruptly, pressing the heels of her hands to her eyes. Rubbing, scrubbing her palms down her face over and over. Trying to erase the nightmare. Not again. It had been years. *Years.* She'd made a new life for herself. New friends. A place. A home.

Now the nightmare was back and recurring. This was the fifth time she'd had it. *Five* times in a row. It wasn't like she lived in a big city. Usually if murder was happening, everyone would know, especially in a small town. But this killer was brilliant. He was absolutely brilliant and that was why he was going to get away with it—unless she brought attention to the murders. Even then, she wasn't certain he would get caught.

She hadn't realized she was rocking herself back and forth, trying to self-soothe. She forced herself to stop. She hadn't done that in years either. All those terrible habits she had developed as a child, that came back as a teen, she'd managed to overcome. Now she found they were sneaking back into her life.

There was no going back to sleep even though it was still dark outside. She'd planned to sleep in. She had few days off even though the season was winding down. She owned the Sunrise Lake Resort and had for several years, turning it around from a dismal, failing business to one that not only made large profits but helped out the local businesses as well. She loved the resort, loved everything about it, even the hard work. Especially that. She thrived on solving problems, and those problems changed hourly, keeping her mind constantly active. She needed that, and first managing, and then owning, Sunrise Lake provided it.

When the owner had decided it was time to retire four years earlier, he sold the resort to her. They'd kept the transaction quiet and he continued to stay the first year as if he owned it. Over time, his visits became less and less frequent. She renovated the main house but kept a special cabin for him so he had a place whenever he came back.

The property was beautiful, high in the mountains surrounding a good portion of Sunrise Lake. Knightly, the nearest town, was located an hour's drive below on a fairly winding highway. The town was small, but that just made the community close-knit.

Stella had made good friends there. She liked living in the backcountry. She felt grounded, connected, alive there. There were all kinds of things to do, from skiing to backpacking to climbing. She fit there. She wasn't throwing it all away on a few nightmares. That would be so foolish. It was just that the nightmares were so vivid, and now they were recurring, becoming more detailed.

It wasn't like there was even a body—yet. She shivered. There was going to be. She knew it. She just knew there would be. Somewhere, a fisherman was going to be murdered in the next two days. There would be no way to prove that he was murdered. She had to stop thinking about it or she was going to go insane.

She rolled out of bed and headed straight for her shower. She had overseen the renovations to the main house herself, paying particular attention to the bathroom and kitchen. She loved to cook, and more than anything, after a long day of work, she wanted to know she had plenty of hot water for showers and baths. Her spacious bathroom was a work of art.

The standalone tub was deep, and the shower larger. She liked space in her shower and lots of jets coming at her from all sides since she was often sore from the work she did, or from climbing, skiing, backpacking or any of the other outdoor activities she chose to do. Even dancing with her friends sometimes went on all night. Her shower was perfect for her.

She'd designed the renovations of the main house for two people, although she didn't believe she would ever have a significant other in her life. She was too closed off. She didn't share her past with anyone, not even her closest friends. She didn't really date. The minute anyone started to get too close, she backed off.

The hot water poured over her as she washed her thick blonde hair. Her hair was the one thing she was a little vain about. She didn't wear it down often, but it was almost silver in color, thanks to her Finnish grandparents on her mother's side. She had inherited that light, light hair color from them, along with her crystal-blue eyes. The thickness of her hair and the darker lashes were a gift from her father's side of the family. He was originally from Argentina. Her mother had met him in college in San Diego, where both had attended school. Her father was from a wealthy Argentinian family. Between her two parents, she had been lucky to get amazing genetics.

The hot water helped to dispel the last of the nightmare and the bile in her stomach. Unfortunately, uneasiness persisted. She just wasn't certain what to do. She'd had those dreams only twice before, and both times reality had ended up being worse than her nightmares. Sighing, she squeezed as much water out of her hair as possible before winding a towel around the mass, and then dried her body off slowly with a warm towel.

Dressing in her favorite pair of jeans and a comfortable tee, she pulled on a sweater and her boots before braiding her hair. She didn't dry it if she could help it, and since she rarely wore makeup or dressed up when she actually had a day off, she was ready to go in minutes.

"Bailey, I can't believe you're still sleeping. Get up, you lazy animal." She put her hands on her hips and tried to look stern as she regarded the large Airedale still curled up in his dog bed right beside her bed.

Bailey's eyes opened and he looked at her and then around the room, noting the darkness, as if to say she was out of her mind for getting up so early. Heaving a sigh, the dog got to his feet and followed her through the spacious house to the front door. On the porch, she hesitated at the door. She had stopped locking her door or setting the alarm some time ago, but lately, that crawling feeling down her spine was back. The churning in her stomach started all over again. Bailey waited patiently for her to make up her mind.

Stella knew it was ridiculous to stand in front of her door like a loon. She made decisions all the time. It was just that giving in to her fears was like going backward, and she'd promised herself she would never do that. She stood there indecisively, staring at the thick, carved door for another full minute before making up her mind.

Locking the door, she set the alarm, furious with herself that she'd given in to the nightmares and unrelenting terror that could consume her when she was asleep. Fear crept up on her unawares, and slowly but surely took over until she was caught up in things best left alone. If she was going to actually acknowledge that a murder was going to take place in her beloved Sierras, no one was going to help with investigations this time. The killer would make it look like an accident. She didn't have dreams unless the murderer was a serial killer, which meant he would kill again. Accidents happened all the time in the Sierras.

There would be no gossip, no whispers or rumors. Before, she'd hated that, the way everywhere she went, murder had been the topic of conversation. Now, if she wanted to stop a killer, she would have to ask the right questions herself. Several of her friends were involved with Search and Rescue. She knew the medical examiner. Maybe she could figure out a reason to ask questions that would make sense and at the same time raise suspicion that the death wasn't an accident.

Stella deliberately avoided the marina and walked in the dark to reach the family pier. This dock was not one the original owners drove their boat to—they used the marina's piers for that. This one was private, one to enjoy the sunrises and sunsets, just as she was doing now. The dock had been positioned perfectly to catch the beauty of the mountains mirrored in the lake as the sun rose or set. She never got tired of the view.

She was so familiar with the layout of the grounds that she barely needed the small penlight as she maneuvered the narrow path that took her away from the main buildings, the small grocery store, the bait shop, the collection of cabins and the play areas designated for children and game areas for adults.

The trail took her behind the campsites and RV sites to an even narrower path that led through a pile of boulders and into a heavily forested area. Once through the trees, she was back to the shoreline. It seemed like a ridiculous place to put a pier, but she liked the peace when she needed it most—like now. Tourists didn't know the way to reach the pier, and that meant precious solitude when she had a few hours—or a day to herself.

Fall had arrived, and with it the glorious colors that only the Eastern Sierras could cloak her with. She loved every season in the Sierras, but fall was definitely a favorite. The cooler weather after the summer heat was always welcome. There was still fishing, and tourists were still coming, but things were slowing down so she could take a breath. Climbing was still a possibility, and she loved climbing.

Then there was just the sheer beauty of the blazing reds, all the various shades, from crimson to a flat, almost purple-red on the leaves of many of the trees. The oranges were the same, all the varying shades. She hadn't known there were so many shades, subtle to brilliant orange, golds and yellows, the colors vying for attention even among the varying greens, until she came to the Eastern Sierras.

The mountains rose above the lake; forests of trees pressed together so tightly they seemed impenetrable from a distance. The mountains stretched for miles, canyons and rivers, amazing forests and scarred, beautiful rock found nowhere else. This was the place of legends, and she had come to love it and the ever-changing landscape.

Stella sat on the end of the thick planks making up the pier and stared out over the water of the icy lake. Fed by the high mountain rivers and snowpack, Sunrise Lake was a huge bowl of deep sapphire-colored water. A light breeze ruffled the surface, but for the most part, the water gleamed like glass. Sometimes the incomparable beauty of this place stole her breath. It didn't seem to matter what time of year it was, the lake and surrounding mountains always had such elegance and majesty to them.

Bailey curled up beside her, close, the way he always did when she sat on the end of the pier. He went right back to sleep, never knowing how long she planned to sit, waiting for the sun to come up. She wished Bailey could talk so she could at least have someone to sound out important things with—like murder—but when she'd tried, the dog gave her a look like she'd lost her mind and shoved his face in her lap, inviting her to scratch his ears. Taking advantage. That was her beloved Bailey.

There was no warning. A hand touched her shoulder and she

nearly threw herself forward off the dock into the lake. Bailey didn't even look up or make a sound. The hand caught her in a firm grip before she could tumble off the pier. She turned her head to glare up at the man towering over her. Sam Rossi was one of those men who could walk in absolute silence. Sometimes, like now, he freaked her out. He was too rough to call gorgeous, with his chiseled masculine features, all angles and planes. His jaw was always covered in a dark shadow that never was a beard, yet never was shaved. He rarely smiled, if ever, and when he did, that smile never quite reached his arctic-cold eyes.

He had a body on him. Wide shoulders. Thick chest. Lots of muscle. He was strong. She knew because she employed him as a handyman and he had to do all sorts of jobs that required unbelievable strength. He had to have knowledge of boats, carpentry, fishing, climbing and most outdoor activities, and so far, he hadn't let her down once.

He had scars. Lots of them. He took his shirt off when it was hot as hell and he had to work outside. Not so much when there were others around, usually only her, or when he was a good distance from others, but she'd seen the scars, and those scars weren't pretty. They weren't the kinds of scars one acquired in a car accident. It looked like the skin had been flayed from his back. He'd been shot more than once. He had a few knife scars, for certain. She hadn't looked closely. She'd made it a point not to stare, although she'd wanted to. She'd never asked and he'd never volunteered an explanation.

"Quit sneaking up on me," she snapped irritably as she reached for the coffee he had in his other hand, clearly meant for her.

He pulled the to-go mug out of reach and sat down, Bailey between them, ignoring her outstretched hand.

"Sam." She practically growled his name. He couldn't bring the aroma of her favorite brew and then withhold it.

He quirked an eyebrow at her. Evidently, he thought he could. He set the mug on the opposite side of his body so there was no way she could lunge over the dog and grab it. Ignoring her, Sam calmly drank from his mug and looked out over the lake. Bailey didn't even help her by biting him. Or lifting his head and growling.

"Did you come out here just to annoy me?" Stella demanded.

He didn't answer. She knew he could keep the silent treatment up forever. It was like his *annoying* nickname for her. He called her *Satine* in that silly voice—*Satine* from the lead character in the movie *Moulin Rouge!* Well, not that he had a silly voice exactly; he had a low, mesmerizing, sexy-as-hell voice. Fortunately, he didn't call her *Satine* in front of anyone else. He didn't talk much, so it never came up when her friends were around.

She was not one to be embarrassed by much, not even when she was caught in a ridiculous situation, but because she harbored a slight crush on Sam, she found things she normally would laugh at nearly humiliating.

She loved the movie *Moulin Rouge!* Loved it. It was her go-to movie when she was in a funk and wanted a pity party. She didn't have them often, but when she did, she played that movie and cried her eyes out. When she wanted to watch something that made her heart sing, she played *Moulin Rouge!* and ate popcorn and cried and laughed.

Stella didn't even know how it happened that Sam had come in while she was having a pity party, but he had. He sat down and watched the movie with her. After that, he'd joined her more than once and seemed to watch her more than the movie. As usual, he didn't say anything, he just shook his head as if she were a little nutty and walked out afterward. She didn't even know if he liked the movie, but if he didn't, he had no soul, which she shouted after him. He didn't even turn around.

She knew every song by heart, and every single morning, when she did her exercises, she played the songs, sang to them and danced. At night she did her fitness routine to them and did a little burlesque show. Naturally, Sam had walked in just as she was kicking her leg over a chair and she didn't quite make it and landed on her butt. That was the first time.

She loved to do aerial silks as a form of exercise. Because the house was two stories and open, she had her own rigging in her home and practiced some nights. Of course, when she'd gotten tangled for a moment and was upside down, desperately trying to get her foot unlocked from the silks, music blaring, he had walked in.

The third time she was doing a very cool and sexy (if she didn't say so herself) booty shake to the floor and back up again. Naturally, he would be leaning against the doorjamb watching, arms crossed over his chest, those dark eyes of his on her. She could never tell what he was thinking because he had no expression on his face.

He took to calling her *Satine* in a low, dramatic movie voice every now and then. She wanted to glare at him but it always made her laugh. He didn't share the laugh with her, but his dark eyes sometimes went velvet soft and her stomach would do a strange little roller coaster loop, which irritated the crap out of her.

"Seriously, Bailey, what kind of watchdog are you?" She sighed as she sank her fingers into her dog's curly fur. There was no getting around the fact that now that coffee was in her reach, she needed it. "Sam, thank you for thinking to bring me coffee. I appreciate it *so* much."

Since she did appreciate him bringing coffee, it was easy to keep the sarcasm out of her voice, although a part of her wanted to be sarcastic. Maybe push him off her private dock into the snow-fed freezing-cold water. He'd no doubt find a way to drag her into the water with him, so she couldn't even get satisfaction that way.

Without a word Sam handed her the to-go mug. She gratefully took her first sip as they both watched the breeze play with the surface of the water. She stole a quick look at Sam's face. Fortunately, Sam never smirked. He was a restful person in that he never demanded anything from her. Sometimes she was so exhausted at the end of the day she didn't want to have to give one tiny bit of herself to anyone.

Those days, Sam would be on her deck grilling vegetables and steak or whatever, as if he knew she'd had a terrible day and didn't want to talk. He'd indicate the cooler and there would be ice-cold beer in it. She'd grab one for herself, hand him one and go sit in her favorite swing chair hanging from the ceiling covering the porch. He never asked anything of her. She never asked anything of him. That was the best part of their strange relationship. He just seemed to know when things were bad for her. She didn't question when he'd show up and make things better or how he seemed to know she needed a little care.

She sighed and took another sip of coffee, her hand moving through Bailey's fur. She'd found a few things made life great. This place and its beauty. Her dog. Coffee. Her five friends. Her favorite movie of all time and maybe Sam Rossi. She wasn't certain what category to put him in. They didn't exactly have a relationship. Sam didn't do relationships. Neither did she. They both had too many secrets.

The leaves on the trees closest to the pier were yellow and red, some orange, and they swayed with the breeze, creating a frame on either side of the wooden planks at the shoreline. Many of the leaves had dropped on the boulders where the lake's waters lapped at the shore. On the pier, where the breeze sent the leaves spiraling down over the wood, it had turned into a carpet of blazing color.

The sun was just beginning to rise and the colors shifted subtly. Rays began to spread across the water. They were low at first. A golden globe barely seen reflected in the deep pools of the sapphire lake. The sight was pure magic, the reason Stella lived here. She felt connected to the real world. Humbled by nature. As the golden sphere began to rise, the trees took on a different look altogether. The ball looked as if it grew in the water, spreading out across the lake, shimmering beneath the surface like a golden treasure.

Stella kept her gaze on the sphere. It appeared to be moving, as if alive. Each sunrise was different. The colors, the way it presented in the water. The magic. She couldn't always get to her favorite spot to watch the dramatic entrance, but she tried. There were always the sounds of the morning accompanying sunrise. The melodies of the early birds. Some were the songs of the males defining their territories. Some birds had beautiful musical qualities while others seemed to be raspy.

She listened for the way the birds sang; some ended on high notes while others let their notes trail off low. Some called out on a single coarser pitch as if they had just greeted one another or called out to say, *I'm here!* She enjoyed her early morning solitude before the sun actually rose and she could see which birds were up with her.

She noticed the hum of bees and skitter of lizards in the leaves. There was always the drone of insects, the cicadas calling. It was all part of nature she could count on there in the Eastern Sierras. It didn't matter what time of year, there was always something that gave her that connection she needed to the earth itself instead of the insanity that made up a world she didn't seem to fit into or understand.

"You gonna talk to me?"

Stella's stomach was already in knots. She needed to talk to someone. If she was going to talk to anyone, it would be Sam, but what was she going to say? She sent him a look from under her lashes, hoping he wouldn't see fear in her eyes. That was the thing about Sam. He was far too observant. He noticed everything. Details everyone else missed.

She wasn't the talking type. What did she really know about him? She wanted to trust him. He was the only man who came and went from her home, but she didn't know him. She didn't know a single thing about his life. She didn't even know if he was married or had children. She didn't know if he was running from the police, although looking at him, she knew instinctively, if he was on the run, it wasn't from something as mundane as the cops. Sam would be hiding from some international crime he'd committed, one the CIA or Homeland Security would know about and no one else.

As a rule, Stella knew everything there was to know about her employees, but not Sam. When she'd asked him to work for her, he had been a little reluctant. In the end, he had said he'd work for cash only. Under the table. She didn't usually go for that. She kept everything strictly legal, but she was desperate for a really good worker who knew the kinds of things Sam knew. At the time, nearly every cabin needed renovations. Electricity, plumbing, walls crumbling. So much work. Motors on the boats. She needed him more than he needed her. She'd hired him thinking it would be for a short period of time. That short period had turned into over two years.

She stayed silent. Took another drink of coffee. Kept looking at the lake. What was there to say that didn't make her look as if she were losing her mind? Nothing. There was nothing she could say. Even if she revealed her past, blew her carefully constructed lie of a life, what would be the point? There was no proof, and she doubted if she could get any proof that accidents weren't going to be accidents and a serial killer was on the loose. As of that moment, even the fisherman hadn't been found dead because no crime had been committed—yet. The killer would strike in two days. She needed to drive around the lake and look for the location.

"Been here over two years now, Stella. You never once locked that door. You don't snap at the workers, especially if they make a mistake. That's not your way."

She didn't look at him again. Instead, she kept her eyes on the lake. The tranquil lake that was so deep and could hold countless bodies if someone weighed them down. Above the lake the mountains rose with all the beautiful trees. So many places to bury bodies no one would ever find. Hot springs. Some of the hot springs were hot enough to decompose a body.

Without thinking, she pressed her fingers to her mouth the way she'd done when she was a child to keep from blurting out anything she shouldn't say. A habit. A bad habit she'd worked to get over, and now it was back. Just that fast. Her fingers trembled and she wanted to sit on them. She hoped he didn't notice, but he saw everything. She knew he did. Sam was that type of man. She dropped her hand back into Bailey's fur. Buried her shaking fingers deep.

"*Satine*, you want help, I'm right here, but you gotta talk. Use your words, woman."

"Did I really do that? Snap at someone because they made a mistake?" She did turn her head and look at him then. "Did I do that to you, Sam?"

His tough features softened for just a moment. Those dark eyes of his turned almost velvet, drifting over her. Unsettling her. "No, it was Bernice at the boat rentals the other day."

Stella pressed the heel of her hand to her forehead. She had done that. Not yelled. But definitely been snippy. Okay. More than snippy. She was not a boss to be snippy or short with her employees. Bernice Fulton was older and had worked for her for over five years. She would take it to heart. "I'll talk to her."

That day was unusually hot, when everyone had been expecting the cooler fall weather. Because it was, those staying in the resort had rushed to rent the boats, wanting to be out on the lake. Unfortunately, that included people who didn't have the least idea how to run a boat, or dock one. Both Sam and Stella spent the better part of the evening rescuing very drunk parties of four and six and couples, as well as a single mom and her two very young children, who, thank heavens, were wearing life vests.

Fishermen had been complaining all day, a steady stream of grouchy, irritable or downright furious people, mostly men, acting superior, although most of them knew her now. They'd come to respect her over the years. Still, they weren't immune to the unexpected high temperatures. Humidity when there was usually dry heat, and all the crazy tourists who didn't have the first clue about how to navigate boats on the lake. Nor did those tourists even seem to have any manners when it came to sharing the lake with those fishing.

Stella had been yelled at, called names and insulted many times, mostly in reference to her IQ and ability to run a fishing camp—which Sunrise Lake was *not*, but she didn't correct anyone. She merely hung on to her polite smile, listened to every concern and complaint and assured them that it would be taken care of—unless they went too far.

Stella had learned a long time ago, when she first signed on as the manager, that if she wanted the respect of the fishermen, she had to stand up to them. She wasn't shrill, she didn't yell. She looked even the oldest, most hardened in the eye when she spoke to them. She knew her facts, fought for their rights, but refused to allow them to push her around no matter how upset they were.

Still, at the end of a very long and trying day, after going out to boat after boat to retrieve mostly drunks who didn't know how to dock a boat, she wasn't in the best of moods and she had snapped at Bernice Fulton. Sam was right. She didn't do things like that. He'd kept his cool. He always did. Sam didn't snap at anyone. Of course, he didn't talk to anyone. He didn't have to. He turned that stare of his on anyone giving him a bad time and they stopped.

When he got aboard a party boat with five women in bikinis, all of whom were throwing themselves at him, he barely glanced at them. He simply brought the boat in, tied it off and didn't even gallantly help the drunk women onto the pier. He just walked off, leaving them to Bernice. Stella knew, because she'd been watching. It had been the only thing she'd laughed at the entire evening.

Stella was having nightmares every night now. She wasn't able to sleep after them, which meant she was getting very little sleep.

That certainly contributed to her growing crankiness. Not being able to discuss her uneasiness and the alarm she felt with anyone added to her irritability. She had no idea what to do in order to protect her friends or those she knew living in the area.

"Bernice will be happy you're clearing the air, Stella, but it isn't telling me why you're upset. What's going on?"

She took another sip of her coffee and regarded the glowing surface of the lake. A little shiver of apprehension went through her. There was no talking to anyone about this. Not even Sam. She had to figure this out on her own, at least until she knew Sam wasn't involved in any way. He'd arrived two years earlier. He didn't talk to anyone. He was a complete loner. He could shove his belongings into a pack and be gone in minutes.

Sam was good at every outdoor activity. He was extremely strong. He had scars all over his body, indicating something terrible had happened to him at some point in his life. Psychologically, what did that do to a person? She'd tried to find out about him on the internet, looking him up, but there was nothing that she could discover. She couldn't imagine Sam being a killer of innocent people, but she had to know before she trusted him enough to talk to him.

She could feel Sam's eyes on her and knew he wasn't going to let it go. She was acting differently. She'd snapped at an employee. She'd locked her house. She was obviously upset.

"What made you decide to bring me coffee this morning, Sam?"

He didn't bring her coffee every morning. He didn't make her dinner every evening. He didn't stop by her house to watch movies every night. She never invited him. He just showed up. When he did, he always cooked dinner. He brought beer. He never asked for anything. Never. He never once stepped over the line to so much as kiss her. She'd been tempted to kiss him more than once, but she never crossed that line with him either. She was afraid he'd just walk away, and she wanted him in her life however she could have him.

Sam liked to both boulder and trad climb. He'd shown up to climb in the area like so many others. He had driven a four-wheel-drive rig containing his possessions and camped at one of the local campgrounds. He didn't ask anything of anyone. He seemed to live off the land for the most part, but he wasn't afraid of work and he was good at almost everything. She'd noticed him right away working in town for Carl Montgomery, the local contractor. Well, the only decent one. If Carl hired him, that meant he was good.

It was impossible not to notice him. Stella noticed everyone. She was detail oriented, which was why she was so good at her job. Sam was a loner, even in the middle of a busy work site. He rarely spoke to anyone, but that didn't stop him from doing any task asked of him. In the end, she decided he would be perfect working at the resort as a handyman. He could do just about any type of job she required.

She offered him a good salary, a cabin year-round and a four-wheel-drive vehicle upgrade. He hadn't jumped at the offer. He'd taken his time, thinking it over. He even came up to the resort and looked it over before making up his mind. She'd liked him even better for that. She'd never once regretted her decision to hire him, even when he was annoying as hell because he almost never spoke.

Stella met his dark, compelling eyes. It wasn't easy. Looking into his eyes never was. Sometimes she thought it was like looking into hell.

"I can be gone, you want me that way, Stella."

He said it so quietly at first the words didn't actually penetrate.

When they did, her entire body nearly shut down. She had to turn her face away quickly, afraid he'd see the burn of tears. Afraid he'd see the panic she felt.

"Why would you say that to me, Sam?" She could barely speak, barely get the question out. "Because I asked you a question? Why would you say that to me?" She wanted to get up and leave him there, but she was afraid if she did, he would shove all his belongings into his backpack and go and she'd never see him again.

Sam was even more closed off than she was. It was possible he didn't feel anything at all for anyone. Did she mean so little to him? Probably. She'd built up their relationship because she needed someone. He was truly self-sufficient. She thought she was, but in the end, she needed the resort, her friends. *Sam.* She needed Sam. The thought of being without him wrenched at her. Maybe she was just feeling so vulnerable because of the nightmares and uncertainty. Because she was afraid for everyone.

"I know things sometimes if people matter to me. You matter to me, so I know when you feel like shit."

Stella's fingers tightened on her coffee mug. That was the very last admission she'd expected from Sam. His tone was exactly the same, that low blend of masculine sensuality that sank under her skin and found her somewhere deep. To other people who didn't ever act on little unexplained urges, his explanation might have sounded ludicrous, but to her, it was perfectly reasonable.

It was the first time Sam had ever said anything that might make him vulnerable. He all but implied he had a psychic ability, or at the very least, a heavy intuition. She wanted to give him something of herself back. It was only fair. Something real.

"I have nightmares sometimes. Bad ones. Once they start, they come in clusters. I can't get any sleep when it happens. Nothing helps." That was all true. She drank a little more of the coffee and kept her free hand in Bailey's fur.

Sam was silent for a long time. When she dared to look at him, he was looking at the mountains. The sun's rays had scattered color through the trees and ghostly mist. The sight never failed to stir her.

"What kinds of things bring on your nightmares? What are they about?"

Those were good questions. She should have thought he might ask her questions like those. He was intelligent and he was a fixer.

"Dead bodies floating beneath the surface of the lake." She blurted the truth out. Or half truth. It came out strangled because a part of her felt like it was a lie and he'd given her something of himself. Made himself vulnerable to her after two years of dancing around each other. He'd opened himself up to ridicule and she was still closed off. He was astute. He knew there was something she wasn't telling him and it had to hurt. She would be hurt.

Stella forced herself to look up at him because he at least deserved that. Those dark eyes of his studied her face. Penetrating. Seeing too much. She knew there were shadows under her eyes. But what could she really tell him? There was no body. Not even an accident yet. She definitely was going to use her day off to drive around the lake and see if she could find the location where the fisherman would be killed if she couldn't prevent it. The worst of it was, there were several lakes in the area popular with fishermen. Still, she was certain the location was her beloved lake.

"Stella, you're the calmest, clearest-thinking woman I've ever come across. I know you're in some kind of trouble." He shrugged. "I'm not going to pry. I don't like anyone asking me questions, so I'm not going to insist you talk to me if you don't want to share. Once you get past being shaken up, you do what you always do, think in steps and tackle the problem one step at a time. You'll find the answer. You always do."

There was absolute confidence in Sam's voice and that steadied her. That gave her confidence. He was right. She wasn't a child, and the killer was on her home turf. Her beloved Sierras. He had no idea she was already onto him and would be coming after him.

# CHAPTER TWO

Thanks, Sam. I don't do well on no sleep. You seem to be a light sleeper and you're able to exist on just a couple of hours. I'm a heavy sleeper and need a good eight hours or I'm cranky."

A ghost of a smile slid over his face just for the briefest of moments and it was as beautiful as the sunrise. She didn't think his smile quite managed to reach his eyes, or it was so fleeting she failed to catch it there. She saw it so rarely. More often, the hard lines etched deep in his rough features were the norm.

"You've never been cranky, Stella, until lately. I'd say the nightmares rather than lack of sleep did that."

"Maybe, but reminding me that I've got a good head on my shoulders helps. I appreciate it. I'm grateful I've got the day off."

"You work too hard, but you seem to thrive on work."

"I love this place. It feels like home to me," she admitted. She'd never had that before. Everything about the Eastern Sierras appealed to her. "Sometimes I sit outside on the deck and just look around me and feel so lucky to be alive. I wouldn't want to be anywhere else."

"I like that you can see the stars at night," Sam said unexpectedly. "I sleep outside most nights and I like to lie on the cot and look up at the sky. You can't see the stars from everywhere anymore. Here, they're amazing, and feel close."

Sam didn't talk as a rule, and just that small revelation from him felt like a gift. She knew he often prowled around the resort at night, checking on everything. He was as bad as the two security guards, or maybe better since he made the rounds nightly and then some.

She knew Patrick Sorsey, one of the security guards, sometimes fell asleep on the job. He was forty-four, had three children and his wife was pregnant with their fourth child, a shocking oops neither expected. He held down two jobs, and she knew Sam covered for him. Patrick was a good man, just overworked.

"It's a little surprising that a few dead bodies floating in the lake would get to you. It's not like you haven't had to deal with bodies, the police and medical examiner more than once, and as far as I know, that's never thrown you before."

That was true. Running the resort and being where she was, she had encountered all kinds of scenarios, from heart attacks to true accidents. Mostly drownings from too much alcohol around water. She had no problem handling any of them and knew what to do and who to call. Several of her friends and acquaintances, including Sam, were part of Search and Rescue. In fact, Vienna Mortenson, one of her friends, was head of the program for their county. They talked often, and after each rescue most of those taking part met up at the Grill to chat about what they had experienced. It helped to learn from each situation.

Stella wasn't certain how to answer Sam because he was right again. He knew her so well. Few things threw her, including dead bodies—only knowing that a serial killer was beginning his work there in their beautiful piece of paradise. But she could get ahead of him. She just had to stay focused and not get thrown.

She wasn't that child. She wasn't a teen. She had skills and training acquired over the intervening years.

She put the coffee mug on the pier and rubbed her temples. "I just need some sleep. I've got a couple of days off. That should help. I'll try to talk to Bernice before I meet Harlow and Shabina. I really do appreciate you saying something to me about snapping at her. She doesn't deserve it because I'm sleep deprived."

"She deserves it because she rented boats to people she shouldn't have, but you don't ever snap at people," he corrected. "I've got to fix the air conditioning in Cabin H."

"You mean Honeycomb Cabin?" She deliberately used the official name given to the larger rustic cabin that had been renovated and was normally rented continually. A couple had left the night before, and they had one day before the next guests would arrive. That was very rare for that particular, very popular cabin.

Sam didn't reply but simply stared at her with no expression.

"You flinch every time I say *Honeycomb*." She couldn't keep the hint of laughter from her voice. He always referred to the cabins as A, B, or C.

"Don't know why you insist on referring to perfectly good buildings with ridiculous names."

"We have to call them something for our guests. They aren't the same as fishing cabins or RVs or the camping areas, Sam. We're attracting a completely different set of people." With a very high income. Those cabins brought in revenue all year round. The winter sports—snowboarding, skiing, and snowmobiling—were very popular, and the resort was the gateway to the mountain above them.

"Will you have enough time to fix the unit before our next guests arrive?"

"If not, I can install another one and fix that later." He stood up. "I don't like that you're having these nightmares, Stella. If they keep up, I'll sleep closer and see if I can help."

He walked around the Airedale in that silent way he had to stand behind her for just a moment. Then his palm shaped the top of her head, the pads of his fingers settling into her scalp. He ran his fingers in a slow caress from the top of her head to her nape, a barely there whisper of a touch, and yet she felt it like a bolt of lightning sizzling through her body. He didn't do things like that. His touch sent a frisson of intense awareness down her spine. Every nerve ending lit up. Sam didn't do casual. He wasn't a casual man.

"I'm just going to put this out there, Stella. I've got certain skills. Swore I'd never use them again, not for any reason, but I've been here a little over two years now and I've gotten to know you. If you're in trouble and you need me, you just say so."

She frowned and craned her neck, turning to look up at him, but he was already walking away without looking back. This time, his walk took on a predatory stalk, or maybe it was her imagination because she was so disturbed by her dreams. What did he mean by *certain skills* and swearing he'd never use them again for any reason? Sam wasn't acting like Sam. She had counted on him without realizing it, and now she found she was a little afraid of him.

She looked down at her dog. Sleeping again. Not paying the least bit of attention. "You know, Bailey, you're supposed to be a protection dog as well as my companion dog. Do you remember me explaining this to you when you were a puppy?" She rubbed the Airedale's ears. He seemed to be a constant in her life she could count on, like her beloved Sierras.

She needed to stay connected to her world. Everything around her was changing too fast. She felt as if the ground itself was shifting out from under her. The Sierras harbored a killer. She knew it with every breath of cool morning air she drew in. She never had the nightmare unless a serial killer was in the vicinity. If the pattern continued, a body would turn up within a day or two. Usually two. Not always. That was a very narrow window of opportunity to stop a killer.

Drawing up her knees, she rubbed her chin on top of them as she looked out over the lake. The fog had reached the very edge of the shore, creeping like shimmering fingers, still with that reddish glow to it. Stella refused to see it any other way than beautiful. Sam was right. She wasn't given to flights of fancy. She stuck to realism and that was how she was going to catch the killer. She wasn't going to turn into a frightened child. Her first order of business was to try to find the spot where the murder was going to take place. That was a huge undertaking, as there were several lakes, not just Sunrise, where many fishermen went out in the early morning hours to fish.

"Okay, Bailey, we've got work to do."

The dog lifted his head, cocked it to one side and looked at her as if asking if she was all right now. She ruffled his fur. "I'm good. Watching the sunrise always resets me. No matter how bad everything is, once that sun comes up it's all good again. I feel like a new person. We've got this. After I have coffee with Shabina and Harlow, I'm going to see if I can sneak in lunch with Zahra."

Zahra Metcalf was her soul sister. It had never occurred to her that she would ever have someone she'd really connect with the way she did Zahra. She was friends with the other women. Liked them. Shared with them. But they weren't like Zahra. She was on an entirely different level. If there was one person in the world Stella trusted, it was Zahra.

She took her time walking back to her house. Thankfully, no one else was up yet. Very few of her guests wanted to get up as the sun was rising, other than those who were set on fishing the lake. She often felt like telling her guests if they just stepped outside onto the porches or balconies provided and watched the sunrise or sunset, they'd understand the beauty of their surroundings. Some of the guests got it. Most had come to get away from the city, but brought the city with them because they couldn't bear to leave their electronics behind.

Stella allowed Bailey to go onto the wide wraparound porch first, watching the dog carefully for any signs that a stranger might have come near her home. There were security gates one had to get through to come to this side of the property, and usually the security guards were "dragons" keeping everyone away unless they had an appointment with Stella. That didn't mean there weren't many other ways to access this side of the property.

She opened her door and went inside with much more confidence when Bailey didn't show alarm. Art supplies were kept in the studio upstairs. She loved the room with its view of the lake. One side was nearly all glass, a thick sliding wall that allowed her to step outside onto the balcony, where she kept a comfortable chair and small table during most of the months. During winter, when the snow came, she brought the furniture inside.

The studio was bright and sunny, perfect light for sketching and painting. It wasn't like she was immensely talented, but she liked to think she was fairly good. She wasn't ever going to sell her work. Like her aerial silks, and bouldering, painting relaxed her. She'd taken quite a few art classes along with her business classes in college.

She kept the journal on her nightmares and the sketchbooks locked up in a drawer beside her bed. She never wanted anyone else to find them. They were the real things of terror. She didn't look at any of the older entries or drawings. In fact, she deliberately began to scrub her mind clean as she'd taught herself to do. She pictured her brain as a chalkboard and erased it over and over until there was nothing on the board. Once it was empty, she pulled up the details of the nightmare. The boulders. The plants. The reeds. Every detail she could remember. She looked at the sky. At the ground. At the edges of the lake itself. She tried to see past the fisherman, past her own terror of what was to come, so she could focus on details and widen her scope of what she could draw. Even the shape of the boulders in the water and the algae covering them might give her clues to where the scene was.

Once Stella was satisfied she had as much detail as possible of the surroundings, she concentrated on the man fishing, trying to see as much about him as she could. His clothing. His shape. His height. As much of his hair as she could see with his hat pulled down the way it was. His hands on his fishing rod. The rod itself. She wrote it all down, everything she could possibly remember, and she was good at pulling up details.

The lake came next, and every tiny bit she could possibly decipher about the surface, the shape, the colors and even what was under the surface. Last was everything about the killer. The way he moved. His body structure. His strength. The way he moved in the water. His wet suit. His gloves. The belt he had around his waist with all kinds of weapons in it.

After she wrote it down in her journal, she took out her sketchbook and began to draw each separate scene, just as she'd written it, making certain of the details. She didn't hurry, wanting to get every fact right. When she finally straightened, her back aching a little, she was satisfied she had reproduced the potential murder scene in her nightmare to the best of her ability.

She flipped back to the first entry five nights earlier to compare drawings. The first one had little detail because it was the least she had gotten, the camera lens shuttered, allowing only a tiny portion of the unfolding horror to be seen.

Her cell played a few notes of a jazz song, jerking her out of her intense contemplation. She dragged the phone out of her pocket, frowning down at it with utter guilt.

"Harlow. I'm so sorry. I know. I know. I stood you and Shabina up. I got caught up in something . . ." She trailed off, knowing Harlow would be sweet about it.

Harlow Frye had grown up in a political family and was used to adjusting to whatever was happening around her. She "went with the flow," so to speak, with grace and elegance. She never got upset over small things, especially when she would assume Stella was busy fixing some problem at the resort.

"We'll try again another time. I'm hoping to come into town tonight. Maybe I can text you to see if you're available to meet up," Stella offered, knowing both women had to work. That was why they had planned to meet for morning coffee.

"Working a night shift tonight. So is Shabina," Harlow said. "We'll meet up though, no worries."

Stella felt terrible for lying. This was how it started. Lying to her friends. Suspecting Sam just because he walked like a predator. Did she suspect him? Not really, but she couldn't just dismiss the fact that he was capable of murder. But wasn't everyone? No, she didn't think so. Not everyone.

She hung up after apologizing again and then texted Zahra, asking her if she had time for lunch. Zahra Metcalf worked at the hospital as an administrator, so she spent most of her time in meetings, figuring out where to spend any money they managed to get their hands on. Stella knew grants were exceedingly important to the hospital. Grants, donations and fund-raising bought up-to-date equipment for the hospital and ensured they had enough doctors and nurses for the emergency room as well as the hospital itself. It was small, but the hospital was very well-equipped. It had to be. They were a good distance from any other help. Zahra was the administrator who ensured the money flowed to the hospital. She was astute and incredible at finding grants and securing them for their hospital. She was very good at thinking up fund-raisers and oversaw executing them, getting the entire county involved.

Harlow had a hand in those as well, although there was something between Zahra and Harlow that neither woman ever talked about. They were always friendly but not super close, which didn't make sense. Harlow had helped Zahra escape from an arranged marriage in her country. Her mother had gotten Zahra a visa and a good job and then eventually citizenship. Zahra never talked about any problems with Harlow, and Harlow never talked about a problem with Zahra. Stella had too many secrets of her own to pry.

Zahra could meet her for lunch, which was perfect. Stella glanced at her watch. She had plenty of time to drive around the lake and look for any spot that might resemble what she'd drawn. She had been around Sunrise Lake numerous times, but it was a big lake and there was no way she could remember every single section of it.

When the snowpack melted, it fed the river and creeks that ran into the lake, which was why it was so cold. The main road leading around the lake was narrow and two laned, paved but chewed up with potholes all year round. The snow and ice kept the asphalt from staying smooth. No matter what was done to protect it, the road disintegrated into mostly a dirty, muddy mess.

Stella tossed a few water bottles into her 4Runner, opened the back for Bailey, waited for the Airedale to leap in and then went around to the driver's side. Her 4Runner was a working vehicle, equipped for every kind of weather. She had enough money to ensure her rig was going to perform no matter what she ran into.

She had the sketchpad with her, although she was fairly certain the murder scene was etched into her brain, never to be erased. She took the main road leading around the lake, but there were a few dozen small dirt roads that branched off, leading down to the shore, and she explored the first six in a row that were the most well traveled. If the fisherman was camping at her resort, he might stick close to the main resort, but if he was a local, or one of the regulars who came often and fished the various lakes, who knew where he would have his favorite spots?

She turned down the first dirt feeder road. It was bumpy and not well-known. Only the locals used this road when they wanted to fish here. The brambles were overgrown, but she could see tire tracks in the dirt. Someone had been through recently, not that it meant anything. If her nightmares held to what they had done in the past, she had another day, possibly two, before the killer struck. That didn't mean the murderer wasn't scouting out his victim right that minute.

She stopped her 4Runner right in the middle of the narrow dirt road, opened the hidden console in the middle between the seats and pulled out her Glock. She had a concealed carry permit, just to be safe, and she was a very good shot.

"All right, Bailey, we're loaded now," she said softly as she glanced in the rearview mirror at her dog. "You ready for this?"

The Airedale had gone on alert the moment she pulled out her weapon and loaded it. She eased her rig into gear and once more started slowly down the narrow lane toward the lake. There was a slight bend in the dirt track, and when she rounded the curve, just ahead, she could see two vehicles—one a dark grayish-green truck, the other a dirty navy SUV. She recognized both rigs.

Stella hadn't realized she'd been holding her breath until she let out her air. Her lungs felt raw and burning. Her hands tightened on the steering wheel until her knuckles turned white as she stared out the windshield at the two men fishing. They were included in the circle of her friends—those she hung out with when she was able to break free of work and have a night off.

Bruce Akins, a man with a dark beard and perpetual scowl, which wasn't at all his personality, was one of the first business owners she'd made a deal with. He owned the local brewery, employing townspeople and trying to keep the economy up and running in a town where there wasn't a lot of work.

Stella had sat down with him, convincing him that she could turn the resort around and, in doing so, help the local businesses at the same time. She used his beer, playing it up as exclusive and creating a brochure, eventually having him give a VIP tour of the brewery, which a few of her higher-end clientele paid handsomely for. His beer was good, that was the thing. If it hadn't been, Stella wouldn't have gotten behind it.

Many of those who came to climb or ski or backpack came from the Los Angeles area and had money. Once they tasted Bruce's beer, they wanted to have access to it, and not just at the resort or in the surrounding towns. Bruce was able to secure contracts with a few of the very private clubs in Los Angeles for his beer, and that meant charging a high price for it. Stella became one of Bruce's favorite people.

Dr. Denver Dawson and Bruce had been close friends for years, at least as long as Stella had been living in the area. Denver was an outdoorsman. He hunted. Fished. He was a strong climber, whether bouldering, trad or sport climbing. He claimed he didn't like winter sports, but she knew he'd gone out to recover bodies in the snow more than once and he'd triggered an avalanche when they needed to bring down a section too dangerous to leave hanging. He wasn't afraid of hard work and pitched in wherever he was needed, often at Zahra's fund-raisers.

Denver was a good man and she liked him a lot. Most everyone in town did. When he hunted, he shared the meat with people who wouldn't get through the winter without help. Same with his fish. He was quietly generous. As far as Stella knew, although Sam seemed to be polite to everyone, Denver was the only one he was friends with, if he had a friend.

Bruce had a thing for Zahra. She was petite and had that cute-as-hell accent and those dark, dark eyes and perfect mouth. Bruce towered over her, a bear of a man. He almost made two of her. With everyone else he was absolutely confident, but around Zahra he could barely say a coherent word. He had reason to be confident. He was six foot six with wide shoulders and kept himself in good shape. His scowl made him look intimidating, but his blue eyes and his handsome face drew all the women like magnets—all but the one he wanted.

Because Denver was supposed to be his "wingman," he was seated next to Stella at nearly every event Bruce attended. Stella and Denver ended up laughing quite a bit over their two friends dancing around each other. Stella really liked Denver. He wasn't smooth and charming like a couple of the other men in their circle of acquaintances, but he could be counted on. He was loyal to his friends. He had a great sense of humor. That mattered to her.

She parked her 4Runner, looking at the colors of the sun shining down on the surface of the lake. The fog edging through the trees gave the sky a shimmering silver effect, amplifying the gold and orange tones spread out over the water. She always wished she could find the perfect colors to paint the visual on canvas. She'd tried in various mediums but could never quite come close to replicating nature.

Stella let Bailey out of her rig. He knew both men, but more importantly, he knew how to behave when men were fishing. He had more manners than most of the tourists that came to the resort. She had actually discussed tips with Roy Fulton, the man who worked at her bait shop for years, putting together a list of common courtesy rules and leaving them in every cabin. She'd asked Denver to add to them when the two of them had been at the bar watching Zahra and Bruce do their careful dance around each other.

The men were a good distance apart, but both had lines in the water. She could see why they liked this spot, especially in the morning hours. Trees grew nearly right up to the shore, giving them privacy and protection from the relentless heat of the sun on the hotter days. There were the inevitable granite rocks, smooth from the years of being in the water with waves lapping at them, shaping them into rounder versions of an egg. Plants grew along the shore, tall reeds rising above the surface, swaying with the waves as the light breeze played over the water.

These two men were her friends. They were a large part of the life in their community and she knew they were at risk. She hadn't thought in terms of any of her friends being at risk. When that realization hit her, she could barely breathe for a moment. She leaned against the driver's-side door and stared at the two men as they peacefully fished in the beauty of the lake. It was so beautiful there with the colors of the sun and reflections on the surface of the water. The shimmering silver of the mist creeping in, and the fall brilliance of the leaves, oranges, reds and greens decorating the trees. The men would never suspect, for one moment, that danger lurked beneath the surface.

Her vision blurred. Bailey pressed his head tight against her hip, and she sank her hand into his fur, reaching back with the other to grip the door. What in the hell was happening to her? A full-blown panic attack? She hadn't had those in years. Just like shoving her fingers against her lips or rocking, she was regressing back to all those childhood habits, but the realization that these two really good men could be at risk was horrifying. Sam fished as well. Most of the men in her circle fished.

"Stella, come here, babe. Just sit down. You need to breathe." Denver wrapped his arm around her and walked her to a camp chair.

She took a deep, shuddering breath as she sank into the chair and managed to drag fresh air into her laboring lungs. "I'm okay, Denver."

He must have tossed his fishing pole and come running. That would be like him, to notice someone in trouble. He was the hospital's anesthesiologist. Dr. Denver Dawson, nicest man on the planet, although his rough exterior put many people off. Make that women. She'd seen it dozens of times. Silly women always went for the smooth charmers, the players, and then they cried when their hearts were broken.

Denver crouched beside the chair, one hand automatically petting Bailey, the other with his fingers over her pulse. That was the other thing about Denver. He could be all business, but he never failed to recognize the animals around him. He might hunt and fish, but he ate what he killed.

"I didn't make you lose your fishing pole, did I?" Stella tilted back her head to look up at him. "And you don't happen to have any coffee, do you? I'm sure I was a little faint from lack of caffeine. I really need to put it directly into my veins."

"I wasn't about to lose my favorite fishing pole," he said, standing and ruffling her hair as if she were five. "You drink far too much caffeine and I'm not sure I should contribute to your addiction."

"I get grumpy without caffeine, Denver. Even Bailey doesn't like me." She didn't want him thinking too much about her panic attack or asking her questions. He would too. Unlike Sam, who had no problem with long silences and rarely asked questions, Denver would get all up in her business. He never seemed to see the barriers she put up, but then he didn't see them with others either. She was certain he was somewhere on the spectrum—a brilliant man with autism, most likely Asperger's, although clearly he was extremely high functioning.

He flashed her a grin and jogged over to the gray-and-green truck. Stella watched him go, a little frown on her face. His body was all muscle, much like many of the men who lived and worked in the area. They were climbers, outdoorsmen, backpackers and skiers, and they kept in shape out of necessity for what they loved to do. Denver had a great body. Very muscular. She'd noticed that before, but for some reason, the way he was moving, it was very apparent to her all over again. Still, even built as he was, that wouldn't keep him safe from a killer lurking beneath the lake's surface.

She scrubbed her palm down her face, trying to think. Could she ask the two men not to go fishing for a few days because she'd had a bad dream? That would make her sound like a lunatic. How could she protect her friends? Her mind raced and her stomach churned. Bailey pushed against her. Her dog always knew when she was upset.

Denver was back with a mug of coffee and another camp chair

under his arm. "I stole Bruce's chair. I'm not even certain he knows you're here. When he's fishing, I think a bomb could go off and he wouldn't know it."

She wrapped her hands around the warmth of the coffee mug. There was a moose with wide antlers on the mug. "It's a beautiful morning, isn't it?"

Denver glanced up at the sky and then his gaze moved slowly over the lake. "Yeah. Nothing like it anywhere else, Stella."

She smiled at him. "That's exactly how I feel." She put her head back and closed her eyes for a moment. "Denver, it's been eighteen months since you lost Suzy. Why haven't you gotten another dog? You've always had a dog." The silence stretched for so long she was afraid she'd offended him. She opened her eyes to look at him.

Denver was staring out over the lake, his expression a little lost. That was another thing about him. She could never read Sam, but Denver was an open book. If he was angry, you knew it. If he was sad, it was right there on his face. He didn't bother to mislead you. If he didn't like you, he made it known. There was no bullshit with Denver. He didn't yell, that wasn't his style, he just looked at whoever was being an ass with utter contempt and then walked away, or he dropped them with one punch and then walked away. He had a bit of a reputation, so most drunks in the bar left him alone.

"I'm sorry, Denver." Stella put her hand on his arm to comfort him. "I shouldn't have asked. Bailey and Suzy were such good friends. When I let him out of the car, I half expected to see her rushing up to greet us. When she didn't, I wondered why you hadn't gotten another dog, but I should have left it alone."

Denver shrugged, a roll of his shoulders. "I think about it all the time. It's just that I had her from the time she was a puppy. I liked that. Now, I'm so busy. I go back and forth on how fair it would be to have a puppy with me. I could take her everywhere but the hospital, but if I'm there a lot, she'd be lonely. I don't like the thought of her sitting alone in a crate all day."

Stella nodded her head in understanding. Bailey, the shameless attention-seeking hound, pushed his way between the two chairs, determined that both humans should pet and scratch him. Stella started laughing. "He's awful and you're just encouraging him." Denver was already scratching ears and chest, two of the Airedale's favorite spots.

Denver grinned at her. "He deserves all the attention he can get for putting up with you, Stella. Why are you dragging him around the lake, especially when you haven't had your morning quota of caffeine?"

Without hesitation, Stella gestured toward the lake. "Do you even see what I do? Take a look, Denver. Try painting that. It's not even possible." She let frustration edge her voice. Who said she wasn't an actress when she had to be? She'd learned to be an actress, hanging on to her smile around all the fishermen who were so disrespectful when she'd first taken over managing the resort. "Sometimes I observe the lake from different angles to try to get a better idea of colors. The shimmer. It changes all the time." That was true. She did drive around the lake, but more because the beauty of nature was inspiring to her.

Denver regarded her for so long in silence she felt herself blushing for no reason, other than the look of admiration on his face. "I learn something new about you all the time, Stella. I had no idea you painted."

"Badly. I'm no artist, which is why I don't tell anyone," Stella said. She took another cautious sip of the coffee. It was really bad coffee. "Who made this?"

Denver laughed. He had a rich, warm laugh that invited others to laugh with him. "Bruce. I told him never to offer to make coffee for Zahra. He was highly offended."

"If I wasn't so desperate for caffeine, I would spit it out, but I can't afford to waste the gift from the gods."

Denver spewed his caffeine out onto the ground. "You're even more insane than I thought you were."

She waved her free hand airily while clutching the mug with the other. "Sadly, it's true, but I don't mind. How often do you two come out here?"

Denver shrugged. "Not as often as we'd like. Bruce is busy all the time now, thanks to you and your scheming. Our laid-back hunt-and-fish days are over."

"I'm not buying it, Denver. You're a workaholic."

She studied the layout of the lake's edge carefully, committing it to memory. The weeping trees. Were they the same? Did she recognize them? What about the rocks jutting out of the water? Her gaze jumped to Bruce. He had waded farther out from shore just like the fisherman in her nightmare. She could see he wore waders. The reeds and plants looked the same, but then the flora was close to being the same on this side of the lake.

"You're going to spill your coffee, Stella," Denver pointed out, his tone mild. He reached out and took the mug from her. "Why are you staring at Bruce like that?"

"I was imagining what it must be like to be a fish." She had to improvise fast. "One minute, swimming along peacefully, looking for a meal, and then the next, some asshole sends a hook down and jabs you in the throat with it. Now you're fighting for your life. If you have a nice little fish family, you're never going to see them again. Bruce looks like a nice enough guy, but under all that niceness lurks an evil fish killer. I have to warn Zahra."

Denver stared at her as if she'd grown two heads. Stella couldn't blame him. She was not cut out to be a detective. She wasn't all that clever. The expression on his face made her want to laugh.

"Nice fish family? Evil fish killer? Good grief, Stella, you have a terrible imagination."

"No, I have a vivid imagination," she corrected. "It's why I don't fish. Or hunt. I will kill the occasional spider, but I mostly practice the capture-and-release program. I trap them and put them outside."

Denver groaned and dropped his head into his hand. "You don't."

"I do. My very healthy imagination tells me all the spiders in the house that are related will rise up in an army and come after me while I'm sleeping. I'll develop an allergy in that single night and it will be a horrible way to go, choking on my own vomit or something equally unpleasant and unwomanly."

Denver burst out laughing. "Unwomanly?"

"Well, yes. When I go, I want to at least look good. Not all covered in red splotches from allergies. That wouldn't be very dignified. If you're going to find me, Denver, I have to look somewhat decent. Vienna is always telling me about these horrible-looking bodies when you find them. I refuse to go out that way. If an army of spiders gets me in the middle of the night and poisons me and I break out in horrid allergy splotches, then I can at least know my corpse isn't going to look hideous. Well, I mean it will if I get attacked and bitten and die that way."

He shoved the coffee mug back at her. "Drink. You're not making any sense." He looked at the dog. "Is she always like this in the morning, Bailey?"

Stella wrapped her hands around the coffee mug, glad she'd diverted his attention again. She took another healthy drink of the bitter brew. "Does Bruce really like this coffee, Denver? Zahra is a coffee fanatic, just like me. I think she might keel over if she drank this, not that I think the two of them are ever going to happen."

The laughter faded from Denver's face, leaving him with that rough exterior that put most people off. There were pock marks on his left side, faint but there, marring the weathered skin. Up close she could see a strange scarring over the pocks, much like a skid mark, as if his cheek and jaw had slid along the pavement.

"Why do you say that, Stella?"

"Bruce is so shy around Zahra and can't bring himself to ask her out. She was raised in a very small village in Azerbaijan. She's been here a long time and she's a citizen, but she spent her life as a child there. Our childhood shapes us, Denver, you know that. She's not going to suddenly be bold and ask Bruce out. She might flirt with him, especially if she drinks a bit, but she won't go any further than that. She might be an American now, but she will never be that bold woman who just asks him out first. Bruce isn't going to take charge like she needs him to. They are, unfortunately, at a stalemate."

Denver stretched his legs out in front of him, his smile back. "That's why she drinks so much. I have to tell you, I was a little worried and kept my eye on her, afraid she might be an alcoholic. I even cautioned him about it once, which didn't go over well."

His smile turned into a grin. He had extremely light-colored brown eyes, almost more amber than brown. His hair was very thick and a light brown with streaks of blond from all the time he spent in the sun. When he gave her that grin, his eyes took on the color of a burnt whiskey.

"Maybe we should lock the two of them in one of your smallest cabins for a weekend and see what happens," he ventured.

Stella burst out laughing, but there was a small part of her contemplating the idea. "If only we could get away with it."

"Does she really like him?" Denver asked, his tone suddenly serious.

"She *really* likes him." Stella matched his tone.

# CHAPTER THREE

Bruce trudged up to Denver and Stella, frowning at them, one hand on Bailey's head as he cast a giant shadow over them. "You're sitting in my chair, Denver, and you gave Stella my favorite coffee mug."

Stella looked him over carefully. The waders were that same olive color that were in her nightmare. She told herself it didn't mean anything. Many of the fishermen wore those same exact waders. It was just that the man in her nightmare wore bibbed denim overalls tucked into the waders. Denver had the waders on but not the overalls, which didn't mean he didn't own a pair. Neither man was wearing a hat, but it was early enough that the sun's rays weren't that strong yet.

"I'm kidding, Stella," Bruce said. "Don't look so upset."

"I was about to tell him to go get another chair out of his truck. He has ten of them in there," Denver said. "Really, Stella, he couldn't care less."

Was she looking upset again? Her nightmares had really thrown her. She'd promised herself she'd get a handle on her behavior. These were her friends. If she was going to save them, she needed to do better. Much better.

"Sorry, I was just thinking about spiders and fish families." She waved one hand dismissively. "Don't ask, Bruce. Denver already thinks I'm crazy. Were the fish biting this morning?"

Denver stood up and Bruce immediately sank into the vacated chair. Denver flipped him off but walked over to Bruce's truck and yanked out another chair.

"Not really," Bruce answered. "I didn't really care if I caught anything this morning or not. I just wanted to come out here and relax. It gets hectic sometimes and my brain can't take the chaos after a while. I need the reset."

Stella thought it was interesting that he thought in the same terms she did. Every morning the sunrise "reset" her. "We all need that once in a while, don't we?"

Bruce nodded. He looked around. "You came on your own?"

Stella kept a straight face. Denver set his chair across from them, looking at her with a little grin that told her he knew exactly what Bruce was fishing for.

"Who did you think was hiding in her rig, Bruce?" Denver asked.

Bruce glared at him. "You're such a pain in the ass, Denver."

Stella pushed out of the chair. "I'm going to look at the water and try to figure out the colors and what I'm doing wrong when I'm mixing my paints. I've been trying to get the colors right for so long and I just can't seem to do it when I'm painting the lake. You two can argue without me." Her art was her best cover, the best reason she had for examining the rocks and grasses so carefully.

She hurried down to the water's edge, doing a careful sweep of the shoreline. She wanted to view it from every direction, the way the camera's lens had done in her dreams each night. She'd gotten multiple views of the lake and the boulders and trees. She should be able to identify if this was the exact location of the upcoming murder. She doubted it. It would be far too much luck to have it be the very first secluded place she checked. This was remote, not known to outsiders, and only a few locals ever went here, which actually made it the perfect place for murder.

She was very glad she'd told Denver she painted, although only a few of her friends knew she did and she was much more comfortable with that. Having told him provided a good reason for her to be studying the shore and trees from every angle. She could commit every detail to memory. Her brain catalogued images for her. Sometimes that was a good thing, but not always. There were things in her past she wanted to forget.

She pushed all thoughts away and began to slowly study each individual section of the fishing area. It would stand to reason that a fisherman would drive in, park as Denver and Bruce had and walk to the area where both had chosen to fish. They wouldn't go much farther. That meant she could concentrate her investigation where they had been fishing. She chose to inspect where Bruce had been first. He had waded the farthest out into the lake, and he'd been among the rocks and into the reeds and plants.

Stella made her way over to the area where Bruce had been fishing. Skirting around the large pile of rocks onshore, she went down to the water's edge, where she could look back toward the ones jutting up out of the water. She told herself to keep breathing evenly. Slowly. It was strange how much trepidation she felt, even though she kept assuring herself there was no way this place would be the same one as the murder site in her nightmare. Still, there was just something in her that knew. She *felt* it.

The rocks were shaped exactly the same as the ones she'd sketched from her nightmare. The more she studied them from each angle, the more her heart beat faster. She looked at the reeds and plants rising out of the water, the way they grew around the egg-shaped rocks, some bent over, some rising toward the sky. There were thick patches and others where the water lapped against the granite rocks. It was like déjà vu.

Not Bruce. Not Denver. Why would anyone want to kill either of them? Both men were well liked, but Bruce did have to let workers go occasionally. What about Denver? He had a few enemies. He got in bar fights sometimes. Bruce did too. Sam did as well, not as many, but he was known to throw a punch now and then. Did Sam fish here? She had no idea. How many other locals fished here?

Maybe she should camp out here. How many days before the murder would occur? One? Two at most. She could do that. Camp right here. No one could use the location as a fishing spot. The murderer wouldn't be able to kill as he wanted to. What would that make him do? Would he realize she was onto him? That would be impossible.

"Stella?" Bruce called out her name. "You hungry? I've got food."

She rose slowly from her crouch. "I'm meeting Zahra for lunch and I'd better get moving, but thanks for the offer." When his face dropped, she took pity on him. "A few of us are going dancing tonight at the Grill. You and Denver are welcome to join us."

Bruce immediately nodded. "We'll be there."

"I have to check my schedule," Denver said.

"We'll be there," Bruce said decisively.

Denver laughed, following Stella to her 4Runner, watching as she opened the back so Bailey could jump in. "He can be very dominant when Zahra isn't around. I think he'd go into the hospital and reschedule any operation just so I could go with him to hang out in a bar so he could stare at his woman all night." He pretended to whisper since Bruce had followed them.

Bruce glared at him. "There's nothing wrong with that."

"She can't be your woman if you haven't claimed her," Denver pointed out. "Scowling at other men to keep them away from her doesn't count."

"It might not count in your eyes, but it works," Bruce said smugly.

"It won't work forever," Stella said as she slid behind the wheel. "You'd better decide soon what you're going to do, Bruce." She started the vehicle and began to back up so she could turn around.

"Wait, what?" Bruce yelled after her. "Are you trying to tell me something?"

Stella waved in the rearview mirror, ignoring Bruce pressing his thick fists to his hips as he shouted after her. He was a grown man. If he couldn't figure it out after all the hints Zahra, Denver and Stella had given him, he didn't deserve Zahra. Stella had the feeling Zahra had already given up and was trying to move on, at least in her head, and Stella didn't blame her.

There really was something to a woman's biological clock if one wanted children. Eggs were only good for so long. She knew because she'd looked that fact up and then resigned herself to a life with no children. She didn't want that for Zahra, when she knew her friend really wanted a family. It wasn't like they were twenty anymore. They'd seen thirty and counting.

The resort was a good distance from town and she had plenty of time to think about what she was going to do in order to prevent the murder of the fisherman while she drove there. The only real solution she could come up with was to camp out at the spot for several days. She could only hope the nightmares predicted the same timeline as the past serial killers she'd dreamt about. That would give her two days before he struck.

If the murderer didn't have access to his chosen murder ground, maybe he would be thrown off his game and have to start all over with his planning. That would give her time to study everything she'd written and sketched without being so terrified. The calmer she was, the more logical and rational she would be in hunting the killer.

Zahra was already waiting at their favorite lunch spot, in the corner booth in the back of the little café the locals knew had the best breakfast and lunch food in town. Mostly it was a deli where people got sandwiches on the go, but there were a few tables and booths located toward the back of the café. The floor was a black-and-white-checked tile. The tablecloths were black-and-white-checked paper over wood so they could be torn off and the next ones spread on easily.

Sunrise Café was owned and operated by their friend Shabina Foster. Shabina was five foot four with thick black hair that fell to her waist if she let it. Mostly she braided it and wrapped it into a figure eight on her head. She had gorgeous skin and unexpected peacock-blue eyes framed with black lashes. Stunningly beautiful, Shabina was amazingly modest. Her father's company had risen to become the number one company called on when oil wells caught fire anywhere in the world. That was how her mother had met him in Saudi Arabia.

Shabina rarely talked about her parents or how their union came about. Shabina once told them her name meant "eye of the storm" in Arabic. Her mother had told her she was aptly named. Shabina implied that meant it had something to do with her family history. Stella did know that her mother never returned to Saudi Arabia nor did her grandparents ever come to the United

States. None of Shabina's aunts, uncles or cousins had ever met her. It seemed they all had secrets, and that was okay. Maybe that was what allowed them all to be friends.

Stella waved to Shabina, knowing she was too busy right now to talk but would come to the booth later when the rush was over. Hurrying to the back, Stella slid onto the bench seat opposite Zahra. "You got off early."

Zahra nodded, her dark eyes looking Stella over carefully. "I had some time off coming to me, and my schedule wasn't all that important that I couldn't move things around. I thought it would be nice to spend more time together."

That wasn't like Zahra at all. She worked. She stuck to her calendar and crossed appointments off as they came. She looked innocent, but then that was half of Zahra's charm. She could look innocent even if she was stealing your car right out from under you. When they went to the gym together and shared a personal trainer, Zahra could talk him into letting her off the hook when it came to the harder exercises, even though Zahra could do them no problem. Stella, on the other hand, thought she was dying and the trainer just made her do more. She didn't have that cute accent or the adorable smile of innocence Zahra had.

"What's going on with you?" Stella asked.

"I needed girl time."

Stella regarded her suspiciously. There was a plate of fried zucchini, one of Shabina's specialties. It wasn't just any old fried zucchini. This tasted light, as if it wasn't fried and couldn't possibly add a single calorie to your body. Shabina could fool you into thinking things like that with her food.

"Perfect. So do I. I'm going camping and need someone to camp with me." Stella pounced. Zahra was a five-star luxury girl. She'd had enough of starving and roughing it to last a lifetime when she was growing up, but she did backpack and climb when Stella twisted her arm.

Zahra narrowed her dark brown eyes. "What does that mean? Camping in one of your cabins? Or in a tent? What exactly are you saying? Because it's cold at night now, or hadn't you noticed?"

"Tents by the lake. I've got the perfect spot already picked out."

Zahra slumped over the tabletop dramatically, burying her face in her arms, groaning. "You're not right in the head, Stella. No one wants to camp in a tent anymore. You have a beautiful house. Cabins. We can go anywhere. Tents by the lake?" She lifted her head and glared at Stella. "Tell me now, you're getting me back for that time I was supposed to hike the JMT with you and I thought I was sick and backed out."

Stella rolled her eyes. "No one believed you were going to hike the trail with me, Zahra. I didn't believe it for a minute. I did think you might summit Whitney because you always talk about it, but no way were you actually going to hike the trail, especially when I was going out for a month. And you weren't sick."

"I could have done it," Zahra stated, salting the zucchini fries, not bothering to deny that she wasn't sick.

Stella took the salt shaker from her. "Not only could you have done it, you would have been far better at it than me. You just don't like inconveniencing yourself."

"I like showers. And toilets," Zahra pointed out. "There's nothing wrong with that. People in their right minds like those things."

Stella laughed and then looked up at the young waitress as she plopped two plates in front of them.

"I ordered for you," Zahra explained. "You always order the same thing. You take fifteen minutes looking over the menu and then you order the exact same thing. It's annoying."

"Um, honey. That's you. You do that. I don't ever look at the menu."

Zahra rolled her eyes and then laughed. "Okay, I'll concede that's the truth. I like looking because everything sounds so good. It's the same shopping for clothes. You go in and you want to be in and out of a store immediately. I like to look for hours. I don't have to buy anything, but I like to look. Shabina's like me. So is Harlow, although she does like to buy. Her mom's a buyer so I get that. Raine is more like you. Just get with the program, she does her research ahead of time. She's back, by the way."

Raine's job was loosely titled programmer. She "sort of" worked for the government, if one could call it that. Raine didn't. Raine was in that first circle of close friends with secrets, which meant they didn't ask too much and she didn't volunteer. She mostly worked for the Marine training base that was about a five-hour drive away from them. Raine was scary intelligent. Wicked smart. Sam had caught on to her right away, and that was saying something because Raine tended to stay quiet and observe. At one time she had programmed missiles when she was in the military, but she was out and now programmed with a code few understood or knew. At least, that was what Stella thought she did. Who really knew?

"Raine likes to camp," Zahra said, twisting her fork around homemade noodles. "She would probably come with us."

Right there, that was why Zahra would always be her best friend. She might not like camping in tents in the cold, but she would do it. Stella smiled at her. "You think she would want to come when she just got back from a trip?"

"Girls' trip?" Zahra flashed her little mysterious smile that men found smoking hot. "Of course she'll want to come. We always have fun. We can ask Shabina too. It's short notice for her, but she might get someone to cover for her. She has a good staff now."

"Harlow has to work tonight. I wanted them to come to the Grill with us and dance. I missed coffee with them this morning."

Zahra shrugged and then closed her eyes, moaning as she ate a bite of her pasta. "I swear I would marry Shabina if I went that way. No one cooks the way she does."

Stella had to agree with her. Shabina kept the menu small, with a few daily specials, but every single thing was perfection. "Vienna may be able to come out. I'll text Harlow and Vienna and see if they can meet us late tonight. I can set up tents for them. If not, maybe tomorrow. I wanted to camp three days."

She hoped three days would be long enough. If the timeline went the same as the other two times there had been nightmares heralding serial killers in her life, then the murderer would be looking to kill in the next two days. She would have a dream for five nights straight and then two days later, the body would be found. That was how it worked. In this case, she hoped to interrupt the killer with her girls' camping trip—hopefully there would be enough of them camping that it would derail anyone looking for a quiet fishing spot.

"We won't be far from the resort, so during the day you can have spa time while I'm working if there's an emergency or something." Stella felt the instant impact of Zahra's gaze. The woman saw too much. Had known her too long. When Stella went camping, she checked out of work. Put her phone away. Didn't want anyone to even talk work.

"I love your spa," Zahra said. "But I'm bringing the tarot cards so each of you can find your inner guide to empower you. The reading will help you find wisdom and guidance to connect with your true self."

Stella kept eating, refusing to look at her friend, who was very serious. She wasn't talking about the other women in their circle, she was talking about Stella. She knew something was bothering Stella, and her way of helping was to give her a reading and let her work the problem through with her own guides. Who knew? Maybe it would help. At this point, she'd take whatever she could get.

"You're going to bring the tarot cards and Vienna is going to want to play poker and take all of our money." Stella flashed Zahra one emotion-laden look, showing her affection briefly, but changing the subject.

"She will. I think she cheats at cards, but I can't ever catch her at it," Zahra declared.

Stella burst out laughing. "Vienna would never cheat at cards, but she is a card sharp. A serious one. She goes to Vegas and plays in some of the large-stakes poker games there. She wins too. Our sweet little surgical nurse has teeth. She looks like a supermodel and no one takes her seriously and that's a big, big mistake."

Zahra looked up, her dark brows coming together in that way that was so adorable men usually fell at her feet, but she never noticed. Stella and the others always did and secretly laughed because she seemed so clueless.

"Card sharp? I haven't heard this term, Stella, and I've been in this country for many years. I play cards."

"You're terrible at cards," Stella pointed out, thinking *terrible* was generous. Zahra only played because everyone else wanted to play and she was a good sport about doing what the others chose to do. Like camping out by the lake when the temperature dropped because she knew Stella was going to do it whether she was alone or not. That was Zahra, loyal to a fault.

"I'm not terrible," Zahra defended and then burst out laughing. "Okay, maybe I am, but poker is so boring. I have no idea what is going on half the time." She took more bites of her pasta and did more moaning. "And I kick your ass if we're playing Durak."

"That's true, because you like that game and you pay attention. Otherwise you chatter. *Incessantly*. I think you're hoping to distract us, which doesn't work."

Zahra's dark chocolate eyes went wide. "I absolutely do not *chatter* during cards." She not only looked but sounded indignant.

Shabina slid onto the bench seat beside Zahra. "Yes, you do, *ya mamma*." She always called Zahra *little mamma*, a term of endearment from Saudi Arabia that Shabina's mother had called her. "But we all love it. You tell us the funniest stories."

Stella burst out laughing at the expression on Zahra's face. Zahra never thought of herself as funny. She got herself in trouble all the time but managed to get out of trouble as quickly as she got into it.

"We're going to the Grill tonight for drinks and dancing and after, we're camping out by the lake for three nights. I have time to set up tents for us," Stella offered as a bribe. "I know it's short notice, but I really need to get away. It's not that far from the resort." Which was still far for those living in town if they had to check on their businesses during the day.

"Definitely in for the Grill," Shabina said readily. "Give me an hour to see if I can arrange for camping. If Vaughn can cover for me, I'm there. I could use a little downtime. And I can help set up tents. I should be off in another couple of hours."

Zahra moaned again as she took another bite. That earned her a couple of very interested looks from the two men at the table across from them, which she missed entirely. Stella and Shabina exchanged knowing looks. They were used to Zahra and the way she attracted men. She couldn't help it. She flirted outrageously and didn't seem to notice she was flirting.

The other man magnet in their group was Vienna. She walked down the street and could cause a traffic jam. The difference was she was aware of it—she just didn't care. She was extremely intelligent and very independent like all the women in the circle of friends. She worked out hard, did the same outdoor activities as the rest of them and they all swore that, like Zahra, she didn't even sweat.

"Good grief, Zahra, if you keep making that sound, you're going to get arrested for indecent exposure or something," Stella warned.

Zahra burst out laughing. "I can't help it. This pasta is that good."

Shabina's face lit up, her dark eyes shining. "That's the nicest thing you could have said to me. A customer demanded his money back after eating the entire lunch, claiming it gave him an upset stomach and it was the worst meal he'd ever had."

"You have got to be kidding me." Zahra was outraged. "I hope you didn't refund his money, Shabina. He was just looking for a free meal. What an ass. Did you call the police?"

"He didn't really cause a disturbance and when I asked him to leave, he did. It seems, though, he did call the police on me." A slight flush slid under the beautiful dusky skin she'd inherited from her mother.

Stella sat back in the booth and regarded her carefully. "I don't suppose a certain detective just happened to show up with a police officer to investigate the complaint. I wonder why that would be."

"A detective investigates all sorts of crimes, including deliberately trying to poison customers, which, apparently, I tried to do,"

Shabina pointed out, her chin lifting and her wealth of very black lashes feathering down to cover royal-blue eyes.

"He actually accused you of trying to poison him?" Stella said, the smile fading.

Shabina nodded. "Apparently Mr. Watson—that was the customer—is certain I am from Iran or Iraq or Afghanistan and have been planted here to get information, possibly on the Marine training center just down the road from us."

"Just down the road?" Zahra echoed. "You mean five hours away? That training center?"

"Wait," Stella said, frowning, looking up to meet Shabina's eyes. "*Sean* Watson? Works for Fish and Wildlife? That doesn't make any sense. Has he always given you trouble, Shabina? You must have crossed paths with him before this. We all know him."

Shabina shrugged. "He asked me out a while back, but there was just something about the way he did it that bothered me. He's attractive. Even my type. I thought about it, but I didn't like the way he was looking at me, or maybe it was the way he worded it when he asked me. I can't tell you exactly why I said no. It wasn't even a hard no. I just said I couldn't make it right then, that I'd have to take a rain check."

"What did he do?" Zahra asked, her dark brown eyes wide with concern.

"He looked me up and down as if I were so beneath him. He had a sneer on his face, like he was really disgusted. He just turned around and walked away. After that, he would come into my café once a week and complain about the food. He'd usually send his lunch back at least twice. I tried to make certain I could slip out the back door if I saw him coming. If I wasn't here, he just ate and left." She hesitated. "Little things started happening about six months ago. Not often, about once a month or so.

Someone took a spray can and wrote all over the outside of the café for me to go back to my country, whatever that means. I was born here. My mother isn't even full Saudi Arabian. In any case, I reported it to the police and we put primer over it and painted that same morning."

"You didn't say a word," Stella said.

"I know." Shabina sighed. "It just left such a bad taste in my mouth. The other incidents were similar. Vandalism, mostly. I've installed more security cameras recently, both inside the café and outside. I asked Lawyer to help me. He installed the cameras for me and put the apps on my phone, iPad and computer to warn me if anyone came near the place."

Zahra continued to frown, looking at Shabina with that same concern. "Why didn't you contact Bale's security company?"

"He's friends with Sean Watson," Stella answered for Shabina. "Remember, Bale dated Harlow for a short time about six months ago. She broke it off abruptly but never really said why. They only went on a couple of dates. Maybe we should ask her."

"He asks her out all the time," Shabina offered. "I've seen him messaging her. Mostly she ignores the messages, but sometimes she'll type a reply and it's very short. Once I asked her why she didn't block him when he has to be driving her crazy with so many messages, and she just shrugged and said she really didn't want to piss him off."

Stella sat back and regarded Shabina's face. She was a beautiful woman. Harlow was as well. They were very different in looks. Harlow was a fiery flame. Red hair, brilliant jade eyes. Freckles over her nose and across her high cheekbones that only added to her beauty. She was tall with long legs and she could move fast when she wanted, although she seemed to be always graceful, even in stiletto heels—training from being a senator's daughter and having to attend endless fund-raisers, she laughingly told them.

"I've texted Harlow and Vienna to see if they can join us after their shifts tonight," Stella said. "I'd love it if we could all get together. It's so rare anymore."

"You know, if we're going to the Grill tonight, we can't possibly go camping," Zahra pointed out. "We'll be drinking, and how will we get there?"

Stella sighed. "I'll be the sober driver."

"You can't be the sober driver," Shabina and Zahra said simultaneously and then burst out laughing.

Stella's eyebrow went up. "What?"

"You're hilarious when you've been drinking, and you hardly ever drink," Zahra pointed out. "We're not missing out on that."

"Well, I'm camping out tonight."

"Text Sam and see if he'll be our sober driver," Zahra suggested with a small impish grin. "Or Denver. Either one would do it for you."

"You're so funny," Stella said, aware of heat rising, the blush starting somewhere low and moving through her body toward her face. "You're such a demon. We're only going to the Grill because you want to see Bruce."

"It's because they make the best Moscow Mules," Zahra corrected. "And I like to dance."

Shabina laughed. "And you like to ogle Bruce and all his muscles."

Zahra rolled her eyes and shrugged. "He's really tall so there's room for a lot of muscle, but he doesn't talk."

"In my experience," Shabina said, "that can be a good thing. The less talk, the more action. Don't you want action, Zahra?"

Zahra sighed. "He has to start somewhere, like asking me out.

He can barely ask me to dance. I think we're having this great time and then he just walks away and we're back at square one. As long as he's around, no one else will ask me out because he glowers at them."

"That's not all he does," Shabina said. "I heard him threaten some dirtbag to leave you alone or he was taking him outside, and he meant it too."

Zahra sat up straight. "He did what? He can't do that. Was someone going to ask me to dance?"

Stella nudged her under the table with her foot. "I remember that night. The guy wouldn't leave you alone no matter how many times you told him to get off you. He kept trying to freak dance you. Bruce pulled him off and had a little chat with him. That was the last we saw of him on the dance floor."

Zahra looked mollified. "Well, I guess that's all right, then." She looked up as another woman joined them, pushing into Stella's side of the table. "Raine. You found us."

"Where else would you be? Best food. Best coffee. Makes sense." Raine nudged Stella. "Camping tonight? After the Grill?"

Raine was petite, a blonde with sun-kissed hair that was usually left loose. She paid little attention to her appearance, which meant she didn't really need to. Large slate-blue eyes framed with golden lashes and brows were the bane of her life, at least she always said they were. Stella thought her eyes were gorgeous.

Everything about Raine was a little on the wild side, as if she were untamable. Fiercely independent, no matter how much she feared something—or because of it—she worked at it until she was able to do it. She loved bouldering, and would spend hours happily working out problems on the rock. Trad climbing was her nemesis. She was actually afraid of heights and didn't trust anyone on the end of her rope. Still, she was determined to climb.

She parasailed even when that scared her and she had ended up loving it.

Raine had hiked the John Muir Trail by herself, taking several weeks in the wilderness to do so, summiting Mount Whitney several times. She had also hiked Mount Shasta and then gone to Europe and hiked the Alps alone. She'd gone to Iceland and climbed into a dormant volcano, and visited ice caves in Romania, hiking around the backcountry. She'd done the same in Thailand.

"You look tired, Raine. You don't have to come camping with us tonight," Stella said. "We're close to the resort. You could stay in one of the cabins and get a good night's sleep and then join us tomorrow night. We were thinking of camping for three nights."

Stella felt guilty for not confiding in her friends, but what could she really say? There was no murder. There was no body. There was no explanation she could give them without turning her world upside down. Nothing made sense to her right now. It had to be an outsider, not someone who lived and worked in the town.

There were so many people with temporary jobs. She pressed her fingers to her temples. People came and went. Even at the resort she hired the same staff, but they didn't all stay year-round. Still, she couldn't imagine any of the people she knew—not even the ones she wasn't particularly fond of—as a serial killer. But an outsider wouldn't have knowledge of a fishing spot that only a very few locals used.

"Are you okay, Stella?" Raine asked.

"Yes, I was just thinking about the things Shabina was telling us. I know Zahra has run into prejudice occasionally because of where she comes from, but it's always been from outsiders. They start asking about her accent and then get all weird with her. I never once considered that someone would be that way with Shabina."

"Let me take a guess," Raine said. "One of four. Bale Landry, Sean Watson, Jason Briggs or Edward Fenton. It's one or all of them. College buddies. Very superior to women. They were mixed up in a fraternity that made lists of female students, particularly ones that appeared to be of different ethnicities. Those in the fraternity were to sleep with as many of the women as they could, any way they could. They would pretend to like them, date them, or they would simply get them drunk at a party. If the woman was innocent, they scored more points for that."

"That's disgusting," Stella said. "There was an entire fraternity of male students at a college dedicated to hurting female students emotionally like that? That's vile and sordid and so disgusting it turns my stomach."

"It was a game to them. They had a point system," Raine said. "If I gave you all the details, it would really turn your stomach. I'd like to say it was college shit, but as far as I'm concerned, by the time you're in college, you're responsible for what you do. Your moral code is developed, and clearly the four of them don't have one when it comes to women. I'm fairly certain they'll cheat on their wives if they get married. I was appalled when Harlow went out with Bale."

"You told her."

"I showed her the evidence. I don't usually do that sort of thing, but I wasn't going to let one of my close friends fall into a trap like that. When she walked, he was really angry."

"Do they know you had anything to do with her finding out about them?" Shabina asked.

"She didn't tell him she knew about his stupid game or even that there was a tie between the four of them. She just ended their dating. Harlow has never really done relationships here so it wasn't a huge leap for him to believe that she might get cold feet and run for it," Raine said.

"Sean asked Shabina out a while back," Zahra supplied. "She declined and he's been terrible ever since. He called the police on her today and accused her of trying to poison him. Guess who showed up to check out the complaint?"

"We are so not talking about this again," Shabina said. "I'm going to get dessert. Raine? Did you order?"

"I wasn't hungry for lunch, but asked for coffee. Would love dessert, whatever you made as the special."

Shabina stood up and did her best to glare at Zahra. "Don't you dare talk about me while I'm gone or you don't get any dessert. It just so happens to be your favorite."

Zahra flashed her impish smirk, the one that let her get away with just about anything. Shabina hurried away, glancing over her shoulder several times, trying to look stern.

Raine burst out laughing. "I take it Craig Hollister came in, and technically, that's talking about him, not Shabina."

Zahra's eyes lit up. "That's true. Yes, Craig came, but she didn't embellish much. You didn't happen to look into Craig's background, did you, Raine?"

Raine looked indignant. "Well, I haven't looked into his background yet because he likes Shabina but I'm not entirely certain she's that interested in him. If I was going to snoop, it would have to be a far more interesting person."

Zahra shook her head. "Sam. I would think you would find him totally intriguing, Raine."

Stella's breath caught in her throat. She didn't want the spotlight on Sam. She didn't know why, but she didn't want Raine to suddenly train her computer skills on him. She kept quiet. Sam was a loner. He could hunt. Fish. Climb. He could use scuba gear. He wasn't an expert in any of those things, but he wouldn't have to be.

Raine made a face. "Sam's boring. He doesn't even talk, Zahra. He's worse than Bruce."

"No one is worse than Bruce," Zahra declared. "Sam doesn't dance with anyone but Stella, and that's romantic."

Raine laughed. "Or she tolerates him stepping on her feet."

Sam had never stepped on her feet. Not once. She couldn't imagine it ever happening. He was far too aware of where his feet were placed at all times—and she wasn't altogether certain Raine was telling the truth. Raine noticed everything about everyone. Sam would be interesting to her just because he was such a loner and he was so quiet, so why wasn't she admitting it?

# CHAPTER FOUR

Harlow and Vienna were able to drive out to the location and set up their tents with Raine and Zahra as well as Stella, staking out the campsite for their own. Stella wanted to make it clear to any of the fishermen that the spot was overrun with campers. They moved the picnic table close to the firepit and pulled out lounge chairs to arrange around the pit, which they filled with firewood in preparation for evening or morning.

Stella knew few people ever went down that particular very pitted dirt road even to fish, so she wasn't worried their tents would be disturbed while they were gone. So if this location was so remote that only Denver and Bruce fished there regularly, was one of them the target?

Her backpack and sleeping bag were in her rig, along with her cooler, when she parked in front of the Grill, where she was meeting Zahra, Raine and Shabina. Vienna and Harlow promised they would meet them in the morning after their shifts at the hospital ended. The music blared loudly, reverberating through the building as it always did, inviting everyone to get up out of their chairs and dance.

Zahra waved wildly, nearly falling off her chair. She'd managed to grab the largest round table closest to the bar just to the right of where the band played. It was their favorite place to sit because it could accommodate most of them and the others could sit at the bar or even on the ledge surrounding the plants behind the table. Bruce and Denver sat at the bar in front of the table. Sam was at the bar as well, but on his usual corner stool. Raine and Shabina were already at the table with Zahra, so Stella waved and then made her way to Sam.

"Hey." She shifted one hip onto the barstool beside him. He was always warm. She didn't know if it was because he was so dense, his muscles making his body thicker than he actually appeared, or if he was just naturally hot. When she got near him, he seemed to elevate her body temperature by several degrees.

His dark eyes moved over her in that way he had, as if he saw everything about her, things no one else saw. "Stella."

"We wanted to go camping tonight. There's a spot we staked out already, our tents are there. I'm worried we'll drink too much and not make it out there." She put her elbow on the bar and leaned her chin on the heel of her hand, looking up at him. She'd never seen Sam drink too much. He'd never had more than a beer, two at most on a hot day. He was a water man and mostly stuck to that, unless it was coffee in the morning. Even that was sparingly.

"You planning on drinking tonight?"

"I wanted to, but I don't have to, Sam, not if it's an inconvenience."

"Where's the campground?"

She told him, watching his face closely. She should have known it wouldn't do much good. Sam's face didn't give much away.

"*Satine*, that isn't a campground. It's a fishing spot. Denver showed it to me a year ago. No one goes out there."

"Exactly. It's a gorgeous spot when the sun comes up. It has a picnic table and firepit and we'll be on our own, no one around to bother us."

He held out his hand. "The four of you? Where are the other two?"

She dropped the keys to her rig into his palm. "Working. They'll meet us there in the morning. Thanks, Sam."

"No problem."

She slid off the barstool and then stopped and turned back, although she didn't know why. She shouldn't have. "Are you going to dance with me tonight?"

Again, his dark gaze drifted over her. This time, she could have sworn there was a hint of possession in his eyes, but it could have been a trick of the light. A frisson of awareness slid down her spine as if every nerve ending suddenly woke up and went on high alert. Her heart accelerated and she just managed to stop herself from pressing her palm over her chest.

She had never asked him to dance before. Never. He'd already called her on acting out of character. This was really out of character. She wasn't certain why she wanted to see his reaction. He hadn't made a fuss over the campsite except for one comment, and now he was looking at her with exactly the same expression on his face, except . . . different.

"Don't I always dance with you?"

He did. One dance. It wasn't what she was asking for, was it? She didn't know. She nodded, suddenly confused. Upset all over again by the nightmares. By the fact that she was so certain a serial killer was creeping close to her friends—Sam included. By her suddenly mixed-up feelings.

Sam reached out to run his palm very gently over her hair. Barely there. A whisper of a touch, yet she felt it like a sword of pure heat piercing her skull and rushing over her to sweep through her body, growing hotter the lower the ball of raging need went. Finally it settled, low and wicked, a seething pool of hunger and passion in her very core, her sex clenching and aching for him. She touched the tip of her tongue to her lip and stepped back, shocked at her reaction to him. What. The. Hell. She hadn't drunk anything, so no one put anything in her drink. She'd just reacted like that to his touch.

Stella hoped he couldn't actually read her mind, as she sometimes suspected he could, because right now it was pure chaos and lust. She turned and hurried over to the table where her friends were already ahead of her, their drinks waiting, chips and salsa on the table. They had her drink waiting as well. Bruce and Denver spun around in their seats in order to join the conversation.

Stella's drink of choice, like the other women, was a Moscow Mule. The chips were homemade, as was the salsa. That was part of the charm of the Grill. Usually the band was good, at least to dance to. They were so far off the beaten path, it wasn't like they got amazing bands vying to come play, but they did get decent ones. There were several good musicians in town playing together, and the locals, Stella included, enjoyed dancing to their music.

"Harlow made some beautiful pottery," Raine was saying as Stella took a seat next to her. "We went over to Judy and Tom's before I left on my last trip and she showed us how to do throw vases. Harlow has such patience for detail. Every single one of her pieces is so beautiful."

Stella knew that was the truth. Harlow could easily sell her work, and sometimes did in Tom and Judy's shop in town. Raine favored smaller, more classic pieces, little bowls or mugs she wanted to perfect that she used in her home or gave to her friends. She never considered selling her pieces, but she did like to give them as gifts at times.

She especially loved animals and would attempt, when making the "perfect" coffee or soup mug for a friend, to include their dog or cat on the pottery piece. Unfortunately, she was very exacting and hard on herself, so she often started a piece multiple times before she was satisfied enough to pass it on.

"What did she make this time?" Shabina asked.

"Glazed vases, but they were stunning, all depicting various places around the lake as the sun was rising. You know how good she is with a camera. She's been collecting pictures of the sunrise for the last few years from various locations around the lake, and she chose the ones she wanted to put on pottery," Raine said. Her voice was filled with admiration.

"I hope that puts her closer to her dream," Zahra murmured.

"Her dream?" Raine echoed. "Harlow never talks about anything in particular she wants to do. Although she does have that beautiful photography studio of hers and she sells gorgeous pictures now and again in the art galleries." She nudged Stella's drink closer to her. "You're behind. You need to catch up."

Zahra shrugged and drank more of her Moscow Mule, her head nodding in beat with the music. "What do I know?" She hopped out of her chair and rounded the table, doing the unthinkable by coming to stand in front of Bruce. "Dance with me."

The big man nearly fell off his barstool to accommodate her. His large hand completely swallowed Zahra's as he led her toward the square in front of the band, already packed with bodies. Lawyer Collins, a man born and raised in Knightly who fixed laptops and sold cell phones and laptops out of his store, immediately came and claimed Raine. Denver slid off his barstool, his amber-colored eyes seeking Stella's, but Sam was there before him, capturing her wrist and smoothly pulling her from her seat, guiding her to the dance floor, one hand on her lower back. She glanced over her shoulder to see Carl Montgomery claim Shabina as Denver dropped back on the barstool, a wry grin on his face.

Sam pulled her close to him, her back to his front, as the music pounded out a beat. The man could dance. He just seemed to have rhythm and knew how to move. More, he kept anyone from stumbling into her, no matter how drunk they were. She'd come in late, and those drinking were already feeling it, inhibitions lowered.

Sam's body was close to hers, close enough that she could feel his heat. He was always so damn hot. His energy was low-key, so why was his body temperature so hot? He wrapped one arm around her, high, just under her breasts, and pulled her body tight against his. He'd danced with her countless times, but he'd never done that before. The moment he did, she could feel every hard line of his body. She was instantly aware of him as a man and her as a woman. That dynamic had been growing between them for a long time, a comfortable, easy bond that seemed natural and strong.

Stella didn't let many people into her world—not the real one. Somehow, Sam had found his way inside hers. He always kept his word. Always. She could rely on him. When he said he would get something done, he always did it. When things went wrong and a guest got out of hand, he would suddenly appear, a silent partner standing right at her side, looking so intimidating, trouble melted away. She didn't know when she began viewing him as someone important in her world. Important to her as a woman. But he was. There was no getting around that.

Toward the end of the evening, Stella slipped onto the barstool beside Denver as she often did when Bruce and Zahra were dancing. She knew she was a little past the point of sobriety, but then Denver looked as if he might be as well. That wasn't exactly Denver's way.

"You okay, Den?"

"Got some news from my family a week or so ago and I'm still processing," he admitted.

Denver never talked about his family. He was speaking low, so she had to lean into him. "I'm here if you want to share."

They'd talked about a lot of things. Denver was better at sharing then she was. She often felt guilty about that. She was closed off for a reason, and that wasn't going to change. She glanced up briefly to catch sight of Sam in his usual corner—drinking water. Waiting to take her and her girls to their campsite. Maybe she could share a little with Sam later if she was going to catch a killer. She had to trust someone.

Denver sighed. "My old man and his brother, my uncle Vern, got into it and they shot each other. Stupid really, but inevitable."

He shook his head, stating the facts as if they didn't touch him, when Stella could see that wasn't the case. His hands shook as he wrapped them around his drink. Normally he drank beer. He was drinking hard liquor.

"They killed each other. Both bled out before anyone could get to them. My mother died while I was in the military, so I inherited the entire fucking estate. All of it. The lawyers contacted me and let me know, that's how I found out they were both dead."

Stella wasn't certain what to say to that. "You weren't close to either of them?"

"Hell no. Joined the service in order to get away from them and pay my way through med school. I was determined to be an anesthesiologist. Always wanted to be."

"You were an officer, right? You'd have to be if you were a doctor in the military in any branch of the service." Stella sipped on her drink and regarded Denver with compassion.

"Yes, that was the only way I was going to get anywhere. My family has money, but they weren't going to help me get an education, or anything else for that matter. Don't think that because people have money their families aren't fucked up, Stella."

Stella had never heard a single note of bitterness in Denver's voice before. She let her gaze drift over his face. He looked the same as he always did, but there was a hint of pain in his eyes. She nodded. "I understand, maybe more than you think I might be able to." That was as much as she was going to give up of her own past.

She came from a wealthy family and her drama had been played out in the press all over the country. If that hadn't been enough, later it had been featured in one of those silly television episode dramas, not very accurately either. She certainly knew that growing up with money didn't guarantee a cushy childhood.

"Well, you did good for yourself, Denver, and that should tell you something about what a strong person you are. That's what I always think. I'm proud of who I am. I hope you are. All of your friends, including me, look up to you. If your family doesn't appreciate you, screw them."

He grinned at her. "That's so you, Stella. Loyal to your friends. I don't exactly have any family left." He gestured around the bar. "I guess this is it. I decided to make my home here when I first came here. It was the only place that gave me real peace."

She understood that. "It sounds like you inherited a lot of money. You could go anywhere."

He shrugged. "I live simply and I like it that way. I make a shit ton of money on my own. I'll think about what to do with the money I inherited. We could use it here for the hospital, and maybe I could set up a foundation. I'll talk to Zahra and Vienna. Zahra knows what the hospital needs, and Vienna knows what we need for Search and Rescue."

"Give it some time, Denver. Even if you had a difficult time with your family, the loss can still hit you at the most unexpected time. I know from experience. We weren't close, but it was still a loss when I lost my mother. You have to allow yourself to grieve and process."

"I suppose so." He sounded doubtful. He drained his drink and held up his glass. The bartender came over to refill it. "What's going on with you and Sam?"

She frowned at him. "Not sure what you mean. He's our sober driver tonight."

"He never dances with you more than one dance. Two at most. And he doesn't have his hands all over you."

Her frown deepened. "I don't recall that he had his hands all over me." She pulled out her cell phone. Did you have your hands all over me when we were dancing?

She watched as Sam took out his phone and looked down at the screen. His expression never changed, not even while he texted her back.

"Yeah, he did. Well, he was dancing closer than he has in the past. You have to be careful of him, Stella."

When I have my hands all over you, Satine, you'll remember it and it won't be in public.

A little shiver went down her spine. She glanced at her screen twice. Yeah. He used the word *when*. It was crazy, but just looking at his text made her body aware of him. Come alive. Too many Moscow Mules, for sure. She needed to stop drinking. She took another sip because the pounding of blood between her legs felt delicious when she'd felt cold and alone and frigid for so long. Sam had slowly awakened her. If he had come at her too fast, she would have run for the hills, but somehow he'd slipped past her guard and found his way inside her.

"I thought you were friends with Sam." She leaned closer to Denver, keeping her face turned directly toward him, afraid Sam could read lips. She'd always thought he could—well, after the first few encounters with him. Either that or he really was as psychic as she was, just in a different way.

Denver's gaze lifted to drift over Sam and then came back to her, his expression concerned. "I'm not saying I don't like the man. I do. It's just that no one can really be friends with a ghost, Stella, and that's what he is."

"Um, no, he's real flesh and blood, Denver. He's sitting right there and he works his ass off at the resort. He's on Search and Rescue with you and never shirks. You're the one who told me that."

"In the military, sometimes men like him are necessary, and they're called in when everything else fails. We sometimes would see them, like shadows, hunting like wolves, but alone, always silent. Most of the time you didn't see them, but you felt them. They cleared the way for you when you were pinned down. Or they got you out of a bad situation."

"Isn't that a good thing?"

He hesitated. "In the right circumstances, yes. But ghosts are used for other tasks as well, Stella, outside the military. They usually don't last long. They die young. They aren't supposed to last long because they're trained for one thing. They're given psychological tests, and when they're proven to be a fit for what the government is looking for, they're trained for specific tasks."

"What you're saying is they're used up as fast as the government can use them."

Denver nodded. "Often, if they do break free, they're hunted down and killed because they're considered too big of a risk to be running around loose."

"You really think Sam is one of these 'ghosts'?"

She was careful not to look at Sam. He had asked to be paid under the table. What would happen if she told him she wanted him to go legit? Would he walk away? She could ask Raine to investigate him, but then Raine would know she was suspicious of him and would demand a reason, and she didn't want that. What could she tell her?

Denver sighed and pushed a hand through his hair. "Yeah, I think he might be. He's too good at everything. Too quiet. Too watchful. I don't even know how to explain it."

"What about his paperwork, Denver?"

"These guys have a million IDs. They have them stashed everywhere and money to go with them. They can be gone in minutes. If he is a ghost, he would have contacts to get him anywhere he wants to go."

"Maybe he just wants to be left alone like the rest of us. We moved here because this place represents peace to us, Denver. You said so yourself. All of us deserve a chance to live our lives the way we want to live them. You have a family here. You belong with us. Sam does as well."

She gestured around the bar to her friends. They were laughing loudly, clinging to one another, happy in their circle on the dance floor. "That's us. We'll figure it out together, right? We always have. I'm so sorry your family past has caught up with you and it turned ugly. I swear to you, I know what that's like. I don't wish that for you, but it happened. Lean on us. You've always been there for us. Let us take care of you. Did you even talk to Bruce about this?"

He put his arm around her. "Babe. Guys don't do that kind of shit. We don't need to get all emotional with one another. It's bad form."

Stella laughed. "Men are so silly. You can't even share with Bruce that you're the last of your family? Did you have cousins? Siblings? Even half siblings? I always wished I had them."

"Not that I know of." He rubbed the bridge of his nose. "Anything is possible, but according to the lawyers, no one has suddenly come forward to say they're related and should get a piece of the pie. It's a big pie. Millions. Hundreds of millions."

Stella pulled back, startled, looking into his eyes. "*Hundreds* of millions?" Suddenly the casual conversation was not so casual. When had the dreams started exactly? The date? Denver fished in that spot. He hunted. He climbed. He was on the Search and Rescue team. What if he was the actual target because he had money? She hated that the thoughts were instantly pushing into her head, but money was a huge motivator. Huge. And hundreds of millions?

"Denver, you have to be careful with that kind of money. Make a will and get it wrapped up in a trust or something. You could be very vulnerable." She took another drink of her Moscow Mule, this time nearly gulping it. It made sense. An outsider might even pay someone to give them information in order to target Denver. A cousin? Even a distant cousin. The lawyer that read him the will? He knew where Denver was. Her head was swimming. She couldn't think straight.

"Babe, don't sound so anxious. No one knows about the money. No one knows where I am, Stella. I swear to you, I'm safe." Denver caught her chin and turned her face to his. He brushed a kiss to the corner of her mouth and then another to her chin.

Stella wished she felt something. Anything. There was no fire. Denver pulled back and smiled at her, his thumb brushing down her face as if he could erase her expression.

"You have to stop or you're going to get worry lines."

She felt Sam's palm slide beneath her hair and curl around the nape of her neck. She knew it was him without turning. He leaned against her back, his fingers massaging the tension out of her, sending little sparks of electricity dancing over her skin. She'd definitely had too much to drink. She had to remain silent or she was going to blurt out something horrible, like he could possibly be the hottest man on earth.

"Why would Stella be getting worry lines, Denver?" Sam asked.

He bent closer so she felt his breath stirring strands of her hair. She needed to hold her own breath to savor that moment. If she breathed too deep, she'd pull his scent right into her lungs, and she didn't dare do that. His voice. That rich, low voice that brushed over her skin and then sank deep into her bones.

"She's worried about me," Denver said, his voice overloud and a little slurred. He turned slightly on the barstool, a frown drawing his eyebrows together. "Uh-oh. That bastard Bale Landry and his rotten friends are here tonight and Sean is staring at Shabina in a way I don't like. I didn't see them come in, did you, Sam?"

Stella immediately tried to push away from the bar, but Sam held her in place. He trapped her body easily with his larger one, his hand still resting casually on her nape, but he was clearly holding her in place.

"Don't go off half-cocked, honey. We need to see what they're up to before you start a war with them."

Denver stood up, staggered and recovered his equilibrium. "They always get ugly with Zahra and Shabina. Mostly Shabina. Bruce is with Zahra, and no one wants to mess with her when he's around."

That was the truth. Bruce was just too big, a mountain of man, mostly muscle. It was known by every local that he crushed hard on Zahra, and saying anything to her could get you on the wrong side of his very powerful fist. Stella could see Bruce dancing in the middle, surrounded by Shabina, Zahra and Raine. They hadn't noticed Bale, Sean, Edward and Jason swagger up to the bar. The four men ordered beers and immediately turned to watch those dancing.

"Why do you suppose they keep targeting Shabina and Zahra the way they do?" Stella asked. "I think Bale intimidates Harlow, and that's hard to do, but they've never really gone after me. I wonder why."

Sam exchanged a look with Denver over her head. Denver sighed and rubbed her arm. "Babe, no one is going to come after you if they think they'll have to contend with the two of us. And they'd have to."

Stella tilted back her head to look up at Denver and then Sam. She'd definitely had too much to drink. Tilting her head back was a huge mistake. The room began to spin. She flung out her arm to look for something solid to hang on to. At the same time, she clutched her drink. It had mysteriously been refilled. Just like magic. She found Sam's arm. He had a very good arm. All muscle. Hard. She petted his muscles.

"I need to get over there, Sam. Someone has to be the voice of reason."

"You're a little drunk right now, Stella," Sam said. *He* sounded like the voice of reason, which annoyed her. *She* was supposed to

be the voice of reason. She didn't get drunk. She got tipsy sometimes, like now, when she was fairly certain her posse needed her
to ward off the bad guys circling their group. There were plenty
of women to choose to dance with, but no, Bale and his desperate
losers had to start critiquing her friends. It was so annoying.

Sam wrapped his arm around her waist. "Woman."

"Man." She glared up at him. "They need me."

"Sam and I can handle it. You sit here and behave." Denver
unexpectedly sided with Sam.

Stella included him in her glare. She should have known he
would switch sides, the traitor. Just because Sam got that impla-
cable look on his face.

"Babe." Denver started laughing and held up both hands in
surrender. "You're shooting lightning bolts out of your eyes.
You're going to fry me. The only reason we weren't banned from
the Grill the last time there was an altercation between your girl
posse and Bale and his boys was because Alek is a little smitten
with you. You saved his bar with your business plan and made the
Grill what it is today, so you're his golden girl."

Stella had saved the restaurant, coming up with the idea for
music at night and the food that was more than bar food. Shabina
had helped with the menu. She hadn't been alone in the planning. Her friends had sat around with her, thinking up different
foods they liked to eat at bars when they were dancing. Stella
wanted a place where those renting her cabins would really love
to go in the evenings.

Raine designed a brochure and a PowerPoint presentation for
Stella to show Alek. It had worked and he had agreed to try the
food and dancing for one month to see if he could bring in the
locals along with those she promised from her resort. The results
had been astonishing, and since then the Grill was so popular

Alek had to hire permanent help along with his temporary workers during the height of tourist season.

Sam leaned down, his mouth close enough to her ear to be able to be heard above the loud, pulsing music. "Stay put, Stella. Bale and his friends are dangerous when they're drinking, especially when confronted by women."

Denver nodded his agreement. "They can't be bested by a woman or they'll need to get back at her in a very public way. You've already had one confrontation with them, you don't need another."

She watched the two men make their way to the dance floor. Denver looked as if he had sobered up. He wasn't staggering at all as he walked beside Sam. Sam just looked . . . predatory. For her, he would always stand out, no matter where he was. It didn't make sense that he was supposedly a ghost as Denver had suggested. Her gaze was drawn to him, that confident way he moved, like a jungle cat stalking his prey.

Stella didn't understand men like Bale or the others. They had thriving businesses, or at least ones that were getting by in the small town. They had jobs where so many had to have three jobs. Why did they think themselves so superior to women? Especially to a woman like Shabina or Zahra? Both women worked hard. Had their only crime been turning down a date from one of these men? Was Bale really harassing Harlow? A senator's daughter? Would he dare?

Stella didn't take her gaze off Denver and Sam as they walked casually up to the bar close to the dance floor and inserted themselves right next to Bale and his friends. There was satisfaction in noting that the taunting smirks faded when the two men showed up, although that didn't stop Sean from calling out something nasty as Shabina danced nearby.

Shabina looked breathtaking. She was naturally graceful and

had rhythm, losing herself in the music as she moved with Zahra, Raine and Bruce. She had her slender arms over her head and her eyes closed. Her long, dark hair fell to her waist and moved around her like a waterfall of gleaming silk.

Stella watched Sean's expression more closely. She might be *tipsy*, but she was aware. He had a look of obsession on his face. There was a reason he continually showed up at the Sunrise Café in spite of the warnings not to keep coming back. He might think himself superior and he could tell himself anything he wanted, but he had a real thing for her friend. She switched her gaze to Sam. Naturally, Sam noticed because he saw everything.

She let her breath out. Sam would be such a great ally to have. He did see everything. He was careful. He listened to her and weighed what she said carefully. If she could rule him out as a suspect—and honestly, she didn't for a minute really think he was a serial killer—then he would be the person she would want to confide in. He fit with her. She didn't know why, only that he did.

She switched her attention to Denver. He had warned her about Sam, but he had done so gently, not in a mean way. She could tell, in spite of his warning to her, he did like Sam and re-spected him even more. He was just careful of her, like a sibling might be. She was closed off to everyone and had put herself off-limits. Denver respected those limits. Sam always had as well. Sam seemed to be stepping over them all of a sudden.

"This seat taken?"

Stella looked up. Carl Montgomery, the local contractor, slid onto the barstool next to her. He was around forty, with dark hair and startling blue eyes. Like most of those living in the town, he was a hunter. He worked hard and expected his crew to as well. Carl had built several of the cabins for her at the resort, and they were exactly what she'd asked for and then some.

She flashed him a smile. "I don't see you here very often, Carl. What a nice surprise."

"What are you drinking?"

She looked at her glass. "Moscow Mule, but I think I've had a little too much. I'm definitely feeling it."

"One night off won't kill you, Stella. You work too hard." He leaned over the bar to get the bartender's attention. "It's packed in here."

Stella looked around. Every table was taken. Every barstool. The dance floor was packed. Along the walls people talked and laughed together, tapping their feet to the music. In the outside covered patio, where the heaters were turned on against the cool night air, she could see those tables were filled as well.

"Yes, it is." There was satisfaction in knowing she had helped to make this happen. She made it a point to visit every business in town in an effort to figure out how she could help them become one of the thriving successes, especially if they were faltering. These people had become her friends, and she believed if they helped one another they could all stay afloat during the lean times.

"You know you stole my best worker." Carl indicated Sam with a nod of his chin. "I had hoped to make him my foreman. Men like him don't come along every day. He knows his way around a build."

She grinned at him. "I saw that. He's good with motors too. You waited a little too long before making him a decent offer. I wasn't going to lose out. He can practically run the resort." She made a face. "Unless he has to talk to a guest, then, not so much. I wouldn't say his social skills match his knowledge of repairing just about anything needed."

She laughed softly. It was the absolute truth. Most of the time, Sam avoided having to deal with the guests. It wasn't his job. She had others to do that. He worked behind the scenes to keep the resort running. He'd made it very clear to her when he agreed to take the job in the first place that he wasn't a people person.

Carl's laughter joined hers. "You're right about that. He isn't much of a talker. Works hard though. I see he's over there intimidating the hell out of Sean and Ed. What the hell is wrong with those boys? If they make one more nasty comment toward Shabina, I'll have to shove my fist down their throats, and I haven't been in a fistfight since I was twenty. Maybe eighteen. I'm pretty sure it was in high school."

"You've known them a long time. Have they always been like that?" Stella asked.

The bartender put drinks and a plate of mixed fried zucchini, mushrooms and cheese sticks in front of them.

"Thanks, Lucca," Carl said, pushing a healthy tip the bartender's way.

Lucca saluted him and hurried down the line, crushing it, the way he did when he was making several drinks at a time. Alek, the owner, had been smart to hire him when he'd first come into town, offering him enough to get him to want to stay.

"Dive in, Stella. I can't eat all this by myself or I'll have to go to one of those obnoxious girlie classes Harlow puts on."

Stella dipped a zucchini stick in marinara sauce. It was good. Not like Shabina good, but good. Alek had his own recipes from his mother's side of the family and they were valuable to the Grill. It wasn't just a greasy spoon.

"Harlow's yoga classes? Wait until I tell her you describe them as girlie. That's rich. Have you ever tried one? Take a private lesson if you're too intimidated to take a class. Seriously, not easy, and that's beginner. People always think yoga is going to be so easy. Your body has to use all the muscles, stretching them . . ."

"Harlow gives private classes?" Carl interrupted.

Stella took a sip of her Moscow Mule. She knew better, but it was going down smooth and this was too good to be true. Carl Montgomery was into Harlow. Who knew? He was always so buttoned down. He rarely came to the Grill, and if he did, he didn't hang out with their crowd. Not really. He was one of the ones on the fringe. She knew him, but not well.

"Yes, Harlow gives private lessons." She glanced toward the dance floor when movement caught her eye. Carl slid off the bar-stool.

Sean was pushing his way through the few people dancing between him and Stella's small inner circle of friends. He strode right up to Shabina, who was dancing, and he positioned himself behind her, his body almost on top of hers. She tried to elbow him off of her, but he yanked her into him, his hips thrusting hard.

Stella found herself trying to run toward the dance floor, but there were too many people between her and the place marked off for the dancing. She squeezed through two men and went around a woman who had paused right in front of her. By the time she got to the edge of the floor, whatever had taken place was over.

Bale, Ed and Jason had Sean by the arms and were escorting him out. Bruce, Sam, Denver and Alek's bouncer, Jeff, watched them go. Zahra and Raine escorted Shabina back to Stella. She flung her arm around her friend.

"That man needs someone to teach him a lesson or two in manners," she said. "Are you all right?"

"Yes. It's not like it's the first time some man wanted to freak dance with one of us. It happens all the time." Shabina smiled at Carl. "I didn't know you were here tonight."

He waved toward the platter of food. "Have at it, ladies. What are you drinking?" Once again, he got the bartender's attention.

Within minutes Carl had them all laughing. Stella appreciated that he didn't refer to the incident at all but rather got everyone back on track having fun. Denver and Bruce joined them.
Sam went to his usual place in the corner, keeping an eye on
them. Before, she had wanted him to be with them, thinking it
strange and creepy that he didn't sit with them, but now, she
liked the idea that he watched over them—that he was sober and
she didn't have to worry about anything but having a good time
with her friends because he was there.

# CHAPTER FIVE

Stella woke with her head pounding. It was still dark, thank heavens. Bailey shoved his wet nose against her face and she absently patted him. Had she remembered to take him out last night before she went to bed? She was a responsible dog owner. Of course she'd taken him out, but clearly he needed to go out again. She sat up, groaning as she did so, pressing her hand to her head. She so deserved everything she was going to get this morning.

Looking around, she realized she was in her own bed. On the nightstand was a bottle of water and two white tablets. Sam. He'd poured the four women into her rig and driven them back to the resort instead of the campsite. On the way back, they sang at the top of their lungs and laughed hysterically, mostly because once Bruce, Denver and Carl had retreated, leaving the four women, Stella had confessed scandalous thoughts she had had about Sam and all the things she wanted him to do to her.

She groaned again and covered her face. Hopefully she'd been whispering when she told her friends over and over how hot she thought he was. He'd been sitting a distance from them, and the noise level in the bar was loud, so surely he hadn't heard. She drank down as much water as possible and slid out of bed.

She was still in her clothes, but no shoes. At least she was spared the indignity of throwing up all over him. She hurried to let the dog out, trying to think whether she'd been facing him while she was confiding to her friends in her tipsy—okay, past tipsy—state about how hot Sam was. She was almost positive he could read lips. She'd be mortified. But then, she had a lot to be mortified about. Leaving Bailey to do his business, she hurried into the shower, hoping to clear the cobwebs.

The Moscow Mules had somehow made the four of them believe they were superb at Cossack dancing. They took to the dance floor, squatting, kicking their legs out with their arms crossed over their chests and laughing hysterically. Unfortunately, all they were really doing was squatting, standing and squatting again. That, and falling on their butts. It had been a fabulous night.

Sam kept his expressionless mask in place as he drove them home, putting up with the four of them making outrageous faces at each other to remind themselves to keep quiet and hide Stella's secret crush. They would all burst out laughing. He was stoic about it, which only made them laugh louder.

Stella dressed in jeans and a tee, trying to remember if the conversation with the girls had taken place in front of Sam or not. She'd definitely asked them if she had inadvertently blurted out how hot he was or how she would "do" him in a hot minute. Had she asked them at the bar or in the 4Runner or at her house? She remembered Zahra assuring her over and over she hadn't said a single damning word in front of him. The others had nodded solemnly, but then they'd spoiled it all by laughing hysterically again and asking how they would know because they were drunk.

She pulled on running shoes after braiding her hair and went out to find Bailey. Sam was usually up long before anyone else. She didn't see him anywhere, so she headed down to the boat rentals. Bernice Fulton was always up early, making certain the boats were clean and all had the required number of life jackets in them. She was meticulous about the care of the boats. She certainly didn't deserve Stella snapping at her a few days earlier.

Bernice and Roy Fulton had worked for Stella for five years and she'd been very lucky to find the couple. Roy was knowledgeable about all aspects of fishing and had been willing to pass that knowledge on to Stella. When she came up with the idea of fishing tournaments, he had been more than willing to help her. They were two of the few year-round employees she kept on staff. Each year, Roy had helped her improve the tournament until fishermen came from all over to participate in their event.

Bernice might not be able to fix motors on boats, but she was skilled with customers. They liked her and she could easily upsell all kinds of items from their selection of paddle boats, rowboats, kayaks, canoes, fishing boats, and of course their cruising boats. They had it all to rent at the marina.

"Hey, Stella." Bernice greeted her with her customary smile. She was in her late fifties and perpetually happy. She had very few lines on her face to show the passing years, and those she did have were mainly from being in the sun. She always wore a wide-brimmed hat and slathered on sunscreen. Her hats were darling, and no one wore them with more style than Bernice.

"Good morning, Bernice. Although I haven't had my coffee, so technically, I can't say if it's a good morning or not," Stella greeted her. "As always, you're looking lovely."

Bernice did look lovely. She wore soft yellow jeans rolled up to her calves and a boat-neck shirt with thin blue, white and yellow stripes. Her yellow boots matched her thick sweater, and somewhere she would have sunglasses that went with her outfit as well.

"Thank you, dear." Bernice took the compliment as her due. "Roy has coffee at the bait shop, but you know it isn't all that good."

Stella was well aware Roy's coffee lacked anything that remotely was good about coffee other than actual caffeine. "I wanted to apologize to you for the way I talked to you the other day. I was way out of line. You didn't deserve me taking out my seriously bad day on you and that's what I was doing. I hope you can forgive me, Bernice. You're a good friend and I know I hurt you by snapping at you the way I did."

Bernice's eyes clouded over and she threw her arms around Stella. "Sweetheart, think nothing of it. I knew that day was terrible for you. Roy told me how some of the guests yelled at you. I hated that for you."

Stella hugged her back. "That's no reason to take it out on you, someone I care about. I'm truly sorry."

Bernice patted her back, sniffed and then straightened and released her. "No worries. I appreciate your apology. It means something to me. Sam said you were camping with your girls for a few days. I think that's good. You need some time off."

"You saw him this morning? Where is he? He was supposed to take us to our tents last night."

"Not this morning. When he brought all of you home last night, he told Roy he was going to spend the night where you would be camping to protect your things, said he was worried about all of you waking up with hangovers. Thought he could get a little fishing in. You know he rarely has the time. Denver might join him if he isn't hungover. Apparently Denver drank more than he usually does, but was planning to meet Sam out there early this morning before sunrise."

Bernice continued to talk, but Stella couldn't hear a word she was saying. She felt the color drain from her face. Sam and Denver were *fishing*. She'd led two people who meant the world to her right to the spot where the murderer wanted his victim to be.

"I have to go, Bernice," she whispered, and ran out of the little building and back down the marina to the main house and to the garage where Sam had parked her 4Runner. She knew she must look insane, but she didn't care. She had to get to the men before something evil happened to them. "Bailey!" She yanked open the back of the rig.

Bailey came running and immediately leapt into his spot. She slammed the door closed and ran around to the driver's side. Where was the fob to her rig? She'd given it to Sam the night before. Where would he put it? Probably on her nightstand. Swearing, she ran back into the house, into her bedroom, and sure enough, it was right there. Sam was predictable when it came to things like that. Water to hydrate. Aspirin for her headache. Her keys.

She drove like a maniac. She knew what her rig could do and just how far she could push it on the road around the lake. Thank heavens Bailey had woken her before the sun came up. It was rising into the sky now and she knew the two men would be fishing, or at least Sam would be if Denver wasn't there yet. The tires slid just a little as she took a tight bend far too fast. It wouldn't do to slide off the road.

She hit the steering wheel with the flat of her palm and sent up silent prayers to someone, she didn't know who. The last time she had watched helplessly as people had died, she'd stopped believing in anyone outside of herself. Still, prayers might help. Who knew? She didn't want to lose anyone else. Not Sam. Not Denver. No one.

Stella made the turn onto the pitted dirt road leading to the lake. Dust rose around her in clouds, forcing her to slow her speed. She came up behind Sam's rig, threw the 4Runner into park, turned off the engine and jumped out. She didn't see Denver's truck. Sam was already fishing. He wore a hat and waders. Just like in her nightmare, he had waded out among the boulders, plants and reeds. She released Bailey and ran toward the lake, calling out to Sam.

The wind had come up and it whipped at her hair, tore tears from her eyes. Maybe it put them there. He was too far away to hear. Her gaze went to the surface of the lake where the wind tugged at the water. There was that dark spot that drew her gaze like a magnet, that exact spot where Sam had dropped his line. Of course he'd hit the spot where the water seemed to swirl just a little bit, making its own lazy pool.

The sun had risen, casting the lake in beautiful colors the way it did every morning. Today it had chosen various shades of purple, from light lavenders to dark purples to burgundies and finally dark, dark reds. Her heart accelerated as she ran. She felt that dark menace creeping closer. It wasn't her imagination. It was there, beneath the surface of the water, swimming toward Sam's hook. Swimming toward him like a silent wraith.

She saw his arm jerk slightly, just the way the fisherman's had in the nightmare. He stepped out farther into the lake, gently battling the fish on his line. Stella felt as if she were running in slow motion. Past the tents. The picnic table and firepit. She kept yelling, trying to tell him to get out of the water. To let go of the line. He was too far out there, away from the safety of the shore. As she ran, she shed her heavier clothes, the jacket, the sweater, so she was down to her tee. There was no getting out of her jeans or shoes; she didn't have the luxury of time.

Sam moved farther out of the safety net of shore, wading

deeper among the reeds, working the "fish" on his line. She could imagine the determination on his face. She kept running as she saw his body jerk and lose balance, something Sam never, ever did. He went over backward abruptly, just like in her nightmare, hitting the back of his head on a boulder.

He was a big man and it took several heaving tries for the killer to drag Sam's unresponsive body underwater, giving Stella the time she needed to cover the rest of the ground. She didn't hesitate, running into the icy water and then diving below the surface.

The lake was fed from the snowpack every year, and the temperature was freezing to her body. Shockingly so. It didn't matter. The cold barely registered as she swam toward the killer trying to hold Sam down in order to drown him. Sam wasn't completely out with his head injury. Instinctively, he was fighting back, his movements slow.

Stella hit the killer from behind, trying to get around his air tank, wishing she had worn a knife so she could sever his airline. She jerked at him, going for his mask, for anything to distract him. He swung around, punching at her face and hitting her cheek. She inserted her body between him and Sam, determined that he wouldn't get to the nearly unconscious man. She swam at the killer once more, trying to tear his face mask off again. This time he drew his legs up, knees to his chest, and slammed them into her hard, driving her away from him with the power of his legs. He swam away fast, disappearing out of sight beneath the deeper water.

Stella tried to move, to swim, to do something, but she couldn't. She just curled up there in the water, her mind sluggish, unable to process what she needed to do next. Sam's hands caught at her before she realized she was nearly completely numb and unable to move in the icy water. They staggered together through the reeds and boulders up to the shore where they lay together, Sam nearly on top of her. He whistled for Bailey and the dog responded, lying down on the other side of Stella at Sam's command. They lay that way trying to catch their respective breath and warm up enough to actually move.

"We need to get you out of your wet clothes," Sam said eventually. "I'll build the fire back up to get us warm."

"I can do it, Sam. Your head. You took a bad hit on the rocks when he jerked you under." She was shivering so badly she thought she might crack her teeth, they chattered so much. She had a terrible image of them fracturing and just disintegrating and falling right out of her head.

"I think, for once in your life, you're going to let me take care of you. I know you're independent and you don't need anyone, but you're going to lie here with Bailey keeping you warm while I get that fire going. First, I'm stripping you and bringing you my sleeping bag." There was pure steel in his voice.

She turned her head to look at him over her shoulder. Something in his dark eyes told her not to mess with him and she was too damn tired to argue. She wasn't sure she could get to her feet anyway. She couldn't control the incessant shaking. She just nodded and laid her head back down passively. Who knew that when he did start talking he'd be bossy?

Sam pushed himself up and reached for the hem of her shirt. "Can you lift your arms up, Stella? If you can't, I can cut this off you."

She put her arms over her head and tried to lift herself enough for him to pull the wet tee from her body. Her bra was next. Then her shoes and jeans. He was gone and returned quickly with a sleeping bag, tucking it around her and once again commanding the dog to lie tight against her. By the time the shaking had ceased, Sam had the fire built back up in the firepit, had changed into dry clothes and had put on water for coffee.

He brought her the backpack from her tent. "At least you have dry clothes."

"The cut on the back of your head is still bleeding." She avoided his eyes. Not because she was naked under the sleeping bag, but because she'd driven out to the lake and acted like a maniac, running to him, diving in, clearly knowing a killer lurked beneath the surface. How was she going to explain that?

"It's letting up. Get dressed and come over by the fire. Have some coffee. With you, that always helps."

"What do you mean, it's letting up? Let me look at it. Does it need stitches? We should have Harlow or Vienna take a look at you. Or go to the emergency room."

"I'll take care of it, Stella." He turned away from her and stalked back to the firepit.

She wasn't going to get a reprieve. She had wanted to tell him. She'd even needed to. He was intelligent. He listened. Really listened. He had a way of staying silent and processing what she told him, not interrupting but really hearing when she talked to him. She had wanted to tell him that she knew a serial killer was going to begin killing in the Sierras and he would disguise his kills as accidents, making it extremely difficult to identify the pattern.

Telling him, talking about her past, meant giving away her secrets. But then, Sam had secrets too. He had a past he didn't share with others. Not even her. She didn't think he would be upset and hurt the way she knew her friends might be. The thought of going back, revisiting all those things that she had buried, made her ill. She had promised herself she would never open those doors again, but how did one ignore a murderer?

She sat up slowly, a little surprised to find that her body didn't want to cooperate. Her muscles felt heavy and battered. Bailey pressed close and she hugged the Airedale to her, grateful to the loyal animal. She could always count on the dog for companionship and protection. Bailey would have plunged into the icy lake after her had she stayed down too long. He'd done it before when she'd rolled her canoe. He hadn't even hesitated.

She dressed in fleece-lined leggings and a long sweater. Sam had left her fur-lined boots he'd found in her tent. She wore them at night to stay warm when she walked Bailey. Standing slowly, she was disconcerted to realize how unsteady she still was. Sam was sprawled in a camp chair by the fire, and the aroma of coffee hit her as she came up beside him and the warmth of the crackling flames.

Stella reached for the coffeepot. Nothing smelled so good as coffee in the morning, especially now, when she was freezing and maybe a little scared. Well, a lot scared. Okay, terrified. Her cheekbone throbbed where the killer's fist had connected with her face, and right under her breasts, where he'd kicked her, her abdomen ached. Her skin burned and her muscles hurt. Thawing out might not be all it was cracked up to be.

Sam casually pulled the coffeepot out of her reach and indicated the camp chair he'd placed facing him. "Sit and tuck the blanket around you. You can have coffee when you're settled." He poured some of the ambrosia into a mug.

She couldn't take her eyes off the rich, dark liquid. In fact, she wanted it so much she didn't even scowl at him for being so bossy. She just meekly dropped into the chair and pulled the blanket around her.

Sam handed her the mug with a slight shake of his head. "You really are a terrible addict."

"I know. There's no hope for me." She wasn't going to lie. She loved coffee. She was a coffee snob. In town, Shabina made the best coffee, but Stella was very, very good at making her own coffee. She'd learned out of necessity. "I don't even care, and I hope I never recover."

Sam gave her a little half smile as he gestured toward the lake. "Someone just tried to kill me and you knew it was going to happen." His voice was gentle. There was no accusation. No judgment. Just a statement of fact.

That was so like Sam. Stella took a sip of coffee, blinking rapidly to clear her vision of the sudden blurring, and looked out over the lake. The capricious wind had died down and the surface looked like a deep sapphire gemstone blazing with beauty as the early morning sun shone down on it.

"You're going to have to trust someone, Stella. It may as well be me. I told you I would do certain things for you I would never do for anyone else, and I meant that, but you have to talk to me. I can't help you if you don't let me in."

"I don't know how. I don't know where to start."

"Look at me, Stella."

She'd almost gotten him killed. She'd been so selfish, wanting her night off, thinking she could set up her camping site and no one would go fishing. The killer wouldn't have a target. Instead, she'd set up Sam to be the killer's victim. She'd done that. Delivered him right into the murderer's hands.

"I could have lost you," she whispered. Tears tracked down her face. She couldn't stop crying when she normally never showed weakness to anyone anymore. She knew better. She'd learned that at an early age. "I almost got you killed."

"Look at me, Stella," he repeated. There was no change in his voice. Not in the volume. If anything, the tone was softer, but there was a firmness to it, that absolute implacability that told her he wouldn't stop until he had his way.

She forced herself to lift her wet, spiky lashes. His features were hard, unreadable, all angles and planes, but his eyes held a gentleness at odds with the ruthless lines carved into his tough features. Her stomach did some serious somersaulting. Roller coasters had nothing on the performance going on. And her heart . . . serious melting.

She didn't trust. That was a given. She had reason not to. Real reasons. How had Sam, over the last two years, slipped under her guard? How had they gotten to this point?

"I wasn't knocked out. When I felt the tug on my line, I knew something was off. I saw you running toward the lake. It didn't take a rocket scientist to put two and two together that you decided on this camping spot for a reason. You didn't want anyone fishing here, did you?"

She couldn't look away from his gaze no matter how much she wanted to. She shook her head.

"I felt someone grab my ankles and yank, so I let them take me under. The blow to my head stunned me, but didn't knock me out. I had my knife, sweetheart. No one was going to kill me. I don't die so easy."

She let her breath out. If she had just stayed out of it, Sam might have killed him, or at least subdued the potential murderer, and it would all be over. She'd rushed in to save him and now the killer was on the loose.

"That just makes it worse. Now he's out there and he's going to kill someone else. He'll keep killing. He isn't going to be easy to stop. I'm sorry, Sam. I didn't realize you'd come out here. I thought if we left the tents here, no one would come to this spot to fish. Both Denver and Bruce were drinking last night and they're the only ones that I know of who really come to this spot to fish."

She rubbed her pounding temples. First her left one and then right. She took another sip of coffee. "I really am sorry."

"There's no need, Stella. Just talk to me. Look at your lake. Drink your coffee and know that you can trust me. Talk to me." He indicated the lake.

Stella took a deep breath and inhaled the Sierras. The fresh morning mountain air. The campfire. Sam. Bailey. Even the smell of her friends' tents. She looked around her at the sheer beauty of her chosen home. The magnificence of it. The trees and colors. Sunrise Lake.

She moistened her lips. "I wish I would sound sane, but I'm not going to, so I haven't decided how I can say this to you and make you believe me." She was as truthful as she could be.

Stella kept her gaze on the lake's surface as the colors went from those beautiful shades of purple to various shades of red. She glanced up to the sky. Clouds had drifted, just little lacy formations, nothing threatening. White and gray, they took shapes in the sky. Little fingers of fog crept from the mountains, emerging from the trees, coming toward the lake in strange ghostly arrows of fine mist. Was that some sort of portent? Did she even believe in things like that?

"Stella, you're as sane at it gets. Talk to me."

She opened her mouth twice to tell him because she really needed to share. It wasn't like Sam talked to anyone. She closed her mouth both times and shook her head. He didn't say anything encouraging. He just waited in silence. A fish jumped and plopped back in the water close to the reeds jutting out of the water by the rocks where Sam had been pulled under. If Stella looked close enough, she'd swear she could see a smear of blood on one of the rocks. Her stomach rebelled. She put her coffee cup down and wrapped her arms around her middle.

"I think there's blood on that rock, Sam." She whispered it.

"Most likely, Stella. We'll have to show the sheriff. We have to report this."

She closed her eyes. She knew he was right. This was going to be a storm she wouldn't get out of. "I sometimes have nightmares."

That was such a great start. Nightmares. She had seen hell in Sam's eyes on more than one occasion and she was fairly certain he knew what real nightmares were.

"I've only ever had these kinds of nightmares a couple of other times in my life. I was four the first time. Four. Five. Six years old. The nightmares were in fragments at first, but then as I got older and the dreams were more frequent, they would be in more detail. By the time I was seven, I could see the details enough to draw them and write some of them down."

She frowned, trying to think of a way to explain. "I didn't realize at first, because I was a child, but the dreams came in a five-day pattern. The first day I would see a small glimpse of a scene as if a clip of a movie or video was playing. Each night the lens would open wider. I was actually seeing a serial killer murder a victim. I would never see the killer, only the setting and sometimes enough of the victim to identify him or her."

She buried one hand in Bailey's fur, needing the comfort of the Airedale. Bailey responded by shoving his big head in her lap. She could feel Sam's eyes on her, but she didn't look at him. She had to find a way to tell him this in her own way.

"Usually, two days after each nightmare, someone would be murdered in the way I would see it in my dream. I was a little girl and had no idea the nightmares were coming true. I told my mother, but she never told me they were coming true. Later, when I asked her why she didn't go to the police, she told me no one would take the word of a child and she didn't want to turn our lives upside down."

Stella rubbed her hands on her legs. She braced herself to look at Sam. To see the condemnation there. The killings had spanned four years. There had been a lot of murders in that time. She should have known Sam would never have judged that little girl. His features showed no emotion. He was all planes and angles, that dark masculinity that whispered he had his own stories to hide.

"My mother wasn't telling the truth. I would tell her"—she lowered her voice even more—"*Mommy, Daddy's doing the bad thing again.* She would get so angry with me. She didn't want me to say that. Or tell anyone. We were very well off and she had so many friends, luncheons to attend, tennis games to play. She couldn't be bothered with nightmares that couldn't be real, even if she knew they were. She fired my nanny so I wouldn't talk to anyone about Daddy doing the bad thing again."

Stella looked down at her hands. "All those lives that maybe could have been saved over those years. The cops most likely wouldn't have listened to a little kid, but maybe one of them might have. My mother started drinking. I was seven when one of my tutors listened to me and took me to the police department. Eventually, my father was caught. My mother drank herself to death. By that I mean she committed suicide. After the media circus died down and there was no one willing to come forward to take the daughter of a serial killer, I was put into foster care."

Sam didn't offer sympathy and she was grateful. She buried her fingers deep into Bailey's fur and kept her gaze on the mist. With the sun in the sky, the wisps of fog had turned from the gorgeous lavender to slashes of crimson, so it looked as if blood spilled in rake marks across the surface of the lake. What should have been beautiful made her shiver. Those arrows of mist looked as if they'd been dipped in blood.

She wasn't going to share that with him. She ran a multimillion-dollar resort because she was level-headed and detail oriented, not fantasy driven. The nightmares were screwing with her head.

"Things were okay for a few years, but then when I was sixteen, I started having nightmares again. They started the same way. *Mommy, Daddy's doing the bad thing again.* I would always hear myself say that very distinctly and then I'd see a part of the murder. Each night a little more would come to me. The fifth night I'd see the murder and then I wouldn't dream. A couple of nights later, I'd hear of a murder committed that exact way. I'd read about it or see it on the news."

She pressed her fingers to her mouth. Her hand was shaking. She was suddenly the scared teenager, knowing if she went to the police the circus would start all over again. If she didn't go, she might be responsible for others losing their lives. She didn't want the notoriety. She detested the spotlight.

Stella forced air through her lungs, remembering how difficult it had been to make that decision. "I didn't want to tell anyone, but I felt guilty that people were dying, and maybe by revealing the dreams, I might save lives, so I went to the police. They laughed at me. I was actually happy that they did, but the murders kept happening. My nightmares kept happening. My foster mother was very compassionate and she put me in counseling. I wanted to believe everyone, that the murders were triggering the nightmares because of my father, but I knew better. I was seeing murders before they actually happened."

Stella sighed and picked up her coffee, took a few sips, grateful for her favorite outdoor to-go mug that kept coffee hot forever. "Eventually, the FBI came to me and asked me all sorts of questions. My foster mother and my counselor both were with me and they insisted the FBI promise to keep me out of it. The agents had me draw details of each of my dreams. They told me when I had a new one to contact them and start detailing everything I could remember. The serial killer was caught and the FBI did try to keep me out of it, as they promised. Unfortunately, my identity was leaked and it was too good a story to pass up for the media. My name was everywhere."

She stole a quick look at him. Sam was looking out over the lake, and the air she'd been holding in her lungs left in a rush. He could be counted on, just like the Sierras. Her place of peace. Her rock. The world might be crashing down around her, but he was steady. Quiet. Confident. The same.

"Eventually, I inherited a large trust fund. There was enough money for me to live however I wanted. I legally changed my name. I got my degree and eventually ended up here. I loved this resort, hired on as manager and turned it around with a lot of hard work. The owner was older and wanted to sell. I made him an offer and bought four years ago, although we didn't tell anyone at the time. I don't like anyone knowing my business."

Sam was silent for so long she wasn't certain he would say anything. He drank his coffee, looking out over the lake, processing what she'd told him. His gaze shifted to her face. "The nightmares started up again."

She nodded. "They did."

"That was why you weren't getting any sleep and you snapped at Bernice."

"That still isn't a good excuse, Sam. I did apologize to her." If she hadn't . . . She blinked back tears and sipped at her coffee. "I couldn't believe a serial killer was here in our beautiful home. He's going to make his kills look like accidents. The first is supposed to be a fisherman. I knew I had one or two days to find the kill spot so I drove around looking like mad. It was pure luck that I found this spot, since it's secluded and no one really comes here that often."

"You had a nightmare that ugly five nights in a row, Stella, and you didn't even mention it to Zahra?"

She pressed her fingers to her mouth and shook her head, keeping her eyes on his chest. "If I told her, I'd have to tell her everything," she whispered. "Sam, you wouldn't have been here if it hadn't been for me."

"That's not the kind of thinking that's going to do us any good, sweetheart. If we're going to catch a serial killer, we're going to have to get out in front of him. Worrying about whether or not you forced me to go fishing when no one has ever forced me to do anything is kind of ridiculous, don't you think?"

"I didn't see any part of him," Stella confessed. "Nothing that would help me identify him. I was so focused on getting to you that I didn't think to even look at his equipment. The water was murky because the bottom had been stirred up and it was difficult to see. I was cold and terrified I wasn't going to get to you in time. I didn't even think to wear a knife."

"He knows about this fishing spot, but a lot of those who come here year after year know all the best fishing spots. When anyone goes to the bait shop and asks, Roy gives them a map of the various spots and even marks how to get to them," Sam reminded.

"That's true," Stella conceded. She hadn't thought of that. "He was wearing a wet suit and swimming in the lake, which means he at least knows his way around it somewhat. If he's local, what would trigger him to start killing?"

"If you hung out with the FBI, you probably know more than I do. My guess would be serial killers kill for a variety of reasons. Anger. Thrills. Money. Even power. Sex. Sometimes it could be seeking attention. That to me all sounds logical enough, but then are serial killers logical? Who the hell knows?"

Stella scowled at the lake. Her beautiful lake. "Whoever thought up this murder went to a lot of trouble to make it appear an accident. We're in a secluded spot. He donned scuba gear and swam under ice-cold water and carried out an elaborate scheme in order to fool the ME, the sheriff and everyone else."

"To be a serial killer, which he would have to be to trigger your nightmares, means he plans on carrying out more than one murder, right?" Sam mused.

She nodded. "I don't get nightmares every time someone is murdered. I have to be in very close proximity to a serial killer. This has only happened twice before this."

"If he wants the murders to look like accidents, we can rule out attention seeking and sex as motivators."

"Denver always fishes here with Bruce. It's their favorite spot. He inherited a great deal of money. When I say a great deal, I mean millions. More than millions. Enough that someone may want to kill him for that money."

Again, Sam was quiet, turning that information over and over in his mind. "If Denver is the target, he would be a single target. Our murderer wouldn't be a serial killer."

"Unless he wanted to cover his tracks by making it look as if Denver was one of many if the so-called accidents were discovered," Stella pointed out. She felt that was a little too far in left field, but who knew what went on in the mind of a killer? "I'm just glad Denver and Bruce were both drinking last night."

She looked up at him and smiled, realizing she was warm again and had coffee. Her dog was right there and even the colors in the lake were once again beautiful and nonthreatening. She had Sam to talk things over with.

Sam shook his head. "Woman."

"Man." The smile faded from her face. "I don't want to count on you, Sam, and then have you disappear. It would be better never to start anything and just let me figure it out on my own than to let me lean on you and you pull out when I think you're going to be here."

Stella let herself look at him, even though it was difficult. She had to know. She wasn't a coward. It wasn't as if his expression ever changed. He was a master at giving nothing away.

"I'm broken, Stella, and I don't let anyone near me. It's not a good idea. But you . . . you managed to work your way in. Maybe because we're both a little broken. You never ask. You never push. You don't mind silence. You just accept me. I came to these mountains and found the first true peace I've had in years. And then the mountains gave me you. Just being close to you brings me peace. If that's all I ever get, I'll take it. You offer more, and I'll go for it in a heartbeat and never be stupid enough to throw it away."

As romantic declarations went, it wasn't up there with Shakespeare, but Stella didn't need a poet. Sam kept his word. If he said he'd stay, he would. If he declared she was it for him, he meant it.

She nodded her head, the smile back. "I want you to stay, Sam. I'm not sure how good I'll be at any kind of real relationship other than what we have, but I'd like to try."

"Wasn't planning on leaving you, Stella, unless you kicked me out or you took on a man. You do know that Sean and Edward are both certified scuba divers and Jason and Bale have been taking lessons from them."

She hadn't known that. "Great. Maybe they're all serial killers." She rubbed her cheekbone. "It would be like them to decide to murder a bunch of people just to see if they could get away with it."

"We have to call the sheriff and let him know what happened," Sam said. "You'll need to write down as many details as you remember and sketch out what you can. I'll write out as much as I can remember too."

"Sam, will your ID hold up?" She really hated asking.

He nodded. "Yeah, no problem. It's all good. I am Sam Rossi."

# CHAPTER SIX

Griffen Cauldrey was the local sheriff's deputy who came out to take their report. Stella knew him very well. Over the last few years, she'd had her share of calls to the sheriff. Dead bodies turned up at various locations in a resort the size of hers, mostly drownings. Alcohol and water didn't go very well together.

Griffen had been with his wife, Mercy, fifteen years, and they had twin sons referred to by their father as the "little hellions," but it was always said with affection. The boys were ten now and could be a handful, but they were respectful and definitely minded their parents, especially Griffen, when he called them to order. Like most families in Mono and Inyo Counties, they loved outdoor sports, and Griffen and Mercy brought their children up with the rules of safety.

Griffen examined the scene in his usual meticulous way, asking them both questions and doubling back without seeming to. He took several pictures of the back of Sam's head and then insisted that he get medical attention, wanting it documented.

"You know better, Stella," he chided. "He should have been seen immediately."

She nodded and indicated Sam with her chin. "Tell him, not me. I figured he might listen to you better than me. He's tough as nails."

"I've called on Search and Rescue to help with searching boats and rigs for scuba gear and also to talk to anyone who might have witnessed someone coming out of the lake in scuba gear. The chances of finding them at this point are pretty slim, but maybe we'll get lucky and someone will have seen something. We just don't have the manpower for something like this. It's all volunteer, and by the time they get here and I get them organized, this man is going to be long gone. You have enemies, Sam?"

Sam shrugged. "Not that I know of."

"Tell me again why you came out so early in the morning." Griffen looked around the campsite with all the tents set up.

She sighed. It was her third telling. "We were going to camp here and we'd set up our tents and left everything here, but we went to the Grill last night. Vienna and Harlow had a shift at the hospital and didn't get off until late, so they weren't going to join us until morning, but Raine, Zahra, Shabina and I were supposed to stay here last night. I realized we were all drinking too much, so I asked Sam if he'd be our sober driver and gave him the keys to my rig. I woke up early, talked to Bernice at the boat rentals and she told me Sam spent the night here in order to make sure none of our things were taken. I felt really awful that he had to do that when he already had to drive us back to the resort and we were a little out of control."

She made a face and sent a look of apology to Sam, hoping she hadn't made too big a fool of herself. As always, there was little expression on his face, although there could have been a hint of amusement in his dark eyes. If there was, it was gone almost immediately.

"I got here, let Bailey out and was hurrying toward the lake. Mostly, I was concerned with getting coffee. I hadn't had any yet and Sam always makes some. He was fishing and was out wading in the reeds. He suddenly went down hard and then was underwater. I didn't think, I just went in. That's when I realized someone else was in the water, holding Sam under. He was wearing a wet suit. He hit me here." She pointed to her cheekbone. "And kicked me here." She pointed to just under her breasts. "Then he was gone. I wasn't even thinking about identifying anything on him. Just getting to Sam. I thought he might be unconscious."

She didn't want to relive those moments again, under the cold water when she thought Sam was drowning and that dark sinister figure had loomed large, rocketing toward her so fast she had nearly somersaulted backward. He had been gone before she'd had time to think.

"Why didn't he try to kill me, Griffen?" She sat up straighter, frowning. "It wouldn't have been that difficult. He had on scuba gear. He could have held me underwater."

"I wasn't unconscious." Sam provided an answer. "I'd pulled my knife from my belt. Granted, I was slow, maybe a little disoriented from the blow to my head, but I was aware of the attack and him going after you."

She hadn't even seen the knife in Sam's fist. Now that she tried to pull up details, she realized it was Sam who was really the one dragging her out of the water, more than her dragging him out.

"I guess I wasn't all that heroic." She sent Griffen a little grin and wrapped her hands around her to-go mug. "I hadn't had my coffee yet or I would have been much sharper."

Griffen spent a few more minutes with them and then left to organize a search for the assailant. Local volunteers were used to coming together to help law enforcement when needed for various tasks. In this case, they would work in pairs, both on and off the water, searching for anyone who might have seen anything that would lead to the identification of the assailant.

HARLOW ARRIVED AT the campsite to take a look at the knot on the back of Sam's head. "Vienna is helping Griffen send all the volunteers out. Denver and Bruce are really upset that they weren't here. Denver says he was supposed to be fishing with you this morning, Sam, but he was a little hungover. He set out to come but had to stop several times because he was sick." She tried not to laugh as she said it. Everyone knew Denver wasn't at his best if he drank too much.

She had a little first-aid kit with her, which she opened and handed to Sam. "Naturally, the two of you would just be sitting here as if nothing happened, drinking coffee. Does anything faze you, Sam?"

"If Stella doesn't get her coffee in the morning."

There was a brief silence. Harlow looked up from where she was gently moving her fingers around the swelling at the back of Sam's head. "Did you just make a joke? I don't think I've ever heard you make a joke."

"It isn't a joke if Stella doesn't have coffee."

"That's so true," Harlow agreed.

"I'm right here, in case anyone hasn't noticed," Stella pointed out. "Sheesh. A little crack on the head and Sam thinks he's a comedian."

"I've always been funny," Sam said without a change of expression. "It didn't take a knock on my head to make me that way."

Harlow burst out laughing. She shook her head. "I had no

idea. I can't wait to tell Vienna. The mere idea that Sam can crack a joke is going to slay her."

"Don't encourage him, Harlow." Stella put her head back and looked up at the drifting clouds. It was good to be alive. "And Vienna doesn't even have good sense. She's a cat person."

That made Harlow laugh more. "What does that mean? Cats have way more sense than dogs do. Bailey would have jumped into that cold water to save your ass and so would my silly little beagle, Misha. Vienna's cat, however, would have turned her nose up in pure disdain. She would have known better."

"She's got a point," Sam said. "Bailey would have."

Bailey lifted his head and looked up at Stella with his brown eyes. She scratched behind his ears. "Because you're so loyal, right, boy? You would have saved me. That cat of Vienna's would have let her drown."

"Are you talking baby talk to that huge animal?" Harlow demanded. "Isn't he supposed to be some badass protection dog?"

"I don't talk baby talk to my dog," Stella denied. She did, all the time.

"She does," Sam confirmed, and reached out to take her hand right in front of Harlow.

His hand was warm. His fingers strong. Whatever Harlow was going to say was cut off mid-sentence when she saw him take Stella's hand. It was the first time Sam had actually made any kind of real public claim on her, if one could call hand-holding a public claim. Sam didn't seem the type of man to hold hands. He was just too reserved for any kind of public acknowledgments or displays of affection.

Harlow bent her head closer to Sam's wound. "This isn't as bad as it could have been. Head wounds tend to bleed a lot and make things seem far worse than they are. Do you have blurred vision?"

"No. A bit of a headache at the back of my head where the knot is. It's centered right there. More of a throbbing, like I can feel my heartbeat there."

Stella was surprised that Sam was so forthcoming and matter-of-fact. Harlow asked him a few more questions and he answered, but now his thumb moved over the back of Stella's hand, feathering back and forth in a little caress that sent strange little darts of fire running through her bloodstream straight to her deepest core, making her all too aware of him. Just that small gesture.

She didn't dare look at him. It had been too long. Way too long. She didn't do relationships and she wasn't certain how to react. The questions Harlow asked Sam seemed far away. Stella heard Harlow say she didn't even have to use glue to close the cut, but after that, Stella concentrated on the way the single gesture, so small, made her body come alive. Or maybe it was the fact that she could sit in her camp chair in the early morning hours with the sun shining on Sunrise Lake, bathing the water in gorgeous colors, knowing Sam was alive. Knowing the killer didn't get his way and the man she cared about wasn't his first victim. There was no first victim.

"Earth to Stella," Harlow called. "That lake mesmerizes you. I need you to listen to me. Sam never does and he needs to take antibiotics. *All* of them until they're finished. We don't know what was on that rock or in the water. I've given him a shot to get started and put antibiotic cream on the wound to be safe."

She held out the tube to Stella, forcing her to pull her hand away from Sam or put down her coffee. Sam solved her dilemma by letting her hand go. She took the tube from Harlow.

"You need to put this on the cut a couple of times a day for two days. Then you want it open to the air."

Sam reached out almost lazily and nearly managed to get the tube of antibiotic cream from Stella before she realized his intent.

"Woman." There was a growl in his voice.

"Man." She glared at him. The growl had an effect on her, but it wasn't intimidation.

"I'm not five."

"That's the problem. Harlow knows you can't be trusted to take care of wounds because you think you're some kind of manly man who doesn't need things like antibiotics the way normal people need them. I'll just keep control of this and supervise you taking the pills too."

Harlow burst out laughing as she took the first-aid kit from Sam and closed it up. "I've got to write up a report on you and then do the same on your injuries, Stella. But this is great. I've never heard the two of you interacting like this before."

"I don't have injuries," Stella objected, frowning at her friend. "Griffen has misled you. The would-be killer punched me, but underwater, it isn't like he could really hurt me that much. It was more that I was startled and it pushed me back and away from him. That allowed him to bring his legs up to his chest and drive his feet into me. He had fins on, but he still got me hard and drove me backward."

Her hand went to her cheekbone. Why did her cheek hurt? It shouldn't have. The water would have slowed the assailant's punch. He couldn't get enough force to really hurt her, yet she felt bruised. It wasn't swollen, but it did feel tender. She brushed her fingers over the exact spot where the would-be killer had connected with her face. There was a small spot that hurt. Not really bad, but it was definitely a little sore. What did that mean? He'd been wearing gloves, but was he wearing a ring beneath the gloves? Something heavy that would have landed just right on the bone like that?

She looked at Sam. His eyes met hers. He knew. That would be another clue. Not an obvious one, but if he had been wearing a ring, it was a heavy one, not a wedding ring. They would have to write that down and she would have to think about how that felt. What shape it might be. Maybe find a way to sketch it.

Harlow's fingers were gentle as she probed over Stella's face. Stella did her best to keep from showing any kind of emotion, mostly because she could feel Sam's gaze on her. She knew he didn't miss much and she wasn't very good at covering her feelings, not the way he was. She didn't want him to know she was hurt, mainly because there was something that lurked behind his dark eyes, an emotion she couldn't quite grasp, that scared her a little.

"Babe," Harlow said. "He hit you right here, didn't he?" Her thumb slid over Stella's cheekbone. "Weird that he could hit you hard enough underwater to leave you sore. There's no real bruising, but I can tell you're very tender here. I'll need you to stand up so I can look at your stomach and ribs."

Stella was reluctant to show her in front of Sam. She found herself putting her coffee down on the ground and nearly shoving her knuckles in her mouth the way that five-year-old child had done so long ago, as if reminding herself not to talk. That was one of those habits she had worked hard to overcome, and now a few nightmares and she was right back to having to fight those old hated patterns.

She pulled up her sweater. "There's really nothing to show. He just kicked me hard enough to get me away from him so he could swim away from us. He clearly wasn't going to be able to drown Sam, and with two of us there, he must have decided to get away fast."

Again, Harlow probed along Stella's ribs and along her stomach and then under her breasts, where she'd taken the brunt of his feet connecting. She did her best not to react when Harlow found the exact place of impact.

"Underwater he couldn't really hurt me with a double kick like that," Stella reaffirmed. "I'm sure it was more to shove me away than anything else." She dropped her sweater back in place.

"I don't understand why he didn't just use a spear or a weapon like that," Harlow said. "He really put himself at risk. Now most of the county is on alert. You know just about everyone carries a gun. The warning went out on Facebook to fishermen. It won't stop anyone from fishing, in fact the lake will be packed tomorrow, both with boats and with men and women fishing around the lake. All of them will be packing."

Stella sighed. "I know." She certainly carried a gun. She had since she'd been old enough to learn how to shoot. She'd never stopped practicing. The images of the terrible things her father and the other serial killer had done to their victims had been burned into her mind. No matter how hard she tried to forget those terrible nightmares, she couldn't. The worst of it was, she knew they were real. Human beings had done those things to other human beings. Her father, a man who was supposed to love and protect her, had done those things to other people's loved ones. How could she ever fully trust anyone again?

She had the feeling the killer was someone who visited the county often, perhaps fishing or hunting on a regular basis. He might even stay at her fishing camp, or one of the many campsites or RV sites she rented out. She could be harboring the killer. He had to be close to her, or she wouldn't be having nightmares.

Bailey gave a short bark of warning to announce the arrival of another vehicle. Sam immediately stood and gathered his gear as

Zahra and Shabina leapt out of Shabina's RAV4, neither looking as if they had been up most of the night partying.

"Where's Raine?" Harlow asked.

"Search and Rescue was called to help look for whoever tried to kill Sam this morning," Shabina said, looking Sam and Stella over. "She's checking boats for scuba gear and talking to everyone out on the water, hoping someone might have seen something strange. Are you two all right?"

"Harlow has pronounced both of us just fine," Stella said, following Sam to his rig. "Are you certain you're okay to drive? I can take you back and have one of the others come with us." She tried to keep anxiety out of her voice.

Sam had the door to his rig open and his gear already tossed on the passenger seat. He turned back to her and unexpectedly framed her face with his hands, sending her stomach into a roller coaster of loops and somersaults.

"I'll be fine. Got work to do. You have fun with your friends, Stella, and don't think about anything for a couple of days. It will do you good. I'll look after the resort." He bent his head and brushed his lips over hers.

It was the briefest of contacts, but hot as sin. A million butterflies took wing. The somersaults in her stomach increased so that she pressed her hand tight there, wondering why she'd never had that reaction in her life to any man she'd been around, or dated. He hadn't really kissed her but it hadn't seemed to matter.

He slid inside the truck, shut the door, eased down the window and looked at her with his dark eyes. "*Satine*, you have to step back so I can go. Not sticking around when the camp is overrun with women."

That made her laugh. "You're running away."

"As fast as I can possibly go."

Stella shook her head and moved away, lifting her hand, watching him back out with expert ease, then turn around and drive away. Almost at once she felt vulnerable, as if eyes were on them. She crossed her arms over her chest and took a slow look around. Someone could be on higher ground, hidden in the trees, a good distance away from them. He'd need binoculars if he was going to really see them clearly from that vantage point. There was the granite cliffside that ran up to the trees. Boulders jutted out and could provide cover. And of course, there was the lake. Anyone with a boat could watch them from the lake or one of the spots along the shore close to them.

"Stella, arc you going to stand there all day in a Sam-induced fog," Zahra demanded, "or get over here and tell us what is going on? Because it looked like he kissed you."

Stella felt color creeping into her face as she walked back to her friends. "I assure you he did not." It took effort to keep from pressing her fingers to her suddenly tingling lips. "I'm not certain what you thought you saw, but it wasn't that." She put her hands on her hips and regarded Shabina and Zahra, studying their clear, glowing skin. "You went to the spa first thing this morning, didn't you?"

The two looked at each other and burst into laughter.

"While I was nearly getting killed by some madman, you were wallowing in luxury," she accused, happy to divert attention from Sam's goodbye to her. "And I don't see any remorse on your faces at all."

Shabina shoved her sunglasses onto her nose. "Girl, if you were hurt, we would be upset, but everything turned out just fine, so there's no reason to be anything but thankful we had a spa morning."

"I had a harrowing experience." Stella threw herself into her camp chair.

"You shared an experience with Sam, the hottest man on earth," Zahra corrected. "That's what she said last night, Harlow. Over and over. She kept saying he was the hottest man on planet earth."

"I certainly did not," Stella denied, afraid she might have. Probably on the way home. With Sam driving. It wasn't like he couldn't have heard. She groaned. "Just kill me now."

Harlow burst out laughing. "Stella, did you drink too much last night?"

"Apparently so. Let's not talk about this anymore. I'm getting a headache just thinking about it." Stella delved into her small backpack to pull out her sunglasses. She needed them to hide behind.

"Perhaps blurting out in your drunken state that you thought Sam was hot paid off," Harlow pointed out. "He did hold your hand."

"What?" Zahra nearly jumped up and down. "You are holding out on us. We're your best friends and you're lying to us. He did kiss you goodbye."

Shabina pulled her sunglasses down to peer over the top of them at Stella. "I'm texting Vienna and Raine right now to keep them in the loop. Kissing. Holding hands. What else happened? All in a couple of hours in the morning too. It is a good thing we went to the spa, Zahra. We're like matchmakers. Without our timely intervention, they probably would never have gotten together."

Stella couldn't help laughing. That was the way it always was when they got together. They could go from serious to funny in a heartbeat, taking each other's backs always.

Vienna and Raine didn't join them until the afternoon. They set up the campsite the way they liked it when all of them were present. Vienna looked tired, and the others suggested she rest while they did the bulk of the cooking when it came to dinner, but as always, she insisted on pulling her weight. They played cards and talked long into the night. Stella still felt uneasy and often walked around with Bailey to see if he was picking up any signs of an intruder close by. Bailey seemed as wary as she did, but he didn't growl or posture, simply stayed alert when he normally would have been relaxed. No one else seemed to notice the ominous feel in the air the way she did. Stella tried to put it down to her nightmares.

One by one the others went to their tents. She stayed outside with Bailey, patrolling around the tents and then down by the lake just to make certain everyone was safe. She even took her gun out of the compartment in her 4Runner, loaded it and put it in her backpack, which she kept close to her at all times.

When she returned to the firepit, the fire had died down and only Raine remained seated, clearly waiting for her. Stella retrieved a blanket and then moved her chair just a little back from the fire, more to keep the light from hitting her face than anything else. She knew Raine had waited up for a purpose—to talk to her alone.

"Is everyone asleep already?"

Raine nodded. "You're restless tonight."

"I just keep feeling like someone is watching us. I know it's probably a leftover thing from this morning, but I can't seem to shake it." Bailey shoved his head in her lap and Stella scratched his ears.

"I made you hot chocolate and put it in your hot chocolate mug." Raine handed her the to-go mug. "That should keep you warm."

"You want to talk about something?" Stella figured she might as well get it over with.

"How involved are you with Sam, Stella?" Raine asked very quietly, looking around as if the others might overhear them even though she'd waited until they were asleep in their tents. She and Stella sat a good distance away, by the firepit, but she was still concerned.

Stella froze. This was Raine. She knew things others didn't. "Why?"

"You two have always acted as if you're very good friends, but now Shabina texted me saying he kissed you and you were holding hands. That seems as if you're more than friends. Are you in a relationship with him? Or was she kidding? At the bar last night he seemed protective of you."

"He's always protective," Stella countered, trying to dodge the question. "That's his nature."

"No, it's not," Raine denied. "Not unless you belong to him. He doesn't claim many people in his circle. Not even us, and we've been around him for a few years now."

Stella tilted her head and studied Raine's face in the light from the waning fire. "You tend to do a background check on anyone who comes close to us. Did you do one on him?" She was curious. If Raine had, she'd never shared.

Raine shook her head and again looked around, her expression cautious. "No."

"Why not? I'll bet you know more about everyone in town than anyone else. Why not Sam? Why wouldn't you check up on him, especially since it's clear you don't altogether trust him?" Stella tried not to sound aggressive or belligerent.

This was Raine. Her friend. She'd known Raine longer than she'd known Sam, and Raine had always been intensely loyal. If Raine had something to say, Stella needed to hear her no matter how much she wanted to be with Sam. Denver had warned her about Sam, but she wasn't exactly certain what he was trying to say. Raine would be truthful and there would be no hidden agenda. Stella might not want to hear it, and it could be painful, but Raine wouldn't intend it that way.

Raine frowned. "No, it isn't a matter of trust, Stella. You're reading me wrong. You're my friend, and I don't want you to get hurt. Sam is the type of person you can count on if you're in his circle, and his circle is going to be extremely small. He won't ever let many people in. If you're one of them, count yourself lucky because he'll defend you with his life. He won't ever lie to you, and he'll stay."

"But. I hear a *but*. There's a reason you didn't do a background check on him, Raine. And there's a reason you're warning me about him, because this is a warning, isn't it?" Stella forced herself to pursue the conversation when she knew Raine would have stopped right there. Raine didn't pry. She didn't push into any of their lives when she easily could have. She didn't gossip and she held confidences.

Raine sighed and pushed at her long sun-streaked hair, a rare gesture of nerves. "I knew I wouldn't have found anything on him and I didn't want to trigger an alert if anyone was looking for him." She hesitated. "Men like him have alerts set for anything like that on their records. They know when someone is trying to find them. He'll have friends that will tip him off if someone is searching for him. I don't want a visit in the middle of the night."

Stella's heart dropped. "What does that mean, Raine?"

Raine rubbed her hand over her leg and looked toward the lake. "He's obviously come here to just live his life, Stella. He wants to be left alone. If I brought attention to him, he wouldn't be very happy and I couldn't blame him. He served his time."

"Denver told me he's what some people in the military refer to as a *ghost*. He more than implied that Sam cleaned up messes, not only for the military but for other agencies as well."

Stella kept her gaze glued to Raine's face. Raine didn't have Vienna's poker face, and right now she was very uncomfortable.

"How would Denver know what Sam did for any agency, Stella? Unless Sam told him—and you and I both know Sam would never do that—Denver doesn't know anything. I'm only taking a stab in the dark and doing so as your friend because I want you to be very sure before you enter into a relationship with him. I'm not saying it's a bad thing, only that you need to know who you're with. You have that right."

"Should I be afraid of a man like that?"

"Are you afraid of Sam?" Raine looked directly at her.

Stella didn't answer immediately. Raine deserved a real answer. Stella thought about all the times she'd been alone with Sam over the past two years. Had she been afraid of him? She had considered that he, like everyone else, might be the murderer in her nightmares when she needed to rule suspects out, but she hadn't really believed he could be the serial killer. She shook her head. "No, I've never been afraid of him. He makes me feel safe."

Raine nodded. "Then you have your answer, Stella, and I have mine. I don't need to do a background check on him."

"I actually don't want you to do one. I wasn't asking you to do one, I just wondered why you hadn't."

"Because he's a dangerous man and I'm not going to tangle with him. I also think he more than deserves to start a new life, which he's done here."

Stella took a sip of hot chocolate. "Did you do a background check on me?" She kept her voice low, sounding calm, but her heart beat so fast and her chest hurt to the point she was afraid she knew what those having heart attacks felt like.

Raine sighed and nodded, not looking away from her. "I'm sorry. It's a hazard that goes with my job. I actually have to do background checks on people I hang out with. I've known you a lot of years, Stella. I've never said anything to you or anyone else. I can keep secrets and I've kept yours."

"Even from our friends?" Stella gestured toward the tents.

Raine frowned at her. "Of course. It isn't anyone's business. If you choose to tell someone, that's for you to decide, not me, not anyone else."

Stella wasn't certain she knew how to feel about Raine knowing who she really was, or the fact that her father was a serial killer. She felt color sweep into her face and was grateful the evening had darkened and she was sitting far enough away from the firepit that the flames weren't throwing light on her face. Raine had always accepted her, and she'd shown intense loyalty to her, but just knowing she knew who she really was, with her ugly past, was disconcerting.

This was how it always started in the past, one person knowing and then her life turning upside down. The whispers. The looks. A media circus. That was so unfair to put on Raine. She'd known for years and never said a word to even their closest friends.

Raine cleared her throat. "I don't know for certain what kind of work Sam did. I don't like to speculate, but let's say Denver is right about him and he's one of these ghosts, for lack of a better word." She pressed her lips together and again looked around and even glanced in the air as if a drone might be hovering.

Stella sat up straighter, all thoughts of anyone finding out about her past gone. If Raine was that nervous, there had to be a reason. Raine didn't get nervous, unless she was climbing at certain heights and she had a panic attack or swore like a sailor.

"Men in that line of work don't usually live long, not because they aren't good at what they do but because they are. They make enemies. They're sent all over the world to take out major targets and, as such, have information that can never be revealed to the public. They're trained in methods of interrogation and killing and they're truly like the ghosts Denver called them. If they're sent after you, they don't stop."

Stella held herself very still. "Shouldn't Sam be telling me these things? Isn't that what you said?"

"Yes, if he's one of these people, and I don't know that he is. But someone tried to kill him this morning in a very strange way. He was fishing, Stella, and they put on scuba gear and swam in very cold water and would have made it look like an accident. A man who has done the kinds of things he's done for his country has made enemies, Stella. Those enemies wouldn't stop looking for him. They can find ways to put alerts on his files so if someone like me did a background check on him, it might give him away. If they found him, they would send an assassin to finish him. If he is what Denver thinks, he might have a target on his back, and if you're in a relationship with him, that makes you potentially vulnerable as well."

Raine put her hands out in front of her, spreading her fingers wide. "I'm not trying to scare you away from him, because I don't really know anything about him, but maybe you should straight up ask him, Stella. He could just be a veteran who has gone through a difficult time and wants to be left alone."

"Would this assassin kill others, making the kills look like accidents in order to cover up what they did?" Sam hadn't in any way indicated to Stella that he thought the killer might have specifically targeted him. And how could he have? Sam wasn't supposed to have been there. But Raine kept looking at the sky. Did that mean some agency had the ability to watch them? Could they find Sam that way? Stella held her breath.

Raine frowned. "No, why should they? They would send a pro. He would hit his target and get out. No one would be the wiser. If there was a witness, he might have to kill the witness as well, but no, he wouldn't indiscriminately kill a bunch of others. Ghosts aren't mass murderers. They take out specific targets that are threats to national security. Heads of drug cartels or terrorist cells. They don't just kill anyone, Stella. Someone sent after them in retaliation wouldn't want attention drawn to them."

An assassin sent to kill Sam wouldn't have known ahead of time that he would have been out at the campsite she'd chosen to set up in order to prevent a murder. Sam hadn't mentioned the possibility because it wasn't a possibility.

"There was no way for an assassin to know Sam would be out here, Raine," she pointed out logically. "It isn't like he fishes on a regular basis."

"Unless they were already following him or watching him, which is a possibility," Raine persisted. "I'm just saying, you might need a conversation, Stella."

Stella nodded and took another sip of hot chocolate. "Thanks, Raine. I do appreciate you talking to me about Sam. You know I'm cautious about relationships. We've been dancing around each other for two years now. I've always been attracted to him."

"Anyone could see the chemistry was there," Raine admitted with a little smile. "The rest of us were taking bets on whether or not you were secretly sleeping with him and just not admitting to it."

Stella's eyebrow shot up. "Really? No, I was careful. I didn't want to ruin what we had. Besides, he had to make the first move."

Raine shook her head with that little smile still on her face. "How was he supposed to do that when you were so closed off?"

Stella couldn't deny that she had been. She was pretty closed off to everyone.

"But he made his move?" Raine prompted.

Stella nodded. "He's indicated that he'd like something more."

After what both Raine and Denver said about Sam possibly being one of these ghosts and on the run, how could they have a real relationship? That left out the possibility of a real future. He would have to be able to pick up and go at the first sign that someone had found him. She loved her resort. She'd made a home here and she'd worked hard for it. She loved the Eastern Sierras. There would never be children if they wanted them, because they couldn't run with children. Sam hadn't once indicated there would be a problem. She definitely needed to talk to him.

"I'm going to bed," Raine said. "Thanks for letting me say my piece without getting upset, Stella."

"Thanks for caring enough to say it." Stella knew Raine was worried about risking their friendship, but she'd still gone ahead, stating her worries.

Stella sat for a long time by herself while the flames in the firepit died down to red ashes. Clouds drifted overhead, occasionally blocking the moon and then moving on. She kept scratching Bailey's ears and head, and then petting him until she finally was so sleepy, she had to retreat to her tent.

VIENNA GOT A call first thing in the morning. James Marley, a local, hadn't come home nor did he answer his cell. He was seventy years old with four children, three sons and one daughter. He had seven grandchildren. He called his grandchildren every day even if it was only for a few minutes. He often took them fishing—his favorite pastime.

James had gone fishing the morning of the attack on Sam and hadn't been heard from since. His daughter, Sadie, had gone looking for him when he hadn't checked in as he always did. She'd gone to several of his favorite fishing sites and eventually found his truck, but she hadn't found him. She called her brothers and they dropped everything and came at once, searching the area and the lake close to where his truck was but couldn't find him. They alerted the sheriff, who called Search and Rescue.

Stella waved Raine and Vienna off, telling them she would break down the tents and take them back to the resort. She had a bad feeling in the pit of her stomach. Had the killer swum straight from Sam to James and murdered him? How far away had James been from Sam's location? She had no idea. She felt guilty. It hadn't occurred to her that the killer might simply abandon one victim for another. She hoped she was wrong and James was just off somewhere, but she knew better. That terrible feeling in her gut told her he was the first victim of the serial killer right there in her beloved community.

# CHAPTER SEVEN

S tella sat in her favorite egg chair, which hung from the ceiling of her porch overlooking the lake. This time of evening, all the boats were in and the marina was quiet. Most of the people were in the cabins for the night. A few heavy partiers were going strong, which always gave her some concern. Alcohol and water didn't mix, especially at night. If one of those partying decided to go for a swim on his own, or just walked into the lake, she would be notifying the sheriff in the morning of another drowning.

It was bad enough that James Marley was still missing. Vienna and her rescue team, including Sam, had gone out two days in a row searching the lake for him. Stella didn't want any other deaths happening, especially if they were preventable.

The lake temperatures were unexpectedly low, even for the time of year. She warned those going out in boats and those fishing, but the partiers sometimes insisted they were "like polar bears" and could run into the lake naked. The two cabins making so much noise had been giving her headaches for several nights. She was happy to know they would be leaving for their homes in the city in two days. Once they were gone, they were closing down and breathing a sigh of relief that the season was over. They'd have a respite for a while.

"I will be glad to see the last of them," she murmured, rocking her chair gently.

Sam turned his head slightly to follow her line of sight. "I've had Patrick and Sonny keep an eye on them at night and I've made sure to do extra rounds myself. We'll get them out of here in one piece." The two security guards were still working the night shift together, but as soon as the last of their guests were gone, the temporary guards would head home and Sonny would take the night shift and Patrick the day shift.

Sam wore frayed jeans with a dark, loose cable-knit sweater. She could see the top of his dark tee under the sweater. His jacket was open, showing the thick Sherpa lining. His hair spilled down onto his forehead, just a little unruly, and his eyes gleamed at her in the darkness. He looked the way he always did, and yet different because now she was even more aware of him.

"You don't ever get much sleep. You aren't a security guard, Sam."

"I don't need much sleep. I never have. It's just a thing with me since I was a kid. Drove my mother nuts."

He'd never once mentioned his mother, but then, until the other day, she'd never mentioned hers. She figured now was as good a time as any to bring things out in the open.

"Sam, I don't like to pry into your past, that belongs to you. It's just that a couple of people have mentioned something to me that is a little concerning moving forward . . ." She drifted off.

She *detested* this kind of conversation. She preferred that he volunteer his past the way she had, not have it forced out of him. Still, she didn't want to hand over her heart to him and then have her world turned upside down. Maybe it was already too late. She'd opened herself up to him in ways she hadn't even to her friends, and it terrified her.

His dark eyes moved over her face with that surprising gentleness that he seemed to reserve only for her. "Woman."

"Man." It was an automatic reply.

"Woman. Don't exasperate me."

She found herself laughing in spite of the seriousness of what she felt. "Someone suggested that you might be something one called a 'ghost' and that you were on the run from the government. You did ask me to pay you under the table and you told me you had certain skills. Granted, I didn't ask you if you were thinking in terms of just having sex together or if we were considering more of an exclusive, permanent relationship, but I guess I was thinking along those lines. I don't let people into my world and I wouldn't just for sex. I mean, I might have sex with you, without all the heart-to-heart."

She wasn't good at this, not when she didn't want to question him in the first place. She had no trouble broaching any subject when she felt it was necessary, but this felt wrong—as if she listened to gossip and was demanding answers from him.

"It's just that, if it was the truth, and these people are hunting you, Sam . . ."

He shook his head. "I don't know how these bullshit rumors start, sweetheart. People like to be in the know and they make shit up just to be important." There was the merest hint of derision in his voice. "If government agencies want to track a person down these days, they can pretty much do it. Even someone with my skills will eventually get caught. Yeah, I worked for the government, but I'm in good graces with them. Not always so much with myself. Sometimes it's hard to sleep at night. As for the agency I worked for, they know where to find me. Occasionally, they still ask if I'll help them out. I always say no and they respect that. I've done my time. They aren't going to send some young assassin after me. It makes for a good movie, but it isn't reality."

Stella hugged her knees to her as the egg chair swung lightly. The moonlight spilled over the lake, highlighting the surface so that it appeared to gleam like glass. The night could have been peaceful had the music from the two cabins not been blasting loud. The conversation would swell, riotous laughter would bounce across the water to her porch and then the sound would be muffled, as if the partiers had gone inside, or closed the doors for a moment.

Sam leaned on the railing, arms across his chest, legs stretched out, looking relaxed when she knew he was aware of everything around him. Maybe that was what made her feel safe. Bailey pressed close to him. From the very beginning Bailey had accepted him, and her dog accepted few people as family.

"As for the two of us and what we're building together, I hope we're on the same page. I want a future with you in any capacity I can get it."

Stella's stomach settled nicely. Denver had been drinking when he'd given his theory about ghosts and Sam. He didn't usually drink that much, and it hadn't stopped him from being his usual friendly self with Sam the moment the two of them had to confront Sean and Bale when they were hurling insults at Shabina on the dance floor. Denver seemed to forget all about his dire warnings after that.

On the other hand, what had Raine said? Raine wasn't given to fantasies, but then she hadn't actually said Sam was one of those people or that the government was looking for him. She had said it was more likely he had enemies looking for him, en-

emies made while working for the government. That did make
sense.

"You don't mind being with a woman who occasionally might
suddenly have nightmares and tell you there's a serial killer on
the loose?" She tried to make light of it, but there was a sudden
lump in her throat and her stomach hurt like hell. Raine thought
Sam might have enemies, but she wasn't any prize. She would
always have the curse of knowing if a killer was too close.

Sam moved then, in that slow, fluid way he had, straightening
from the railing, covering the scant few feet separating them to
stand with his legs right up against the egg chair so that all movement ceased. He bent down, framing her face with his large
hands, looking her right in the eye. "I told you, Stella, and I
meant it. I'll take you any way I can get you. You accept me the
way I am. It doesn't bother you that I'm a little broken myself.
You don't need me to talk all the time. You just let me be. That's
a rare gift. You're a rare gift."

His thumb slid over her lower lip, a barely there caress, but it
was intense and intimate, just like every touch with Sam. Maybe
she fell so hard for him because Sam knew who she really was,
not the mask she hid behind, that person she'd created. He knew
all of her, even the panicky, ugly parts, and he seemed to accept
those in her.

She didn't know who leaned first. It could have been her. He
was that compelling. The next thing she knew, she was on her
feet, her body tight against his, her mouth welded to his, his
hand on the back of her head, holding her still while fire flared
bright and hot and out of control.

No one had ever kissed her like Sam. The world disappeared
and the only anchor she had was her fists clutching his shirt.
There was something beautiful and surreal that went with that

rush of fire, every nerve ending in her body responding to him, coming alive for him. She was alive. The real Stella. Little sparks of electricity seemed to leap all over her skin to arc over his and jump back to her. She felt the pull of him. The way her body went boneless and she seemed to melt into him because the fire had gone that hot.

Sam lifted his head first, his arms steadying her. "Let's take this inside before we can't stop, Stella."

She wasn't altogether certain she could walk on her wobbly legs, but then she didn't need to. He just swept her up easily, cradled her against his chest and carried her inside. Stella wasn't certain if she actually floated into the bedroom or he really carried her, but she did know there was a fire roaring in the pit of her stomach and molten lava rushing through her veins by the time he set her down. Her hands were desperately trying to find the hem of his T-shirt to pull it off him. She needed skin-to-skin contact. He was always so warm. Hot. A raging fire to match the one inside her.

Then she had what she wanted—what she needed. Just the two of them. Finally. She should have known he was just the way he was outside the bedroom. In charge. Patient. Skilled. Generous. Demanding. He believed in burning slow and raging fiery hot. He was intense and thorough and very Sam. He didn't say a lot verbally, it was all with his body, and he was very good at talking that way. And he said everything she needed and wanted him to say and more.


STELLA LEANED ON the railing and stared out over the lake. Bailey, the treacherous dog, was with Sam, which didn't really surprise her. She should be happy that Sam walked the property so much, making certain drunken partygoers didn't fall into the lake and drown. He didn't let them take out guns and shoot at the sky in some bizarre celebration.

Sam didn't like dealing with the guests but he could repair anything. He would never see to the taxes or business end of the resort, but he would make certain security was tight and everything was running in top condition. If the roads needed plowing, Sam would get it done. She had come to rely on him in a short time without even realizing it.

She had always loved the night and never felt in the least bit nervous or anxious when she was alone until her nightmare had woken her. Sam had helped alleviate that, but for some reason, she felt a sudden chill go down her spine and goose bumps rose all over. It felt the same as at the fishing spot, when she thought someone was watching.

Straightening slowly, Stella walked to the stairs and whistled for Bailey. He would come to her the moment he heard that whistle no matter what. She'd just feel safer knowing he was close. She inched her way into the shadows, wishing she'd brought out her night binoculars. She didn't have the porch light on, but that didn't mean if someone was out there they wouldn't see her even in the dark. They could have night-vision binoculars just as easily as she could.

She waited, growing more and more uneasy. The minutes seemed to creep by slowly. If there was really someone out there, Sam would know. He had some kind of sixth sense about that kind of thing. He hadn't been at the campsite when she'd felt eyes on them. What if someone had harmed him? What if he was lying somewhere hurt right now? Or in the lake? The cold water? Her imagination was getting the better of her and she had to stop. Bailey would be sounding the alarm.

She took several deep breaths. She had trained for this. She knew how to use a gun. She was trained in self-defense. She could use a knife if necessary, or at least do her best to defend against a knife attack, knowing she would get cut. Preparing for those situations didn't always transfer to the reality of the circumstances. She hoped they would.

She backpacked and climbed and she trained for those sports. She particularly loved bouldering. She was careful to keep her body in good shape and to do her best to know what she was doing when she climbed. She didn't just decide to hike a mountain, she trained for it. Stella hoped that same care she applied to her backpacking and climbing also went into her training for any situation she might run into when it came to self-preservation. She went to the gun range twice a week. She had an instructor in hand-to-hand fighting as well as a weapons instructor she trained with three times a week. Hopefully the running she hated and all the fitness work she put in morning and night would stand her in good stead against an attacker.

Bailey suddenly burst out of the darkness, rushing up the stairs to press his nose against her. The relief she felt was tremendous. She dropped both hands into his fur and crouched down beside him. "Baby, you came back to me. Where's Sam? Is he all right?"

"Right here, sweetheart." Sam's voice was soft, coming to her out of the night.

He wasn't on the porch, rather down below it, just looking up at her through the rails. He didn't look out of breath, but it was clear he had either run or jogged to get back to her.

"Someone's out there watching me. I can feel him," Stella warned, certain of it, keeping Bailey between her and the open just in case the watcher had binoculars.

"I believe you're right," Sam said. "I can't locate him and neither can Bailey."

She was grateful he didn't try to coddle her. She would have hated that. "Could he be on the water? In a boat?"

"It's possible. He could be in any one of the little rocky coves that look straight at this house if he's got binoculars. Or he could be in one of the cabins. Bailey went with me several times around the empty cabins, checking them, but we didn't find anything."

"When you woke up, you knew someone was watching, that's why you called to Bailey," Stella guessed.

"Yeah. I slept about two hours and when I got up to make my rounds, I took him with me. I didn't think you'd mind. I locked you in, not that you stayed." He gave a little shake of his head. "Should have left you a note."

"Do you think it's the killer?"

"Why would he be watching you? He can't know about your nightmares, Stella."

"Because I was there at the lake and I stopped him from murdering you."

Sam's fist clenched around the thick spindles that made up the fancy railing on the porch. "There is that. You did draw attention to yourself by diving into a freezing-cold lake to save me."

"I couldn't possibly know you weren't knocked out, Sam, and that you had a knife and were about to do him in."

He reached up and cupped the side of her face. "Did I sound upset with you instead of grateful? Because believe me, Stella, I'm very grateful you cared enough to put your life on the line for me."

"I think I just feel guilty that I got in the way." She gestured toward the lake over Bailey's back. "He's still out there. If he really killed James Marley, and he does what the other two killers

I've encountered have done, he's going to kill again very soon. If I hadn't gotten in your way, maybe you could have stopped him."

"You can't think that way, Stella, and you know it." Sam sighed. "It's too cold out here. Go in with Bailey. I'll go around to the back and go in that way. We aren't going to find him tonight, whoever he is, and there's no use in losing any more sleep over him."

"You don't have to sleep at my house if you'd be more comfortable in your cabin, Sam," Stella forced herself to say. She felt far safer with him there, but just because he'd made love to her once, she didn't want him to think she was presuming he would want to stay with her.

"I've got my gear here and there are very comfortable rooms, Stella, if you don't want me in your room. Don't worry about me. I'd rather we be together while this is all happening."

She nodded, not certain she liked his answer. What did that even mean? That he'd leave when it was over? That he'd not want to be in the main house any longer? When had she become someone who didn't just come out and ask? Why was she so reluctant? Because she wasn't good at relationships. Why didn't she just tell him she wanted him to sleep in her bedroom?

She'd been friends with five women for several years and none of them knew who she really was. That should tell her something right there. Raine didn't count because she hadn't known Raine was aware of her true identity. Even Zahra, her best friend, hadn't known who she was. She didn't give anything of her true self away. She was guarded and careful at all times.

She stood up, murmuring to Bailey to stay at her side, not wanting the dog to give away Sam's presence. Once inside, she leaned against the heavy door and waited, not arming the alarm system, knowing Sam would when he came in through the back.

She didn't turn on lights because that was the first thing taught to her. If windows were lit, whoever was outside could see inside, and she couldn't see out.

"What are you doing, Stella?"

She nearly jumped out of her skin, even though she was expecting him. She put a hand over her wildly pounding heart, pressing hard. The house was much warmer than outside, and her sweater was almost too hot. It could have been that Sam had gotten too close to her, towering over her.

"I'm just thinking." She looked up at him. "I've really come to rely on you around here. I didn't realize how much."

His dark eyes moved over her face. "How is that a problem?" He held out his hand to her. "I'm a reliable kind of man."

She found herself staring at his palm. There was an odd scar across it. She put her hand in his and let him close his fingers around hers. His hand was large and completely engulfed hers. He tugged her into the bedroom and indicated the bed.

"You change and I'll make you hot chocolate. That always gets you back to sleep."

Stella watched him leave and then pulled off the sweats and got into her thin pajamas. She didn't like heavy clothes at night. It was odd how much Sam knew about her. When had he discovered that hot chocolate helped to put her to sleep, especially if she was restless? He always knew when she was having a bad day, even if they hadn't seen each other. It was odd how he was so tuned to her. The only other person that came close to knowing her so well was Zahra.

She sat in the middle of the bed, up high by the headboard, and thought about what she would do if Sam left. She had done that a few times when she worried that Zahra might decide to relocate somewhere. She knew sometimes Zahra worried that she wasn't as free as she thought she was from her past, and she would get the sudden urge to run. Stella only knew part of her story, that Zahra's parents had arranged a marriage for her—a common practice in her small village—and she had fled. Stella knew the consequences were dire and Zahra could never go back, could never see her family. They had disowned her. Whenever she thought about losing Zahra, she would panic, just as she felt panicky at the thought of losing Sam.

"What's going on, *Satine*?" Sam asked, handing her a mug of chocolate. "Talk to me."

She made a face at him. "Relationships are difficult when you've never had them."

He took the chair across the room from her, sprawling his long legs out in front of him. She was pretty certain he wasn't drinking hot chocolate in his mug.

She shrugged, trying to be casual. "I do rely on you in a lot of ways. The thought of you leaving scares me a little."

He took a sip from his mug and regarded her through the steam. "Why would you think I would leave?"

"I don't know. Everyone leaves, don't they?" That sounded lame and not at all like her. She was honest and she wanted honesty between them. "I didn't understand when you said you'd rather we be together while this is happening. That implied when this is over, you intend to move on."

His dark eyes held hers captive. "Babe, try to keep up. I'm in this for the long haul. I made that very clear with you. I moved into your house in order to keep you safe and be here if these nightmares persisted, not to make you uncomfortable. I don't want you thinking I expect anything from you. Do I prefer to stay? Yes. Hopefully I'll manage to seduce you into letting me stay in your bed with you before you kick me out. If that doesn't happen, I'll need to work a little harder."

Okay then, so much for insecurities.

"VIENNA FOUND THE body," Denver said. He put his hand on Vienna's shoulder in sympathy as he explained to Stella what had happened on day three of the search.

Vienna kept her head down, looking into her drink, her beautiful features an unreadable mask. No one would ever suspect that behind that gorgeous face with its classic bone structure and her runway body, she could easily be a member of Mensa and had held several patents that she sold, turning her ideas into gold mines. She made money playing cards in Vegas, and was quite passionate about playing poker.

She excelled at being an emergency and trauma nurse. Her love of the Sierras kept her in their small town. She was head of Search and Rescue and had been for the past few years. Due to her organizational skills, she had managed to get much-needed equipment and funding for them as well as new recruits. Those recruits, like Sam and a few others, were very skilled on various terrains.

"We have to be sworn in as a sheriff's deputy when we work on the team," Bruce pointed out. "I always sort of wonder if Sean and Bale won't get hit by lightning when they take the oath. Both of them were fishing out on the lake the morning of the assault on Sam. They had Bale's boat out. Griffen's people searched their boat and truck for scuba gear. Neither man was wet, he said, but by the time anyone got to them, the sun was out." He sounded disappointed that Bale or Sean wasn't the culprit trying to kill Sam.

"I always forget they're part of Search and Rescue," Stella said.

Vienna looked up. "Bale and Edward are local boys and both are good in the snow. They hunt and fish. They grew up here and know the area. Jason and Sean have been their friends since college and have been members of the community for a few years. They're all pretty tight. They're solid when it comes to rescue, particularly Bale and Edward. They're all business."

Denver nodded. "That's true. As much as they annoy me sometimes, never during an actual search and rescue mission. They all knew James Marley. We all did."

"He was a good man," Raine said. "Loved his family. There's no way this was an accident, not with it being the same way Sam was attacked. I looked at the rocks where he was fishing. Griffen took tons of pictures. There was a kind of skid mark where it looked as if one of his waders slid along the algae on the rock."

"I saw that," said Sonny Leven, the younger of the two security guards from the resort. He had been born and raised in the small town as well. He'd never left, not even to go to college. Stella knew he supported his father and that was why he hadn't gone away to school. He'd never had that opportunity. Like many, he had worked multiple jobs before becoming a full-time security guard at her resort. "There was blood on another rock where Marley hit his head."

Stella glanced at him sharply. He sounded a little strange. She'd forgotten that he lived in close proximity to James Marley, just down the street from him. She vaguely recalled that there was some kind of feud between Marley and Leven's father, but she didn't know what it was about or when it had taken place. Not while she'd been living there.

This was what they did after one of the rescues turned into a recovery. The members came together at the Grill and talked about the mission in low voices, especially if they knew the deceased. Stella knew it helped them to get rid of some of the aftermath of their grief.

"We had to walk in those reeds for what seemed forever," Carl Montgomery said. "We all knew he was there and we didn't want to face his family without bringing him home, but those reeds were so close together, choking the water and preventing any sight."

"I stepped on him," Vienna said in a low voice. "I felt so awful stepping on him, but that's how I found him."

Stella felt the delicate little shudder that went through her body. That shocked her. Given all the things Vienna faced, all the surgeries and trauma victims, all the rescues and dead people she brought home to families, she hadn't expected her friend to be so shaken. Still, James Marley wasn't just anyone. He was well liked and respected. He had been a friend.

"An accident is one thing," Vienna continued, "but to think that someone would viciously target a man like James is so ugly."

"The worst of it is," Harlow said, "it really does look like an accident. He slipped, hit his head. He has that injury on the back of his skull, which easily could have made him disoriented or even unconscious. He didn't have signs of a struggle, nothing that would indicate someone drowned him. He had a finger broken in two places, but there was fishing line wrapped around it. Cause of death was drowning."

"That fishing line was everywhere," Denver said. "It was around the reeds and partially around his wader, anchoring him underwater. It looked like he rolled a couple of times with the waves and that was what wrapped him up in it."

Bale came in and ordered a beer, seating himself a few barstools over from Denver, who immediately acknowledged him.

"Came to pay my respects to the old man," he muttered. "Helped me out when I was a kid a few times."

"Yeah," Carl said, "I have to admit, he did me as well. Loved his family and got a little crotchety as he got older, but always did the right thing in the end."

"Loved those grandkids of his," Raine said. "Heard he called them every single day. Even the younger ones. Liked to take them fishing with him. He had patience for them."

"I do business with his sons. They're good, honest men. Don't know his daughter . . ." Carl trailed off, as if he might have heard things he didn't want to repeat.

"She lies," Bale said. "Always did, even in school."

Stella wondered if that was the truth. She glanced at Carl. She tended to believe him. He didn't make a reply, but then he didn't deny it either.

"Why did it take so long to find him?" Sonny Leven asked. "I mean, his family looked in the water all around that area because his truck was there, right? They searched before we did. Why do you suppose they didn't come across him?"

"The reeds are really thick there, Sonny," Vienna said. "We didn't actually see the body, and it was close to the surface. The reeds hid it."

"There are rocks all through there as well," Bruce said. "The reeds choke out everything so you can't see the rocks. The rocks are green under the water."

"But wouldn't the fishing line have been at the top of the water where they could see it?" Sonny persisted.

"You don't think his own family did him in, do you?" Carl asked.

Sonny shook his head. "No, it's just weird that no one could see him when he was in such shallow water, even with the reeds." He was the newest member of Search and Rescue and trying to learn.

Stella knew this was their process, but still, it sickened her. She didn't know why she felt so guilty, but she did. All the rescuers were hurting. She stood up and moved away from them, needing fresh air. Although intellectually she knew it wasn't her fault, guilt still weighed on her. She told herself there was no way she could have foreseen that the murderer would have rushed from attempting to kill Sam straight to another fisherman. James had been miles away, so there had been a boat involved. Boats meant launching into the lake. Pulling behind a vehicle. Someone had to have seen something—someone. There were so many people out that morning.

She slipped out of the bar into the evening air. Temperatures were already dropping, especially at night. Folding her arms across her chest, she walked briskly up the street just a little way from the bar's entrance to try to stay warm. She didn't plan to go far.

This was a town where most of the locals hunted and fished. They owned guns. Now that one of their own had been most likely murdered and word had gone out from the sheriff's department to be on the lookout for someone in scuba gear, it hadn't stopped anyone from fishing. Instead, they were fishing in pairs, and all were packing guns and looking for the killer.

She hadn't gone halfway down the block when Jason Briggs, Bale's friend, came up behind her. "You shouldn't be out here alone, Stella. It isn't safe."

She whirled around at the sound of his voice. Of all of Bale's friends, she knew Jason the least. He rarely said much, particularly when he was with his friends. He stayed in the background. He'd gone to college with the others, was an engineer and liked the Sierras enough to want to stay. He was a strong climber, one of the main reasons he relocated to the area.

"It can get stuffy in the bar. Tonight the rescue crew is talking about finding James Marley. It makes me feel so sad for him and his family."

Ominous gray clouds towered toward the moon, stacking up in formations blocking out the stars. The weather was definitely changing. Winter was coming with a vengeance.

"I didn't know him. Bale and Edward did. They said he was a pretty cool guy most of the time. Edward and he had a few words a couple of months ago, but that was over his daughter's mouth. Apparently, she didn't like something Edward and Sean were talking about in the parking lot of the hardware store. She overheard them and told them to be quiet. Something to that effect. They told her to go fuck herself, that she had no right telling them what they could or couldn't say in a public place. The exchange got heated and they left. They thought it was over, but she ran to her daddy and he was really pissed."

Stella couldn't tell if he was relaying the incident the way it really happened, or the way he heard it happened. She didn't like Sean or Bale, so in her mind, they were always at fault. Just because she didn't like them didn't mean they were always the ones in the wrong. If they were having a private conversation outside and James Marley's daughter overheard it, she really didn't have the right to ask them to stop talking.

"That's too bad that they would have a bad experience with him when James was such a good man as a rule. He was fiercely protective over his family, and they were the same about him. I just can't understand any of this." That much was true. She couldn't.

"People don't always make sense," Jason said. "I hope it really was an accident and no one murdered him."

Music suddenly blared louder as someone opened the door of the Grill and allowed the sound to escape. Sam moved toward them in that easy way he had that made him look like a menacing jungle cat.

Jason glanced toward the bar and then leaned into her, but kept his eyes on Sam and his voice a whisper. "Tell Shabina to stop going out into the forest by herself looking for birds. Not a good idea right now." He walked briskly away, continuing on down the block as if he'd been walking all along and had never stopped.

Stella stared after him, her heart pounding, her mouth suddenly dry. Shabina was an avid bird watcher and she did go into the forest, hiking the trails, looking for various rare birds and their nests. It wasn't like she advertised she was a bird enthusiast. She was very quiet about it. Someone was watching Shabina's movements closely. Sean? Most likely. Jason would know. Sean seemed obsessed and not in a good way, if there was such a thing. Things were getting more and more complicated. What had happened to her peaceful town?

"You forgot your jacket, Stella," Sam said as he held out her coat, expecting her to slip her arms into it.

Sam never seemed like the gentlemanly type, so the unexpected gestures always moved her. She let him bundle her up, not realizing how cold she was until she was zipped in her jacket. He handed her the gloves that had been in the pockets of her coat. Again, he waited for her to speak, letting her decide what she wanted to tell him, but his gaze followed Jason as he went down the street.

Sam wasn't the only one watching Jason. She noticed that Denver had come out of the bar as well, presumably to check up on her. He stood leaning on the corner of the building, head turned in the direction Jason had gone. She moved closer to Sam, turning her face up toward his to tell him what Jason had said, when a sudden chill crept down her spine.

"Sam?" His name came out wobbly. She glanced up, toward the roof of the bar. There was movement. Someone was watching them. They'd seen Jason and Denver as well.

"Keep looking at me, sweetheart. No one else is here but us. I clocked them the minute I came out."

"What is going on? Why is everyone we know acting so weird? Do you know who is on the roof?"

"Bale and Sean are on the roof. Edward is on the other side of the street, a block up in a parked car. I don't know why they were watching the bar. They know Search and Rescue always comes to the Grill to talk things over and process. Sometimes they even come in and listen, even if they don't participate. Bale stayed inside until you left. He went out the back and Denver followed him. He must have climbed up the fire escape ladder to get on the roof to join Sean."

"How do you see all that? I came out here and didn't see anything. Jason startled me when he came up behind me. He told me to warn Shabina not to go off by herself bird watching. She goes into the forest all the time. Someone must be following her, Sam. He said it wasn't safe. He whispered it to me, as if he knew we were being watched."

"He probably knew his friends were watching. He took a chance warning you. I don't think Sean would be very happy with him. Shabina should be careful. I think Sean's fixated on her."

Stella sighed. "All this time I thought my little piece of paradise was as perfect as it could get, but there are all these ugly things going on that I didn't know about."

He put his arm around her and turned her back toward the bar. "Do you want to go home?"

She did. Talking with the others about James Marley only made her feel guiltier that she hadn't considered the killer would murder another victim knowing the sheriff would realize the death wasn't an accident.

Sam walked her to the 4Runner and opened the door for her. Stella got in and put on her seatbelt automatically, a frown on her face as she tried to puzzle it out. "Sam, why wouldn't the killer care that the sheriff knows he murdered Marley? I guess I presumed, since he went to the trouble of making it look like an accident, that he wouldn't want anyone to know it was murder, but maybe I'm wrong."

Sam glanced at her as he started them on the way back to the resort. "Not necessarily. He's smart. What difference does it make if Griffen knows or anyone knows, but can't prove it? If he kills several other people but there's no evidence, if every other murder looks like an accident and no one is the wiser, he's still in the clear. He can still thumb his nose at everyone."

"Do you think he's local?" Stella asked in a low voice. She held her breath, afraid of the answer. "I mean he could be someone who comes up here on a regular basis, right?"

"I thought that would be likely. Someone who came to fish or hunt or both. Maybe does climbing and fishing. The Sierras offer all kinds of activities. He might have been coming here for some time," Sam said. "Something triggered him to kill and he's started here, or maybe he was already doing it someplace else and is now bringing it here."

Stella wanted it to be that, but it didn't *feel* right to her. "Do you think he killed before this?"

Sam drove in silence for nearly half a mile. "He laid out his plan meticulously, Stella. I can't imagine that it was his first time."

"Don't you think he panicked when he saw me underwater trying to save you? Would a seasoned killer panic?"

"Was he panicked or did he just want you away from him because you weren't his chosen victim?" Sam asked. "We don't know if he chooses victims yet. Maybe he doesn't kill women. Or beautiful women. Or ones with curves. Or blonde hair and blue eyes. We have no idea."

That was all true. They had no way of knowing. Stella sighed. They just had to wait. She knew there wasn't going to be a way for the DA to make a case for murder no matter how diligently the sheriff investigated. What did they have to prove that James Marley had been murdered? It really did appear as if he'd slipped on a rock and hit his head and drowned. They had the killer's earlier attack on Sam, but that could have been entirely unrelated. Not likely, but it could be argued. There was no evidence left behind to point to any person.

As always, they would have to wait until the killer decided to strike again.

# CHAPTER EIGHT

*Mommy, Daddy's doing the bad thing again.*

It was very dark and suddenly the sound of laughter erupted and a light went on, illuminating a campsite. The young man checked the woman's backpack to ensure it sat perfectly where it was supposed to so that when they did the miles of hiking they'd planned on this leg of the trail, she would be as comfortable as possible. She didn't appear to be as used to hiking as he was. Clearly, he wanted her to really enjoy it.

He had light brown hair, trimmed neat, as if he might have gotten out of the military recently, or maybe was a police officer. He held himself very straight, his shoulders perfectly aligned. He had a trim body with a lot of lean muscle. He moved easily around the woman, making sure her water bottle was full.

She had her blonde hair in a ponytail, the mass coming out the back of the hat on her head. He handed her gloves and she pulled them on. The gloves were the same color as the thin neon-pink piping on her jacket, boots, hat and shades. Both wore headlamps to illuminate the trail when they began their hike.

The lamps showed colors of fall bursting overhead as leaves of gold, red, orange and green cascaded in, weeping waterfalls in every direction. The leaves swirled to the ground to cover the floor of the campsite. There seemed to be the dark sheen of water in the distance, but the man shut off the lantern, plunging the campsite into darkness again. Abruptly, as the two backpackers started along an unseen trail with only their headlamps on, the man leading the way, the camera lens shut down.

STELLA WOKE, GASPING, choking, twisting, clawing the bedsheets, fighting for air. Not again. She sat up and put her head between her knees, trying to combat the nausea. She wrapped her arms around her middle and began to rock herself, trying to soothe the child in her, that little girl who saw those gruesome murders. The one who told her mother, but no one would believe.

She was alone. She had to be alone. No one could know. She could never tell anyone. *Don't you say one word, Stella.* Her mother's voice rang sharp in her ears. *If you tell anyone, they'll take you away and throw you in a deep dark pit and feed you to the lions. Do you want that? I won't be able to find you. They'll cut off your hair and chop you into little pieces so those lions can eat you. I took you to the place where the lions are. You saw them. The way they looked at you. That's what will happen if you tell anyone.*

She remembered that place to which her mother had dragged her, right up to the cage where the lions were roaring with hunger and rage. The man took the money from her mother, lots of it, and had her stand in the doorway of the cage with raw meat in her hands, all bloody. Her mother told her it was another little girl who didn't know how to keep her mouth shut. The lion leapt at the doorway and the man thrust the meat inside with a long instrument, laughing as she screamed and screamed.

She pushed her fist into her mouth and tried not to choke on the sobs. She'd never gone to a zoo again. Never. Not as a child. Not as a teen. Never as an adult. She'd never told anyone what her mother had done.

Now she had to contend with another murderer. He was going to kill again. A couple? The man? The woman? Where were they? Backpackers. They looked so happy together. How could she stop him?

"I'm right here, sweetheart." Sam's voice came out of the darkness. Steady. Calm. Reassuring.

She felt the weight of his body settle on the mattress beside her and then he was pulling her into his arms. Onto his lap. Rocking her gently, his chin on top of her head. Bailey pushed his head onto her thigh.

"Another nightmare?"

She nodded, gripping his leg hard. She needed to feel the steel of his body. That tough infrastructure that was Sam.

"She told me not to tell anyone. I tried to forget that. I never let myself remember if I could help it." She turned her head to look up at him over her shoulder.

He tightened his arms around her and kept rocking her gently. His lips were barely there on her temple, a soft brush of encouragement.

"When I was little and would try to tell her, she would say it wasn't real, Daddy would never do such a thing, it was all in my head. Later, she would get angry with me and say I was never to speak of it and it would ruin our family. Sometimes she would grab my head and hold me very still. She'd look into my eyes and make me repeat over and over that I would never tell anyone that Daddy was doing the bad thing."

"How old were you?"

"Four when the nightmares started. Five when she told me

not to tell. I remember she wanted me to have tutors. And she told me never, ever to tell Daddy I knew." Because it was so fresh in her mind and her heart was racing, her mouth dry, she forced herself to recount the visit to the zoo and the terror she'd endured. She'd believed she held another little girl's body in her hands to feed to the lion.

Sam was silent for so long she thought he wouldn't speak. He simply held her, rocking her in his arms, his face in her neck. She could feel his warm breath on her shoulder. When he lifted his head, he gently brushed a kiss along her pulse and then her ear and temple.

"You must have been a very brave child, Stella. You were alone and terrified. You still wanted to do the right thing. Over the years, the things I saw, my moral compass wasn't always the best, although I can honestly say I tried to always have justice in my mind, not revenge."

His words warmed her a little when she was so cold inside. There was true admiration in his voice. Still, she couldn't shake the nightmare and the aftermath that always came with it.

Sam took another deep breath as if he were fighting down demons and reached for the bottle of water on her nightstand, uncapped it and handed it to her. "Did you ever say anything to your father?"

She tried to control the tremors that wracked her body. "No. The images I saw in my nightmares were horrific. He tortured his victims. I was a child and those images were burned into my brain. I became terrified of him, and the last thing I would ever do would be to talk to him about what I saw. My mother had to figure out ways to explain why I was afraid of him when he came back from his business trips. Fortunately, he wasn't all that interested in children."

Sam didn't try to get her to tell him anything else. She didn't know if she could have. She hadn't told anyone about her mother telling her not to speak of her nightmares or that she came into her room at night and coached her over and over not to talk. She'd forced herself to forget.

"I didn't want to remember," she murmured. "The things my father did were bad enough, but now, as an adult, I can see that by my mother's silence, by forcing me to be silent, she was complicit. She didn't want to give up her status. She knew, better than I did, what would happen to the family of a serial killer, and because she didn't want the taint of that, she let people die."

She laid her head back against his chest. "That's what I'm doing now. Staying silent so I can keep my resort and my happy place. My safe haven. I'm doing exactly what she was doing. I hate myself right now. If I don't go to Griffen and tell him who I am and that I'm having these nightmares, that there's a killer here, we won't catch him, Sam, and more people are going to die. He's making his kills look like accidents. If he hadn't been so upset at missing his first intended murder, he wouldn't have used the exact same method killing James Marley."

"At best they can say his death is suspicious at this point because of the attack on me," Sam said. "But it does look like an accident. This killer is good. Had he not missed, no one would be the wiser. Our ace in the hole is you. He doesn't have a clue that you're onto him. If it got out that you are who you are, that goes away. If you do tell Griffen, we can't let this get out to the media or anyone else, and you know it would. They already know murder's a possibility because of the attack on me. They just can't prove anything. This situation isn't the same, Stella. We need to be silent in order to have an edge or we don't stand a chance of catching him."

That was fine by her. She didn't want it to get out. The more people who knew, the more her life would be turned upside down. Griffen Cauldrey was a friend, at least she had come to know him pretty well over the last few years and she felt he was a fair man, but he would have to inform the sheriff, and the sheriff would have to call in the FBI.

She took a deep breath. "Sam, I have to tell Zahra. She's my best friend and she'd be very hurt if I didn't tell her who I really was. I've thought about sharing a million times, but didn't because . . ." She trailed off, remembering the feel of her mother's fingers biting into her cheeks. She hadn't realized until just now that those childhood memories had played a part in deterring her. "I have to tell Zahra."

He was silent for a long time. Too long. Long enough that she knew he didn't approve. She knew why. Zahra tended to blurt things out. She could overshare at times, but she also could keep confidences when it mattered. If Stella asked her not to breathe a word to anyone, she would go to her grave never speaking a word. That was Zahra. In any case, she didn't need Sam's approval. She wasn't that woman.

"Do any of your other friends know who you are?" Before she could answer he sighed, his long fingers moving to the nape of her neck to begin a slow massage. "Raine. She did a background check on you and she would be thorough about it."

She attempted to turn her head, but his fingers felt too good and they prevented all movement, so she just held still and let him soothe the tension from her. "How do you know that?" Raine knew about Sam. Sam knew about Raine. She just wanted to go back to scheduling her events at the resort. She thought that was complicated. Now she had killers to worry about.

"She won't run her mouth."

"As opposed to Zahra, who might?" This time she didn't care

about the soothing massage, or the fact that he was the only person who had ever helped her in the middle of the night when the world had come crashing down. Zahra was her best friend, completely loyal to her, and she wasn't going to have him act as if Zahra couldn't be trusted.

"Woman." His dark eyes caught the moon through the window, glinting at her with amusement.

Her stomach did an unexpected roll. He didn't look like that ever. His harsh features softened, eyes drifting over her face as if he might want to devour her.

"Man," she whispered back.

"You think I can't see inside her? I spent most of my life reading people to stay alive. Not only does she love you, but she's as loyal as they come. I think she'd chew off her own arm before she'd tell someone who you are."

His straight white teeth flashed in the briefest of smiles and she nearly fell out of his lap. He didn't do that. Smiles were so rare they felt like a gift. She touched her fingers to his mouth. "What was that for?" Because she was going to do it again. Often. She liked that he "read" Zahra and recognized she was loyal.

"You have such a nasty little temper. Cracks me up sometimes."

"My temper cracks you up?" Her eyebrows drew together in the darkest scowl she could summon. "I don't have a temper. If I do, it's a very tiny one."

"Turn around and let me massage your shoulders. You get very upset when anyone is threatening your friends. Even a perceived threat."

"There was a *but* in there when you were giving Zahra a compliment. I could hear it in your voice. What was that?" She turned around because she wanted the massage. Who would turn that down?

He took the water bottle out of her hands and put it on the nightstand before settling both hands on her shoulders. He had big hands and strong fingers. "When she drinks, she's totally un-inhibited. She has no idea what is coming out of her mouth."

"You can say that of anyone, Sam."

He leaned close, his mouth next to her ear so that his lips brushed against her lobe. "That's not so. You might blurt out how hot you think I am, but you would never talk about your real identity."

Her entire body turned red, she was certain of it. She tried not to choke. She *had* said it to the others right where he could hear it. She knew she had.

"She wouldn't have any reason to tell anyone."

"Not even Bruce?"

"She wouldn't tell Bruce," Stella told him with absolute confi-dence.

He was silent, continuing to massage the tension from her while she sat in his lap, Bailey resting his large, heavy head on her leg. She petted the Airedale, her fingers in the curly fur, lis-tening to the sounds of the night, realizing Sam had managed to distance the nightmare from her with his presence, letting her talk and then distracting her with their discussion.

"No, she wouldn't tell Bruce," he agreed eventually, and easily lifted her by putting his hands around her waist, to set her on the mattress. "I'm going to make you hot chocolate. You can sketch what you saw and write out the details in the journal you keep. When I come back, if you're ready, you can tell me about it."

He hadn't even asked her to tell him about the nightmare. She waited until he was out of her bedroom before snapping on the small lamp beside the bed and unlocking and then reaching into the drawer where she kept her journal and sketchpad. She visualized everything she saw in her nightmare. There were no faces, but she saw the woman's blonde hair and athletic clothing. She'd been stylish, as if she'd chosen her clothing more for looks than because they were the best for hiking the trails. A newbie? She wasn't his normal partner then, that was why he fussed over her, making certain her backpack sat just right. He looked comfortable; she didn't, but was willing. This was something she wanted to do with him.

There was so little she could get from the first glimpse. She pushed herself to see as much as she could. *Concentrate, Stella.* The woman's backpack. His. Their hiking shoes. He had a watch on his wrist—she didn't. They both wore puffy jackets. His was expensive, a good outdoor brand. Her jacket wasn't a brand she recognized. Maybe one of her friends might know. Someone might recognize her, or him.

She sketched the two people in relation to their height and weight, trying to guess as accurately as possible given their bulky clothing and surroundings. Then she sketched the very little she could make out of the campsite, her impression of water in the distance behind them, the trees and colors, the leaves on the uneven ground. There wasn't much. When she finally lifted her head, she realized that Sam was back in the room with her, looking at the drawing over her shoulder, and the hot chocolate was in her favorite to-go mug sitting on her nightstand.

He studied the sketches in silence for a while. "I don't recognize that campsite, but I'm not a backpacker. You and Raine tend to backpack more than anyone else of our group."

She'd never heard him include himself in their group. It was true. Raine tended to be the one to backpack with her, especially if the hike was a long one. The two of them liked to go on one- or two-week hikes into the mountains and forest and camp. Sometimes, if they could get off work, they would go for longer stretches.

"I've looked at it over and over, especially the large impression of water in the background, but I just come up blank. I thought I could show it to Raine, see if she recognizes it." She pushed back her hair and then reached for the chocolate. "It's incredibly frustrating to see so little, Sam. It's next to impossible to identify a place with no real identifying markers." She rubbed her forehead. "That's nothing. This is the Sierras, with thousands of miles of trails and so many campsites."

"At least you have somewhat of a warning. That's something. If it wasn't for you, we'd probably never know this killer was at work here. Who knows how many murders he would get away with?" Sam sounded the way he always did. Calm. Steady. A rock.

She took a deep breath. "You're right, I have to look at things from a different perspective if we're going to catch this man."

Sam paced across the floor restlessly, when he wasn't a restless man. She observed him carefully over the top of her mug. "What is it?"

"I get that you have to talk to Zahra, but, sweetheart, you can't forget for one minute that this man is a murderer. If he knows that you're a threat to him, he's going to set his sights on you. That's the last thing we want. You aren't going to be of any use to anyone if you're dead."

"I'm not likely to forget what I'm dealing with," she assured. "I've had dealings with serial killers twice before and that was already enough for me. I don't want to get anywhere near one. Zahra won't say anything, Sam. I'm more worried about telling

Griffen than Zahra. He'll have no choice but to tell his boss, who would call in the FBI. Then it's a circus."

"We don't exactly have anything to share with Griffen at this point." He hesitated. "It's possible I can use a couple of my contacts to help us."

She looked up quickly. Her nightmare had woken her in the middle of the night, and if it hadn't been for the moonlight streaming through the window, she wouldn't have been able to see his face from where she sat. As it was, most of his features were in the shadows, giving him a predatory appearance. She almost wished Denver and Raine had never said anything to her. Already, with her nightmares and the memories of her past so close, she was edgy, and she didn't ever want to see Sam as the "ghost" one had called him and the other had implied.

If what her friends said about his career was true, then Sam would have relentless enemies tracking him. Harlow had told her that men in the DEA who had gone undercover and shut down rings were hunted, as were their families. If that was the case, she could imagine that someone like Denver and Raine described would be pursued to the ends of the earth. He shut down terrorist cells. Drug cartels. Getting in touch with his friends in order to help her would be a huge risk to him—a sacrifice he would make for her. He didn't put it to her that way, of course, because he downplayed his past, but she was fairly certain she wasn't far off.

"I don't think that's necessary yet, Sam. What can we tell them that we can't tell Griffen? Helen McKay is a local trail runner and peak bagger. She logs hundreds of miles and is familiar with so many of the trails around here and throughout Yosemite."

Sam loomed over her, shaking his head. "Stella." This time her name was a clear warning.

"I thought I could show her a sketch and tell her I'm drawing and have this vague memory of this cool place I want to paint in detail, but can't remember where it is. She might know."

Sam thought it over and then nodded. "That's a good idea, sweetheart. If she has any friends who trail run, she might ask them as well, but maybe wait until you have a little more detail."

There wasn't much more she could do. This was always a wait-and-see game with a killer. That was the worst part.

"I'm going to take a walk around the property. Do you want to come with me?"

He did that every night. Sam didn't seem to need sleep the way others did. She nodded and jumped up to pull on warm sweatpants and a sweatshirt over the skimpy clothes she'd been sleeping in. She didn't need to look glamourous for Sam. He didn't seem to care one way or the other. If she dressed up, she could tell he liked it. If she didn't, he still seemed to think she was beautiful—at least he always made her feel that way.

Bailey followed them outside, although she could tell her dog thought they were a little crazy for interrupting their sleep to the extent of wandering all over the property and walking out onto the pier when they could be in a comfortable bed. It occurred to Stella that it was the first time in her life that she'd ever had one of her terrible nightmares and ended up feeling content and even at peace after.

ZAHRA SAT ACROSS the table from her, dipping the fried zucchini into Shabina's incredible and very secret sauce that had everyone coming back to her café. Stella watched her closely. Usually, Zahra was an open book. She had a pixie face, with her dark expressive eyes and pretty, very pouty mouth. Right now, she kept her gaze on the sauce and the zucchini, as if that would give her all the answers she might need.

Stella sat back in her chair and looked around the café. They'd deliberately met late for lunch, almost at closing time, Stella wanting the crowd gone so they wouldn't be overheard at the back of the café when they sat in their favorite spot. No one was close to them because the section was cordoned off. She'd asked Shabina ahead of time if they could sit there. Shabina hadn't asked questions, just gave her permission and said she'd clean up after, not involving her crew.

The silence seemed to stretch on forever, along with the tension. Finally, Zahra flicked her gaze up to Stella's. "Did you think this revelation about your father would change how I feel about you?" Her voice was very low, her accent pronounced.

Stella started to press the pads of her fingers against her mouth and then realized she was doing it. "No, I didn't say anything because I was trying to get away from that little girl and her family. The things my mother trained me not to say to anyone. I built the life that I wanted for myself and was happy in it."

Zahra's gaze went back to the zucchini. She dipped another piece in more sauce and swished it around. "Why did you decide to tell me now?"

Stella took a deep breath. "The thing with knowing about my father started with nightmares. I was a little kid, but I would have these dreams. I'd have five in a row and each one would give me a wider picture of what was happening. The dreams would stop and, two days later, someone would die in that exact way. I was just a little kid, and I'd tell my mother."

She found herself rocking back and forth and she deliberately forced herself to stop. She wasn't a little kid. She had allies now. She had Zahra, who sat across from her without judgment, ready to help without knowing what was wrong. There was Sam. Raine. She could do this.

"Essentially, you saw the murders before they happened."

Stella nodded. "When I was a young child, it went on for years. The nightmares started when I was four, and my father wasn't arrested until I was eight, almost nine. My mother was a terrible alcoholic by that time and she killed herself when he pled guilty to avoid the death penalty. The media circus was too much for her. She was very certain he wouldn't be found guilty and she could continue her life in society. When she was ostracized by her friends, she became bitter and angry, mostly at me because I told on my father and she'd said not to.

"When I was a teenager in a foster home, I suddenly began to have similar nightmares. I didn't want to believe it, but I realized there was a serial killer at work in close proximity to me again. The pattern was the same. Five nights of dreams and then one or two days of silence and then the kill. I tried to stay out of the limelight, but the media got ahold of it just like when I was a little kid. It was hell. I vowed never to go through that again. I changed my name and found a place of peace where I could just live my life."

Stella took a piece of zucchini, but her appetite was gone. She dropped it on her plate and looked at Zahra with stricken eyes, unable to go on.

Zahra sighed. "The sudden desire to camp when we already had plans to go to the Grill. That didn't make sense. Bruce told me that was his favorite fishing spot. He and Denver go there all the time. You had a dream and you were keeping them from fishing there, weren't you?"

Stella nodded. "But I had too much to drink. I thought Sam would drive us home and just stay at the resort, but no, he had to be too nice and go watch over our things. He doesn't get a chance to fish because he's always working, so he thought he'd put in a little time in the early morning hours before we got there. Bernice told me he was there and I jumped in my rig and raced to the site, terrified I'd be too late."

"He would have murdered either Bruce or Denver if we hadn't put up the tents and driven them out of their favorite fishing site," Zahra said. "They don't always fish together because Denver has to work so much at the hospital and can't get away. Bruce can only go out in the early morning. Most likely, he would have been the victim. You probably saved his life."

"I didn't save James Marley's life. I never even saw that coming. What did he do? Go straight from trying to kill Sam to targeting James and then getting away that fast? How? Sam called the sheriff after the attack. They searched boats and trucks for scuba gear."

"The killer would have dropped the gear to the bottom of the lake, Stella. It's a big lake, and by the time the sheriff gets out there and the word goes out, come on, realistically, if he's been around here at all, he'll know it wouldn't be easy to get a decent search crew together. He had hours to get away."

Stella knew Zahra was right. Unfortunately, it had been a good day for fishing, and there were boats on the water and many fishing from shore all around the lake. It wasn't like the sheriff had hundreds of men he could deploy to search. She hadn't expected the killer to go straight from attempting to kill Sam to killing another fisherman using the exact same method.

"What are you going to do?" Zahra asked.

Stella shrugged. "I don't know. There's not really much I can do without evidence. According to everything I'm hearing, there isn't enough evidence to build a case for murder. As it stands, the only reason they're even considering that it wasn't an accident is because there was an attempt on Sam and we saw the assailant in the water, but of course, we can't identify him."

"Are you even certain it was a man?"

Stella nodded. "Absolutely."

Zahra sighed. "If Bruce was the intended victim, at least it's not some woman out to kill him because he isn't paying attention to her." She sent Stella a little mischievous half smile. "You can't really tell the police anything, can you, and you shouldn't at this stage, Stella. If it got out who you are, it would only tip off the killer and we'd lose any advantage we have in trying to catch him."

"That's what I think too. Sam does know. I had to tell him when the killer almost got him and I suddenly showed up out of the blue and dove into the lake to save him. The *freezing*-cold lake. I really think he should remember that."

"I'm sure he's appropriately thankful. He did kiss you, after all."

Stella wasn't touching that. "Raine has to do background checks on anyone around her because of the type of work she does. She knows about me and has known for years. She's never said anything. She keeps everything confidential."

Zahra's head snapped up, her eyes darkening almost to a black midnight. Her brows came together. "What do you mean, background checks?"

"It's a requirement for her job. Anyone she's close to. That would be us. She doesn't talk out of turn, Zahra," Stella soothed, seeing the near panic on Zahra's face.

"How much can she know?" Zahra's dark eyes were bouncing all over the place, as if she might suddenly get up and make a run for it. She looked really alarmed.

Stella realized Zahra had her own secrets, maybe as shattering as her own. "I have no idea. My past was very well documented. I don't know how well documented yours is. Whatever you're worried about, if no one knows about it, or wrote it down, or had pictures of it, she wouldn't be able to find it."

Zahra took a deep breath and let it out. "That sucks to be her. She must feel like a peeping Thomas."

"Tom," Stella automatically corrected. "It is difficult for her. I'm sure that's part of the reason she stays a little apart from everyone. But in any case, what I was trying to say in regard to the serial killer . . ." Stella frowned as she dipped the zucchini in sauce and took a bite. "It isn't like we have a huge circle to draw on and we can't talk to anyone else about this. No one, Zahra, not Bruce, not anyone."

Zahra nodded. "I get it. I come from a place where the wrong word can get someone killed. I'm not about to mess up when it comes to your life. This is one of those situations where we can't trust anyone until we know for certain they're clear, and how do we know that?"

"I had another nightmare this morning. This time it was two backpackers. It was such a small, tiny piece of a campsite that it was impossible for me to recognize. I know I've been there before, but there's thousands of miles of trail in the Sierras, and the campsite I know I've seen, but it was so dark. I believe the killer is going to stay close to home, stay in our county, so odds are I might be able to identify where he's going to strike."

Zahra wasn't a dedicated backpacker. She would camp occasionally, and go out on weekend backpacking trips, or day trips, but not week- or monthlong trips. She didn't want to hike the John Muir Trail. That wasn't her thing at all. She would generously resupply her friends if they were hiking the JMT, but that was the extent of her "hiking" expertise.

"You have four more chances to find the right place he's going to strike, right?" Zahra asked.

Chances. Stella had never considered each nightmare a "chance," but that was what it was. Another clue. Another reveal of the larger picture. "If this goes the way it's always gone in the past, then yes, I should have a nightmare every night for the next four nights and see more of what the killer sees."

"Wait." Zahra sat up straighter. "Do you actually see through the killer's eyes?"

Stella shook her head. "Not exactly. It's like I'm a bystander, a witness, watching from somewhere apart from them all. In this instance, I'm behind the couple. I can't see their faces. It's frustrating. I can't shift positions to see any more of the trail. There's no way to move the lens of the camera."

"Is it an actual camera lens you're looking through?" Zahra asked.

Stella had never thought of that. She'd been a child and then a teen. No one had ever asked that question. She wasn't a photographer. She didn't know anything about cameras. She could barely take a selfie with her phone. The rest of her friends laughed at her efforts when she tried. She did have hundreds of pictures of Bailey on her phone. And the lake. She loved the lake, especially at sunrise.

"I don't know. It's a dream, Zahra, how would I know, and what difference does it make?" Stella asked, looking around, suddenly needing coffee.

Shabina was busy cleaning her machines, but she looked up as if she had a sixth sense when it came to her customers. She moved quickly to catch up her coffeepot and bring it all the way to the back of the shop to pour the aromatic liquid into Stella's mug.

"Thanks, Shabina. You're a goddess."

Shabina laughed. "It's a new pot, just for you. That's why it's a mini-pot." She turned and left them to it, not even asking why they needed to meet alone where no one could overhear them. She didn't seem the least upset that she wasn't included in their conversation.

Stella took a sip of the coffee. It was very hot. Too hot, just the way she liked it. "Why would it make a difference? I've always concentrated on what I've seen through the lens, not on the lens."

Zahra leaned closer. "What if you could make the lens wider yourself, Stella? If there were details on the lens you're looking through, the camera itself, you might be able to adjust it, shift the view a little each time. I don't know, it's just a thought. When I dream, I can sometimes change my dream a little." She shrugged and dabbed the zucchini stick in more sauce.

Stella sat back, staring at Zahra in shock. In a hundred years she would never have thought of trying to change her dreams. Not those dreams. She was too shocked by them. Too terrified. "That's brilliant, not that I know the first thing about cameras or lenses."

"But you do know how to draw what you see, and Harlow knows a lot about photography. She's good, Stella, really good. If you can get any details at all, she might be able to tell you what you're looking through and how to widen your view or move it even a little."

Stella bit down on her lower lip, trying to recall all the times she saw through the lens. She'd always concentrated on *what* she saw, the vivid details, training herself to see everything she could, not what she was seeing through. Now she tried to narrow her vision, block everything out but that lens.

"Honestly, I'm too scattered to recall anything about the lens,

Zahra, but you might be onto something. The thing is, if you are, and I can find something on the lens to help identify it, then I'd have to go to Harlow. As you well know, Harlow, like everyone in our circle of friends, is extremely intelligent and quick on the uptake. She's going to know something is up, especially after the attack on Sam. Everyone now suspects James Marley was murdered but no one can prove it."

Zahra shrugged. "Maybe, but how is your asking about a certain type of lens going to have her connecting those dots?"

"I've never asked about a camera in my life, Zahra. I have zero interest in them. I've gone to see her work and that's it. You all laugh at me and I'm good with that. I don't make any effort to get better. She knows that," Stella pointed out.

Zahra gave her that little mysterious, intriguing smile that got to every single man within miles if they saw it. Stella always thought she was beautiful when she flashed that particular secretive smile that told anyone seeing it exactly nothing, but they would want to know more.

"You can't purposely taunt Harlow, Zahra," Stella said. "You're such a minx sometimes. What did Harlow ever do to you?"

"Harlow was very good to me," Zahra said staunchly. "If it wasn't for her, I wouldn't have made it into this country. I wouldn't have gotten my citizenship or gotten into college. I owe her a lot. She's been a good friend to me."

"But?" Stella prompted.

Zahra shook her head. "I've never changed the way I've felt about her. It's just complicated between us. I tease her occasionally and she takes it with grace."

"She never goes home. Never. Her mother comes here to see her, but she never goes home." Stella didn't make it a question, because if Zahra knew why Harlow's mother visited but her very popular senator father didn't, she didn't want to put her on the spot.

Harlow was a talented surgical nurse, but her first love was photography. She'd gone to school for it and not only taken classes at college but interned with some of the masters, both digital and old-school. She'd been making a name for herself when all of a sudden she'd gone to nursing school and seemingly become passionate about that career. Then she'd gone to the High Sierras and stayed. She was needed there and she could take the photographs she loved and do the work she felt was important.

"Tonight I'll see if I can get any details on the lens, Zahra," Stella promised. "If I can, I'll write it down, sketch it, and see if Harlow can help me. Thanks for understanding, but mostly, thanks for being my friend. I really needed you. As your friend, I have to tell you, that's the same zucchini stick you've had for the last half hour and you're dipping it into the sauce. You may as well pick up the sauce container and drink it."

Zahra made a face at her and dropped the zucchini onto her plate. "The sauce is excellent."

"I was getting that."

# CHAPTER NINE

*Mommy, Daddy's doing the bad thing again.*

The man kept up a steady pace in the very early morning hours, the young woman right behind him. It was still dark and both wore headlamps clamped to their foreheads. He cast a few glances over his shoulder, as if anxious that she was all right. She looked around her more than she paid attention to where she was putting her feet. The light whirled and bobbed as she tried to take in her surroundings even in the dark.

The wind blew viciously, cutting at them both, tugging at their clothing, whipping at their jackets and her hair in spite of her baseball cap. Leaves swirled around the couple as they advanced along the trail. The man had a good gait, easy and natural along the climb. The woman seemed to struggle. There were rocks beneath the mat of leaves and she rolled them beneath the soles of her hiking boots, mostly because she wasn't paying any attention to where she was going or what she was doing.

The woman's bobbing light shone on the trees surrounding her and then, when they gave way, to granite walls rising above her and rocks on the ground, with leaves of all colors clinging to them. She turned this way and that, at one point whirling around so fast she tripped and went down on one knee. Instantly, the man turned back and hurried to her. He helped her up and they consulted for a few minutes. He insisted she drink water, which she did, while he stood close to her. He gestured back the way they'd come, but she shook her head and gestured the way they were going. He nodded and resumed the hike, albeit reluctantly.

The climb seemed to be going steadily uphill. Twice, he turned, saying something, and she nodded and took drinks of water. He was keeping her hydrated. That meant the hike was a long one. She was a little more cautious, keeping the light on the ground, just ahead of where she was stepping, although after a few minutes, she couldn't help herself and began to look around again, showing various views of the rocky formations. Just flashes as her light bobbed and weaved through the section they hiked.

Abruptly, the lens began to close. It hadn't even gotten light. Stella wanted to shout that it wasn't fair, but she forced herself to be aware in the dream. Not to be a passive observer, or a terrified one. For the first time, she tried changing the dream, maintaining it longer by staring at the lens only, trying to see if she was holding a camera and looking through it, silently cursing herself for not caring about photography. What was wrong with her when every other person in the world seemed obsessed with selfies?

She tried to study the lens from every angle, to see if she could see even a part of the camera itself. Was that a dial on it? A button of some sort? Did it look like a knob? She tried to study it so she would be able to sketch it accurately. The lens closed abruptly.

IN SPITE OF how composed she'd been, she heard that child's voice very distinctly reverberating through her mind. She began to fight to get herself to the surface, to pull herself out of the nightmare.

Her heart beat too fast. Blood thundered in her ears. Her breath hitched, lungs burning raw, desperate for air. She woke fighting the sheets, kicking frantically to get them off her legs. She sat up abruptly and gulped in air.

Stella looked around her bedroom, her eyes a little wild, trying to take in everything familiar to anchor herself. Bailey was there, curled up in his bed across the room. Sam sat in a chair straight across from her, a silent sentry, looking strong and invincible. He had that expressionless mask, the one that was intimidating as hell. She'd never viewed him like that, and she knew that look was there to keep anyone from thinking they could harm her.

"Stella?" Sam's voice was gentle, moving over her like a caress.

This was the first time she wasn't sobbing hysterically or rocking back and forth. She had held the dream longer by just changing it slightly with her will. She had refused to view it as a nightmare, but more as a chance for her team to identify and catch the killer. To keep him from killing more victims.

"I think I'm okay, Sam," she said. Her voice trembled and she wasn't certain she was telling him the truth, but she wanted it to be the truth. She pushed back the damp hair tumbling around her face. Her hands were shaking.

Little beads of sweat had formed on her skin, running unattractively down her forehead and between her breasts. She had fought the sheets, but she hadn't gone to sleep with a slew of blankets, knowing from experience what was coming. She wasn't screaming. She wasn't catatonic. She was thinking, her brain processing.

"You're the strongest woman I know, Stella," Sam said. Respect was in his voice. Admiration. "Of course, you're okay. You've got this, sweetheart."

Just knowing he believed in her was half the battle. She wasn't alone in this fight. She had Sam and Zahra and even Raine if she needed to call on her. Raine would believe her and help in any way she could.

"Tell me what you saw while it's fresh in your mind," Sam encouraged.

She liked that he didn't coddle her. There was no, *Don't think about it.* He was all about, *Get it out. Go over it a dozen times if you have to. Write it down. Draw it.* That was Sam.

"It was dark. I couldn't see much. They both wore headlamps. She kept moving hers around so I caught a few glimpses of the terrain, but not much. At the end, when the lens was shutting down, I did my best to force the dream to continue and I studied the lens. I think I can draw a couple of features I saw around it. I don't know if that will help or not."

That expressionless mask softened and his eyes lit up. His mouth curved. "You were right about Zahra. She really came through, didn't she? Whether it pans out or not, she had a couple of really good ideas."

"She did point out that Harlow knows cameras and photography better than anyone in the county. She's really good, Sam, but if I went to her, that would be bringing another person into our circle," Stella said a little reluctantly.

Sam had been so adamant about keeping the number who knew about her past very low so there was no way the killer would discover Stella's true identity. She didn't want others to know about her, but on the other hand, she didn't want to be like her mother, going to any length to protect what she had and letting others die when she could possibly have saved them. She knew going to the police wouldn't do any good at this point, but perhaps bringing Harlow in might help if she really was able to find something about the camera to widen her view.

Sam tapped a rhythm on his thigh, his dark eyes drifting moodily over her face and then taking in her thin racerback tee that she'd worn to bed. It was old and ratty but it was soft and comforting and she'd needed it when she knew she was going to have a nightmare. The cotton was damp from her sweat and clung to her skin, revealing more than it covered.

"Don't like that you have to go through this, Stella, but your friends are women and we know the killer's a man. These women have been your friends for over five years, some a little longer, and they're all loyal to you. I can't imagine any of them selling you out to the media, especially Harlow. If we bring her in, I want to be with you. They're your friends, so it's your call, but I want to be there."

She lifted an eyebrow. Her nerves were beginning to settle. Just talking to Sam did that for her. "Why?"

"I scare people, sweetheart. Haven't you noticed? I don't have to say anything, I can just sit next to you instead of a few seats down and they'll get the message."

Stella frowned, trying to analyze his tone. His voice had a velvet quality to it, almost as if it brushed over her skin. At the same time there was a note of menace, something very sinister and frightening, when he never raised his voice at all. He spoke low, but his instructions were always carried out. She'd noticed if he talked to a drunk causing a problem, the drunk listened immediately, no matter how far gone they appeared to be.

"What message, Sam?" She looked directly into his eyes, challenging him. Daring him to tell her. She wasn't afraid of him. She would never be afraid of him.

"Not to fuck with you. They do and they'll have to answer to me. That's something they aren't ever going to want to do."

His honesty sent a little frisson of heat curling down her spine. She lifted her chin at him. "Did you know that Raine is required to do a background check on anyone she hangs around with?"

He folded his arms across his chest, looking more relaxed than ever. "Doesn't surprise me."

"She's done one on everyone with the exception of you. Said she didn't want to raise any flags in case you had enemies that might have alerts on your file. She also said she didn't want you paying her a visit in the middle of the night. Is there a possibility of that if she had alerted an enemy? Or if any of the people who find out about me do rat me out?"

"Yes." There was no hesitation.

Stella's restless fingers gripped the sheet. "I don't want that for you, Sam. You said so yourself, you put in your time. If something goes wrong, I'm a big girl, I can handle it. We can handle it without you going back to that place, whatever it is or was. We both came here because the Eastern Sierras offer something beautiful and unique, something we couldn't find anywhere else. It's my place of peace, of happiness. I think it's yours as well. We started over here and we've got something good. Nothing can take that away, not even this serial killer." She sent him a small smile. "You get me?"

His answering smile was slow in coming. "Woman, you're about as good as it gets. A gift. Write up your report and make your sketches. I'll make your hot chocolate for you." He stood up, took a step and stopped, turning back to her. For a moment he just stared at her with those dark, fathomless eyes.

"What?"

Sam shook his head. "Don't want to lose you, woman. Not for

any reason. If I lose my mind and fuck up, you hang in with me and let me know what I did and how to fix it." He stood a moment longer and then turned his back on her and sauntered out of the room as only Sam could.

Stella let her breath out. As declarations went, it was a good one, a Sam one, and she'd take it because he always meant every word he said. He could melt her heart when he did unexpected things like grill salmon for her at the end of a long day when she was so tired she just wanted to curl up in her egg chair and forget everything. When he brought her an ice-cold beer, or watched her favorite movie for the tenth time without complaint, those were Sam things. He bought books she liked, treats for Bailey, he remembered to get the particular kind of chocolate she loved. He was quiet about it. The books would show up occasionally, the chocolate would be in the kitchen and Bailey always had treats. Sam was thoughtful and he kept them uppermost in his mind.

Stella switched on her lamp and pulled the drawing pad and journal out of the drawer of her nightstand. The moment she illuminated the bedroom, she had that eerie feeling she didn't like, the one that told her someone could see in. She wished she'd gotten black-out screens for the windows instead of the shades that allowed her to see through them to the lake. She loved her views and hadn't wanted to compromise them.

She glanced at the window. She was being silly, wasn't she, letting her imagination get the better of her? The aftereffects of the nightmare. She put one hand in the air and it was still trembling. It wasn't as if she could say she wasn't still freaked out by her dreams just because she was being proactive and Sam and Zahra were helping her.

She forced her mind to be meticulous about remembering every component she could, writing it all down, and then she began to sketch. She was better at drawing. The details emerged when she fleshed out her illustration. She got lost in the picture, no longer thinking in terms of it being a serial killer's view, or a witness's view, but simply an artist's rendition of two backpackers on a trail in the very early morning hours as they started on their journey.

It was dark and she filled in that darkness with charcoal, adding the woman's brief spotlighting of the floor of the trail, various rocks and the walls by putting each separate image in its own square, much like a graphic novelist might do. By treating each of the pictures as an individual drawing, rather than one as a whole, she could concentrate on details of what the light revealed to her. Veins in the rock. Crevices in the wall. Leaves from the types of trees or bushes. Stella always found that when she drew what she'd seen in her nightmares, she recalled quite a lot more detail. Her subconscious mind picked up far more than she realized.

She turned to a new blank page and began to sketch the lens she had peered through, adding in the features she had noticed on the sides. What might have been a partial round knob that didn't mean anything at all to her but hopefully meant something to someone else. This wasn't a cell phone she was looking through. She put as much detail into that fractional view of the button as she had the other pictures, right down to the strange little vee-shaped mark in gold that ran through the black rounded-looking thing she thought might be a knob one could turn.

When she looked up, Sam was standing well to the back of the room, out of the light spilling from the lamp beside her bed. Just the fact that he hadn't come close to put her chocolate on the nightstand or see what she'd drawn sent more chills walking like fingers of doom down her spine.

She glanced toward the bank of windows that overlooked the

lake. With a little sigh she turned off the light, once more plunging the room into semidarkness. Even with clouds drifting across
the moon, the lake reflected enough light to allow her to see well
enough in the bedroom.

"You feel it too, don't you, Sam? Someone watching again."

Instead of answering, he set the mug on the table between the
two armchairs. "Come get the chocolate. Keep Bailey with you.
I'll arm the security system when I go outside. You have a gun in
the bedroom with you, don't you? I know you keep one in the car."

She nodded, keeping her face turned away from the window.
"I have a small compartment built into the wall just to the right
of the bed. It's difficult for anyone to notice. I keep several weapons there so I have them close."

"Get your gun out. Have it loaded, one in the chamber, but
don't shoot me when I come back inside." There was a trace of
amusement in his voice. "Bailey acts up, you know it isn't me."

"Be careful, Sam." What else could she say? Was it the killer
out there? Did he know who she was?

She leaned over and pushed the journal and sketchpad into
the drawer beside the bed and closed and locked it before slipping
off the bed and going to the opposite end of the room. When she
neared the corner where Sam was, he suddenly reached out and
caught the front of her T-shirt, his fist closing on the thin fabric.
She could feel the brush of his fingers against the swell of her
breasts. Her heart accelerated and her gaze jumped to his. He
pulled her slowly, inexorably, to him.

Her breath caught in her throat as he bent down toward her,
his head descending, those dark eyes burning with desire. With
something close to an emotion she was afraid to name, not when
he was going out alone and the serial killer could be waiting for
him. She couldn't cloak him in armor, in a net of invisibility like

she wanted. Instead, she gave herself to him. Surrendered completely, kissing him with that same unnamed emotion she saw in his eyes when he looked at her.

"Could he be here for you?" She whispered the query, her palms flat against his chest. "Because he missed you? Could it be a matter of pride?"

"I'm not easy to kill, Stella," Sam reassured. His lips brushed over hers one more time. "The gun. I want it right next to you. Keep Bailey in the same room with you."

She'd rather he take Bailey with him. They were going to have to get another dog. She watched him go, the hot chocolate in her hand, her heart in her mouth. She realized he hadn't actually answered her. There was no real way of knowing who was out there watching, but someone was and it was too big of a coincidence to think that the serial killer had arrived on the scene and someone else—a peeping Tom—was stalking the resort.

She walked back to her bed and put the hot chocolate down on the nightstand before leaning down out of sight of the window to press the pad of her thumb over the button that would release the door cleverly hidden in the wall. Her thumbprint would open the safe quickly. She'd practiced over and over until she could find the button in her sleep. During the day, even though she knew it was there as well as the door to the safe, she had to look for it because it was so well hidden in the wooden walls.

She removed her gun, quickly loaded it and placed it right beside her, keeping it out of sight of the window, just in case the watcher could see into her bedroom. She picked up her hot chocolate and sipped it slowly. Bailey pushed his big head onto her bed, sensing she was uneasy.

"You don't like it when he's out there alone either, do you, big guy?" she crooned, scratching the dog behind his ears. She sighed, sipping at the chocolate, leaning back against the headboard and trying not to think about Sam being alone outside. She should have insisted on going out with him. "Since when do I stay inside, Bailey?"

She wasn't the type of woman to just sit in her room on her butt while other people took the risks, so she leapt up, ignoring Bailey's startled whine, and unhooked the night-vision binoculars that hung by the largest window facing the lake. She liked the view. The house sat on higher ground, allowing her a good view of not only the lake and marina, but a good portion of the front half of her property—the beautiful half. She wasn't looking at the cabins and RV park or campsites or fishing camps. This was all beautiful land surrounding the lake.

She leaned against the window and put the binoculars to her eyes to do a slow sweep of the lake to see if anything looked suspicious. Next came the marina and docks. She continued the slow perusal of her land, moving the binoculars inch by inch along the shore. Something moved just under the trees down near the boat rental building.

As she adjusted her view, Sam's frame leapt out at her. There was another man, thinner and a bit shorter, holding a gun on him. Two other men emerged from behind the trees just as Sam moved with blurring speed, sweeping the legs out from under the one holding the weapon. As he went down, Sam stripped him of the gun. He took down the other two men using a vicious swipe of the barrel to the side of one's head, sending him to his knees, and pulling the other to him with an arm around his throat and the gun tight against his skull.

Stella watched them, tension coiled tight in her gut. The two on the ground remained there, not trying to get up or move. After a couple of minutes, she had the feeling Sam knew all three men, or at least the one he had the gun pressed up against. Suddenly, Sam dropped his arm and stepped back, releasing his prisoner.

The man he'd hit with the gun remained seated on the ground, his head in his hands. The younger one, who Sam had originally swept the feet out from under, jumped up and put distance between them. Dressed in jeans and a sweater, his entire body posture screamed belligerence.

The third man, the one with the impeccable suit who had had the gun at the back of his skull, seemed unfazed by everything. He did all the talking. It was very clear he was in charge. He seemed to have a lot to say, gesturing toward the lake and then up at the sky, shaking his head once. He waited as if for a response from Sam and then went on, moving his hand as if to include the entire resort, marina and Sam's cabin. Then he gestured toward her house.

Sam remained very still, not moving a muscle. She'd seen him like that hundreds of times. She could have predicted the look on his face. Expressionless. Those eyes, flat and cold. Lifeless. He listened, but he wasn't going to give anything away.

Stella had watched him for over two years, secretly studying Sam's every move. She knew by the loose way he held himself that he could explode into action, just as he had when he'd taken the younger man's weapon from him. There had been no reaction from him to anything the older man was saying until he'd gestured toward her house. Sam hadn't looked toward the house, hadn't followed the gesture in any way, but there was a slight difference in the way he held himself. She had the feeling he had gone from being neutral to being a threat, but the change in his demeanor was so subtle she couldn't say why she thought that.

The man sitting on the ground must have felt the threat too

because he suddenly looked up and then climbed to his feet, moving away from Sam and back toward the older man almost protectively. The younger man circled around behind Sam warily. Sam didn't deign to glance at him. He kept his attention fixed on the older man. The younger man gave Sam a wide berth as he made his way to the older man's side.

Stella tried to puzzle out what it all meant. She forced air through her lungs. Sam had known those men were out there. He hadn't thought a serial killer was out there watching the house. He had her get the gun out because he knew who was out there and he didn't want them coming into her house and talking to her.

This wasn't the first time he had gone out alone into the night when she'd been certain someone had been watching them. Had these same men been there then? Had they been watching her and her friends camping out at the lake? She suddenly wanted to lock Sam out of her house and just sit alone with Bailey and her wildly beating heart. Unfortunately, Sam had the code to get in. Was she afraid of him?

Sam's head suddenly came up alertly and all three men turned toward the path leading to the boathouse. Stella swung her binoculars in that direction. Sonny Leven sauntered along the trail on his rounds, patrolling the compound at night. He generally stayed away from the main house, but did make a pass along the marina several times a night. He was still a distance away, but he was coming at a fairly rapid clip. When she looked back at Sam and the others, they had completely disappeared.

Stella searched everywhere, moving the night-vision binoculars carefully along trees and shrubbery, but not a thing seemed out of place. There was no evidence that the men had ever been on her property or that they'd met with Sam. So much for her two security guards. They had no idea of secret, clandestine meetings in the middle of the night.

"What do you think, Bailey? Should I shoot Sam when he walks in and tell the sheriff I thought he was an intruder?"

She hung the binoculars back where she always kept them and retreated to her bed, her hand finding the reassuring grip her palm was familiar with.

"This is the very reason I don't let people close," she told the dog. "Now we're in this big mess. I'm blaming you. You liked him right from the start. If you'd growled and gotten all protective, I would have passed on hiring him."

At least she knew the killer wasn't watching her. That was a relief. And Sam had a chance to tell her the truth. He might come in and tell her he met with three men he obviously knew and had a little chat with them. What were the chances?

Minutes crept by, but it seemed like hours. Stella imagined all sorts of things, including the three men murdering Sam and hauling his body away with them. She had no idea how they got onto her property or how they were leaving without either Sonny or Patrick Sorsey, the other security guard, knowing. Still, she was grateful neither guard had confronted those three men. She had the feeling they were lethal.

Bailey's head went up alertly. The dog went to the door of her bedroom and stood right at the entrance, looking into the hall. She glanced at her device and saw the back keypad had been unlocked. Her fingers tightened around the grip of her gun. No one had murdered Sam—yet.

He came into her space looking coolly confident and, as always, composed, calm and completely relaxed, as if he'd been on a midnight stroll. His dark eyes moved over her face, drifted lower, took in her body and then her hand on her weapon before coming back up to meet her eyes. Bailey nudged him and he automatically scratched the dog's ears, never once taking his gaze from hers.

Stella waited for him to say something, but he didn't. She should have known he wouldn't. Sam was all about silence. He'd never been big on talking. He didn't give himself away. Usually, the silence had been companionable between them. Not this time. The tension stretched until it could have been cut with a knife.

Sam shook his head and then sank into the chair across from the bed, reaching for the water he'd left on the small table there. "You going to put the gun away or use it, Stella?"

The little note of male amusement annoyed her enough that she deliberated on the benefits of putting a bullet in the wall right next to his ear, but she knew he wouldn't even flinch.

"I'm still considering."

He swallowed water, his gaze never leaving hers. He didn't look in the least worried, but then he never did. He remained silent, not offering her anything, not even an explanation.

Stella went over his every action—or rather inaction—as he'd stood under the trees with the three intruders. He hadn't seemed bothered by them until the older man had gestured toward her house. That was when the subtle change had come over him. It hadn't been just her that knew it; the others had as well.

She studied Sam. There was so much there she didn't know. She'd never asked. She'd taken him on faith and he'd never once let her down. She'd been shaken tonight because she'd had a nightmare and they'd been sorting it out when they both knew someone had come on the property—someone was watching. Sam still hadn't let her down. He hadn't done anything to change her opinion of him.

She didn't ask him what had happened out there because she

was afraid he might lie to her. He wasn't her mother. He wasn't her father. He wasn't the friends in school abandoning her the moment they found out who she was. He was Sam.

Stella unloaded the gun and locked it in the safe. "I really did feel like nearly clipping you for that stinking superior male sense of humor you have."

"I'm well aware you have a bit of a temper, Stella."

The dark eyes glinted with humor, catching the light off the lake. She didn't get to see that very often and the sight gave her a ridiculous melty feeling in the pit of her stomach. She rolled her eyes.

Again, there was a silence. Her silence. He was going to make her ask. She didn't know if she had the courage. She couldn't bear it if he lied to her. If he let her down. His silence was normal. He didn't tell anyone—including her—his business. He would consider those men his business.

She gathered the sheet between her fingers, looking down at it, twisting it back and forth, telling herself she needed to know now, before it was too late. Another part of her whispered she was being silly, Sam didn't tell lies. More than likely, he wouldn't answer if he didn't want her to know something, but he wouldn't lie.

"Woman." He sounded exasperated.

"Man."

"Spit it the hell out."

She lifted her lashes and looked him directly in the eyes again. "Who was out there?" She could feel her heart pounding too hard. Too fast.

"I've been contemplating whether it's a good idea for you to know or not."

She blinked. She hadn't expected that answer. He'd already been considering telling her. That was something. And no, he

wasn't going to lie to her. Relief swept over her. She had trust issues, big ones. Him. Her friends. She needed to get past them.

"Were they here before, Sam?"

"No. This is the first time. Because they were out there, I
couldn't be sure someone else wasn't watching the house as well.
It felt like it when I first went out."

That frisson of fear crept down her spine. "Do you think those
men were the ones I felt spying on my friends and me when we
were camping? Because someone was."

"I don't know." There was a distinct edge to his voice. "I told
them not to come here again and definitely not to go anywhere
near you or your friends."

Her stomach was suddenly in knots. "They didn't threaten any
of my friends, did they?" She was more worried about her small
circle of friends than she was about herself.

"One of them mentioned meeting Raine. He was offhand
about it, but I didn't like it and I let him know."

Sam had only spoken to the older man, but he'd swept the legs
out from under the younger man when he'd been talking. It had
to have been him, the younger man, and Sam had retaliated, taking him down and then taking his weapon. Stella had thought it
was because the younger man had held a gun on him.

Protectively, she put her hand to her throat. "Why would he
say anything about Raine?"

Sam shrugged. "He was testing me. It didn't work out in his
favor."

A sudden thought occurred to her. "Do they know who I
really am like Raine does?"

He sighed. "No, Stella, they have no way of knowing. Even if
they did, they wouldn't say anything unless they thought it would
get me to do something they wanted me to do."

She pressed her lips together. "They wanted you to leave, didn't they? That man, the older one, he wasn't trying to get you to take another job somewhere. He wanted you to leave."

In one of those rare Sam moments, his lips curved into a real smile. It was breathtaking. At least for her. He just didn't smile that often. It changed his entire demeanor.

"You were watching."

"Someone had to back you up just in case you got in over your head."

He laughed. That was even more exhilarating. The sound was beautiful. "Yeah, sweetheart, we had a little argument over that."

"It didn't look so little to me. Sam, who were those people?"

"I give you this, Stella, you give me your word first that you stick with me." All humor had vanished from his face, leaving him completely expressionless again.

"My father is a serial killer, Sam. I had to confess that to you and I'm still having to come to terms with telling my friends." She already knew he'd worked for the government in some capacity. It wasn't like she was going to be shocked.

"You better keep your word, because I'm holding you to it."

She'd never seen Sam tense. Never. She almost didn't want him to tell her. She knew what it was like to protect secrets and keep them hidden for very good reasons. Some secrets didn't need to come to light. Sam traveled around, looking for a new life, a new beginning. He had just wanted to be left alone.

"Were they government agents, Sam?" She gentled her voice, trying to convey to him that no matter what, even if they were trying to convince him they wanted him to come back and work for them, she would understand.

Sam shook his head. "No, not even close, Stella. The older man you saw out there, that was my father, Don Marco Rossi. The one I put on the ground was his underboss, and the mouthy one was a bodyguard." He fell silent, his dark eyes on her face while she absorbed his statement.

Stella frowned. "Sam. I'm not going to pretend I haven't heard of him, but why would you be so upset over telling me who your father is when my father is sitting in jail right now for what he did?"

"Your father killed how many victims over four years? Five? Who do you think taught me most of what I know, Stella? Do you think I learned to be what I am from the training I was given when I joined the military? That was my father's training. That was what I was taught from the time I was in the cradle."

Sam took another long drink of water and rubbed Bailey's fur while Stella thought about the tense way everyone had acted when his father had gestured toward the house. Had he threatened her? What had Sam been close to doing? Surely he wouldn't have attacked his own father.

"What went wrong between you and your father, Sam?" she asked.

Sam screwed the cap onto the bottle and then pressed the bottle to his forehead. "My family owns quite a few strip clubs, and my father saw no reason not to partake in the joys of the back rooms there. He did so often. My mother was sweet, Stella. The best. Loved big gatherings with lots of friends and food. She cooked meals herself. We had money obviously, but she did everything herself. She poured love into everything she did. And she loved him. She made everything in that house perfect for him."

Stella couldn't help noticing that he spoke of his mother in past tense. Her heart hurt for him. He looked alone and too far away from her. She suspected that, like her, he'd spent most of his life alone.

"She asked him to stop so many times or let her divorce him. He told her it wasn't her business, there was no divorce, that he gave her a nice home and he came home at night. That should be enough. I tried talking to him when I was really worried about her, but he had a couple of his men beat the hell out of me for interfering in what wasn't my business. He said I didn't have any right when I was often at the clubs, and that was true enough. I was doing a lot of business for him at that time. Too much. Doing things that I look back on now and realize how easy it was to become what he shaped me into because as a kid I admired him and wanted to be like him."

Stella knew what it was like to want a parent to love you, to seek their approval. She had done so time and again. It was natural.

Sam shook his head. "They had a terrible fight one evening. He was going to the club after she'd made a special dinner. It turned out it was her birthday. She wanted him to stay home with her, but he said no. There was some new girl at the club he wanted to try out. He didn't tell her that, but he refused to stay and Mom got very upset. The fight turned physical, at least she slapped him and he slapped her back. I interfered and he left."

Stella pressed her lips together to keep from giving him sympathy. He needed her to listen, not talk.

"I held her while she cried and then she got very quiet. She told me she was tired. So tired. She told me to please never treat a woman like he treated her—that if I found a girl, to make certain I really loved her enough to stay with her and only her or don't bother. I made her that promise. She told me she loved me and then she went upstairs."

Stella felt her heart start to accelerate. She had a bad, bad feeling.

"My father didn't come home for the first time that I could ever remember until that next morning. I had just gone upstairs to call Mom when I heard him come in. I knocked on her door and she didn't answer. I pushed open the door and I could see her sitting in her favorite place by the window. It was a window seat overlooking the garden. She was slumped over and still in the clothes she'd been wearing the night before. There was blood on the bench and cushions as well as pooled on the floor. It looked like it was everywhere.

"I ran to her, even knowing it was too late. She'd sat there and quietly bled out after cutting her wrists. I picked her up and held her to me, rocking her, and when he came in and tried to take her, I wanted to kill him. I told him it was his fault. He had done that to her as surely as if he had made those cuts himself. I left right after her funeral, joined the service and made it into the Rangers. After that I was offered a job that was high risk, lucrative, but much more satisfying if you were looking for redemption, which I was. It also kept me impossible to find, even with my father's resources. Once I got out, I drifted, mostly needing to figure out how much of me was him. I've done so many things, Stella, things that I can never take back. I don't want to be anything like him."

"Come lie on the bed with me, Sam. We might not get any sleep, but at least we'll be close. Tonight, for the rest of the night, we need close. At least I need it."

"I told him to stay the hell away from you." He bent to remove his shoes.

Stella scooted under the covers but left the comforter for him. When he lay beside her, one arm around her, she put her head on his shoulder. "Why was he so upset?"

"He found out about the killer trying to drag me underwater. He wanted me to come home."

She was silent, thinking that over. "He must care for you, Sam, or he wouldn't have come in person to try to persuade you."

"I have no doubt that he cares for me. He cared for my mother. He can sit down to a meal with you and your friends, Stella, and then go home and order one or all of you tortured to demonstrate that it isn't a good idea to fuck with our family. The worst part is, I'm totally capable of doing the same thing."

His arm tightened around her. "I came here to find a different way of life, to be a different person. Not the way I grew up, and not the person I'd been for our government. I found this place and you."

"No one is going to take that away from you, Sam." Stella said it fiercely, determined she spoke the truth.

# CHAPTER TEN

Harlow Frye had flaming-red hair and jade-green eyes. Freckles dusted her nose and high cheekbones, scattered across her shoulders and arms generously, adding to her beauty. She was tall with long legs and generous curves. By turns she could look elegant, a temptress or girl next door, depending on what she wore and how she did her hair and makeup. Even with all the varying looks she had, she always appeared to be a fiery flame. There was no getting around that, not with her hair.

Today she wore her thick mane of red hair up in a simple ponytail. She had little makeup on, jeans rolled up and a golden sweater buttoned with tiny pearl buttons. Her boots came up to her calves, a soft golden leather that matched her sweater. Stella could never figure out where she found her clothes or boots.

Harlow studied the sketch that didn't really show much of anything while she digested what Stella had revealed to her of her true identity. Beneath the artist's table in Harlow's studio, Stella pressed her fingernails deep into her own thigh through her jeans. She'd told Sam she wanted to talk to Harlow alone, so after a curt nod that clearly conveyed his displeasure over her decision, he had stayed at the resort to ensure the last of the guests renting the cabins had left without mishap. They were officially closed for the season, a true relief. Tonight there would be a party for her longtime employees. They certainly deserved their break, and then she and Sam would have time off as well. Hopefully they would have time to develop their relationship and catch a serial killer.

"When you have these nightmares, Stella, you're aware that you're dreaming? Are you an active participant in the dream?" Harlow asked, still studying the sketch. She was frowning in concentration.

"I've never been before," she admitted. "I was always terrified, but I was a little child the first time and a teen the second. The first series of nightmares was so unexpected, about the fisherman, I was just concentrating on trying to find the place around the lake where it might be. Zahra suggested I might be able to widen the lens. I never thought of that. I never even considered looking at the lens itself."

"Have you ever changed a dream?"

"I've woken myself up by telling myself I was dreaming, but I never changed anything significant. When I liked a dream, before I went to bed, I told myself I wanted to dream that particular dream again and I did," she admitted.

"I'm sorry about your father, Stella." Harlow looked up for the first time, meeting her eyes, looking sincere. "We can't choose our parents, can we? Thankfully, they don't necessarily have to reflect who we are." She looked down again at the sketch. "This doesn't really give me a lot to work with, but you could try experimenting. I know you're not a camera person." She glanced back up at Stella, who shuddered and made a face. Harlow burst out laughing in spite of the seriousness of their conversation.

Stella covered her face with her hands and peeked out between her fingers. "You're going to make me touch a camera, aren't you?"

Harlow studied her. "Why do you have such an aversion to them? Do you think it was because you grew up surrounded by the media after they found out about your father?"

Stella took her hands down, considering Harlow's question. "No, there were always reporters around. My mother was involved in multiple charities and sat on several boards for opera, ballet and theater houses. She was big in the arts. That translated to numerous articles in newspapers and magazines. At the time, my father was considered quite the handsome philanthropist. They were quite a couple and made a splash everywhere they went, always camera ready. I had to be as well if I went outside the house."

Harlow nodded in understanding. "I know what that's like as a child. My father was always in politics as far back as I can remember." She made a little face. "God forbid you get dirt on your shoes or scuff them up in the garden in case someone needs a family photo. That's one of the reasons I don't do portraits."

Stella knew Harlow rarely took photographs of people. When she did, the pictures were private ones, only of her friends and their activities. It was her landscapes that were considered breathtaking and captured so much attention.

"That was definitely my childhood and then some. My mother had very strict rules in place for what I could wear and what I couldn't. That's probably why I wear jeans all the time and little makeup now. She had a camera my father had given her for Christmas one year. It was the latest thing and all her friends had cameras. She didn't use it, she liked to keep up with whatever they had."

Stella couldn't just sit at the long worktable. She had to get up and walk around. There were so many beautiful things in Harlow's studio to see. Harlow was an extremely creative woman. It always amazed Stella how she could make such beautiful pottery and take exquisite photographs that looked as if they were so real you were right there too. Stella had one framed, a beautiful picture taken from above the lake, early morning just as the sun was coming up and the colors were extending out over the water. It was gorgeous. Stella wouldn't give it up for any amount of money. She could never quite equate the creative side of Harlow with the pure practical side, the nurse who worked in the hospital and didn't blink when sewing up wounds.

Harlow was a strong climber. Like Stella, she preferred bouldering, but she did trad climbing with her friends, which Stella could do but didn't enjoy that much. Harlow's dog, Misha, a beagle, lay curled up in a doggy bed beside the door leading to the yard that opened to the canal, where Harlow walked her every couple of hours. Misha seemed to know the schedule and didn't let Harlow forget it. Right now, she watched Stella wandering around the studio.

"Misha and Bailey are good friends, Harlow, but she's looking at me very suspiciously, like I might try to make off with one of your art pieces any minute," Stella couldn't help but point out. "No treats for you, Misha, thinking I might be an art thief."

Misha wagged her tail, thumping it against her dog bed at the sound of her name and the word *treats*.

"Misha eyes everyone suspiciously in here," Harlow agreed. "Her idea is to drive us out so she can do her favorite thing, which, as you know, rain or shine, is to go for a W.A.L.K. In her case, R.U.N."

Stella laughed. "That dog is too smart. She's going to learn how to spell."

"She's only smart when she wants to be. Stop stalling and tell me about the camera your mother had. She didn't use it, but something happened to it."

The smile faded from Stella's mouth. Reliving old memories wasn't fun. How had this serial killer brought so many things back? She hadn't even thought of them in the months of therapy she'd gone through as a teen. Nor had she when she had gone to therapy while she'd been in college. Suddenly, now she was remembering her childhood, things she had deliberately put in a room and locked the door on. Some things should just stay that way, behind doors one barricaded.

"I'm remembering so many things I deliberately locked away, Harlow. I don't want to remember these things about my mother, let alone my father. She started drinking too much as a way to compensate once I started telling her my nightmares. At first, she was just trying to cope with a child having terrible nightmares, but then she realized what they were. Maybe she suspected all along, I don't know."

Harlow stood up as well and crossed to the window. "We think in terms of our lives, the way we are now, but women weren't nearly as independent. My mother reminded me it was a different time when our parents were young. Our mothers were raised differently and there wasn't as much help for women as there is now. Some of their parents believed that if you brought children into the world, you had the right to do anything you wanted to them."

Stella had to agree. "The camera always sat on her dresser. It was beautiful to me and one day I just couldn't resist. I always sat in her room when she was getting ready to go out. I liked to watch her put on her makeup and jewelry. I asked her if I could take her picture."

Harlow turned around very fast to face her. "Was this before your nightmares started or after, Stella?"

"I was so young." Stella frowned, rubbing her forehead, trying to think back. She looked out the window toward the canal, wishing she was outside. She felt closed in. Felt as if someone was watching her again. She was driving herself crazy. "I don't know. I remember being happy with my mother in her room when she was getting ready to go out with my father, at least some of the time. And then it wasn't good anymore."

"You started having the nightmares when you were four? And then they really started when you were five. That's a fact. When he was caught, that came out in the story. He wasn't caught until you were older, but the nightmares started when you were that young." Harlow went across the room to one of the shelves and started looking at the cameras she had on display there.

Stella's heart dropped. She deliberately stayed where she was, close to the window on the opposite side of the room. "Yes, I was five."

"So, you could have been as young as four when you wanted to take your mother's picture. You might even have memories as young as three of going to the theater with your mother. Of the ballet. Your mother would have taken you. You would have heard talk, gossip, all the time to reinforce memories of your mother being on boards for various arts. I've noticed you retain almost everything. It seems to be a gift you have."

"It's a curse," Stella muttered. "This entire thing is a curse."

"Not if you can catch him and save lives."

"I didn't catch my father, or Miller when I was a teen."

"You did eventually," Harlow pointed out. "You couldn't expect to right away. And you can't now. You're going to have to understand that none of these deaths are your fault. He's out there, and if you didn't know about him, he would be killing without anyone to stop him. As a nurse, I know I'm not going to save everyone. I'm not. Not even my favorite patients, no matter how hard I try. No matter what effort I put into it. Every police officer has to come to terms with that same thing at some point. Every man or woman in the military."

"Death just feels . . . unacceptable to me. I almost feel like I'm being taunted and I fail these people, these very human people with families who love them."

"I feel the same way. I'm certain most doctors feel the same way. These nightmares you have are simply clues, a way to catch him. He doesn't know who you are and that you're already looking for him. Hopefully he doesn't find out until we have him. That's the big thing, Stella. Be careful of who you bring into the circle. I know you're going to be tempted to bring law enforcement in, but if you do it too soon, he'll disappear. Just fade away. This place is made for that. You have to know who he is before you inform them."

"I don't want to be my mother, Harlow. I don't want to trade my peace of mind for lives."

"Telling law enforcement too soon would be doing just that, Stella. Think about it. If you tell them, the FBI shows up, the serial killer fades away and you get your world back. He goes somewhere else and kills. No one is the wiser because he has a new playground, making every kill look like an accident, and you aren't there to tell them any different. He would never stay here. Why should he? Especially if he's a temporary visitor."

Stella crossed her arms over her chest and leaned against the long bank of curved floor-to-ceiling windows. Of all the arguments to keep from telling Griffen, this was the best because Harlow was right. Stella felt it.

"You're making sense, Harlow, but then you usually do. Sam doesn't think I should say anything yet. Zahra feels the same way. I haven't talked to anyone else about it. I'm considering what to say when I do. I'm going to talk to Raine about the backpacking trails and campsites. She goes all the time with me. She knows the trails even better than I do."

"I've got a couple of cameras that were popular when your mom was young, Stella. I'm going to look in a catalogue and see if there were any knobs on them that look anything like you sketched."

Naturally, Harlow would do that for her. She was observant and knew exactly how much Stella disliked taking pictures, let alone touching an actual camera. "My mother gave me permission to take her picture. Of course, I had no idea how and she didn't show me. I just probably played with it, looking at her and telling her how beautiful she was. She smiled at me over and over and then held out her hand for the camera. I gave it to her. Later, when she put me to bed, she kissed me several times and told me she wasn't angry with me for breaking her camera. I told her I didn't break it. She said, *Remember, you dropped it?* And then she kissed me again and told me accidents happen. My father was standing in the doorway and had a frown on his face. She told him not to be so angry, that I was just a little girl. She even flung her arms around his neck and kissed him."

Stella could still remember the chilling way her father had looked at her. She'd been afraid of him for the first time. She knew she hadn't broken the camera. It was the first time she realized that her mother lied. That frightened her and she'd felt very alone. She didn't remember how old she was.

"It's never a good time when we find out our parents might be monsters, like your father, or have feet of clay, like your mother," Harlow said, her gaze glued to the catalogue she was scrutinizing. She glanced up for a moment. "Do you think any of us comes from normal? I mean anybody alive? Do we even know what normal is, or do we just make it up in our heads because the movies and television convinced us there is a normal?"

Stella raised an eyebrow. "That's a good question, and one I don't have an answer for, but I don't think most people have serial killers for fathers."

"I think the camera thing with your mother happened *before* the nightmares, Stella, so in a way, you can thank your mother for helping you stop serial killers. I know it sucks to be you when it happens, but at least you stop them eventually from killing. There is a similar-looking knob. In your next dream, try twisting it a little to the right and see if it widens your range of vision. If it doesn't, no worries, we'll keep working on it. You're using your mind, not actual fingers, so you really can't hurt anything. Don't panic in your dream thinking you're going to harm anything. If you have to, pretend I'm with you, taking the photographs for you. Just imagine that I'm twisting the knob to the right."

"You're so brilliant, Harlow." Stella meant it too. "Misha is out of her bed and pacing. I think she's trying to tell you something. I'll get Bailey if you're ready." She was more than ready to stretch her legs.

At the lake she spent hours and hours picking up trash after everyone left. She was lucky that when she had a clean-up day, volunteers showed up with their own supplies to help—that was the kind of community she lived in—but there was always trash. She walked Bailey every morning and took a trash bag. In the evening she did the same after the last of the campers left and they closed everything down.

She was used to being extremely active. Sitting even for a short period of time made her antsy—especially now. During the season, there was no time to do anything but work. If she took a day off, she climbed or hiked. She needed the time away to clear her mind. She was busy every minute of the day from sunrise until well after midnight. Sam had taken a great deal of pressure off her, and she had gathered the best staff and crew together over the years. That helped tremendously. They worked hard and she appreciated every single one of them.

Misha leapt at the back door as Stella went out the front door to get Bailey out of her 4Runner. He was already waiting for her, eager for the walk. He waited for her release command before leaping out and then he raced around the studio to the back to meet with Misha, who was already eagerly yipping her joyous greeting.

Stella found herself smiling. Happy. That was one of the things she loved about dogs. They lived in the moment. They took joy in whatever they were doing. Both Misha and Bailey loved to run along the canal, and they knew the way Harlow and Stella jogged or walked. Neither needed a leash. Everyone knew them and who they belonged to. They could play tag together and find every interesting crawling creature and rodent available.

It was much warmer at the lower elevation and Stella wore a light sweater over her T-shirt. She could always tie it around her waist if she got too hot. The October weather cut down on the mosquitoes, which was helpful, but she was always careful anyway, carrying repellent with her. The same with tick repellent, although, if truth be told, she was more vigilant with Bailey than herself. Her dog was always protected.

"Where's Vienna today? I thought she had several days off in a row. Wasn't she going to try to train her cat to go for a walk with Misha?"

"Vienna was called into work just before I got your call, an emergency. Denver had to go in as well. Big accident, two trucks, head-on. It sounded bad."

"That's awful."

"As for her cat and canal walking, yeah, that didn't go so well. Her prissy little princess wanted to ride on Misha's back, claws dug in deep, not walk on the ground."

The two women looked at each other and burst out laughing. The cat was the love of Vienna's life and spoiled rotten. The animal ruled, although she never admitted it. She always indicated she was determined to have the cat come along on their adventures with the dogs. The cat never did. She lived in a "palace" and was snobby, turning up her nose at most food and demanding to be brushed and petted when Vienna was close. She would get annoyed if Vienna was gone too long and turn her back on her owner for long periods of time in a little snit. They all thought the "princess" was aptly named and loved to hear stories about her.

Walking along the canal was peaceful, even at the brisk pace Harlow set with her long legs. Stella didn't mind walking fast, although she was no runner. If she had to jog for her dog's sake, she would, and she did run under protest to stay in condition, but she wasn't one of those people who loved it. She would never be a peak bagger—running up a trail and then a mountain to "bag" the peak. She could hike a trail steadily for hours, days, weeks, months, but running, that was a big fat *ugh*.

The trees swayed gently in the breeze, a few leaves slowly shaking loose and swirling lazily toward the wide trail or the water below. Everywhere was an explosion of color. Reds and oranges with various shades of greens and browns. The fields around them appeared gold. The grasses were so tall they tipped over. Some stalks still held a bluish or greenish tint, but most were brown or that gorgeous shade of gold.

A lone great blue heron walked the canal on tall spindly legs, searching for something to eat. "Are you lost?" she called. "You should have left already. You'd better get moving, my friend, before the weather turns."

Harlow sent her a little grin. "Do you always talk to the wildlife?"

"Pretty much," Stella admitted. "They can't talk back to me."

Both women laughed as they continued along the canal with their dogs.

NIGHTS THREE AND then four Stella did her best to do as Harlow had said and twist the knob on the lens to widen her view of what she was seeing. Night three was a complete bust. She couldn't make the knob do anything, and she was so anxious she barely got any new details. She ended up being more frustrated than ever. The lighting was better than the night before so that promised to be better the next night.

*Mommy, Daddy's doing the bad thing again.*

The couple appeared to be moving forward on the trail, not staying in the same place. Even in the dim lighting from the woman's headlamp, Stella felt as if she had hiked that same trail more than once. She even felt the familiar weight of a backpack on her. This time, on day three, she felt eyes on the couple. While she was an outside observer watching them make their way up a steep trail, someone else was watching as well. She could only observe.

A shudder of awareness went through Stella's body. He was there. Stalking them. Couldn't they feel him? How could they not feel him? His presence was menacing. His energy powerful. Was he closing in on them? She tried to shout out a warning to them. Icy fingers crept down her spine. Was she going to see him kill them right now? So early? It was too early. He couldn't do it yet. He had a timetable and this was too soon.

She desperately tried to widen the lens, hoping to trap the killer, to see him. The darkness enfolded him, hiding him. The more she shook, the more the lens shook. She was terrified he would realize she was there watching him. Seeing him. He would know he wasn't alone. If she could see him, could he see her? The idea was chilling.

Just as abruptly as her nightmare started, it ended, the lens shutting down, snuffing out the scene, leaving the couple alone in the early morning hours with a serial killer stalking them, determined to end their lives and make it look like an accident.

"No, no. Don't stop. Damn you, don't stop."

She woke fighting, tears pouring down her face, horrified that she hadn't gotten anything that could help. Angry with herself for not being able to warn the couple. She sat up fast, trying to take a breath when no air could find a way into her burning lungs. Her heart pounded so hard her chest hurt.

"Stella, you're here. Open your eyes. Take a deep breath."

She shook her head. He didn't know. He couldn't know what it was like. He could sit across the room in his stupid chair feeling calm and superior with all his training and do whatever it was he did to disassociate but she couldn't. She just couldn't. She was rocking again, arms going around her middle, uncaring that she was having a complete breakdown.

Then Sam was there, lifting her up and onto his lap, his arms around her, holding her tight, pushing her head against his chest while he rocked her. He didn't ask her any questions, he just let her cry as he held her. That was so Sam, uncaring that she was a hot mess. He cupped the back of her head in his palm and rubbed strands of her hair between his fingers.

Finally, she was able to quiet and give a couple of loud sniffs.

He handed her a tissue so she could blow her nose. "I don't feel anyone watching tonight, do you?" It was the only thing she could think of to ask when her face was red and splotchy and she looked awful. She'd gotten his shirt all wet.

"You're right. It's quiet outside and no intruder."

She breathed a sigh of relief. It felt good to be surrounded by Sam. To breathe him into her lungs. She felt like she'd breathed in the serial killer and couldn't get the cold chill out of her bones when she first woke, but Sam drove him away.

"This is the first time since the attempt on your life, Sam, that I haven't felt someone watching me. Do you think it was your father or someone he sent? Is that why they're gone?" She rubbed her cheek along his chest and then settled her ear over his heart.

He hesitated. "I wish I could tell you I thought so, but no. Last night was the first night they were here, and I believe he was as well. Or at least, someone was watching. That doesn't mean it was the serial killer. He has no reason to be watching you or me. Maybe me because I got away. I've never stayed in one place this long. I knew eventually my father would find me if I stayed, but you're here, so I'm here."

Her heart jumped. He stated it so matter-of-factly. "I'm so sorry about your mother, Sam. I really am. I saw your father gesture toward the house and you were really upset. Do you think he wants you to come back and work for him?" She moistened her suddenly dry lips, but she had far more confidence in her relationship with Sam. "Did he threaten me to try to get you to come back?"

Sam was quiet for a moment, his fingers rubbing strands of her hair together. "Stella, I always want you to look at me the way you do, like I'm a good man. I came here with that intent. I always want to be a good man. If my father or those men with him had threatened you, you can believe all three of them would have been dead. Right then. All of them."

He went silent, obviously waiting for her reaction. Stella wasn't certain how to react. She knew where he came from. She knew, or thought she knew, what he'd been for the past ten years. He had instincts and skills others didn't. He would definitely protect her if someone threatened her.

She nodded to show her understanding. "What did he want then, coming here?"

"He wanted me to come back," Sam admitted. "And to give him a chance to repair the relationship."

She couldn't help the way her body reacted, freezing in place just a little. She wanted him to have a relationship with his father if that was what he wanted, but she didn't want him to leave. Not ever. "I see. And when he gestured toward the house?"

"I said I was never going to work for him again. That my woman was here and my home was with her. I found peace and I needed it. You are that peace, Stella. You and this place. He wanted to meet you. I said another time. He tried to insist and I wasn't polite. You've got enough on your plate with this serial killer. They came in the middle of the night. I told him that. He admitted he thought I wouldn't want to see him and was afraid I would take off again and they wouldn't be able to find me." His fingers continued to rub the strands of her hair.

It was a lot to take in. Stella rubbed her cheek over his chest again. "What are you doing?"

"Your hair's like silk. Really love your hair, Stella." He dropped a kiss on top of her head. "Thought I'd let you know, I'm contemplating sleeping with you tonight instead of on the floor in front of your door."

Her heart jumped. Raced. "Is that where you've been sleeping? I thought the guest room. I have guest rooms."

"I wanted to make certain I heard if you had a nightmare." His hand continued to stroke her hair, fingers rubbing the strands together.

She nuzzled his chest, afraid to look at him. "You would have heard." He had instincts like no one else, especially when it came to her.

"Maybe." There was a smile in his voice. "You going to let me?"

"Let you what?" Could her heart pound any harder?

"Move into your bedroom." He paused. Kissed the top of her head. "Permanently. I don't do things in half measures, Stella. You're mine, then you're mine. You're not ready for that, it's okay. I can wait." His normally low voice had an edge to it. His body had more than an edge to it.

She slid her arms up his chest and linked her fingers behind the nape of his neck, lifting her head to meet his eyes. Her breath caught in her throat at what she saw there. His eyes were alive with emotion. So much. All hers.

"Say it, Stella, then there's no taking it back." He brushed his lips over hers and looked down at her again, those dark eyes alive with that same intense emotion she wasn't certain she'd ever get used to seeing, the one that turned her inside out.

"Absolutely, I want you here with me in my bedroom."

"And . . ." he prompted, his hand fisting in her hair, tilting her head back, his eyes darkening even more.

She smiled at him. "I'm yours. You're mine. We're together. Living in the same house. In a relationship, however you want to put it. Just kiss me and get on with it."

He raised an eyebrow. "Get on with it?"

"I've been kind of waiting a long time."

"You gave no sign after the one time. And that took forever before you gave me the green light. I don't want to let that amount of time pass again."

"I didn't want to ruin our relationship."

"You wouldn't have let me close to you if we'd had sex," he corrected. "I wouldn't have gotten my foot in the door."

That was true. So true. He knew her so well. But then she couldn't think because he was kissing her senseless in that way he had. It didn't take her long to realize why his body was always so hot. He burned up the night with that same restless energy he used to prowl around the resort, only turning his considerable skills on her body until she was gasping for air, too tired to move, sated and sprawling over the top of him like a blanket, only to have him wake her two hours later to start all over again.

NIGHT FOUR WAS different in that now Stella had Sam to talk to her when she went a little crazy trying to prepare for her nightmare. She went to bed thinking about it. Planning for it. She visualized it ahead of time. She was so anxious that she was sick before she went to bed.

Sam was his usual calm self, talking matter-of-factly to her. "It doesn't matter if it works or not, Stella. Do what you've always done. Pay attention to every detail and record it. That's what you do. When you wake up, write it down and sketch it. You'll show it to Raine. She couldn't come yesterday, she was out of town, but she'll be here tomorrow and she'll meet with you to look at the sketches. If the two of you can't figure it out, then you show it to the woman you said was a peak bagger. Tell her you're painting, just like you said. If you and Raine know where it is, we'll get there."

It was so comforting, just to have him there. She didn't want to miss a detail because she was trying to change something in her nightmare, but she really thought it was such a good idea to try to widen the lens, so she lay there for a long time, thinking about how to just turn the knob gently to the right as she tried to fall asleep.

She stared at the ceiling, terrified of a repeat of the night before. That had been *such* a disaster. Well, until after. But that was because Sam had saved the day. She could hear the ticking of a clock. Did Sam breathe? Was he alive? He wasn't snoring. Did she snore? Bailey did. She turned on her side. Stared at that wall. Started to turn toward Sam's side.

His arm came across her belly, preventing a full roll, keeping her on her back. "Woman." There was a warning in his voice.

"Man, you took my side of the bed." She made it an accusation, as if it was his fault she couldn't sleep.

He moved fast, stripping her of the covers that had been keeping her warm when he'd insisted she sleep without clothes. No one slept without clothes—except maybe him. He was bossy in bed, she'd discovered, but there were benefits, and she'd reaped them all.

"You sleep in the middle of the bed, Stella. You don't have a side. I sleep by the door to protect you. That's the way it is."

Before she could think to protest, he yanked her thighs apart, wedged his wide shoulders between them and then his mouth was there and she was in another galaxy. Sam didn't believe in doing anything by halves. Much later, she was exhausted, sated and unable to move, not even to pull up the covers. Sam was the one with the warm washcloth and towel. He wrapped himself around her, tucking her so close to his hot body she didn't think they really needed the layers of covers he pulled over them.

"Go to sleep now, sweetheart," he murmured, and kissed her temple.

The heat of Sam's body, the natural sounds of the night, the drone of the insects and the lapping of the waves against the shore lulled her to sleep.

*Mommy, Daddy's doing the bad thing again.*

Stella was prepared this time for the couple on the trail. It was light. Early morning, grayish light. Almost foggy. The couple moved at the same steady speed, dictated by the female. Was there snow, or just the promise of it?

No more trees. Just rock. The rock towered above the couple as they hiked along the narrow trail that would widen in spots and then suddenly narrow again. What kind of rock? Granite. Definitely granite. The fog seemed to move around the couple like steam—or breath. To Stella, it seemed alive.

The fog gave her a creepy feeling but then she realized it was because she was feeling him—the killer. They weren't alone on the trail. The killer was right there. She could almost smell him. He was definitely stalking them. She tried to figure out where he was just by holding very still and turning her head this way and that like a divining rod to see if any direction produced a stronger chill.

Stella had hiked the John Muir Trail alone, had spent nearly a month in the wilderness. She wasn't someone who spooked that easily, but everything about this morning on the trail felt ominous to her. She heard muffled footfalls. Muffled voices. Wait. What? Were there others close? Could she hear people? The murmur of other voices? Was someone coming down the trail toward the couple? Others walking up it? *There were others on the trail.* Maybe Stella could see and sketch the other people and identify them. Surely the killer couldn't murder two people with witnesses so close, could he? Was he one of those people?

Heart pounding, Stella tried to widen the lens just a little. *Cooperate, you piece-of-junk camera.* Why was she so inept that she couldn't make it move? She could gladly go hike the trail and confront the killer but she couldn't move a knob? She kept watching each new detail any light revealed, recording it in her mind to sketch later, but it was the killer she was trying to get impressions of as well as the trail.

What had Harlow said? In her dream, maybe Harlow was photographing the trail, and Stella was just watching. If Harlow was behind the camera, could she widen the lens? Stella put Harlow behind the lens in her dream. That was easy enough to do. If Harlow was around, she was always taking pictures of something. It would be odd to see Harlow without her taking pictures, mostly with her cell phone when she was with them on their camping trips.

To her astonishment, Stella began to see a slightly wider picture. Granted, it wasn't much, but triumph swept through her. It was a little bit of a victory. She could record so much more of the trail and it was definitely recognizable to her. She would sketch it and show it to Raine first thing. Now, if she could just get an image of anyone else as well. Even a shadow. In the early morning fog, she doubted that would happen. Abruptly the lens snapped closed and her dream ended.

STELLA'S EYES OPENED and her mind was instantly clear. "Sam. Sam, are you awake?" She turned, realizing he wasn't there. Wasn't in bed with her. She should have known. Sam didn't sleep long.

"Waiting on you, *Satine*. I can see you've got something."

"They're on the main trail of Mount Whitney. I've hiked that twice with Raine. She's been on it more than I have. It has ninety-nine switchbacks and they're on the switchbacks heading for the summit. People are lost up there quite often, more than you think. Raine might be able to pinpoint more precisely where the killer plans to hit them."

"I'm part of Search and Rescue in Mono County, sweetheart. I'm well aware. Most of them really are just lost and thankfully aren't dead."

More and more inexperienced hikers were attempting the climb without knowing what they were doing, and hiking without the proper gear. The death toll was rising.

"Only so many permits are issued," Stella said. "It's possible we can find them that way and stop them before they even start the climb, although they'll think we're nuts telling them a serial killer intends to murder them."

"We could offer them an insane amount of money for their permit," Sam suggested, "and I could take his place."

"You mean *we* could take their places."

He was already shaking his head. "Not happening, Stella. You're not putting yourself in danger."

"He's stalking them. He would know the moment you changed places," she pointed out. "It wouldn't work. We need to find them and get them to leave."

"He'd choose someone else. We have to offer someone in their place."

She hated that he was right. "Let's find them, Sam. While we're looking, we can decide what we're going to do."

# CHAPTER ELEVEN

Raine O'Mallory shook her head, frowning at the series of pictures Stella had sketched. "Babe, I don't think this is the main trail. I think they camped at upper Guitar Lake and set out from there. It's hard to tell because you're only seeing tiny glimpses, but I think they're coming up Mount Whitney from the other side. If you're right, and she's not as experienced, it's much shorter for her. They'll hike to Trail Crest and drop their backpacks with their bear cannisters and just take a day pack to summit."

Stella frowned. "They still have their regular backpacks on."

"You have tonight. If they have them on tonight, I'm wrong, but some of this beginning terrain looks much more like they started out near upper Guitar Lake to me. He's a seasoned hiker, Stella. Would he take an inexperienced backpacker up Whitney and then hike the JMT this time of year? He wouldn't. The answer is no."

There was that. Stella knew Raine was right. It wasn't snowing—yet. But it would eventually, and once it did, the female wasn't dressed appropriately at all.

"He knows weather can turn up there fast. The wind can be a

real bitch. You know what it's like in lightning storms. He started her out super early in the morning. It wasn't until night four that you heard others around them. He's done this hike before, probably more than once, and wants to make sure she makes it without a problem. You said they're hiking at her pace. He isn't trying to make her go too fast. I'm just guessing that he took the easiest route to show her the Sierras he loves without her taking on too much."

"I'm so glad I showed these to you. I really thought the switchbacks. The granite."

Raine turned the last sketch to several different angles. "I believe you're right they're trying to summit Mount Whitney. You said you heard others."

"I couldn't see anyone, just heard them."

"If they drop their backpacks at Trail Crest and keep going with day packs to the summit, you know there's a very dangerous place, narrow, drop-offs on both sides. They could be shoved off there. There's one more switchback. It wouldn't be hard, even with others around. Feigning an accident. Trying to help if she got altitude sickness. So many things can go wrong up there."

Stella dropped her head in her hands. "Sam's trying to find out who can help with figuring out who has a permit, but I told him the couple has one for the main trail." She texted him. "I don't know if it's even possible for him to do that."

"I might be able to," Raine said. "I can hack almost anything. I'll do my best to track them down." She put the sketches on the table and leaned back in her chair. "So, how are you doing? This is rough. Really rough."

"Let's just say I'm not getting much sleep. I don't want to lose them. I can feel him. He's right there and I can't call out to them and warn them, but there's a feeling." She gave a little shudder.

"The first couple of nights he wasn't there, but last night he was close to them."

Raine jumped up. She wasn't very tall, but she had a powerful, forceful energy that could take command of a room—or a conversation—when she chose. Stella had seen her go from a quiet almost-shadow in a corner of a room to a formidable explosion of energy, her brilliant mind suddenly on display, razor-sharp, challenging someone, most often a man, who put down someone else with a pompous display of superiority on some subject he thought he was familiar with. She would start out softly, but she could annihilate her opponent the moment they underestimated her—and they always did.

Raine looked young, with her strawberry-blonde hair that fell as straight as a board nearly to her waist. She was always careless with it, pulling it back in a ponytail or braid to get the silky mass out of her face. With her slate-blue eyes, golden lashes, dusting of freckles across her nose, and lips defined and curving upward, many people, on meeting her, made the mistake of thinking she looked like a pixie or cute little fairy, due to her size. Anyone who knew her laughed at that description. She was a fighter, an Amazon.

Stella looked around Raine's single-story house on the outskirts of town. She had an acre of land surrounding the house, with neat little gardens and a greenhouse because she liked to grow her own food year-round. She also loved to get her hands in the dirt.

Her property reflected who she was. The three-bedroom home was always neat but overrun with workout gear. She had some kind of gear in every room, including her office. The office was huge, with state-of-the-art computers in it, and banks of screens, but also a treadmill with a TrekDesk. Raine actually did walk on her treadmill while she worked. Stella had tried it and it was no joke even walking at the lowest possible setting.

Raine liked to mountain bike as well as backpack. Like Stella, she wasn't into running and she didn't do peak bagging, but she bouldered and trad climbed when pushed. She was a problem solver, so bouldering afforded her, like Stella, that continual occupation of the mind she needed.

The thing that Raine really loved about her house other than the acreage that allowed her gardens was her secret indoor pool. She loved to swim. She joked that when she was younger, she had permanently green hair from constantly swimming in chlorinated pools until she could figure out how to take care of her hair and swim without damage. The pool was heated too, so in the winter Raine's house was the place to go when the friends wanted to get together. Stella had to admit, she'd grown fond of that pool.

Bailey's very best friend in the entire world was Daisy, Raine's Jack Russell. The little female went everywhere with Raine as a rule, even when helicopters came and picked her up and took her off to work, or she hiked hundreds of miles. Sometimes, it was true, Daisy rode in Raine's backpack, but the energetic dog usually ran circles around them all when they went hiking or camping together. When Daisy couldn't go with Raine, she usually stayed with Stella and Bailey at the resort. Right now, Daisy was running around the yard with Bailey, occasionally giving a yip of pure joy as the two animals dashed together in one direction then the next, discovering every little insect and lizard that dared take up residence in Daisy's territory.

Stella couldn't help but smile. "Those two out there, they are so cute together. I love their friendship. They live life without all the complications. Sam seems to do that too. He doesn't worry about things that haven't happened yet. This thing that's happening, Raine, it's really shaken me. I've built a good life here. It isn't just that for the first time I've actually found friends I love, and that's true. I've never had that before. It's that I've found peace up in the Sierras. There's something about that country that calls to me."

Raine nodded slowly. "I do understand because I feel it too. That's why I settled here. I could work from anywhere, but this is my happy place. There's a reason I backpack so much. Being in the forest and hiking along the trails at ten thousand feet, taking in the ever-changing nature, is an incredible experience. I feel more alive than I do anywhere else, but like you, that same peace. This is a glitch, Stella. The Sierras have been here for thousands of years. We're like little ants crawling around on it. This killer is nothing. He's come and you'll eventually catch him. The Sierras will remain, and so will their beauty. You can count on that and the peace they bring to you because that will never change. He can't change that. Nothing can."

Stella kept her gaze on the two dogs now rolling around on the golden grass, legs in the air, kicking wildly. Bailey looked like a bear next to the petite Jack Russell, and rather silly too, with his giant legs in the air. She laughed at the two dogs. They certainly weren't concerned with a serial killer.

"You went to UC Berkeley, right? After finishing high school, you were accepted straight into the university."

Stella turned to face Raine, hearing the speculation in her voice. "Yes, why?"

"Do you realize there was a serial killer at work in the area near the university at the time you went to school there?"

Stella nodded slowly, wrapping her arms around her middle, her stomach dropping. She suddenly wished Sam was there. Her mind shied away from where she knew Raine was going. Sam let her get away with it; Raine wasn't going to.

"Yes, of course, it was all over the news. He had a particular type. He went after mothers of children playing sports. The mothers who stay home, take care of their children, drive them to practices and all of their games. He followed them home, tied the child or children to chairs and made them watch while he tortured and then killed the mother. He left the children alive, but very traumatized. How could anyone forget that?"

"But you didn't have nightmares. You weren't in any way involved, yet it was close to you, right in the same city."

"It's a big city."

"Stella." Raine's voice was gentle. Low. She shook her head, those gray-blue eyes compassionate but steady. "Not so big. He struck close several times. The killer was one of the security guards right there on campus."

Now Stella's heart was beating too fast. Galloping wildly like a runaway horse. *Don't say it. Don't think it. Don't say it.* If Raine said aloud what Stella was pushing out of her mind so it could never be true, then Raine might make it true. She opened her mouth to tell Raine it was a big campus, but her throat closed, threatening to choke her.

"Why would you have nightmares when you were such a little girl, a five-, six- and seven-year-old? Then again when you were a teenager? You were a teen when you began having those same nightmares again, Stella. You were in a foster home, in high school, getting good grades, powering through school, and suddenly it was happening all over again. You knew there was a serial killer before anyone else. The nightmares started when you were fifteen, but no one believed you but your foster mother. She took you straight to the cops."

"She was pretty cool. I don't know what I would have done without her. My world had spun completely out of control when my birth mother committed suicide and I was put in foster care. She was the emergency home, but she ended up keeping me permanently. I don't know why I was such a mess."

Stella hadn't thought about those early days ever. She never let herself go back to the time when, at nine, she'd found her mother dead from a mixture of alcohol and pills. Anne Fernandez was wearing her best dress, her makeup and hair perfect. She even had on her favorite pair of silver heels and the jewelry she loved most.

"My foster mother, Elizabeth Donaldson, had a dog, a great big bear of a dog, and she let him sleep in my room every night. She was the most amazing woman. By that time I didn't trust anyone, especially adults, but she didn't seem to mind when I refused to talk or give anything of myself to her. When I did start opening up, little by little, she always listened. She stopped whatever she was doing and acted like it was the most important thing in the world to hear me out. She never dismissed a single thing I said. Eventually, we had discussions. I didn't know what a discussion was until she so very patiently taught me. So, to answer your question, when I told her about the nightmares, she believed me and took me to the cops. *They* didn't believe me."

"Even though they knew who you were?"

"*Especially* because of who I was. I was a girl in high school who wanted attention. What a perfect way to get it, right? Because what girl wanted to bring that kind of attention to herself?" Stella tightened her arms around herself. "I detest looking into my past. Others might have bright, happy memories, but mine suck."

"Not all of them," Raine pointed out. "You had Elizabeth

Donaldson as a foster parent. She sounds like she was a lovely woman."

Stella had to concede that point. She was guilty of trying to block those memories in order to close the door on her previous life, the life of Stella Fernandez. She had started her life in college as Stella Harrison and just moved forward from there. She hadn't meant to leave Elizabeth behind. She'd only changed her name and used her trust fund after Elizabeth died from breast cancer. She'd stayed with her until the very end. It had been Elizabeth who had discussed the possibilities of legally changing her name. She owed everything to her foster mother and yet she'd left her behind.

"I did have Elizabeth and have so many memories of her. Even when she was so sick, she was sick with such dignity and grace. I was terrified of losing her." Stella blinked back the sudden tears. "Thank you for reminding me, Raine. I don't want to lose any of the memories I have of her. She taught me so much."

Raine nodded. "I'm glad you had her, Stella." She took a visible breath. "She faced life head-on and I see that in you. She gave that strength to you, didn't she?" Her voice was very gentle, compassionate even, but there was no hiding from her observations.

"I see where you're going with this." Stella rubbed at the goose bumps rising on her arms. "I've thought about the why of my nightmares a million times. Why one serial killer and not another. If it was just the close proximity, then yes, I should have dreamt of the one while I was in college, but I didn't."

That familiar little chill went down her spine, the one she got when she knew she was on the right track—and she didn't want to be. She bit her lip and avoided Raine's eyes, her stomach churning again.

"Obviously, I had a physical connection to Jose Fernandez, my father. I lived in the same house with him and he picked me up. We were a family," she said.

"There was no obvious connection to the second one, when you were a teenager, Stella," Raine said. "I searched. I got into the FBI files and couldn't find anything. I even went back to the original police files when your foster mother took you to them to report your nightmare. There was nothing to indicate you had any physical contact with the killer."

Stella pressed her fist against her chest. Admitting it aloud meant that she knew *this* serial killer. That she'd *touched* him. She'd known it, of course, somewhere deep down, but she hadn't wanted to admit it to herself just yet.

"Elizabeth loved her coffee and she would take me to this one shop all the time. It was where we would go for our discussions, as she always called them. I think she wanted to make them fun, so it was always an outing. He was a customer there. He was there a few times when we were there. I only noticed him because he dropped his wallet going back to his table. I had been in line behind him. I picked it up and brought it to him. When I put it on his table, he thanked me, and when I went to turn away, he caught my arm and asked if he could buy our coffee. I thought that was sweet, but said no and thanked him for the offer. So, he had touched me. It wasn't much of a connection, but there had been physical contact."

"You said you saw him more than once in the coffee shop. Did you ever have physical contact again?" Raine asked.

Stella nodded. "He wasn't there often when we were. Maybe four or five times. Elizabeth never spoke to him. I don't think she even noticed him. But I slipped on some spilled coffee when I went up to get our drinks and he caught me, kept me from falling. I remember laughing and saying we were even for the wallet."

"That was before he started killing?"

"As far as I know. It was before the nightmares started, at least a year before. Elizabeth was diagnosed and our world was turning upside down." She swallowed hard. "We thought she had beat it. She had a double mastectomy, did chemo, and we were told she was good to go. She followed up, but everything looked good."

"I'm so sorry, Stella. I can see why you wouldn't have even thought about having ever laid eyes on the killer."

"He looked different at the time, but I recognized him after they arrested him. I never saw him in one of my nightmares. I just didn't think it was pertinent to tell the FBI that I'd seen him in a coffee shop after he was arrested. I just didn't care, not with Elizabeth so sick. All that mattered to me was getting her better."

Raine sighed. "The serial killer here has to be someone you physically have come in contact with."

Stella nodded. "Unfortunately, that's most likely the case, but I come in contact with a lot of people during the season, Raine." She tacked on the last because this killer wasn't one of her friends. It absolutely wasn't. She had to believe that.

"You're certain it's a male."

"Yes."

"And he's not Sam." Raine didn't take her gaze from Stella's, looking her steadily in the eye. "You're absolutely certain the killer from this dream isn't Sam."

Stella didn't hesitate. "I'm absolutely certain. Sam would protect me with his life."

Raine visibly relaxed, taking her at her word. "You have good instincts. I'm grateful you have him, because he's a huge asset to you. So far, who have you told about this?"

"I still have to bring Shabina and Vienna in. I'm trying to go slow and tell only those who need to know so there's no chance of tipping off the killer. I have no idea who he is, but even if he doesn't live and work here, if he's a temporary, he's still here. It's hard to keep one's facial expressions from showing anything if you know ahead of time it's murder and not an accident."

Her greatest fear was that the killer was a local, someone they all knew.

"You have to bring Vienna into the loop. She's head of Search and Rescue, Stella. She has to know, if she's called, what she's facing."

Stella rubbed her suddenly pounding temples. "And then what? She treats it as a crime scene instead of an accident? What if the killer is watching? What if he's close enough and that makes her a target? I don't want him suddenly putting his sights on her."

"Vienna always treats every accident as a crime scene, you know that. She's careful. Everyone knows that about her. She's going to be first on scene if we can't save these people. She'll know what to look for. She'll be able to preserve evidence. We have to trust her."

"I trust Vienna implicitly," Stella assured. "She's always putting herself at risk, Raine. Of anyone, her life is on the line on these rescues. She's the one hanging off a cliff when some idiot climbs way beyond their level. She goes out in a snowstorm, risking her life, to find a family who should never have gone for a drive in the snow. I know what Vienna is willing to do to keep others safe. She doesn't keep herself that safe. The minute I tell her what's going on, she'll find a way to be on Whitney."

"I think we're all going to find a way to be on Whitney," Raine agreed. "Tell her tomorrow after your dream. That way you'll know whether the couple dropped their backpacks at Trail Crest and have their day packs on. I'll try to find permits and go through them for couples that might be planning to summit Whitney in the two days after tomorrow to see if we can get ahead of him. That's all we can do, Stella." She glanced out the window. "The dogs have been patient with us. We can take them for a walk and get all this out of our heads for a little while."

Stella was more than happy to do just that.

MOMMY, DADDY'S DOING *the bad thing again.*

There was no mistake about it, the two backpackers were making their way up to the top of Whitney, day packs on their backs. Stella could make them out in the early morning light. Gray streaks glimmered through what had appeared as unrelenting darkness and both turned off their headlamps as they continued at a steady pace.

Occasionally the woman seemed to call out to him to stop and both would look at the wide, sweeping views. Stella had been there more than once and she knew what they were experiencing. The climb was worth every strenuous moment. There was nothing like the beauty of the Sierras, and from atop Whitney, aside from the achievement, the breathtaking views felt like sitting on top of the world. The trail was only two or so miles from Trail Crest to the summit. There was only the one switchback left that could give the two climbers any trouble, and so far, Stella didn't feel the killer's presence. He hadn't followed them from Trail Crest. Perhaps he was waiting for their descent?

Her heart started to accelerate and she immediately calmed herself. This might be the last night for her clues, but she wouldn't panic. That was the point of all this, gathering every piece of information she could get in order to save these two individuals. She forced herself to be that onlooker, taking in every single detail, looking for the tiniest shape of a rock or an outcropping she might be able to make out in the dim lighting so she could sketch it and hopefully find the exact location if they missed them at Trail Crest.

The female hadn't shown any signs of altitude sickness. She might be a relatively new backpacker, but she had trained for this hike. Her partner must have stressed the importance of it, or she was a natural at this kind of altitude.

Altitude sickness was nothing to mess around with, and many seasoned hikers fell prey to it. One had to recognize the first signs of it. Headache, nausea, shortness of breath. Legs refusing to cooperate no matter how hard you commanded them to move. Stella knew, she'd had it happen. She'd been careful, going slow, eating the right foods, but still, anything over eight thousand feet was always a risk, a fifty-fifty shot for her. She would try to camp every thousand feet or so if she could when she was preparing for a mountain like Whitney, but it didn't always guarantee she was going to dodge the altitude sickness that sometimes prevailed, even if it was mild.

The woman said something again to the male and he stopped, came back to her, and they looked out toward the early morning sunrise. It was still too early for the sun to climb high enough to illuminate the granite. He indicated the summit, clearly telling her that if they could make it to the top to watch the sunrise, it would be worth it. She nodded and they started out once again.

Stella felt him then. Just a thin, ominous threat carried on the wind blowing across the open trail. He was like a dark film infiltrating the beauty of the early morning. Sly. Cunning. A sinister presence creeping into the picturesque setting. She couldn't tell where he was. Behind them? In front of them? She should be able to see him. Why couldn't she?

She took several deep breaths in an effort to remain calm. It wasn't like there were places to hide. The early morning light was beginning to reveal more and more, and the killer couldn't hide in the shadows for much longer. She found herself straining to see through the gray, looking for him.

The couple continued upward toward the summit, and as they came around the last switchback, there was a person huddled right on the edge, rocking back and forth, head in hands, pack beside him, clearly suffering altitude sickness. It wasn't uncommon to get so close and not be able to make even the last five hundred feet, or think one couldn't make it. She'd had it happen where her legs just refused to work.

Stella observed the individual as the couple approached him. Clearly it was a man, although it was impossible to tell his size or even his build. He wore a dark rain hoodie over his jacket, the hood covering his hair and shielding his face. The closer the couple got to him, the more that ominous, pervasive feeling of menace grew.

She tried to yell to the couple to stay back, but already the male had hesitated in his forward progress. He obviously spoke to the killer, who shook his head and indicated he felt sick.

The male took out his water and walked over to the killer, the female trailing behind him. Stella cried out a warning, but nothing could be heard. She could only watch helplessly as the killer, who had feigned altitude sickness, rose suddenly. In a blur of motion, he gripped the male with both hands and turned so the male hiker teetered on the edge of the cliff. Oddly, it looked as if he reached out and caught at the hiker's left ring finger as he shoved him.

The female stood frozen, in clear shock. It had taken the killer all of two seconds or less to throw the male over the side. She probably had no idea what actually happened. The killer turned to face her and she opened her mouth to scream. Before a sound could escape, he was on her, one hand slamming over her mouth as he shoved her right to the very edge. He held her there a moment.

Stella couldn't imagine how the poor girl felt, looking down, knowing she was going to die. She didn't understand what the killer was doing, but he appeared to hold her finger, the way he'd done to the male, slowly, cruelly, tipping her over the edge. Then the woman was gone, out of Stella's sight, and only the killer remained, crouched down, looking around him to make certain there were no signs that he was there.

He didn't go up to the summit but, head down, body slumped, began to make his way back down as though he'd already made the climb and was on his way down to Trail Crest. The lens snapped closed and she couldn't stop it, although she tried.

SHE HAD NEVER gotten a clear view of him. Not his face, not his size. Not one identifying mark. He could have been anyone. He was faceless, shrouded in his hood, stooped over, and no doubt if he met anyone on the trail he would feign altitude sickness. If he heard them coming, he would lie down, curl up, and wave them on, assuring them he would be fine, he was hydrating. They would never see his face or actual build.

She woke, wanting to scream out her frustration, but at least she knew the couple would drop their backpacks at Trail Crest. There would be a two-day window for the killer between this nightmare and when he struck. They would have to monitor Trail Crest for couples in those two days, but surely they could stop the couple from climbing.

She tried not to think about James Marley and how the killer had murdered him when he hadn't been able to kill his first victim. If they saved the first couple, would he simply select someone else to kill and take them instead?

"Stella, you already know you have to work through this," Sam's calm voice came. Always reassuring. "You write it down and sketch it. You're going to talk to Vienna today. Raine said she'd look for permits. Vienna and I will go up Whitney. It makes sense for us to go. We're the ones they'd call for Search and Rescue and we can easily make an argument that we need to figure out faster and better methods to get to people in trouble. Vienna will be able to get us onto the trail both days."

Stella knew he didn't want her there, but she also knew that made perfect sense as well. "You're right, it's just hard to see him murder two innocent people. He pretended to have altitude sickness and they were going to *help* him. I hate that doing something nice for someone got them killed."

"I know, sweetheart," he said gently. "We're going to stop him."

Stella hoped he was right. It was just that watching the killer, he seemed so invincible somehow. So completely bold, hiding in plain sight. Usually, there were several people on the trail that early in the morning, but somehow his luck held.

Vienna Mortenson was tall, blonde and gorgeous, with the looks of a supermodel. Her Scandinavian ancestry was very evident in her pale hair and large green eyes. She hadn't come from money, but she made it by playing cards, and she'd put herself through nursing school with her earnings. She was a serious card player, eventually playing high-stakes poker in Vegas, although she kept a fairly low profile when possible. She said it was never good to get the wrong people interested in you. Some were very sore losers.

Stella knew very little about Vienna's life other than that she had a mother she sent money to, paying her rent and utilities in Las Vegas. She knew her mother lived with someone, but Stella didn't have a clue who that person was, if they were related or anything about them, and Vienna never said.

Vienna's house was small but very neat, everything in its place. Every single piece of furniture had been chosen with care. She took her time deciding on what she wanted in chairs for her living room or the kitchen table. She wasn't a person to be rushed over personal decisions, yet she could think fast in a crisis, making decisions that saved lives when others depended on her.

Her cat ruled the household. Princess, the white Persian, had a bed in every room. She had a climbing castle and scratching walls everywhere, in every possible shape that could please the finicky animal. The smug little feline strutted around to show Stella she was the boss, especially since Stella "stunk" of Bailey.

Stella didn't dare bring Bailey into Vienna's home. Bailey had good manners and would have curled up in a corner and calmly waited for Stella and Vienna to finish their visit. She knew because they'd tried. Princess would have none of the invader in her home. She'd attacked him, chomping on his giant paw, racing up his hind end, clawing her way to his back to try to ride him to the front door.

Bailey had made it abundantly clear that unless he got to retaliate in a big way, he was staying in the 4Runner and Stella could visit Vienna and her vicious cat alone. He was *not* protecting her.

"Bailey looks miserable out there," Vienna said, turning away from the window to give her cat the best glare she could muster up. It wasn't much of one.

Stella feared for any children Vienna might have if she ever ventured down that path. "He's just fine. He's sulking. Princess is the only cat that's never fallen in love with him. He can't understand why she thinks he's a barbarian."

"I'm sorry about your father, Stella," Vienna said suddenly. She crossed the living room again to look down at the sketches Stella had made. "He's in prison?"

"Yes. I don't have any contact with him, but I make certain to know what's going on with him so I don't get blindsided if suddenly, by some miracle, he gets out."

Vienna sank down into one of her beautiful and very comfortable chairs. No leather for Vienna. She liked material with extra padding in her chairs, a thick wall of stuffing draped over a sturdy frame that promised to last for years; her chairs either glided or raised to give one a nice foot rest. Where she managed to find her furniture, Stella didn't know, but it came from taking her time and not settling.

"I think Sam is right, the two of us should go up there. It would be natural for us to go up there together. No one would question it, Stella."

"Do you have time off?"

"I've got tomorrow off and can trade. It's done all the time. I can say I have a chance to do this and the weather is holding. The holidays are coming up so someone will want to trade with me."

"It's terrifying to think that he'll just switch victims like he did with Marley," Stella said. "That's another huge fear. That I save two victims and condemn someone else to death."

"You didn't do that," Vienna reprimanded. "You can't let yourself think that way or you'll go crazy. This is an opportunity to save lives. Maybe not this time or the next time, but if we don't catch him, think how many people he will kill."

"That's what Sam and Raine say."

"They're right. In any case, if we can't stop the couple, Sam and I will start up from Trail Crest. Thanks to your dream, we know what to look for. It's possible we can prevent any other hikers from trying to help a lone male feigning altitude sickness. We'll sit a distance from him and just talk to him. That should frustrate him to no end."

"He's lethal."

"I'm counting on your Sam being lethal. Is he?"

Stella thought about that. She nodded slowly. "I believe he could be, given the right circumstances. If anyone tried to harm you, Vienna, then yes, he would be."

"Good to know."

"Meaning, if you go up there with him, don't let yourself get separated from him. You have to stick right with him no matter who else is with you. No matter who else you know and how well you know them."

Vienna's light wheat-colored eyebrows came together. "What does that mean? Do you suspect our friends? Or someone we know?"

Stella sighed and rubbed the sudden goose bumps covering her forearms. "It makes me sick to admit this, but I think the only way it works for me to get these nightmares is if I've come in physical contact with the serial killer. I've been in close proximity to a serial killer before and not had nightmares, but each of the killers I've had nightmares about I've actually touched physically."

Vienna looked at the sketches and then crossed one elegant leg over the other. She was dressed in soft burgundy-colored straight-legged yoga pants. The pants had little twists at the bottom that made them look classy. At the back was a band of crisscrossed ties in a darker shade of burgundy. Her cable-knit sweater was cream with dots of various sizes and shades of burgundy. Everything about Vienna screamed classy, sophisticated and stylish, yet she was a super-skilled outdoorswoman.

"That sucks, Stella."

"You're telling me."

"It could be anyone, though, right? You check in all the men and women who compete in the big fishing tournament every year at the fishing camp. And you check in the people who rent the cabins at your resort. When you're here in town, you're at the businesses all the time, talking to everyone and picking up brochures, refining them. It doesn't have to be someone in our immediate group of friends."

"No." Stella kept rubbing her arms.

"Why would someone we know suddenly start killing?"

"I don't know, Vienna. Why does anyone do anything? I don't think my father killed those first few years of my life, but he certainly did after I was five. Why would he start then? He's never said."

"Were you ever tempted to ask him?"

Stella shook her head. "I couldn't bear to look at him. I closed the door on my childhood and I've been afraid to open it. This has been hard enough. I've been remembering things about my mother I haven't wanted to look too closely at. The last thing I want to do is confront him."

"I can relate to that," Vienna said. "I'm all for moving forward and letting the past stay where it belongs. Sam and I should be up there tonight. If that couple hits Trail Crest around two in the morning, we need to be there. I can't tell by the sketches what time it is. Did Raine give you a list of permits?"

"Yes. Everyone who has a permit for both days. I'll have her send them to your phone." She was already texting. She sighed when she got a reply back. "Poor Raine. They've sent a helicopter for her again. She's going to try to make it back to my place before morning to wait with me, but apparently she has to work. She'll send you the list of permits, Vienna."

"Something big must be up."

"Whenever there's some kind of terrorist thing going on somewhere that I'm reading about, Raine suddenly is nowhere to be found," Stella said, lowering her voice, although she didn't know why. It wasn't like anyone was around. "Please be careful up there, Vienna, and don't leave Sam's side. Promise me."

"I promise. This guy scares the crap out of me."

# CHAPTER TWELVE

S tella, there's a couple of men at the gate saying they want to see you. Man by the name of Marco Rossi?" Patrick Sorsey said, his voice sounding tinny as he called up from the security gates. "He asked for Sam first, but Sam's nowhere to be found and it's damn early for visitors."

Stella glanced over at Raine. At least she wasn't alone. Raine had just gotten there, before the sun came up. She had the feeling Sam wasn't going to like this, but she couldn't turn away Sam's father. Besides, it was a welcome distraction while they waited for news on whether or not they were successful in reaching the couple before the killer had.

There were so many names on the permit list for the two-day window the killer might work in. So many question marks. Vienna and Sam had gone up to Trail Crest to see what they could do to find the couple and hopefully stop them from getting killed.

"Please escort him up to the house." That would give her just enough time to change from her pajamas to jeans and get the fire going in the living room. It was too cold to make him stay outside on the porch, although Sam would probably insist that was what she should have done—or just waited for him to get back before allowing his father to visit.

"Sam's father is here," she hissed, dragging down her pajamas, tossing them on the bed and yanking up her favorite jeans. She found a cable-knit sweater to pull over her T-shirt and then hurried into the living room to get the fire going.

"Sam has a father?" Raine asked.

"Very funny." Stella took the time to glare at her over her shoulder. "He isn't going to be happy with me for letting him in. They kind of had a falling-out. I've never actually met him. Do you have a weapon on you?"

Raine raised an eyebrow. "Of course."

"Just checking." Stella scowled. "This is crazy. I'm already out of my mind waiting to hear from Vienna and Sam."

"Then this is a good distraction." Raine was practical.

"He's mafia, Raine. You might want to go out the back way. He'll have a bodyguard with him and I don't want you in trouble with your work."

Raine raised her eyebrow. "You do know my family is originally from New York, right? It isn't like I don't know what goes on. We did eventually relocate to California, but I was already grown by that time."

Raine rarely gave insight into her family, other than she'd had a happy childhood. Stella knew her father was dead, but her mother was still alive. Raine didn't ever go home for holidays. She spent them with Stella, Shabina, Denver, Vienna and Zahra and, recently, Sam in the Sierras. Stella had always enjoyed having the others there to celebrate with. None of them were ever alone. They'd formed their own family.

"It isn't like I think he's dangerous or anything, it's just that he came in the middle of the night and Sam was really upset with him for doing that."

"I can imagine, especially with what's been going on." Raine remained strictly neutral. She looked out the window. Bailey had alerted and Daisy was leaping up and down, giving her joyous welcome. The little Jack Russell loved everyone until she realized they were strangers, and then she would by turns growl and eye them suspiciously.

Stella signaled Bailey to his corner to remain on alert, letting him know he was on guard. He would ignore Daisy's antics and keep his eyes on their guests, waiting for a signal from her to attack, or any indication from them that they were going to hurt either of his charges. Raine put Daisy in the bedroom and closed the door with a sharp order to stay quiet.

"Do you want me to make coffee?"

"Let's see how this goes first," Stella said, and went to the door. Taking a breath, she opened it at the first knock.

"Stella, this is Mr. Rossi. He was here to see Sam, but asked to see you when I told him Sam wasn't here," Patrick informed her, repeating what he'd told her before. He was obviously curious and very disapproving.

"Thank you, Patrick. I can take it from here." She waited for Patrick to reluctantly leave before turning her entire attention to Sam's father. He was studying her intently with dark eyes. Sam's eyes, although he didn't have the same intensity that Sam did. "I'm Stella Harrison. Would you like to come inside?"

"Marco Rossi. This is Lucio Vitale." The older man introduced his bodyguard. "Thank you, I'd appreciate a few minutes of your time."

Stella stepped back to allow the two men entrance into her home. Marco was a handsome man, his dark hair streaked with silver. She could see that his son took after him, although Sam had much harder edges. Marco appeared powerful while Sam was . . . disturbing. His bodyguard, Lucio, was more like Sam in that he had that same dark energy flowing from him even though he appeared relaxed.

Lucio's eyes took in everything in the room, moving from Stella to Bailey. He noted windows, doors and exits. She was certain he knew she was armed, and then Raine walked into his line of vision and a flicker of heat and recognition slid into those dark, merciless eyes as they settled on her.

Lucio moved ahead of Marco, the suit he wore every bit as expensive as the one his boss wore, but somehow, even though Marco exuded power in that suit, Lucio was the more dangerous. Even Bailey's eyes followed him.

Stella smiled a welcome at Sam's father. "Was Sam expecting you?"

Marco shook his head. "I was staying in the town about an hour from here and decided before I leave for home, I'd like to speak with him one more time. It's been years since we had a chance to talk."

Stella waved the two men toward the chairs facing the sofa. "This is my friend Raine O'Mallory. Raine, Marco Rossi, Sam's father, and Lucio Vitale."

"A pleasure to meet you, Mr. Rossi. I've met Vitale before," Raine said. "I'm originally from New York." She settled on the sofa with an enigmatic smile on her little pixie face toward Marco, barely sparing Lucio a glance.

"You aren't Sean O'Mallory's daughter, are you?" Marco asked as he took the chair opposite Stella, giving his bodyguard the one across from Raine.

"Yes, Sean was my father."

"Shame about his death," Marco said. "He was a good man. Always kept his word when he did business. When he moved out to California, I thought he was retired."

"He was. Someone wasn't willing to let things go."

"How's your mother? She's a lovely woman."

"I haven't seen my mother in years," Raine said, no change in her expression or tone.

Stella had her gaze on Lucio, who had Sam's mask and flat, cold eyes, but at Raine's declaration, something crept into his eyes and then was gone. She had thought his eyes were black, but she realized they were actually navy blue, a dark, dark blue. Now they were fixed on Raine's face. Stella wanted Raine to stop talking.

"There is a punishment, the ultimate that can be given out when one betrays the family. It can be worse than death. You are thrown out of the family, declared dead. Your name is never spoken by any family member again. You are not seen by them even if you are standing in front of them, begging forgiveness. There is no forgiveness for betrayal."

Marco raised his eyebrow. "I can't imagine how you could have betrayed your family."

She gave him that same enigmatic smile. "In those days, I had no knowledge of what my father's business entailed. I was very young and female and considered, I guess, without a brain."

"No, no, Raine, protected. He protected you. All fathers want to protect their daughters."

"From sharks? From men who would use them to get information to ruin their families? To destroy their father? I very naively fell for the wrong man. I thought it was love. Do you have any idea how truly silly that sounds when my father is dead and my family lost to me? The thing is this though, I do have a brain.

A very good one. Had my father told me, I would have watched out for sharks. Now that I've learned that lesson, I know men lie all the time to women. More, I made certain to gain as much knowledge and understanding as possible about the circumstances of his death."

Stella hoped Raine wasn't challenging Marco in some way. Surely, she didn't think Sam's father had anything to do with her father's death. She felt completely lost by the conversation and she still couldn't keep her eyes off Lucio for some reason, and his reaction. He hadn't said a word, but he was no happier with the direction the exchange was going than Stella was.

"No, no, Raine." Marco leaned forward. "This is very risky. You shouldn't be looking into such things."

Raine's eyebrow shot up. "This is truly fascinating. Are you telling me, Mr. Rossi, that if someone murdered your father, you wouldn't hunt the one who ordered his killing? Because we both know whoever killed him was ordered to do it. The actual hitman is beside the point, merely the weapon. Whoever is behind the killing is the real murderer. Surely you would hunt for that person."

"That is different." Marco waved his hand in the air expansively.

Stella groaned and covered her eyes for a moment, knowing that was like waving a red flag at Raine.

"Because I'm a woman and you're a man? Because I shouldn't love my father the same way you love yours? I shouldn't feel the same loyalty toward him? Tell me why, Mr. Rossi," Raine persisted. "I don't quite understand."

"Simply put, Raine," he said gently, "even looking into it could get you killed. You need the right resources. You need to know what you're doing. And if you were to find your answers, you'd have to be able to follow through."

She smiled at him, that same sweet Raine smile that meant nothing and yet everything. "And who's to say I don't have those resources, and that when I find the answers, I don't have resources to follow through as well? Never underestimate women, Mr. Rossi. That's what ultimately gets men in trouble in the end."

Marco stared at her for the space of thirty seconds and then burst out laughing. "You certainly are your father's daughter. Sharp as a tack. I don't think I'd want to argue with you very often."

"No one does," Stella agreed. "Would either of you care for coffee?"

Both men nodded. Raine immediately offered to make it. Lucio made a move as if he might get up.

Raine lifted her chin. "I don't need any help. It will only take a minute. Anyone take cream or sugar?"

Stella got the feeling Lucio and Raine were definitely not friends. She hadn't realized that Raine was "dead" to her family. When she spoke of them, she always talked about them so lovingly. She'd described her childhood as happy. Stella wanted to weep for her. How could she be blamed for falling for someone and talking about her family when she had no idea what her father did? She couldn't know she was giving away information she wasn't supposed to tell anyone. To permanently disown her seemed horribly harsh. How could her mother and brothers do that? Stella didn't understand, but then her own mother had left her to face life on her own after it came to light that her father was killing people.

"Your friend is an interesting woman," Marco said.

"She's brilliant," Stella said. "IQ off the charts."

"What do people do up here?" Marco looked around her living room. The windows all had views. "I've seen for myself how beautiful it is, but you're all young. Is there really work up here to support everyone? Do you all make enough money to live?"

She sat back and curled her legs under her. "I'm not going to pretend I don't know who you are. You wouldn't have come here to see Sam without first investigating me. You know I own this resort and the fishing camps, and the property around the lake. Sam works for me all year round. I employ another couple as well as security guards, full-time. Everyone else is temporary."

"I only discovered my son was here a short time ago. I came quickly, afraid he would move on. We've not been on good terms for years, and this is the first opportunity I've had to really talk to him. It wasn't smart of me to come at night."

"Why did you?"

"I thought he would be embarrassed for you to know who his father is." Marco shrugged. "I'm not embarrassed, but we parted on very bad terms."

Stella nodded. "I can see why you would do that. Did you tell him your reason?"

He sighed. "No. We got off on the wrong foot immediately."

"I watched from the window. He definitely wasn't happy with any of you." She looked at Lucio. She was going to make certain Raine knew all about his downfall and how Sam had taken his gun.

The monitor for Search and Rescue went off and Stella's breath froze in her lungs. "Sam." She whispered his name and jumped up, feeling the color drain from her face. "Raine," she called, taking two steps toward the kitchen. The door was wide open and Raine came into view, her expression compassionate. Stella couldn't move.

"I'm sorry, honey, Search and Rescue was called to Mount Whitney."

Stella bit hard on the end of her thumb. "Sam? Vienna? Has either of them checked in with you?" She could barely breathe.

Raine shook her head. "Not yet. You know Sam. Nothing is going to happen to him and he won't let anything happen to Vienna."

"What the hell's going on with my son?" Marco demanded.

Stella whirled around. Marco was on his feet. She'd all but forgotten Sam's father. Bailey growled low in his throat at the tone, warning the man to stay put. Lucio had his gaze on the dog, one hand inside his jacket. Stella signaled to Bailey to stand down.

"Sam's on Whitney today with our friend Vienna," Raine said smoothly, covering for Stella, who couldn't look at either man. "Vienna is head of Search and Rescue and Sam is part of that organization. I believe they were up there to try to improve the ability to rescue on the mountain. A call just went out for rescuers. Both are good climbers and hikers. They know what they're doing. More and more hikers are trying to make that summit and they don't know what they're doing, so experienced climbers like Vienna and Sam have to help them."

Raine was just talking, saying whatever came to mind in order to give Stella time to pull herself together. Her cell vibrated and she all but yanked it out of her back pocket to stare down at the one word that meant everything in that moment. *Safe.*

Her legs threatened to go out from under her. She looked up at his father, blinking back tears. "He's safe. It wasn't him."

Raine stepped all the way out of the kitchen, her blue eyes sympathetic. "Two hikers went off. Vienna has called for the sheriff."

Stella shook her head. "That can't be. They were going to stop them at Trail Crest."

"Stella . . ." Raine began gently.

"I know. I know. I'm grateful it wasn't Sam or Vienna. I just need a minute. I feel like I can't breathe." She couldn't stay there, cooped up in her living room, afraid she'd cry her eyes out or say something she shouldn't in front of total strangers. "If you'll excuse me."

Adrenaline poured through her body, until she wanted to run to get rid of the energy making her shake. She turned toward the front door. "Bailey, with me." She could only hope Raine would forgive her for leaving her with two strangers as she went out the door with her dog beside her. She got as far as the porch. It was very cold, and although she was in jeans and a sweater, she wasn't dressed for outdoors.

Leaning against the railing, she covered her face with her hands. The serial killer had won after all. After all their careful planning, he'd still managed to murder two innocent people who only wanted to summit Mount Whitney and take in the sunrise. How could they have missed them? Vienna and Sam had been at Trail Crest. Right there. Waiting for the couple. What could have gone wrong?

Bailey shoved his large head against her hip and she automatically dropped one hand down to rub his ears.

"Stella?"

She nearly jumped out of her skin. She should have known the dog was warning her that she was no longer alone. She whirled around to face Sam's father. He looked at her with concern.

"I'm not going to pretend to understand what's going on, but it's clear something terrible has happened. Is there anything I can do to help?" He handed her one of her jackets. She kept them on hooks beside the doors to her home so she could grab one at any time during the day or night in an emergency around the property.

"Thank you," she murmured automatically. "No, there's really nothing you can do. I'm sorry for acting so silly. Sam's fine. Some of the hikers coming up from the city have been clueless about what it entails to summit Whitney. Vienna and Sam were trying to figure out how to protect . . ." She waved her hand, unable to lie. She didn't know what to say. "He won't be back now until late."

"I've been diagnosed with a heart condition," Marco blurted out. He glanced toward the closed door as if he didn't want to be overheard even by his bodyguard. "I've decided to retire, which in my line of business can be risky. I have no heir other than Sam."

Stella turned completely around, her back to the lake and the rising sun with all its shades of gold. She hoped he didn't think Sam was going to step into his shoes.

He shook his head. "I know what you're thinking. Sam wants nothing to do with my business. He got out a long time ago. No, I'll name someone else to follow in my footsteps. I want to retire close to my son though, and have the chance to repair our relationship."

"Why didn't you go to him before this?"

"I'd like to say it was because we're both stubborn, but the truth is, even with all my resources, I couldn't find him." He sounded as proud of Sam as he was frustrated. "I didn't know if my only child was alive."

Stella could understand why he would approach Sam in the middle of the night when he found out where he was. Marco had probably really been afraid his son would take off at the first sign that he'd been found.

"I know I'm a stranger to you, Mr. Rossi, but I have to ask you, just how ill are you?" Because she might advocate for him if necessary. There were years of separation. If Marco was dying, Sam might never forgive himself if he didn't at least sit down with his father and talk to him.

"I'm not dying yet. I had a heart attack and the doctors have told me that my eating habits and lack of fresh air and exercise have contributed to my very unhealthy heart. I made up my mind if I found my son I'd retire and try to talk him into at least living close to me. Knowing he has a lady makes it easier. It's beautiful country up here, although I've never lived in the country, nor have I ever seen the appeal."

She found herself smiling in spite of the circumstances. He was city through and through. She couldn't imagine him ever considering settling in the Sierras. "It isn't like there's tons of company up here, Mr. Rossi. If you did decide to make this your home, or at least in the town, it isn't like a city." She tried to make it a warning.

Marco nodded. "I'm well aware." He hesitated. "I met someone two years ago. We don't live together, but I think if I did retire and moved away from the city, she might consider moving with me."

Meaning out of harm's way, Stella interpreted. Whoever the woman was, she wasn't part of what he'd been doing all of his life. Stella honestly didn't know that much about what he did, but she did know Sam. He wouldn't be too happy with his father coming here and talking to her without him being present.

"You do know Sam will want to talk to you about all this himself."

Marco sighed. "Yes, but he won't be very receptive. I was hoping you would advocate for me if my son refuses to cooperate, Stella. I think he'll listen to you."

She could see his charm, his appeal to women, a powerful, handsome man, asking for help. He knew what he was doing, what he looked and sounded like. She had the feeling that he had practiced that charm many, many times over the years.

"When he comes to see me, insist on coming with him. He'll be much more cautious how he treats me, what he says. We'll have a better chance of making amends with each other with you present." He sounded perfectly sincere and appealing.

Stella shook her head with a faint smile. "Here's the thing, Mr. Rossi. I would never, under any circumstances, go behind Sam's back. I wouldn't mislead him or try to persuade him one way or the other. Sam is a grown man. He's intelligent and I don't believe he's hotheaded or does anything without thinking it through. If he was stubborn when he was younger, he isn't that way now. He's thoughtful and calm. I believe he will listen to you and whatever is between you and will honestly try to resolve it. You won't need me there for that. If Sam wants me there, of course, I'll go with him."

Marco Rossi was not a man people said no to very often. That was plain on his face, but he managed to cover up his annoyance with a small false smile. "I hope you're not one of those women who believes your man tells you everything."

"I'm not certain what that means. I don't ask Sam to tell me everything. That's not our relationship." She indicated the door with a little shiver. "It's very cold out here. Perhaps we should get back inside." She didn't wait for him to go in front of her. Instead, she led the way, opening the door and sending Bailey in first and then stepping back so Marco could enter.

Raine looked the same as she always did, sweet and innocent, as if she were that little pixie, sitting with her feet curled under her and the fall of red-gold hair haphazardly pulled back, making her look younger than ever. Stella was never certain if Raine purposely cultivated that look or if she was just naturally born that way, but it worked. The majority of people bought in to it. They never viewed Raine as a threat. Stella's gaze jumped to Lucio.

She wasn't so certain he was buying in to it, but maybe it was simply the tension in the room.

"Are you okay?" Raine asked.

"Yes, have you heard any more news?"

"No, I didn't expect to, honey. They're going to try to recover the bodies. It will take some time."

Stella sighed. "I'm sorry, Mr. Rossi. Sam will most likely be on Whitney for the rest of the day. I don't know when you're planning to return to New York, but he'll be exhausted when he comes back. They'll have to climb down the side of the mountain to recover the bodies."

Even saying it made her feel sick. She still didn't understand how it could have happened. How could the couple have been missed at Trail Crest?

"We can stay another couple of nights. I'll leave the information for where we're staying with you," Marco said.

Raine's cell went off and she answered, jumping off the couch and pacing away toward the kitchen. She could be heard even with her soft almost-whisper.

"I'm in the middle of something. I just left there. I worked all night, General. I haven't had any sleep and what I'm doing is extremely important." A small silence. "Give the job to Jack. He's good. He can do it."

Raine listened for a moment, leaning against the counter in the kitchen. Stella could see her through the open door. She looked exasperated. "This is not a secure line. You called me on my cell phone. Yeah, because I'm not home. No, I told you . . ." She sighed heavily. "It's always a matter of national security. Fine. It would take me an hour to drive home. Send the helicopter for me in an hour so that gives me time here to finish up. Tell Dante he'll have to take me home. I'll throw some things together and he can take me from there to you. That's the best you're going to get. I've got a life, in case you were wondering, and it doesn't always revolve around you." She made a face. "Very funny." She shoved the cell in her back pocket and joined them again.

"Sorry, Stella. I've got about an hour and then work calls again."

"You haven't slept for days," Stella objected. "They need to give you a break."

Raine shrugged. "Lots of hot spots right now."

Marco frowned at her. "Someone sends a helicopter for you? You're speaking that way to a general? As in the military? Secure lines? National security? What in the world do you do?"

Raine laughed softly and waved her hand in the air, looking innocent and young as only she could. "It does sound very dramatic, now that you put all that together. I'm a contract worker for the government, so yes, sometimes when they need me to work on something they need done fast, they send a helicopter because I live so far away from everything. The rest of it though, that's just hogwash."

She made a face. "I'm not certain how best to describe Peter. He likes to be called *General*. I wouldn't be able to talk to a real general that way, right? Not without getting in trouble. Peter is very, very dramatic. He plays a *lot* of video games so he gives orders in terms of his ridiculous video games. The pay is great, and in the end we're both happy."

Stella didn't think either man looked entirely convinced, but Raine gave a little eye roll as if Peter were the silliest man on the planet.

"What do contract workers do?" Marco persisted.

Raine shrugged. "I don't know what others do, but in my case, I am very good at a certain computer code. When programs go down and they want them up and running fast, it's always an emergency, although it really isn't. I go in and troubleshoot. Most of the time I can do it remotely, but lately I've had to go to the main office and fix the program there."

"Some sort of virus?" Marco asked, sounding knowledgeable. "You would think government computers would have the best protections against something intrusive like that."

Stella held her breath, hoping Raine wouldn't eat him up and spit him out. She didn't. She smiled serenely, widening her eyes as if Marco were giving her the best piece of advice possible. "Why didn't I think of that? I'll have to talk to Peter about it."

Marco was silent a moment and then he burst out laughing. "You are a true O'Mallory. Of course, you thought of it. So, not a virus."

Raine smiled at him. "No, not a virus. Sometimes in a program, someone adds an enhancement and doesn't think of all the combinations that might cause the program to crash. Sometimes a crash can happen due to a loss of connection while transmitting data and the data is unreadable." She shrugged. "Not exactly the most exciting stuff in the world, but it's a good job and good steady work."

Marco nodded. "I don't know much about how computer programs work, only that they do and we rely on them now."

Raine had to agree. "Probably too much." She sipped her coffee. "Lucio, you haven't said what you've been up to lately. Judging by the suit, looks like your impressive skills have paid off."

Marco lifted an eyebrow. "Which of your many impressive skills is she referring to, Lucio?"

"I have no idea." Lucio sounded bored.

Stella studied his expressionless mask. His eyes weren't lifeless. There was something hot and lethal smoldering beneath all that dark blue, a promise of retaliation that made Stella worry for Raine. Clearly, the two were enemies—bitter enemies. Marco seemed unaware of the fact, and Lucio didn't seem inclined to enlighten him.

"When I was in New York, he was quite the ladies' man, Marco," Raine said. "He could lie with the best of them. Had women eating out of his hand. It was an easy way to climb the ladder, I think you said, Lucio. It's been a long time, so I'm not quite certain, but I thought that was what your sentiment was. Women are so easy."

Stella raised her eyebrow. "I suppose when we're young we're pretty gullible. We believe in all that fairy-tale crap."

"Comes from being protected by our fathers, Marco," Raine pointed out, ignoring the fact that Lucio hadn't responded. "It's better to know men lie than to learn the lesson the hard way, don't you think?"

"Girl, you're letting yourself be too cynical," Marco objected.

"I don't think so. I believe in being realistic, don't you, Stella? I'd rather see the truth than be taken in by lies. Seriously, Marco, if you had a daughter, wouldn't you want her to know the truth about what she was getting into when she was being married off to some man who would cheat on her? Or if she dated someone she believed loved her when he really was out to impress you? Would you want her to be so disillusioned that her world would come crashing down at some point? Better to go into it with eyes wide open, right?"

Marco frowned. "You young women are so independent. What do you think, Lucio? Do you believe women should be protected? Would you protect your daughter?"

Lucio's white teeth flashed in a brief smile that failed to light those dark blue eyes. "I have no children, Marco, nor do I have a woman of my own. How could I possibly weigh in on this decision with any real wisdom?"

"I suppose that it is the wise man's answer when he is with two beautiful women. We should go. Thank you for seeing us so early in the morning, Stella." Marco stood and Lucio did as well. "It was wonderful to meet you both."

"I enjoyed meeting you as well," Stella said, walking the two men to the door. Relief poured through her as they moved off the porch and began walking toward their car. She hadn't realized just how tense she had been with the two men in her home.

Once they were out of her sight, she closed her front door, leaned against it and faced Raine. "Thank you for staying. I would have had a very difficult time without you here. I know it put you in an awkward position. Clearly, you and Lucio have some kind of history."

"I knew him back in New York when I was a kid. I was Irish. He was Italian. We were both Catholic. Suffice it to say the two didn't mix." Raine gathered up the coffee mugs and took them into the kitchen. "He was very aware back then of how good-looking he is and he's just as arrogant now. He actually had the nerve to try to tell me what I can and can't do the minute the two of you went out the door. Like we were still kids and he thought I would fall in line and do whatever he said."

"Were you ever a 'thing'?" Stella asked, following Raine into the kitchen and leaning against the counter.

"One doesn't have a 'thing' with Lucio. He isn't that type of man. He makes that very clear to any woman he goes near."

"You have a lot of animosity toward him, Raine, and that's unusual for you. You can be full of contempt when men get arrogant and try to act like they know what they're talking about when they don't, but you're never downright hostile toward them like you were with him. Not that I think Mr. Rossi was aware of it."

"He was aware. Not much gets by him. Don't let him fool you, Stella, he's not a nice man. He may have come here to see his son, but he's been head of a crime family for years. He's committed all sorts of crimes, from things very small to murder. I don't know if men like him do the actual killing, but they certainly order it. These days they try to fly under the radar of law enforcement, so they don't do the kinds of things they did in the past, but that doesn't mean they aren't committing crimes."

"I'm sorry about your father, Raine. I had no idea. And your family. You speak of them so lovingly. It must be so hard not to see them, especially your mother."

"I've come to terms with it for the most part. There are moments it hurts like hell and I cry myself to sleep. It's her choice. She made that choice never to see me, knowing I didn't know the circumstances of my father's business." Raine stuck her chin in the air and shrugged. "As much as I'd like to undo the things that led up to my father's death, I can't undo them. They happened. I met someone, I fell for him and I told him I could see him this one evening because my father had gone out to check on things at the warehouse. I had no idea that was information he had been waiting to hear. I went to see my supposed fiancé and he was beating the shit out of my father at the warehouse and killing his men. They took his shipment. We left for California. Someone put out a hit on him anyway."

"Do you believe it was Mr. Rossi?"

"At this point, I have no idea who did it. For all I know, it was one of my father's business partners. They lost men, sons. Brothers. Cousins. And a lot of money. They should have put the hit out on me. It would make more sense." Raine sighed. "That's why

I live in the Sierras, Stella. I find my peace here. We've formed our own family. We might be strange and a little dysfunctional with all of our secrets, but we work and we're loyal to one another."

They could hear the sound of the helicopter in the distance. It would set down in the meadow far enough from the house. Raine glanced at her watch. "I'd better free the hound. Daisy is going to have to do her business and run around like a maniac before we get on that bird."

"Be safe, Raine."

"You too. I hope Sam doesn't get too upset about his father being here without him."

Stella hoped for that very thing as well.

# CHAPTER THIRTEEN

W as everyone from Search and Rescue in the near vicinity?"
Stella whispered to Sam. "That seems a little unusual."
She tried not to look suspiciously at Sean, Bale, Edward and
Jason.

Sean had every reason to be in the park. His work took him
there, after all. She supposed Bale, Edward and Jason could go
see him while he worked. There was nothing that said they
couldn't. Yosemite was beautiful and the various campsites would
be closed soon. She just pictured them leering at all the female
campers.

Denver often guided hikers through the park to some of the
off-the-beaten-path trails and he, apparently, had taken a small
group into the park, so he was close when the call went out for
Search and Rescue as well.

Stella's nighttime security guard, Sonny Leven, had taken his
brother out to the park for a hike. They had a permit to hike up
the back side of Whitney. What were the chances?

"Not everyone, but it was good they were close to help," Sam
said. "The recovery wasn't easy." He sounded tired and Stella
leaned into him. She knew that he was just as upset over the fact

that they were unsuccessful in saving the two hikers—maybe more so.

"Vienna examined both bodies as we waited for the sheriff to get there. Multiple broken bones of course, you'd expect that. The strange thing was, because you had said that about the killer grabbing at their fingers, she really paid attention and both bodies had two breaks in exactly the same place on the ring finger of their left hand."

Stella frowned and laid her head on his shoulder. Sam wrapped his arm around her. Immediately there was a small silence. Several others at the bar had ceased conversing and were staring at the two of them in astonishment. She realized it was the first time Sam had ever really shown any kind of public display of affection toward her. She didn't move and simply waited for the Search and Rescue crew to begin their normal dissecting of their operation in the way they did.

"Didn't James Marley have two breaks on his finger as well from the fishing line or something like that?" she asked.

"I don't think it was from the fishing line, Stella. I think the killer has a signature, but we can't risk being overheard here."

She turned her face into his neck, keeping her voice very low. "You're right, but I just have to know how they were missed at Trail Crest. It doesn't make sense, Sam. You and Vienna were there."

He nuzzled her temple and then her ear. "They had a permit for three people. His brother was supposed to be with them and couldn't make it at the last minute. We were only looking through the database for couples with permits."

She closed her eyes. Such a simple mistake. The permit had been for three people, not two, and Vienna and Sam had been focused on looking for permits for couples only.

"We need to talk about my father showing up and you letting him in."

"I think I got that it wasn't such a good idea, Sam." She sat up straight and took a sip of her mojito. It suddenly didn't taste so good and she pushed it away.

The Grill was filled with members of Search and Rescue, sitting at the bar or at the big round table, eating from the platters of the various appetizers Alek Donovan, the owner, had created in his kitchen to serve before his simplistic bar-style foods. The lunch room was almost at full occupancy, but Vienna had called ahead of time and Alek had saved them their spot, even though he didn't take reservations in the bar.

"I'm not good at turning anyone away," she admitted. "And Mr. Rossi being a relative of yours made it even more difficult. He was very polite. Raine was with me and I kept Bailey in the room the entire time. I didn't text you that he was there because I knew what you were doing was dangerous, or I would have. I wasn't trying to keep anything from you."

"I'm aware of that, Stella." He waited, his eyes on her, trusting her to let him know what his father had said to her.

"He told me he's retiring, and that he'd like to live closer to you. He said he wanted me to come with you when you go to talk to him in order to keep you calm."

Sam's expression didn't change. He kept his gaze fixed on her face. "What do you think?"

"I don't think, I *know* you don't need me to keep you calm, Sam, and I told him that. I don't go behind your back. He might really be ill. He said he'd had a heart attack. I don't know him well enough to know what's true and what isn't, you'll have to determine that for yourself."

"Did he scare you?"

"Not at all. He was very polite. Very charming. He had another man with him. Lucio Vitale. Do you know him?"

"I knew him back when we were both kids. He was from a very poor family. Had to work his way up. His father and two brothers were murdered. He was responsible for his mother and a sister, I think, from a very young age. He fought his way up the ladder, and I mean that literally. It wasn't easy for him. I wasn't that surprised to see he'd made it all the way. My guess, he's an underboss or capo, not Marco's bodyguard, although they introduce him that way."

"You took his weapon."

"Marco handicapped him by telling him he didn't want me shot or killed. There's that. There's also the fact that I spent most of the intervening years fighting for my life. Lucio didn't. He might train, but when your life is on the line every day, you keep your skills honed. Don't underestimate him for one moment."

"I wasn't underestimating anyone. They did help to pass the time. And Raine was with me. She had known Lucio in New York apparently. Her father was in the Irish mob. He supposedly retired and moved to California but someone put out a hit on him anyway and he was killed. Her family blames her and she's dead to them. Literally. Your father knew her father."

Sam shook his head. "This is getting complicated, Stella. I'll go talk to him, but I'd rather you keep your distance until I find out what he's really doing here."

"I have no problem with that." Having a serial killer around was enough for her to contend with.

Zahra inserted herself between the bar and Stella's barstool. "What are the two of you whispering about? Sam's looking very serious and dictatorial."

Stella studied his expression carefully. "You could be right, Zahra."

Sam's eyebrow shot up. "I look dictatorial? What do you mean by that, Zahra?"

"I mean exactly what it sounds like, Sam, that you look like you have a tendency to tell people what to do in a tyrannical way." Zahra gave him her impish smile. "Fortunately, you never speak, so you can't actually be bossing Stella around. You just look like you are."

"That is fortunate," Sam murmured.

Harlow draped herself over Stella's shoulder. "You three are looking cozy over here. Stella, you're not drinking your mojito."

"It's all yours." Stella indicated the drink. "I think my beloved coffee will do today. It always feels so weird drinking alcohol at lunch."

Harlow picked up the drink and took a healthy swallow. Zahra watched her, a little frown on her face. She suddenly reached out and took the glass from Harlow.

"Babe, what's wrong? You don't drink in the afternoon either. Not like this. Do you want to go to a table?"

Harlow looked stricken. "I'm just upset for you. Worried. I don't know what to think. Have you been following the news? The war started up again between Azerbaijan and Armenia for that strip of land."

"The president signed a deal to stop the fighting," Zahra said.

Harlow nodded. "That's exactly right. He did. And I asked some of my sources to dig a little deeper just to make certain everything was staying calm. It's been years, but getting you out of the country was difficult, Zahra. That man was so determined that he wouldn't ever let you go and he's so high up in the military now.

He's got his own resources. If that conflict is ending and he asks the commanders or president or whoever to give him help, they would, wouldn't they?"

Stella went very still, watching the color drain from Zahra's face. She felt Sam's fingers tighten on the nape of her neck. Suddenly, it seemed as if her entire world was falling apart. In the space of a couple of weeks, the serial killer had turned not only her world but also her friends' worlds upside down—or at least it felt that way.

"Who is this man, Zahra?" Sam asked.

Zahra shook her head. "It isn't entirely his fault." She lifted her long lashes and looked at Harlow. "It isn't. In our village, which is very small, Ruslan was the son of the village elder. His mother was from a family in Turkey. He had been educated in Russia. His life wasn't easy. He had a name that although considered perfectly part of Azerbaijani culture, was more Russian culture. And then because he was educated in Russia, some of the elders looked at him as if he might not be completely loyal to us. To make matters worse, he was difficult to read. He had been in a tough school and learned not to show emotion."

"Zahra, you don't have to defend him," Harlow said.

"I'm not, I just want everyone to understand, life is very different where I grew up. Women don't have passports. We don't come and go whenever we want. We wear the clothes our fathers and then our husband deem respectable. Marriages are arranged. It is very rare for a couple to fall in love first, at least in the village where I grew up."

"Is it easier for the men? Do they have a say in who they want to marry, or do the elders arrange the marriage?" Sam asked.

"Sometimes they are allowed a say," Zahra said. "Not always. In this case, I believe Ruslan went to his father and asked for me.

His father, as head of the village, could demand any unmarried woman for his son. It would be idiocy to refuse him."

"But you don't know for certain if this Ruslan went to his father or if his father insisted," Sam persisted.

Zahra shook her head. "I have no real way of knowing. I woke up one morning during a break from my college classes to my father suddenly telling me that I was no longer going to school and that I was to be covered from head to toe always if I went out of the house. When I protested, he became quite violent. It was shocking and unexpected, to say the least."

For a moment she looked as if she might cry, but she pushed back her hair and lifted her chin. "That's when he told me I was to marry Ruslan Islamov and he wanted me to be covered at all times, to learn my place as his wife. My father said Ruslan told him it was his duty to teach me my place, that I was running around in improper clothes, speaking my mind and acting like a whore. Ruslan told my father I was shaming my family." She looked down at her hands.

Harlow put her arm around Zahra's shoulder. "You weren't shaming anyone, least of all your family. You didn't do anything wrong. You weren't even dating anyone."

"So, what happened? Why would this man still be a problem for you, Zahra?" Sam persisted.

Stella thought it was interesting that Sam's quiet voice held such persuasion. He spoke in that calm way of his, but it definitely had what Zahra had jokingly described as an authoritative tone. His voice was so low and gentle, yet so perfectly in command, that it was hard to resist answering him.

"It was like being in prison after so much freedom. I tried to do as my father asked me, but it was very difficult. I have always thought for myself and I don't censor very well. I knew if I didn't accept the marriage it would be difficult for my family, so I was determined to go through with it, but I felt like I needed to at least talk with Ruslan. I didn't know him and I thought if I just sat down with him and asked what he expected of our marriage, I might be able to come to terms with it."

She looked up at Harlow almost helplessly.

"It was fortunate I had come to visit her. I had already scheduled the visit and it was considered an honor to have a senator's daughter in their home, so her father wasn't going to suddenly tell her I couldn't come after all."

Zahra nodded. "I went to Ruslan's house late at night covered completely from head to toe, only my eyes showing. He opened the door and believed me to be someone else, someone he was expecting who had betrayed him. Before I could speak—" She swallowed hard, shook her head and tried again. "Things didn't go well and I nearly was killed. I just managed to get out of his home and I ran, messaging Harlow. She told me where to meet her and she'd have a car waiting. She had use of a car and driver. It was the first time I was grateful I was completely covered from head to toe and no one would know who I was. Harlow, with her family's help, managed to get me out of the country and into the United States. I was just so lucky, and I'll be forever indebted."

That wasn't telling Sam or Stella what Ruslan had done to her, but there was stark fear on Zahra's face and her voice trembled when she related what happened. To Stella's astonishment, Harlow moved even closer and wrapped her arm even tighter around Zahra very protectively. As there had appeared to be some kind of a rift between the two of them, Stella was happy to see Zahra respond, cuddling close, even though that meant her friend was very upset just at the memory.

"I want to be certain I fully understand, Zahra," Sam persisted. "Ruslan Islamov has ties to Russia and Turkey as well as your native village and Azerbaijan. It's important."

Again, Stella noticed his tone was low, but quite compelling and firm. Zahra reacted to the gentle dominance in his voice, her small teeth biting down on her lower lip as she nodded.

"Yes, and he rose to power in the military fast. He had specialized training because he went to military school almost from the time he was a little boy."

"Did he ever train in Turkey? Is he older than you?"

"Yes, he's about ten years older." She whispered the affirmation. "I always noticed when he was back home with his father. It was difficult not to notice him. The men were careful around him. It was the way he carried himself. Some of the women were flirtatious and wanted to be with him. They asked their fathers to go to his father, but he always turned them down. I ran into him on the street, literally. I was out running and I had looked away from the trail and crashed right into him. He caught me before I went down. The way he looked me over, as if I was so beneath him, dressed the way I was, was humiliating. He didn't say anything at all, but after that, when he was back, he would . . . watch me sometimes and it made me uneasy."

Zahra always talked fast and far too much when she was nervous.

Sam stroked one hand down the back of Stella's head. "Zahra, do you remember if anyone ever mentioned Ruslan going to Turkey to train with the military there?" He repeated the question in that same gentle, calm voice.

Zahra's dark brows drew together. "He did go to Turkey several times. His mother's family was there. He would stay for extended periods of time, but I didn't pay attention."

"Raine should be able to track him for you," Stella couldn't help interjecting.

Harlow nodded right away. "That's right. Raine can find anyone."

Zahra's chin lifted. "I don't know why I let just the mention of his name throw me. It's kind of silly to think that after all this time he would be looking for me. He's probably found another wife and has three or four children by now."

"Raine could find that out for you as well," Harlow said.

"What's going on in this little corner?" Bruce demanded as he shuffled up, crowding Harlow to be closer to Zahra. "Everything all right, Zahra?"

Denver came up beside him, grinning, shaking his head, giving Stella and Sam a look that said there was no stopping Bruce from checking on his favorite girl.

"Perfect," Zahra said, flashing a smile. "How's it going with you? Work still going good?"

Bruce nodded. "Production is up. We keep getting new orders, so that's good, but it also means I need someone I can count on to help me out. Denver's only interested in human beings, dead or alive. I even offered him a partnership."

Stella raised her eyebrow and nudged Denver with her foot. "Dead or alive? Surely Bruce isn't referring to your rescue work. That would be so inappropriate right now."

"I'm not that insensitive," Bruce objected, directing a dark scowl at Denver, as if the turn in conversation was all his fault.

Denver shrugged, a roll of his shoulders, but he looked a little lost. "I'm going through my midlife crisis. I like what I do at the hospital, but sometimes, all these rescues, it doesn't feel like enough, you know? I tried riding with Griffen to see if I'd like switching careers to law enforcement. I went out with Sean for a while to see how I'd feel about working for Fish and Wildlife. I talked to Vienna about it and she suggested I ask Martha to work with her occasionally, doing autopsies. I still don't know. Maybe I should go back to school and become a surgeon."

"You are screwed up," Bruce said. "Drop all the creepy stuff and be my partner in the brewery. If you give up Search and Rescue, you'll stop thinking about all those people who put themselves in harm's way. You know most of them bring that shit on themselves anyway. Then you have to go out there and put your life on the line and try to save them or recover their bodies for their families."

Bale, Edward and Sean had joined the circle, Bale jumping into the conversation. "That's an ongoing argument we always have. Where do you draw the line, knowing you're risking too many people's lives in order to save someone who should have known better?"

Vienna pushed her way through the men to wedge herself close to Stella. "That's something every rescuer has to ask before they risk their life to help someone else. All of you know that."

"Vienna," Bruce persisted. "Look at the amount of people who are coming up from cities to climb Whitney with absolutely no experience. They have no business doing it. None. They read about how cool summiting the mountain is, look at a few pictures and think they can do it. They don't bring the necessary gear or even dress in the right clothes."

"He's right," Bale said. "Sadly, that's the truth. Every time we turn around, there's some idiot hanging off the side of the mountain and one of us, usually Sam or Denver, has to climb down to them, risking their lives, to get to them. Are they even grateful? No. They want to know if they got pictures."

"How many of these vain idiots fall because they're taking selfies?" Sean asked. "Vienna, you had to stop those two girls from letting go of the cable on Half Dome last year so they could take selfies. It was just sheer luck that you were climbing that morning."

Vienna couldn't deny she had to stop the two girls from letting go of the cable when they were climbing. They had pulled out their phones to take each other's photograph. They'd even argued with her until she'd gotten tough with them and all but ordered them to keep climbing. One girl had teetered for a moment as she tried to replace her phone, and that had sobered both girls instantly.

"It is becoming a bit of a nightmare," she said. "But we can't abandon people, Bruce."

"I don't want to lose any of my friends," Bruce said.

"I've never seen this side of you." Zahra's big brown eyes looked up at Bruce.

"I'll join Search and Rescue right now if you want me to, Zahra," Bruce said hastily. "If you think the men and women who come up here and trash the trails and blithely go up the mountain without properly preparing so that our friends risk their lives should be saved, I'm on it."

"You don't climb, Bruce," Denver pointed out. "We'd have to rescue you."

They all laughed, including Bruce. He shrugged. "Doesn't matter, I'd try." He looked down at Zahra, clearly sincere.

"It's a good point Bruce is making though," Bale persisted. "Helicopter crews have to make that call all the time."

"It's true," Vienna agreed. "More and more that's a question that's going to be considered, even if we don't like it. The risk to how many others when one person has been so careless."

"I'll admit I was an idiot once," Edward muttered. "Decided to ride out a hurricane. Man, was that a bad idea. Because I do search and rescue, I realized what a risk it was going to be for anyone coming to rescue me and I got myself into big trouble. Fortunately, I was able to get out of it, but it was touch-and-go there for a while."

"You were an idiot once?" Bruce teased, nudging him. "If that's all you got, you haven't lived long. I've managed plenty of times."

"Bruce, getting back to your problem with the business getting too big," Stella said, "what are you going to do? You have a good manager. Will he be able to help you keep up?"

Bruce shook his head. "I need a partner. Genesis doesn't have that kind of know-how and he doesn't want it bad enough. I need someone with skills."

"An anesthesiologist fits that bill?" Harlow teased.

Bruce grinned at her. "Denver can do just about anything if he puts his mind to it."

"Told you, buddy, not interested," Denver declined. "As much as I'd like to help you out, I'd be crazy in a week."

Bruce nodded toward Bale and Sean. "Jason Briggs is an engineer and a darn good one. He's got the mind for it and his kind of work can be scarce up here, especially during winter months. You know him. He's a hard worker. I've been taking a hard look in his direction."

Stella was shocked, to say the least. Jason was the last person she expected Bruce to name. He would take one of the mean boys as a partner in his brewery? She looked at Denver, her eyebrow raised, hoping to convey to him that he might need to talk to his friend. Denver sent her a look that said he'd already done so to no avail. He felt guilty, but he wasn't going to make matters worse by taking a partnership he knew he'd end up screwing up.

Sean and Bale broke into smiles. "Jason is one of the hardest-working men you'll ever find, Bruce," Bale said. "Ask anyone he's ever worked for."

"I have," Bruce said. "I've been doing background work on him. He knows it. I didn't tell him I was asking around because I was looking for a partner. He thinks I need work done."

"No, seriously, Bruce," Sean said. "You'd never regret having Jason work with you. He's smart. He loves it here and wants to stay and settle down. He's got his eye on some property to purchase."

If she didn't know Jason was firmly entrenched with Bale, Sean and Edward, Stella would almost have been convinced to have Bruce give him a chance, but the four men were really horrible when it came to the way they treated women. She didn't want Bruce to be anywhere around them, especially since Zahra was from another country, and for some reason that was a trigger for the four men. She couldn't imagine that they would influence Bruce, but it would be a tragedy if they did.

Denver seemed to know what she was thinking, but they'd been friends for several years. He shook his head slightly, as if to say it was impossible. He nudged Zahra with his foot. "What's going on, shrimp? You're looking sober this afternoon."

"Some of us work," Zahra said. "You docs just pretend to. I'm heading back over to the hospital. Go right ahead and pickle your brain."

"You're just jealous, sweetheart."

She flashed him her killer smile. "You know I am." She looked up at Harlow. "Thanks for everything. I really appreciate it."

"I'm texting Raine."

"Have at it," Zahra approved and waved at the others as she moved out of the circle.

Bruce trailed after her. "I'll walk you over to the hospital, Zahra." He fell into step beside her before she could protest.

"Are you really looking to change jobs, Denver?" Stella asked. "It isn't like we have too many anesthesiologists around here. You're kind of a big deal."

"It isn't like I'd quit my day job," he answered. "But Martha's work is fascinating."

Stella gave a delicate little shudder. "You sound like the vet tech, Vincent, when he talks about doing surgery with the vet. He gets all enthusiastic. Spare me the details."

"I always forget what a baby you are about certain things," he teased.

Stella wasn't a baby about most things. She had to deal with bloated, dead bodies in her lake when partiers insisted on drinking too much and falling into the water when no one was around. Still, she wasn't the person dissecting them. She hadn't been great at dissecting frogs. She'd done it, but she hadn't liked it. She certainly wasn't going to dissect human bodies.

"Is that what you really want to do?"

Denver shrugged. "No. After being there a few times, I realized I wouldn't want to do that day in and day out either. I think I'm just restless. Maybe I need a long vacation."

Stella laughed. "Everyone comes here for vacation, Denver."

His brows drew together. "That's right, they do."


STELLA HAD RARELY been nervous alone on her property. Long before she had hired Sam, she had handled many of the difficult drunk partiers in the middle of the night alone, or with one of her security guards. She just wasn't a person who panicked. But now she found herself uneasy, pacing through her house looking outside, feeling as if maybe she'd been followed back to the resort.

Sam had stayed in town in order to talk with his father. She'd run a few errands, picked up groceries and made the hour-long trip back from Knightly without incident. Her resort was up higher in the mountains, so it was decidedly cooler. The elevation assured she received snow and ice when the town was often spared.

It wasn't that late by the time she returned home, but the sun had set and it was already getting dark. She had checked, but no one appeared to be on the road behind her. Still, the feeling of uneasiness had begun to grow in her, and now that she was home and had put her groceries away, that feeling persisted.

"What do you think, Bailey? Should we stay trapped in here or take a little walk around the property?" She dropped her hand onto the dog's head. He seemed as restless as she was, but just the way she was acting could convey anxiety to the animal and put him on alert.

He padded to the window and looked out as if to answer her. Stella sighed. This wasn't the night for Sam to be gone, but he had family issues that were important for him to deal with. She was certain the watcher was out there. She'd set the alarm, but that didn't mean anything. A good sniper could shoot right through the many windows she had and kill her if that was what his intentions were. She hated the feeling of being trapped in her house.

Finally, she decided she would go outside with her security guard and just walk around the property, something she did often. If the watcher knew her at all, he wouldn't think she was doing anything much different than normal. Sonny was on duty and she texted him. He would be there already, making his rounds. He always answered immediately and he would come up to the house and meet her.

She waited, scratching Bailey's ears, grateful she had her dog.

Sonny didn't text her back. Time seemed to slow. She called him, her heart beating. Sonny *always* answered. He was reliable. He liked his job. He was thorough. He might even be considered overeager. Unlike Patrick, he didn't miss a single area when he checked the resort at night. He knew every inch of the property, which made him valuable when they were looking for missing partiers or a child who wandered off.

Sonny didn't answer his phone. Now she was more than worried. That was totally unlike him. She checked the log-in she could access from her phone. He'd gotten to the resort before she had and relieved Patrick on time. Swearing softly under her breath, she did the only thing she could do under the circumstances. She sent a text to Sam.

Sonny not answering. Afraid he's hurt. Am going to look for him. Calling Griffen.

Wait for Griffen.

Sonny could be hurt.

She couldn't take the chance and Sam knew it. They had to rely on one another. She put the call in to the sheriff's office and hoped they had someone available. Most times, they could get someone there in ten minutes.

Stella armed herself with two guns just in case, slid a knife into her boot and went out the front door. "Bailey, find Sonny." She gave the command and turned him loose.

Bailey took off fast, rushing into the gathering darkness. Stella jogged after him, sending up a prayer to the universe that Sonny was alive and okay, that he was out of range, even though her text had been marked *delivered*. The dog skirted around the lake and then made a rush toward the heavier trees, where he disappeared from her sight altogether. There was no path or trail to run on to follow him. The ground was uneven, and even though it wasn't completely dark, running could be perilous. She didn't want to trip and fall or sprain an ankle. She kept jogging, but she slowed her pace enough to pay attention to where she was putting her feet.

Bailey roared a challenge, the sound shocking in the night, rising to a horrible crescendo, and then just as suddenly he shrieked in pain, over and over. The breath left Stella's lungs, but she increased her speed, throwing caution to the wind. Bailey had never sounded like that, never once in all the years she'd had him. Not that scream of agony that was wrenched from him. It was worse when he went silent.

Once she hit the grove of trees, she slowed, pulled her gun and also her phone, shining the light over the ground. "Sonny? Bailey?" She called to both of them, uncaring if the attacker heard her. He would see the light. She held her weapon close to her body. If he saw her, hopefully he wouldn't see she was armed.

She saw a splash of blood on the leaves first and her heart nearly stopped. Still, she resisted the urge to go rushing in without first taking a cautious look around with her light. She shone it completely around her and then up into the trees before taking steps farther into the grove. Bailey lay on his side, panting in pain, blood pooling on the ground under him, his coat matted with it. Beside him, Sonny stirred, tried to sit, groaned loudly and dropped his head into his hands.

Stella rushed over to them, but again shone the light in a circle to make certain the attacker was gone. He couldn't be too far away. Bailey had four stab wounds that she could see visibly. Cursing, she took off her jacket and then her outer shirt to tie around him tightly.

"Sonny, how bad are you hurt? A sheriff will be here any minute. I've got to get Bailey to the vet or he won't survive. I'll take you down with me to meet the police or you can wait here for the sheriff."

Sonny looked out of it, but she couldn't see any stab wounds on him. There was no way she could leave him alone, not if the attacker was close by. Why had the watcher stabbed Bailey and not Sonny? Sonny looked like maybe he'd been hit on the head.

Sonny put his hand to the back of his head and looked up at her, moaning again. "What happened?"

"Someone hit you, I think. I've got to get Bailey to the vet." She'd already texted the vet to meet her at the clinic, that it was an emergency. She hoped Bailey would survive the hour-long trip in. He had lost so much blood.

A powerful light burst over them. "Stella?" Griffen Cauldrey's voice bellowed loudly. "Where are you?"

"In the grove," she yelled back. "We need help, Griffen."

She heard two sets of boots running, then Griffen was kneeling beside her and another deputy, Mary Shelton, was beside Sonny. Stella was grateful to turn over Sonny's care to Mary so she could concentrate entirely on Bailey.

"Get a tarp. We'll slip it under him and carry him to my rig. Let the vet know he'll need blood," Griffen said. "I can make it down the mountain faster than you can. Mary? Can you handle Sonny?"

"Yes, go," Mary answered. "I've got this."

"The attacker could be close," Stella warned.

"I'll be careful," Mary said.

Stella was fast when she needed to be, but she had no doubt that Griffen knew what he was talking about. She ran to the shed and caught up a tarp and raced back, feeling as though too much time was passing. She just wanted to pick up her dog and run, but he was too big, and when a dog was in that much pain, he could be dangerous.

She talked softly to him while they maneuvered the tarp under him. It wasn't easy, and even Sonny and Mary had to help. He bared his teeth, but he didn't snap. Stella thought he didn't have the energy because he'd lost too much blood, and that terrified her.

"Put your jacket on," Griffen reminded before they started to lift Bailey onto the tarp.

She'd forgotten she'd taken it off. She'd forgotten her gun, which was lying on her jacket. She holstered the weapon and put on her jacket, unaware she'd been cold until that moment. They carried Bailey to the sheriff's rig. She texted Sam to meet her at the clinic and then she texted Zahra, asking her to tell their friends. If Bailey didn't make it, she didn't know what she was going to do. Bailey had been her constant companion for years. Her family.

"He's strong, Stella," Griffen said.

"He lost so much blood," she whispered.

"What the hell happened?"

"I don't really know. I had this really eerie feeling that someone was out there watching. It wasn't the first time. Sam has felt it too. I texted Sonny and he didn't answer. He always answers. Then I called him. He didn't answer his phone. I immediately called your office, but I couldn't wait for you to come just in case Sonny was hurt and needed attention. I gave Bailey the command to find him. I heard Bailey roar as if he had gone into attack mode, and then he was screaming. When I got there, I found Bailey on the ground bleeding and Sonny was just waking up. He was trying to sit up. No one was around that I could see."

"Damn it, Stella, the attacker had to be close by. He could have gone after you."

"I know, Griffen. I did have weapons on me. I was afraid he might kill Sonny. I had to go. Believe me, I made certain you were on your way."

He didn't reply, but he drove fast and got them to the clinic in record time.

Dr. Amelia Sanderson had bought the clinic from old Fiddleson, who had retired nearly two years earlier. The town had tried to entice several veterinarians to come, but they were remote, and those with families had decided against it and those without felt they didn't have much of a chance finding a partner.

Amelia had wanted the practice, but being fairly new out of school and her internships, she was without the necessary funds, so a couple of the locals had put up the money, Stella being one of them. No one was concerned about losing their money. Nearly everyone in town had pets, and the farmers and ranchers had livestock. Hunters had dogs. They desperately needed a vet, and Amelia was a hard worker. Vincent Martinez, her technician, was grateful to have his job back, and she employed two other full-time workers as well as a part-time one. That was good for the town.

Amelia never turned anyone away no matter the hour of the emergency. She took one look at Bailey and she, Vincent and an employee she'd called in, John McAllister, rushed the dog into the operating room.

For Stella, it was the longest night of her life. She sat waiting, feeling hollow and empty. Sam was already there, waiting for her. He looked grim when he saw Bailey, exchanging looks with Griffen and then Amelia. Stella could see that they weren't holding out much hope. Sam put his arm around her and then took her to the one comfortable couch the office had.

"He was so little when I got him from the rescue," she whispered.

"He's strong," Sam said.

Zahra arrived about an hour later, bringing coffee and blankets. She tucked a blanket around Stella and handed Sam and Stella coffee before taking the chair beside the couch. She didn't ask questions but sat quietly, reading her tablet.

Harlow and Shabina came next, bringing desserts from Shabina's café. They had them on a platter they put on the little coffee table where the magazines were, along with a large carafe of coffee. Both took chairs by the windows, keeping vigil with Stella and Sam.

Vienna and Raine arrived fifteen minutes after Harlow and Shabina, taking the last two chairs next to the doors, murmuring their love to Stella and looking to Sam for some kind of encouragement. He couldn't really give them any, so they followed Zahra's example and just stayed silent, reading and waiting.

Denver and Bruce came last, two hours later, filling the waiting room to capacity. They had to bring in chairs from their vehicles, using the actual "office" part, where the receptionist met with the clients. It was the only part of the waiting room open to them.

No one left in spite of the fact that Bailey's operation took most of the night. Amelia came out to talk with Stella around four in the morning, looking exhausted. She looked around the waiting room and shook her head.

"Bailey's alive, Stella. He's very strong and a fighter. That's what we have going for us. That and, shockingly, the knife missed most vital organs. He lost so much blood, though. If you hadn't gotten him here as fast as you did, he wouldn't have made it. It was good thinking, tying your shirt so tight around him. That saved his life. He'll need to stay. There's one wound I don't like the look of. He's not entirely out of the woods yet. I'll stay with him tonight around the clock. If I need a break, I'll have Vincent stay. He's volunteered, anyway."

· "I can stay if you tell me what to watch for," Stella volunteered.

"No, hon, you go on home. Let me do this. I'll stay in touch and you can call me anytime to ask questions," Amelia assured. "Do you know who did this, or why?"

Stella shook her head. "I have no idea. None. It makes no sense."

"He's a beautiful animal. I'll watch over him for you. You all need to go on home."

Stella and Sam stood, knowing that if they didn't, everyone would stay. The food and drink were mostly gone, but they indicated to the vet that she was welcome to have something if she wanted it. Stella was just grateful Bailey was still alive. She looked around the room at all her friends, friends who were like family to her. When she tried to thank them, she choked up.

Denver dropped a kiss on top of her head, held the door open for the others to file out and then said simply, "It's Bailey, Stella."

That really said it all.

# CHAPTER FOURTEEN

Roy and Bernice Fulton, the only couple who lived and worked on the property full-time, had left a note on the front door for them. Stella was too tired to even ask Sam what it was about, although she should have, because poor Sonny might have been really injured. Although he seemed to be talking to the deputy, Mary Shelton, quite a bit by the time Griffen was helping her prepare Bailey for his ride down the mountain. Sonny even had a flirtatious note in his voice.

Stella collapsed in her bed and cried herself to sleep, vaguely aware of Sam sliding in beside her, wrapping his body protectively around hers. She fell asleep cocooned by his warmth. As always with Sam, she woke to exactly what she needed. He had her coffee and the latest news on Bailey. Her dog had lived through the night, had another blood transfusion and seemed stronger. He'd been stabbed four times, and each wound had to be stitched inside and out. Fortunately, none had been to his chest cavity or he never would have survived. The idea that someone had attacked him in such a vicious manner sickened her.

Sonny was fine. Mary had taken him to the hospital just to be certain he was okay. He had a small bump on the head and some bruising around it, but there was no laceration. He was told to go home and rest. That was a relief, that he hadn't been really hurt. Bailey must have interrupted whatever the watcher had planned on doing to Sonny.

She showered and dressed while Sam made breakfast. "Scared me last night, woman," Sam said as he put the plate with the egg scramble in front of her. "I detested the fact that I wasn't home with you and couldn't get to you and Bailey when you needed me most."

She wrapped the scramble in the warm tortilla like a burrito. "You might have been stabbed instead of Bailey, Sam. Do you think this person watching us is the killer?"

"I've asked myself that a million times. It seems too coincidental for it not to be. The timing is just too close."

"But that would mean he would know who I am." She tried not to look or sound alarmed.

"Not necessarily. He could have other motivation for stalking you. The Fultons left us a note last night. It was pinned to the front door. The alarm went off while we were gone. Right after the deputy left with Sonny, which means the watcher was hanging around waiting for them to leave. He came up to the house and tried to get in. The alarm was on."

She nodded, her mouth full of food. He was really a good cook. It didn't seem to matter what meal it was—morning, noon or evening—he could whip something great together.

"He wanted in the house. He tried the doors and then the windows, but was good enough to keep from actually getting caught completely in the security cameras. When he couldn't get in, he tried breaking a window at the back of the house. One of the mudroom windows."

Stella put down her breakfast burrito and regarded him with

shocked eyes. "He got in?" That seemed such a violation. She looked around her kitchen. "Do you think he was in the bedroom?"

"No. The minute the window broke, the alarm went off. The sheriff's office was alerted and so were the Fultons. Roy and Bernice immediately drove over to the house to see what was going on."

"They could have been killed. I didn't even think to text them about Bailey and Sonny," Stella said. She covered her face. "What's wrong with me, Sam?"

"There was a lot going on last night, Stella. You had your hands full trying to save Bailey. I made certain they were aware. I did tell Roy that it wasn't a smart idea confronting whoever was trying to break in, but you know Roy. He wasn't going to let someone get into your house. I don't know if the alarm going off scared him, or hearing the sound of Roy's truck, but he was gone by the time Roy got here with his double-barrel shotgun. Bernice was armed with hers as well. After hearing what happened to Sonny and Bailey, if they weren't already, I think they're now itching to use those shotguns."

Stella picked up her burrito. "I wonder what he was looking for?"

"I have no idea, but now we know he wants in the house. I checked the window. The glass is spider-webbed, but it held. I've called to get it repaired. We don't want it like that through the winter. Nor do we want him to know there's any part of this house that is vulnerable."

"He must have known you weren't here, Sam."

Sam nodded. "That wouldn't be difficult. I park in the same place all the time. If he was watching before you came home, he would have seen you drive up alone. Until this is over, we'd better stick together. Especially since we don't have Bailey right now."

Stella's stomach dropped. She put the burrito down and took a sip of coffee. "There was so much blood, Sam. I didn't think it was possible to save him."

"But he's alive. Amelia's a really good veterinarian. The town is lucky she decided she wanted to live here."

Stella nodded. "We were actively looking for a vet after Fiddleson retired and he couldn't get anyone to take his place. It's so beautiful here and the clinic was so successful we thought it would be a piece of cake, but evidently, there are reasons people don't want to raise families here. And long hours don't appeal to everyone. Also, there seems to be this idea that not everyone can find a partner here."

Sam flashed a small smile at her. "You do have quite a few female friends, all rather good-looking with great jobs, who don't have partners, Stella."

"By choice, Sam. Not everyone wants to settle down with a man."

"You certainly didn't. I had to go very carefully, never let you see I had my sights on you. You would have run like a little rabbit."

"You didn't have your sights on me."

"From the first time I ever spotted you. You were wearing your favorite pair of jeans, which, by the way, you still wear. You had on a little black-and-white sweater with squares all over it. Your hair was up in some kind of messy knot that kept falling out and you'd put it back up every now and then. You wore black boots and you had Bailey with you. You were standing across from the jobsite where I was working and you were talking with Zahra and Shabina. You kept laughing. You have the most beautiful laugh."

Stella was shocked that he remembered what she was wearing

and that she'd been with two of her beautiful friends and he'd looked at her instead of them.

"I made it my business to find out about you. Wasn't that hard. Everyone in town knows about you. You're royalty. You've helped so many businesses. I just had to listen. It was clear you didn't date anyone and you didn't have a partner. I just kept to the background and observed you, trying to figure out why and what you needed."

"Did you figure it out?"

"You need a patient man."

Stella found herself laughing, and that astonished her. Right in the middle of the worst time, with Bailey in the hospital, she could sit at the breakfast table and laugh. "I suppose that's true. I can't believe you remember what I was wearing." She took another sip of coffee. "How did things go with your father?"

"Better than I expected. Marco is complicated. He's used to being the complete authority. Everyone is supposed to fall in line the moment he decrees something. He has it in his head that we're going to have a relationship, which is fine, but he wants it on his terms. He's had time to think about how it's all going to play out. He doesn't know me at all. The last he saw of me, I was young and impulsive. He still thinks of me that way."

"Surely after meeting you again he has to know you're nothing like that, Sam."

"Marco doesn't let go of his authority easily. I let him talk. The more someone talks, the easier it is to understand them and hear lies. He's good at mixing truth with deceit."

"Is he doing that?"

"He always does it. He's had to do it in order to stay alive. In his business, you can't trust too many people. Modern-day business is much more under the radar than it used to be, but there is always somebody who wants to take away what he has. He told me about his heart. I could tell he wasn't lying about that. He seems to really want to retire. That's always a scary proposition. Sometimes you can in that business, other times you don't get to. He knows that."

"Why?"

"He knows everyone's business. Secrets. Things that can put others behind bars. He's always been notorious for being close-mouthed."

"What about Lucio Vitale? Is he really his bodyguard?"

"I don't think so, although he would protect him. I think he's much higher than a mere bodyguard. Still, Vitale could very well take out a gun and put a bullet in Marco's head. That entire business is twisted when it comes to loyalties, although I believe Vitale is loyal to Marco for whatever reason. And if he isn't, having met me, he would think twice before killing my father."

"Do you think Marco will really retire and settle here?"

"He knows if he does he'll have a better chance of staying alive," Sam said. "He's pragmatic about that kind of thing. He claims he met someone that he believes would move here with him and be happy."

"How do you feel about him coming here, Sam?"

"I don't really have an opinion one way or the other. My father is going to do whatever he decides to do, Stella. There's no stopping him. I'm going to live my life the way I choose. Hopefully with you. You're my choice. If he fits in once in a while, that's good, but if he doesn't, he doesn't. I don't know him anymore, and he doesn't know me. We'll see how it works out."

Stella nodded, biting on her lower lip for a moment. Sam knew his father better than anyone, and she had the feeling his father was used to manipulating people. Sam wasn't a man to be manipulated by anyone. She always wanted to be Sam's choice. Always.

"That's good, Sam. We'll work around that." She rubbed her hands on her thighs, detesting that she was showing her distress. "I hate that Bailey isn't here and I can't be there with him. He's been with me practically every minute of the day since I got him as a puppy. It feels off without him. I know he has to feel like I've abandoned him."

"You know better than that, Stella." Sam's voice was so gentle it turned her heart over. "I talked to the vet's office first thing to make certain Bailey had made it through the night okay."

"You know I'm going to want to talk to Amelia myself."

He smiled at her. "Of course, I know that. I'd be shocked if you didn't. She was actually sleeping when I called. Vincent answered. He said she'd be awake by ten."

"I don't know what I'd do without Bailey." She swallowed the sudden lump in her throat and picked up her coffee cup.

"He's a tough dog, Stella. Amelia's a good veterinarian. She hung in there last night and fought for him."

"I knew she was good. I sat on a committee and we read everything about her. She was at the top of her class in school, then interned for some of the best vets for livestock and then small animals. Everywhere she worked, she was given glowing recommendations. She had come to the Sierras often to climb and backpack, so when the clinic came up for sale, she was interested, but couldn't quite swing the loan on her own. We knew she'd have that money paid back immediately. Her work ethic was too good. I'm so happy we went after her so aggressively. If we hadn't . . ." She trailed off.

"Bailey's going to make it, Stella," Sam said.

The confidence in his voice steadied her. She nodded. "Did you talk to the sheriff yet? Or Sonny?"

"Sonny. He says he feels fine. A little headache, nothing more. I went down to the site to look for tracks. Whoever this watcher is knows what he's doing. I think he's lived here a long time, Stella, maybe was born here. He knows how to move on rough terrain without leaving a footprint. I found a few things, broken and bruised limbs on brush, twisted leaves, but little else. Nothing that I could follow."

"I still have to ask myself what he would want in the house," Stella said. "Maybe all this time he was watching the house in the hopes we would leave."

Sam gathered the empty dishes and took them to the sink. "I'd like to think that, but we're often at the Grill. He would have had ample opportunity. It's only been recently that you've been locking the house. I think it would be a good idea to put your journal and sketches in the safe with your gun. If he does get inside, you don't want him to easily access those."

She rose as well, clearing the rest of the table. "You think he must be the killer."

Sam shrugged. "I don't know, but the timing is just too coincidental. I think it's far better to be safe."

MOMMY, DADDY'S DOING *the bad thing again.*

A riot of sounds hit first, birds calling back and forth. So many different types, Stella was aware they were various species. Insects droned and inevitably frogs croaked. Early morning brought with it the continuous cacophony of nature. Somewhere an owl screeched as it missed its prey before retiring. She heard the continuous flutter of wings and the skitter of rodents and lizards among the leaves on the forest floor.

The terrain appeared steep, long grasses thick, colored mostly gold and brown with some green still in evidence in spite of the cold. Trees rose toward the sky, a forest of them, some trunks thick, others mere saplings, many with their leaves already falling to the ground. Beams of color burst all through the branches to hit the rotting vegetation on the ground. Bushes were thick, matting together, while ferns and shrubs added to the wild landscape.

The lens focused on one tree, the trunk sturdy. The camera seemed to go up and up until she could see the bottom of what appeared to be a steel or aluminum frame jutting out from the tree with a pair of muddy boots on the floor of bars. One boot was planted flat while the other had the toe pressed firmly into the bars. She could see just the edge of heavy hunting camo pants coming down over the boots as the camera lens began to close in that abrupt way it had of doing long before she was ready.

STELLA SAT UP quickly and kicked off the covers. The room was surprisingly warm, a fire going in the fireplace she rarely used. Sam sat in the chair across from the bed, his dark eyes on her, waiting to give her whatever she needed. That expressionless mask was becoming a little more readable to her and he looked—wary.

She took several deep breaths and shoved both hands into her hair. She'd braided it to keep it away from her face, but she felt as if she'd sweated and it was all over the place. "He's accelerating, not taking any time between his kills."

"He's got a taste for it now, or whatever triggered him has

made him so unstable he's getting out of control. If that's the case, he'll make mistakes."

The killer didn't appear to be making too many mistakes, not as far as she could see. There had been other backpackers around on Mount Whitney, yet he'd calmly faked altitude sickness and murdered two people.

Stella wrapped her arms around her middle and rocked back and forth. "Thank you for the fire. I don't even know when I'm cold anymore."

"It's getting cold up here. It will start snowing soon," Sam said.

She was grateful that he stayed in the chair across from her, where she could see his reassuring presence, but didn't touch her. He always seemed to know what she needed. When she first woke up after one of her nightmares, even though she was handling them better, she was close to panicking—too close. She needed to allow herself the time to breathe. To admit she was afraid. That she detested she was able to connect with a serial killer, even if it meant catching him and preventing him from killing more people.

Sam let her be who she was. He didn't "fix" her. He didn't ask her if she was all right. He knew she wasn't. He just simply let her work through the nightmare the way she had to, and he was there for her, staying silent until she needed to bounce her ideas off him. If she wanted to talk about it, he'd talk about it. If she wanted to divert attention to something else, he would go along with it. That was Sam, exactly what she needed. She was coming to see, more and more, just why they fit together.

She missed Bailey pushing his head into her lap. She missed being able to scratch his ears, giving her something else to concentrate on while she processed. He made her feel safe. He had always given her companionship when she'd lived alone for those years.

"When I first took on the resort as manager, it was really run-down. I lived in the big cabin, which was a wreck, by the way. I got Bailey from a rescue place. He's a mix, mostly Airedale, but the breeders were upset because another male had gotten in that wasn't all Airedale, so they gave the pups to the rescue place. He was the sweetest little puppy. I didn't go anywhere without him. This little bundle of curly fur."

She rubbed her thigh where Bailey usually positioned his head when he was trying to comfort her. "I called Amelia a dozen times today and she assured me he was doing so much better. She didn't want me to visit him because she said I'd get him too excited and she'd never get him to calm down again. I just wanted to bring him home. He has to be there several days and needs to be very quiet."

She knew Sam was well aware she'd argued with Amelia over visiting with Bailey, but in the end complied with the vet's wishes. She was babbling and Sam just let her, the way he always did. She sighed and forced herself to get to the main topic.

"I didn't get much at all. I'll sketch what I did, but I had no idea what I was looking at. You might know. As for the part of the forest, there was no identifying path or trail that I could see. I could hear all kinds of birds. Shabina knows so much about birds, particularly in our area. If she has recordings of birds, if I listened to them, I might be able to tell her which ones they sounded like. She could maybe identify them and also the area for us."

"That's a good idea."

She scrubbed her palm over her face as if she could erase the sinister feeling that always came when she had the nightmare. A little shiver went down her spine. She found herself looking around, wanting to get her gun out of the safe where she kept it and just have it on the bed beside her. She took another cautious look out the bank of windows.

"Do you think he's out there again, Sam?"

"Yes. He's keeping his distance. While you were sleeping, I took a walk around the property, inside the gates and all around the cabins."

"Sam," she protested. "After what he did to Sonny and Bailey, you can't take chances like that. I don't care what you did in the military. This person is really scary. There's something wrong with him. People like that are . . ." She stopped herself from saying *invincible*.

Sam's dark gaze was fixed on her face. "Sweetheart."

The way he said that single endearment turned her heart over, but it didn't change the truth. Whoever was out there was playing for keeps. He had a knife and he'd plunged the blade four times into Bailey. He might have done so to Sonny had not Bailey attacked. Stella was certain he wanted Sam dead. She didn't know why she was absolutely convinced of it, but she was. That brought her up short.

"Sam, if this man is the serial killer and he's after you or even me, why hasn't he targeted either one of us recently? You just said it yourself. You went walking by yourself at night on the property. He could set you up, draw you out. He hasn't done that. He could make your death look like an accident if that's his thing. You go out every night, sometimes several times a night."

Sam hesitated.

"Just say it."

"Lately, I've had Bailey with me. Now, Bailey's incapacitated. We might see that change. The killer might target me now."

She dropped her face into her hands. "This gets worse and worse."

"No, it really doesn't, Stella. We still have only a couple of things we're dealing with and we take them one thing at a time. You do your sketch and journal like normal. See if Shabina has any recordings of birds and can help identify where the next murder is taking place. As for this watcher we have, he's been around now for a little while. We're both getting a feel for him."

Stella had to admit Sam was right about that. Sometimes even when she went into town, the hairs on the back of her neck would stand up as if she felt the watcher close.

Sam continued. "He's got some vantage point. In the morning I'm going to scout around and see if I can find his tracks. He's got to be up high across from us. There are only a few places that would give him a good view of the house. He's good at hiding his tracks when he wants to, but he might not think about it when he thinks he's safe."

"Could he be on a boat?"

"I thought of that, but he would be too low to see much if he was on the water. I would imagine it would be too frustrating."

"We'd see the boat, even if he didn't have running lights, most likely," she agreed.

"I think he's a good distance away. He might not think I'll go looking across the narrow part of the lake up on the slope. That's where I think he's established himself. If I'm lucky, he's sloppy there. Has a nice little blind set up for himself where he feels safe. Brings food and water. If he's left anything behind, I might be able to get something with fingerprints on it."

She looked up quickly, hope blossoming. "Do you think that's possible?"

"Anything is possible, Stella. No one is perfect. Everyone makes mistakes. He stabbed Bailey four times, and those stab wounds were deep. When you use a knife like that, often you can get cut yourself.

He may have been bleeding. He might have retreated to his 'safe' place in order to see when everyone left so he'd have access to the house. If he cut himself, there might be blood and anything he used to clean up with."

"I never thought of that." But of course, Sam did. He was like that. He seemed to think of those little details that would never occur to her. "It's hard to believe he'd have the guts to return after what he did last night," she added, trying not to revert to rocking back and forth. It was such a bad habit. "You'd think he'd want to at least take a night off."

"Apparently, serial killers and assholes don't ever get tired," Sam said.

To her utter astonishment, Stella burst out laughing. "Apparently not. Do I get hot chocolate while I'm sketching and journaling?"

"I suppose you deserve it." He got up, came to the side of the bed, leaned over and brushed a kiss to her temple as he trailed a finger down the side of her cheek to her chin.

His touch was barely there, like a whisper, but she felt it all the way through her body, the way she always did whenever Sam touched her. Abruptly he turned and stalked out, moving with his silent grace, reminding her of a panther. She watched him go, nearly mesmerized, until he was out of sight. Even before they were in a relationship, he'd always managed to catch her attention when he moved like that. He would go from being perfectly still to looking as if he were flowing across the ground. He really did disappear into shadows.

Stella leaned down and pulled open the drawer in the nightstand containing her sketchpad and journal. She switched the bedside lamp on dim and began to meticulously recall as much detail as possible from the dream. As always, when she first started, it never felt like she could get enough from the tiny portion the lens of the camera showed her, but when she actually began to draw, and the picture took shape, there was more than she thought.

The grass was long and textured, blues, greens, yellows and reds. It was thick as it ran up a slope and into the trees. The trunks of the trees were round and heavy with saplings struggling to grow in between the larger ones, most faltering, choked out by the heavy brush and towering trees around them. She only had the impression of tall trees; she couldn't actually see the tops of them. Leaves and needles lay on the ground, and some of the branches she could see were clearly losing the fight with the wind.

It was the strange metal frame she wasn't familiar with, jutting out from the tree with the grid on it, the two boots resting on it, with just the very edge of camouflage pants showing, that baffled her. She would have to look that up on the internet if Sam didn't know what she was looking at.

As soon as she finished sketching, she switched to the journal and wrote down as many of the details as she could remember, specifically the birds and insects she heard. Every sound counted. She really hoped Shabina could identify that for her.

Sam placed the hot chocolate on her nightstand. "Gave you whipped cream tonight."

She picked up the mug. "And chocolate sprinkles." She flashed him a smile. He was staring down at the drawing. "Do you have any idea what that is?"

"Sure. Hunters use them. They sit up in a tree and wait for deer to come to them. Deer. Elk. Whatever they're going after. It's called a tree stand."

She frowned. "How come I haven't heard of them?"

"You're not a hunter."

"But nearly everyone around here hunts for their food, Sam. They don't talk about tree stands. How high up are they put in the tree?"

"Anywhere from twelve to thirty feet, maybe. It depends on the amount of cover there is. This time of year might be more difficult to find good cover because the branches are dropping leaves."

"How does one climb into the tree stand?"

"Hunters use all different methods. Climbing sticks are very popular."

She raised an eyebrow.

"I'll show you on the internet. That would be the easiest, but just from the little that you've picked up, it looks like he's definitely going after a hunter."

"Sam, practically everyone we know is a hunter. That's how most people get through the winter. You hunt. Denver hunts." She put her mug down and pressed her hands to her temples, wanting to scream in frustration. "Sonny hunts. Even Griffen. Mary does. Without hunting they can't feed their families."

"Those boots look too big to be a woman's boots," he replied, calm as always. "We can rule out the women we know who hunt. We can rule out any hunters who aren't sitting up in a tree stand."

"How do we know who hunts from tree stands?" Stella wrapped her arms around her middle again, rocking herself back and forth.

"Sweetheart, there's no reason to get upset this early. We have to outthink him. We have to think of this like a puzzle we're solving and you've already got pieces he doesn't know we have. He believes he's clever and no one could possibly be onto him." Sam retrieved the mug of chocolate and held it out to her. "Drink your chocolate. It always helps you think."

Stella took the mug from him. "If the person watching us is

the same as the one doing the killing, don't you think he's watching because he already knows who I am?" She looked up at Sam, the knots in her stomach tightening. "It's possible I was his trigger. He found out who I was and wanted to pit himself against me."

Sam sat down on the edge of the bed. Stella tried not to think that Bailey was usually on that side of the bed, shoving his big head against her. To keep from acting like a baby, she sipped at the chocolate and forced herself to keep her gaze steady on Sam's. He was a man who told the truth no matter the consequences. She might not always be able to read his expression, but she could count on knowing he would answer her when she asked him his real opinion.

Sam's eyes darkened until they looked almost like black velvet. He reached over and switched off the lamp. "There's no need to help him see anything. Let's put your drawings and the journal in the safe. When you lean down, I'll shield you with my body so it's impossible for him to see what you're doing even if he has night vision."

Stella leaned over to put her mug of chocolate on the nightstand. At the same time, she scooped up her sketches and journal. Sam shifted to block her body from the sight of anyone watching from the window as she pressed her fingerprint to open the door built into the wall.

"That's an interesting theory, Stella, that finding out your identity might have been the trigger for a serial killer. It would fit with someone watching you, trying to discover what your next move might be." Sam sounded thoughtful but pragmatic, the way he always did, as if the idea might have some merit but it didn't in any way get under his skin.

Stella wondered what it would take to get him riled up. Not

that she ever wanted to see him angry or upset, but the idea that she might have triggered a serial killer into murdering random people sickened her. How Sam could be so calm about it shocked her. She stuffed the sketchpad and journal in the safe on the shelf below her gun and closed the door before straightening, trying to look composed.

"Does anything ever get to you?" She tried to keep the challenge out of her voice.

Sam gently tucked stray tendrils of flyaway hair that had come loose from her braid behind her ear. "You get to me. Anything upsetting you gets to me. A man stabbing Bailey gets to me. I learned a long time ago that thinking things through requires a calm mind. Anger gets in the way and clouds judgment. In order for me to stay alive, I had to learn to always keep my mind clear."

"That's a lot easier said than done, isn't it?" She sipped the chocolate. That was always her calming go-to formula. That, Bailey, and now this man she was learning to love.

"My body was turned into a weapon. I learned to use all kinds of various weapons, but do you know what the greatest weapon we have is, Stella? Our brain. We all have one. The trick is to actually use it. We can't panic. We can't freeze. We have to be able to use our brain in a crisis. More often than not, that's what keeps someone alive when others die."

Stella knew that to be true. She had taken enough self-defense classes to have had instructors drill that into her over and over. Her brain was her greatest weapon. Use it. She also was taught to be observant. Don't be looking down. Don't look at her phone as she walked or ran. Look around. Pay attention to her surroundings. She had always followed those instructions.

"It's difficult to stay calm when I know that horrible killer might have started murdering people because of me. But you're right, and I know you are."

"I don't believe he's aware of who you are, Stella. If this watcher is the serial killer, he's here for another reason."

There was something in his tone Stella didn't quite understand. Speculation? An underlying darkness? A hint of a threat? "What would that be, Sam?" It would be interesting to hear what he had to say, especially since she had the feeling he wouldn't want to tell her. "Why do you think he would come around then, if he doesn't know who I am?"

He sighed and moved off the bed. It was the first time ever that she'd seen Sam act uncomfortable. "I think we need to get privacy screens to black out the windows, at least in the bedroom, Stella." He paced across the room. "If he had a sniper rifle, we'd be sitting ducks."

She leaned back against the headboard. The weird feeling of being watched had slowly begun to fade. "I think he's leaving. Or he left."

"We still need to get screens. I don't like the idea of having someone watching us if I'm touching you, sweetheart."

A little shudder went through her. That idea hadn't occurred to her and it should have. She was a very private person. "I think you're right. I'll order them tomorrow morning."

She waited. He kept pacing, reminding her of a tiger locked in a too-small cage. "Man."

His eyes locked on to her. Like a target. It should have been uncomfortable, but that gaze only held a deep emotion that set her heart pounding. A smile tugged at the corner of his mouth. "Woman."

"Spit it out," she ordered.

"You won't like it."

She raised one eyebrow.

"I don't like it."

"You're most likely wrong. We're only guessing," she reminded him.

"I don't think I'm wrong. You've got enough crap to contend with. I should just keep this particular speculation to myself."

"Samuele Lorenzo Rossi." She called him by the full name he'd given her on his employment record, the one she couldn't find anywhere on the internet.

He winced visibly. "Only my mother called me that when she was really upset with me and I was in trouble. Mostly between the ages of two to seventeen."

"That's your actual name? And the real spelling?"

"Yes. Why would I lie to you? I knew I was staying. I told you. The minute I laid eyes on you, I knew you were the one. I checked to make sure you weren't taken and then I set out to win you. Pay attention, *Satine.*"

She rolled her eyes. "Why couldn't I find you on the internet? You should be there, at least your earlier life with your father."

"Type of work I did, didn't want anything leading back to my family."

That made sense. "I am not letting you distract me, as charming as I find you, especially knowing your mother used your full name to chastise you. What is your theory of why the serial killer might be stalking me if he doesn't know anything about my past?"

Sam sighed and once more came to the side of the bed and sank down, his weight shifting the mattress so she nearly tumbled into him. He put his arm around her to steady her, or offer comfort, she wasn't certain which. Now, she braced herself, wondering if it had been such a good idea to insist on knowing his theory, especially since he really didn't want to tell her, which meant he was reasonably sure he was right.

"This man has met you, Stella. He doesn't have to know you very well. He could have met you in passing. You don't realize it, but you're considered somewhat of royalty down in town. There are businesses thriving because of you. That means jobs. You don't notice, but you go into a restaurant and you're seated right away. Others have to wait. You don't have to pay. The owner waves off your money because you saved his ass when he was going under. Now he's making it through the winter with cash to spare."

His assessment of her embarrassed her. She had saved a struggling fishing camp. When she'd taken over management, the place was going under, and every single cabin, RV and fishing camp, dock and piece of equipment was in desperate need of repair. The owner had money, but he was tired and didn't have the staff or the energy to keep his beloved business going. He had hired her as a last-ditch effort to keep his fishing camp open. It was Stella who had come up with the idea of a high-end resort and a first-class fishing tournament, two things that didn't sound as if they would mesh at all. She got the locals on board and turned their businesses around right along with the one she was managing.

"He could be a temporary worker here or in town. He might have been one of the campers or a climber you talked to when you were out bouldering. You're friendly, Stella. You talk to people. You make them feel like they matter. You get coffee when you're in town and you stand in line and he could have stood in line next to you and talked to you. Obsession starts that way. Some stalkers fantasize they're in a relationship with the one they're obsessed with."

Stella pressed a hand to her churning stomach. "Great. A serial killer might be fantasizing he has a relationship with me? That's what you think?"

He nodded slowly. "That's why you felt him at the campsite and in town. That's why he's out here some nights. He could have been trying to get into the house to get a few of your things to take home with him to feed his illusion."

By now, she could tell, whoever had been outside was gone. It didn't matter. The idea that Sam might be right was repulsive. "I don't want to think about this anymore, Sam." She wrapped her arms around his neck and pulled his head down to hers. "Just kiss me."

Kissing Sam was never enough. He slid her under him and then the world disappeared until there was only the two of them and she couldn't think, only feel, because Sam had a way of setting her world on fire.

# CHAPTER FIFTEEN

The formal dining room in Shabina Foster's home was large, the ceiling high and the walls made of what appeared to be white marble with thin gold veins running through them. If one looked closely, that was exactly what they were made of. The ceiling overhead had heavy beams of redwood quartering the deep insets of subtle gold. The floors matched the subtle gold of the ceiling and pull the very thin, jagged veins of gold from the walls. The room defied description, but then Shabina's entire house did.

She owned the local café and worked from early morning until late afternoon serving customers, some very surly. Even the car she drove, a RAV4, was modest for the area when one could afford the best, and yet when she went home, few knew the home she went to was behind closed ornate gates. The drive led to a three-car attached garage with radiant floor heating. The garage was attached to a four-bedroom, four-full-bath home with a library, game room, chef's dream kitchen and formal dining room as well as a smaller, more intimate dining room and many other appointments, including an indoor pool and exercise room. Mostly,

Stella knew, it was the kitchen and the grounds Shabina had fallen in love with.

Outside the two-story mansion, a gray-and-white stone pathway meandered through beautiful, well-kept gardens with several water features before going up three long round stairs that curved around the front of the deep verandah. The lanai was long and was shaded by a roof to keep the unrelenting sun off those enjoying an afternoon breeze. Screens fit along the railings to keep out insects, protecting the occupants from nasty bites.

Stella loved Shabina's home. At first glance, it might seem pretentious, but it was warm and homey and always welcoming. If she'd had Bailey with her, he would have been right in that formal dining room, nose to nose with Shabina's handsome boys, three large Doberman pinschers: Morza, Sharif and Malik. Her dogs accompanied her everywhere. Stella had been shocked when Jason had issued his warning about Shabina not going into the forest alone. She always had her very well-trained dogs with her. Didn't everyone know that? Would someone shoot her dogs like they had stabbed Bailey?

"What are you thinking about, Stella? You're looking at my boys like they might suddenly come out of their dog beds and attack," Shabina said, putting one of the sketches back down on her gleaming cherrywood formal dining table.

The table was massive and sat beneath a tiered chandelier that appeared to be dripping a multitude of chains of raindrops. Stella had never considered it odd that Shabina had dog beds in every room for the three Dobermans. She was a dog person. Bailey usually went with her, and if he didn't go into a home, he was out in her rig. Most of her friends wanted her to bring him inside. Vienna's cat was the only exception, and Vienna was mortified over her princess acting so snobby. She was determined that someday the silly cat would come around and appreciate the dogs. Her friends all knew that was never happening.

"Remember I told you Jason whispered that warning to me about you going into the forest alone? You always have the dogs with you. Someone stabbed Bailey. Do you think he meant they would hurt your boys? All three of them? They would have to in order to harm you, Shabina. I don't think they'd run away if someone came at you."

Shabina's eyes, those strangely colored, intense royal-blue eyes, stared directly into hers. "No, they would never run away. Aside from being my companions, they're trained personal protection dogs. I love them dearly, and they're rarely away from me. At the café, they're in a room with the door open so they can see me at all times."

"How did I not know that all this time? Bailey knows some commands, but he wasn't trained by a professional. Were they?" Stella looked at the three Dobermans.

"Yes. And then I was trained to handle them as well. I've had them from the time they were puppies, but we were given strict instructions on how to interact as they got older."

"Why would you need them, Shabina?"

Shabina shrugged. "My dad works all over the world. He used to take my mother and me with him. We'd spend months in one place. Sometimes there were factions that didn't like Americans. When I was fifteen, I was kidnapped on my way home from school. My bodyguards were killed and I was taken by some pretty vile men."

For a moment, her lips trembled and she turned away from Stella. Stella could barely believe what she was hearing. In all the years she'd known Shabina, she'd appeared composed and confident. For just that brief instant there was a crack in that perfect serenity, but she recovered fast.

"How awful, Shabina. I had no idea."

"My father and his company didn't let the news get out. They felt if they gave the kidnappers publicity, it would only make the situation worse." Shabina's left hand stroked her throat with trembling fingers.

All three dogs lifted their heads. The largest, Morza, padded over to her and pressed against her legs, clearly in tune with her. Stella knew dogs were sensitive to their owners, and Shabina's recall of those memories couldn't be pleasant.

"Were they looking for money?"

"They demanded a ransom, of course. My father paid. They didn't return me. They had all kinds of demands after that. It was clear to everyone, me included, that I was never going to get away from them unless I was rescued. The odds of that happening were very slim. They moved me all the time." Her fingers continued to stroke her throat as if it hurt. "I managed to escape once on my own, but they found me. I was out in the middle of nowhere. No shoes. My ankles were messed up. I could barely walk. They were seriously pissed at me when they found me. I thought they would kill me. I wished they had."

That didn't sound good. Stella frowned, nearly mesmerized by those fingers stroking her throat. "How long did they have you, Shabina?"

"I was fifteen when they took me and sixteen and a half before I was rescued. Nearly a year and a half." Now all three dogs surrounded her. Shabina suddenly seemed aware of them. She looked down at them and smiled. "I'm all right, boys. Just taking a trip down memory lane. Sorry, Stella. I don't usually go there.

In fact, I try to keep that particular door closed and locked as best I can."

"And I thought I had a lousy childhood. I'm really sorry, Shabina."

"It was hard on my parents. They didn't want me out of their sight once they got me back. I didn't want to be away from them. I slept in their bedroom until I was nineteen. My father had a contingency of bodyguards around my mother and me at all times after I was back home. I still didn't feel safe."

She looked down at the dogs and smiled. "But then I saw a woman training several personal protection dogs when I went with my father to the security company where he hired the bodyguards. She was down in this long field the offices overlooked. I was so fascinated. It was the first time I felt like I could breathe. I didn't want to leave and I was very fortunate that the owner of the company allowed me to go down to meet her."

Stella knew what she meant. She'd felt that way when her foster mother had allowed her to have a dog for the very first time.

"Meeting Lisa Fenton and learning about personal protection dogs changed my life. Lisa worked with me and gave me an understanding of how the dogs worked and how I needed to interact with them while they were working and when they weren't. I could tell her dogs were totally bonded to her, and yet when she was training them, they were like precision machines. She liked the Dobies for me because they were so sensitive and she felt I needed that."

"I had no idea. They're so sweet," Stella said. "They hike with you, go to the boulders with us, and camp. I've never seen them act aggressive at all. They've alerted, but then all the dogs do on occasion."

"Personal protection dogs aren't supposed to act aggressive until they have to, Stella," Shabina said. She signaled to the dogs and they left her side. "I do my best to be as independent as possible. My parents visit often and we talk together online, but I needed to establish my own space and feel like I could make it on my own." She smiled at Stella. "I came to the Sierras backpacking. I wanted to hike the JMT alone to see if I could do it without panicking. Then I met you, Stella. You were such an inspiration, just like Lisa."

Stella had no idea.

"I thought if you could be so brave as to take on a job like managing a failing business, then I should at least try my dream of opening a café. I had the money. There was nothing stopping me but fear. I had the necessary skills and the business background. My father made certain of that, even when I couldn't attend classes. He made me take them at home. I couldn't walk out the front door for a very long time, and when I did try, I often failed."

"But you kept trying," Stella pointed out.

Shabina nodded. "I did. My parents encouraged me, although, like I said, my father surrounded me for a very long time with a wall of security. I needed it at first. Once I came here, I felt at peace. There's something real here. I feel connected to nature. My mind is still and calm. I love to hear the birds sing and the wind move through the leaves on the trees. Meeting you and then Zahra, Vienna, Harlow and Raine settled it for me. I knew I belonged here."

"That's how I feel. We all have these strange backgrounds. I thought all of you would look at me differently knowing I have a serial killer for a father, but instead, all of you showed me why you're my friends. I'm kind of ashamed of myself for thinking you would look down on me."

"It would make sense to want to walk away from your past, Stella," Shabina said. "I never talk about what happened to me. We all came here for various reasons, and thankfully we've formed our own family of sorts. It's been good for me and I appreciate it. I'm okay with whatever any of you want to share or not share. I'm just grateful I discovered the Sierras were right for me and that all of you accepted me into your circle."

Shabina picked up one of the sketches. "What did the vet say about Bailey?"

Stella instantly smiled. "He's stronger today. I can go see him. She wants to keep him another few days so he'll stay quiet. He's on antibiotics and pain meds. Once I bring him home, he won't be allowed to move around other than to do his business. He'll need to stay on his meds and wear the cone of shame."

"That was one frightening night," Shabina said. "I kept thinking it could have been one of my boys. We all love Bailey. He's such a sweet boy and he was protecting Sonny."

"Sonny was on his rounds. He's very thorough. He never saw his attacker. Griffen Cauldrey, the deputy sheriff—you know him, right?" At Shabina's nod, Stella continued. "Griffen thinks Sonny came up on him, the attacker heard him coming, hid, and knocked him out. I just happened to text Sonny right then and he didn't answer, so Bailey and I went looking for him. Bailey charged and the man stabbed him with the knife."

"Bailey must have bitten him," Shabina said. "There's no way that dog didn't get his teeth into his attacker, not if he was stabbed four times. Even if he isn't a trained attack dog, Stella, he's big and powerful. He's not afraid. He'd fight."

Stella hadn't thought of that. She should have. Bailey had been trained by a professional, not the way Shabina's pack had been trained, but he'd certainly had lessons with a trainer. He knew his commands and he had good instincts. She'd heard that roar, that challenge. Of course he would have managed to get his teeth into his opponent.

"Whoever attacked Bailey and Sonny had to have been bitten, and probably severely. No way would they go to the local clinic or hospital, but they might contact one of the nurses. You might talk to Vienna and have her put out the word at the hospital to everyone," Shabina said, tapping her finger on the tabletop.

"I wondered why he didn't stick around and just kill me and then kill Sonny. It didn't make any sense to me at the time, but if he was hurt . . ." She broke off. "He couldn't have been too hurt. Later, he tried to break into my house."

"How much later? Do you know what time it was? You had to get Bailey down the mountain, right? What about Sonny? Who took care of him? Did an ambulance take him to the hospital? How long did it take before he was out of there?"

"That's a good question. I didn't think to ask. I was so involved with Bailey and then came home to that. It was pretty awful. I should have considered how much time had passed before the break-in and everyone had left." She frowned. "No doubt Sam did. He's always one step ahead of me in that kind of thing."

"He thinks differently, is all," Shabina said. "That's good. The more people thinking about this and coming at it from different directions, the better. I also think it's a good thing everyone is used to the way we women get together often. So, if we're together to throw out ideas, no one else in town is going to think anything about it."

"Sam *really* thinks differently," Stella conceded. "And he stays calm. After these nightmares and Bailey and this horrid man watching me all the time, I need that calm. You know me, I don't get creeped out, but this person has managed to do it. I'm not just afraid for me, I'm afraid for Sam and for all of you."

"I thought a lot about Jason giving you that warning. I go hiking every single day with the dogs. They need it and so do I. It's made me very leery. I always put the dogs on alert now, where before, it was their fun time. Now they're working. I hate having to do it, but I know it's necessary. It's also made me consider Jason might know more than he's saying."

Shabina ran her finger over the trees and grasses in the sketch. Stella had been very accurate in her portrayal of the colors. She'd taken her time filling them in after the second night. The camera had widened to show her more of the terrain, but little of the actual victim. She could see more of his legs and the camouflage pants he wore, that was it. She'd concentrated on drawing the trees and brush she saw and the grasses that were everywhere.

"I doubt he'd give me any more information if I talked to him, especially if Sean, Bale or Edward were involved in any way."

Shabina sighed. "They are a strange group. Sean is difficult to figure out. He won't stop coming to the restaurant. I let him come and told myself no matter what he said to me or how mean he was about the food, I'd be nice and eventually he'd stop, but it only seemed to make things worse. I have no idea what he gets out of being so abusive."

"I always thought Sean had a thing for you, but that kind of behavior isn't going to win any points with you."

Shabina shook her head. "I think I mentioned he did ask me out once, but I was busy on the night he wanted to go to dinner. I hesitated, because I was tempted. I hadn't dated anyone and I had told myself that it was time. I was truly going to ask for a rain check but then he got angry with me when I said I couldn't go that night. I don't do very well when anyone yells at me. I think I just froze for a minute. I couldn't believe he would get so upset when I told him I was busy that night."

"And that's when his harassment started?"

Shabina nodded. "He began coming in and sending food back and making loud comments. At first I was nice about it, but he only got worse. I don't know what his problem with me is, but sometimes I'm afraid of him. I don't know if it's because of my past, or if I have good reason to be."

"Have you spoken to the police?"

Shabina nodded. "Bale and Sean were both born here. They have ties to people in the department. That makes it a little tough. I'm not saying no one listened, because a couple of cops did. Craig Hollister, one of the detectives, is very aware of the situation. He's talked to me about it a few times." She glanced at Stella. "Don't look at me like that. I don't have a crush on him like everyone thinks."

"Then why are you blushing?"

"Because all of you give me those eyes whenever his name comes up and I can't help it. He did tell me to be careful and not to be alone with Sean. But Sean works for Fish and Wildlife and I'm in the forest a lot. Since you told me Jason gave you that warning, I've been a bit of a wreck. I actually considered asking my father to send a security team, but I knew if I did I would be regressing. I can't do that. I've fought hard to get to this point of independence. I refuse to let Sean mess me up."

"The season is over and I'm off for a little while. I'd be happy to go with you, Shabina," Stella volunteered. "Between the dogs and my guns, I doubt Sean can do us much harm."

Shabina smiled at her. "You're a good friend, Stella. Thank you." She looked again at the drawings, assembling them in order. "The trees here are ghostly white. There's about a hundred acres of dead or dying trees around the area near Horseshoe Lake due to toxic gas. The roots are unable to take in oxygen. There are signs up warning people to be careful in that area because the gas is dangerous to us as well, especially belowground, in pits or poorly ventilated areas."

Stella nodded. "I was fairly certain from the first couple of nightmares the intended victim is hiking in the D7 zone, where the gas from the magma leak occurred. D7 is very popular with hunters for various reasons, at least that's what Sam tells me."

Shabina laid the first two sketches representing the first two nightmares down in a line.

Stella pressed her hand to her forehead and then rubbed her temples. She felt like she'd had a headache from the first moment she had tried to figure this one out. She already knew it was an impossible situation. "That is a *huge* area."

"Once you hike in about six miles, you're into forest. Horse-shoe Lake is there. It *is* a huge area, and you're right, Stella, they could be anywhere, but if your hunter has one of these tree stands and he's packing it in, is he going to go that far? I don't know how heavy they are, but it doesn't seem too rational to think they're that lightweight. He has to have something to climb the tree with, right? Like sticks or a ladder? He has to pack that in as well. His rifle. We're talking a lot of gear here."

"He can't be from around here," Stella said. "None of our guys would do that."

"No, I can't imagine that they would."

Shabina arranged the next two sketches with the lower part of the tree stand, boots and partial hem of the camouflage pants next to the first two drawings. Even with the pictures beside each other, there was nothing extraordinary to make the area stand out. And there wouldn't be. The wilderness surrounding Horse-shoe Lake was massive. How were they going to find one tree? One hunter?

They both stared down at the drawings for a long time, knowing it truly was an impossible task to find a single hunter in the Inyo National Forest. It didn't matter how many trees and varieties Stella drew, there was no way to identify a single area by looking at them.

"I played various recordings of birds singing to you, and the ones you heard were from the area in the D7 zone closest to Horseshoe Lake. Those are migratory birds. I would say this is definitely the place, but the area is huge, Stella."

Stella bit down on her lip. "I just don't understand why he targeted this particular hunter. Why him? What is it about these random strangers that sets him off?"

"Does he need to be set off?" Shabina shook her head. "I studied those men who took me. At first, I wanted to think they had kidnapped me for some higher cause. At least an act of revenge. Then the money. But they were just vile, disgusting men getting off on a power trip. There was no real reasoning behind any of it. Some were worse than others."

"Did they have other prisoners?"

Shabina nodded. "Occasionally. Those prisoners never lasted long. Over time, I learned that the least little thing could send one off into terrible violence while another might still have a shred of decency left in him. I knew that wouldn't last long being around the others, but it was interesting watching the process as they took a new recruit down their path of complete and utter depravity. I suppose one might call them serial killers. Certainly, they were murderers and rapists."

Stella shook her head and paced across the room, suddenly restless. "I have a very bad feeling about this one. Right from the beginning, I felt like I didn't really have much of a chance of saving this victim. I don't see how the killer is onto me, but given what happened to Bailey, it's possible. Ever since the night we were camping together, I felt as if someone was watching me. If he knows who I am, it could be that he's playing some vicious game with me."

She went over to the window and stared out into Shabina's beautiful gardens. Even in October, the grounds were filled with a riot of color. In spring, the various shades of green were amazing. Stella hadn't known there were so many colors of green. Now it was golds and reds.

"When I was a child, I remember thinking if I could be good enough, then my father would stop doing those bad things. If I obeyed the rules. If I didn't get dirt on my new shoes. If I didn't spill anything on my dress. If I didn't cry when I fell down and it hurt. I would go to bed without protesting. I made all kinds of promises to myself to be better. I'd be so good so Daddy wouldn't have to do those bad things."

Bailey. She needed that dog. She put her hand out and it wasn't Bailey who pushed his head under her palm but one of Shabina's Dobies. "There's my boy. You always know when I'm feeling blue, don't you, Sharif?" She scratched his ears just as she did Bailey's, grateful Sharif had always included her in his circle. All three of Shabina's dogs did, but Sharif in particular liked her.

"It is funny what we take on ourselves as kids," Shabina said, coming over to stand beside her. "After I escaped and they found me, they were really angry. I was beaten severely and thrown into this awful pit. Every single day they would beat me. The nights were worse and then it would be that pit. There were rats and bugs. But it got so I believed I deserved it. I wasn't worth anything. I wasn't grateful enough for the things they'd provided for me, the way they had treated me before, which, by the way, hadn't been much better. Most of all, I deserved it because I was responsible for forcing my father to work the way he did, in those countries."

Stella half turned from the gardens. That sounded insane, but children did think the strangest things. She stayed quiet, letting her friend tell her how her teenage self came to those conclusions.

The other two dogs came close to Shabina, one on either side of her. "I started thinking if I hadn't wanted my father to buy me new shoes for school, or a new backpack, he wouldn't have wanted to start a company that made so much money. It was my fault that he needed to make that kind of money. I grew too fast and they had to keep buying me new clothes all the time. If I wasn't growing, he wouldn't have to work so much. We wouldn't have to travel to so many other countries and put us at risk."

There was silence as the two women looked out into the gardens. Stella loved her own house, but if she had to choose another one, just for the grounds alone, she would have wanted to live here. Once the gates were closed, it was as if they were in their own world. She felt that way at the resort.

"You were so lucky to find this place, Shabina. It's really extraordinary."

"Raine found it for me."

"I didn't know that."

Shabina nodded. "In those early days, I was still very much afraid. I was determined, but afraid. You know Raine and her computer skills. She knew everything there was to know about me in probably two-point-five seconds. She knew I was looking for a house, a piece of property, with some grounds to it. I had told the real estate people I wanted gardens and enough land to walk and exercise the dogs, but I think Raine knew what I needed. This was a private sale. She got me a tour. The moment I saw it, I knew this was what I wanted. The kitchen is a chef's dream. The grounds are unbelievable. And there are suites so when my parents come, even though there's a guest house they won't stay in, they can use one of the suites."

"They won't stay in the guest house?" Stella repeated.

"Nope. Not a chance. My mother says she refuses to give up the late-night girl talks, and if I'm truthful, I enjoy them. I don't want to give them up either. Dad says he doesn't want to give up raiding the refrigerator, that he starves without me in the house to cook."

"I thought your mother cooked."

"He claims she's given up cooking the *good* dishes in favor of the kind that are supposed to be healthy." Shabina laughed. "Naturally, he says this in her hearing so she chases him around the room, just so he can let her catch him."

"Your parents sound lovely, Shabina."

"They are lovely. So many couples wouldn't have survived the trauma of their only child being taken and gone for so long, but it made them stronger. They have a bond that seems unbreakable. I want that for myself but . . ." She broke off and shook her head. "I think one has to actually go out with or be friends with a man before they can have an unbreakable bond."

Stella laughed. "That's true. Poor Sam, to hear him talk, he waged a secret campaign for the last two years because I was so closed off to the idea of a relationship."

"Sam is so impossible to read," Shabina said. "I would watch him at the Grill when we all got together. He always came. He and Denver seem to be good friends. And it's very clear that Carl Montgomery likes him. Carl wasn't too happy with you stealing Sam out from under him. He told me it's hard to find good workers, and Sam was one of the best he'd ever had. Skilled and had a good work ethic. Around here, with the dirtbags coming in, you just don't get that combination often."

"We were dirtbags, Shabina," Stella said. "We came here and didn't even know we were considered dirtbags."

"I showered daily." Shabina burst out laughing. "I rented a house because of the dogs. But we were talking about Sam. He always sat on that one barstool just a little apart from us, one barstool over or just away from our table. His face was in the shadows. Did you notice that?"

"I noticed everything about Sam," Stella admitted. "Denver usually sat next to him. Sometimes, if Carl came in, he did. And once in a while, Craig. I'll bet you noticed when Craig came in, although he wasn't in uniform." Stella nudged Shabina.

Shabina laughed again. "You're awful. See why I always end up blushing when any of you mention poor Craig? The point is, it was impossible to tell what Sam was thinking or feeling. He was just there, but not in this creepy way, more like a protective way."

That surprised Stella. "You got that feeling from him?"

"Most of the time, yes. Unless Sean and his crew were insulting me on the dance floor, and then he just walked over and intense menacing vibes would pour off him. He didn't have to say anything. He just looked at them and they usually left or went back to the bar. He could be scary. I ought to know, I've had protection details most of my life."

"I just stared at him and hoped I didn't blurt out something stupid like he was utterly gorgeous or impossibly sweet," Stella admitted. "Zahra likes to ply me with Moscow Mules when I go to the Grill with her, or worse, mojitos, because I drink too many of them without realizing I'm doing it, then I say things I shouldn't."

"He's sweet?" Shabina asked.

Stella nodded. "These last couple of years, while he worked for me, he never asked me questions. Never put me on the spot. If I had the worst day ever, with some of the guests yelling their heads off at me, I'd go home and he'd be on my deck, grilling the best dinner ever. He'd point to a cooler and there would be ice-cold beer in it. He wouldn't expect me to talk. He didn't talk. I could go in and change, put my feet up and sit in my swing chair while he made dinner. We ate and he'd leave. Sometimes he'd do the dishes. Sometimes, if the day was really bad, he'd watch my favorite movie, *Moulin Rouge!*, with me. I think he thought I was an idiot for crying, but he'd just hand me the box of tissues."

"Wow, who knew it was the silent types who could be all sweet when it was needed?"

"And he loves Bailey, which was essential, and Bailey loves him back. You know how Bailey is with everyone. He likes people, but he's completely devoted to me. He included Sam with me. Kind of like we were the same person. I don't even know when that started happening. I didn't notice or I might have gotten jealous."

"How is Bailey?"

Stella sighed. "Poor baby wants to come home and I want him home. Sam keeps telling me that we want him to have the best care possible. I know Amelia is giving that to him, but he doesn't like being away from us."

"While you're working on this, I suppose it's a good thing to be somewhat mobile and not tied to the house," Shabina said, looking down at the sketches again. "I wish I could be of more help. This is definitely the D7 zone. Your hunter hiked in the six miles. I don't think he went too far in, because he's hauling too much gear. I doubt if he's local. Maybe if you can figure out how the killer is actually going to manage to murder his victim, it would help. I mean, he is high up in a tree. He can't sneak up behind him and climb up without being seen. He can't shove him out of the tree, again because he's too high up. How does he actually kill him? Do you have any idea?"

That was a good question and Stella had wondered that herself. If she was sitting up in a tree stand, safe from a serial killer, how would the killer get to her? If he tried to climb the same tree, the victim was armed. Wouldn't he shoot? Or would he feel threatened? How would the killer make it look like an accident? Most of the time, a hunter would harness himself into the tree stand. Stella knew, because she'd read all about it once Sam told her what it was.

"Someone that high up in a tree should be able to see anyone coming at them, right?" Shabina asked. "I don't know all that much about tree stands, but in order for them to be of any use they have to be pretty high up in the tree."

"Sam said twelve to thirty feet."

"Then how does the killer expect to get to his victim without the victim fighting him off?" Shabina asked.

"He wouldn't know he was a serial killer," Stella pointed out. "He's just another friendly hunter passing by."

"Do hunters visit with one another? Doesn't that defeat the purpose? If the guy waits up in his tree stand for a deer to come by and another hunter stops under his tree and starts talking, wouldn't he scare off all the deer?"

"Maybe we have it all wrong and the serial killer is the one in the tree stand," Stella ventured suddenly. "Could that be? He sits up there waiting and along comes an unsuspecting hunter. He lures him over with some kind of deer sound and then murders him and makes it look like it was his tree stand all along. Is that plausible?"

Shabina scrunched up her nose. "I don't know, Stella. What about the purchase of the tree stand? That would be traceable. It isn't like the killer could figure out a way to put it on the victim's credit card. Even if he paid cash, that's a big jump."

Stella gave a little cry of sheer annoyance. "This entire thing is so frustrating. It's a big jump to think that we could find a single tree in an entire forest. If this serial killer really is playing a game with me, he's got to be laughing his head off right now."

"I just don't think he's onto you."

"That's what Sam says, but why not?"

"Because how could he be? It isn't like you're that same person."

"Maybe he went to high school with me. I can't have changed in looks that much. I've never run into anyone I went to school with, but it's possible they saw me and I didn't see them."

Shabina sighed. "Honestly? I didn't think of that."

Stella bit down on her lower lip. "Do you have any idea how many people come here to climb or backpack? There are a million things for people to do and it's so beautiful. We get visitors all the time. I'm always busy during the season. I wouldn't notice someone from those days, not when my foster mother had cancer and a serial killer was on the loose. My world was falling apart again."

"You told me the serial killer has to be someone you've physically come in contact with or you wouldn't be having the nightmares. That was one of the reasons you didn't want to tell any of our male friends," Shabina pointed out.

"I might have come in contact with someone I went to high school with," Stella said. She doubted it. In those days, she stayed to herself. She didn't trust anyone and she didn't have friendships. If she was face-to-face with someone from her high school, close enough that she would physically touch them, would she remember them? She thought so. Her mind tended to be obsessive about details.

"I want it to be someone from my past, Shabina," she admitted. "But I don't think it is. I think it's someone close to me here. Someone from town. One of the businesses."

"Like Sean."

Stella tried to picture Sean as a serial killer. He was incredibly strong. Most of the climbers were, and Sean was a forester. He knew animals, but then again, most of those in the area were hunters. They knew the anatomy of animals.

"What about Edward? What do we know about him? Bale's the leader of the group, and Jason sort of hangs out on the edge. Sean is an ass, but Edward is right there in the thick of it, yet he is so quiet I overlook him," Stella said. "He climbs. He hunts. He does a lot of winter sports, right? That's kind of his thing."

"He was born right in town," Shabina said. "I hear everything at the café. He was raised by his grandmother. Still lives in the same house, from what I understand. He inherited it after she died. One of the women in town was talking to her friend at lunch one day—this was a couple of years ago—and she mentioned that he took her back to the house after a dinner date. She said the house was super creepy. There were lace doilies everywhere, that the furniture and pictures and everything seemed out of time, as if nothing had been touched since his grandmother's day. It was dark, with old heavy drapes covering the windows. She didn't like the way the house smelled, like old moth balls or something. In any case, she couldn't relax and ended up going home before anything happened. She never went out with him again."

"How strange. He seems like a modern man. He's got all the

latest toys and equipment," Stella said. "His truck, his climbing gear, snowmobile, all of it is the latest and greatest."

Shabina sighed. "Let's go for a walk in the gardens. This isn't getting us anywhere. I'm sorry I can't be of more help."

"It was a long shot. I knew it when I brought this to you," Stella admitted. She followed Shabina outside, the three Dobermans rushing out with them. Inhaling the crisp October air, she took a moment to savor the fact that she didn't feel anyone watching her. She could relax. Maybe she just needed to move in with Shabina for a few days for some respite.

# CHAPTER SIXTEEN

The body of the hunter, Victor Bane, was found nearly immediately by his brother, Lawrence, who had gone looking for him just before sunset. It appeared as if Victor had fallen from his tree stand and broken his neck. His brother was very confused by the "accident," as Victor always took safety precautions and wore his harness faithfully.

Lawrence had packed in Victor's gear himself. Lawrence had been the one to set up the tree stand and see to it that Victor was comfortable and had everything he needed before Lawrence left his brother to his favorite sport. Victor was good at hunting. He was the one who usually provided the meat for winter, and he was proud of his skills. He had multiple sclerosis and it was all he could do to hike and backpack the trails at times, but he did it. He hunted from a tree stand now, but he was still accurate. He never took a shot if his hands were shaky.

Nothing about the "accident" made sense. Lawrence kept repeating it over and over to anyone who would listen. Victor wouldn't have tried to climb down without him being right there. If he shot a deer, they used walkie-talkies to communicate. Lawrence would have come. If there was an emergency, he had a satellite phone.

Vienna told them all that the ME found it suspicious that the left ring finger had two breaks on it in exactly the same places as the climbers and James Marley. She even had the sheriff come in and take a look. He didn't seem to think, even with four people having the exact same breaks on the exact same finger, that he could build any kind of a case. Falling from tree stands wasn't all that uncommon, and when you added multiple sclerosis to the mix, it stood to reason that an accident was an accident. The ME had a drink with Vienna and voiced her concerns. She said four people with exactly the same breaks on exactly the same finger was pushing the boundaries of coincidence for her. When Vienna had pushed her, asking what she was considering, the ME had backed off, shrugging, just shaking her head.

Stella couldn't blame her. What were the odds of a climbing accident on Mount Whitney, a fishing accident on Sunrise Lake and a hunting accident in the Inyo National Forest being in any way tied together? If the sheriff didn't think broken fingers were enough to build a case—and she knew he was right—then what was she going to do? Stella didn't blame him either. Even if he did think there was cause to think Victor's death wasn't an accident, there were no witnesses. There was nothing whatsoever, no evidence to suggest a serial killer had murdered him. That was the danger of this killer. Other than his "signature" of the broken finger, there was no way to identify his kills.

Stella cried over the hunter, but she'd all but resigned herself to the fact that she wasn't going to be able to save him. There just weren't enough clues to find him in time.

Shabina called and asked if Stella wanted to come for a girls' night at her place. Sam insisted that she go, that she needed at least a night off before Bailey was back and the killer struck again, as his timetable seemed to be getting shorter and shorter. Sam was afraid that meant he was unraveling.

It felt good to just climb into her favorite pair of leggings and a long shirt, eat pizza and be with her friends. Stella found it strange to be without Bailey, but Shabina's Dobermans, Raine's Jack Russell and Harlow's beagle were all there. Zahra had lost her dog two years earlier and continued to vacillate between getting another dog or a little black kitten. Where she got that idea, no one knew. She'd been heartbroken when she'd lost her beloved rough-coated half–Pyrenean Shepherd and half something no one knew. Her energetic gray, black and white Elara had been twenty pounds of sheer fun. Zahra continued to say if she got another dog, she would get the same combination, although she swore Elara wore her out "forcing" her to take her out for runs a hundred times a day. All of them knew Zahra didn't like to run. She shared Stella's view of the pastime. Jogging was okay, but running was just the worst possible thing in the world. For her dog, she sacrificed with much complaining.

Stella sat tailor-fashion on the floor of Shabina's great room with its luxurious carpet that one could practically swim in. The huge stone fireplace was lit, the flames burning orange and red, casting images on the walls. Instead of sitting on the cozy sofas and chairs, all six women sat on the floor, using the furniture as back supports. Over the last few years, they'd gotten comfortable sitting that way. In the center of their circle were bowls of popcorn and small chocolate bars Shabina had made for the evening.

"I'm going to gain so much weight tonight," Zahra moaned as she chose another one of the bars. "I wouldn't eat it, but just looking at it puts weight on my thighs, so I might as well enjoy it."

"There is this thing called exercise," Stella said. "Miguel, our personal trainer, is still on speed dial."

"Don't speak his name to me," Zahra sniffed indignantly. "He no longer exists. Not after telling me I have to swipe my badge at the desk if I want in his class."

The other women burst out laughing. "You never swipe your badge, Zahra," Harlow pointed out. "In fact, you don't bring your badge."

"If he doesn't know who I am by now, there's something seriously wrong with him." Zahra's dark eyes were passionate as they normally were when she was very serious about a subject. "Miguel Valdez can take his badge swiper he's so fond of and shove it somewhere he doesn't want to talk about. Besides, he's so *mean* to me when he's making us do our workouts."

Stella rolled her eyes. "Don't even go there. You make one little complaint and for you he changes the workout, but he makes me do the same hideous and extremely difficult program no matter what. And it's always easy for you. You never sweat and I look like I dove into a swimming pool. My face is lobster red, even my eyelashes have sweat on them, and Miguel is over there helping you up and staring into your big brown eyes."

The others burst out laughing. Harlow tossed a piece of popcorn at Zahra. "Stella has a point. I work out all the time and you just lie around complaining about how hard it is to run and then you just go out and run, talking the *entire* time, never running out of air or things to say while I'm keeling over."

Zahra raised her dark eyebrows and stared at them all soberly, looking serious and innocent. None of them were buying into it.

"You're a flirt too," Vienna accused. "There isn't a male in town, no matter the age, who isn't enamored with you. I was juggling three bags of groceries and you had one. *One.* Two silly teenage boys come up and it's, 'Oh, Zahra, can I carry that for you?'" She used a teen voice and rolled her eyes.

Zahra shrugged and examined her fingernails, a little smirk curving her lips. Even that was attractive. "I can't help it if these boys are polite, Vienna. You glare at them when they try to help. You speak of women's independence. I only want to be independent when it suits me. Taking out trash doesn't suit me. Doing Miguel's torture exercises and swiping my name badge certainly doesn't suit me. And I despise running unless I have my dog with me, which I no longer do, so running is a chore. I even hated it then, but I did it for her."

"I swear, I'm getting you another dog," Harlow groused.

"I've been thinking I should be a cat lady like Vienna. She has a white cat and I'll get a black cat and call her Matilda."

"You need a dog to run with you," Raine said firmly. "Eat another chocolate bar."

Zahra obediently chose one and took a bite, again moaning as if she were in ecstasy. "Who needs a man when we have Shabina's bars?"

There was another round of laughter. Stella leaned her head back against the sofa, grateful that she had such good friends. Sam was right, she'd needed them—needed the closeness of them. The laughter they shared. Still, they had gathered for a purpose. She could tell there was an underlying tension that ran between them. They wanted her comfortable and mellow, in a soft, trusting, open mood.

She took one of the chocolate bars and regarded her friends. "You may as well get to the main subject, because I know you want to talk to me about something. None of you has a poker face with the exception of Vienna." She laughed at her own joke. It was a little significant that none of them really laughed with her. They smiled, but they didn't laugh. If anything, they looked uneasy.

Stella sat up a little straighter. She looked around Shabina's living room at all of her friends. They looked troubled, and no one seemed to want to bring up what was bothering them. She looked to Zahra. She never understood what it was about Zahra that she'd gravitated to right from the beginning. They had very different personalities, but she knew, even if it sounded weird, they were soul mates. She could count on Zahra.

"What's going on? We all have our drinks. We're comfortable, or should be, but you look like someone is about to do in your best friend. Me, I've had a lot of blows the last few weeks, so just get it over with. Tell me."

The women exchanged long looks between them. Stella took a drink of her margarita and wished she had Bailey to comfort her.

It wasn't Zahra, but Vienna, who was the one to answer her. "I spoke to Amelia Sanderson, the vet, about Bailey and his wounds."

Immediately, Stella tensed, fearful Amelia might have given Vienna bad news she wouldn't have given Stella, maybe long-term effects that Bailey would suffer.

"Given the number of stab wounds on his body, his size and power, the fact that he was stabbed while attacking and yet no major damage was done to his internal organs, whoever used that knife on him had to know what they were doing. They knew anatomy."

Stella frowned, her eyes on Vienna's, trying to comprehend what her friend was getting at. "You're saying whoever stabbed Bailey didn't want to kill him."

"Amelia says the attacker had a big knife and he could have

killed Bailey, but he didn't. He punched down about two inches and raked, opening lacerations but avoiding any internal organs. Bailey had charged, probably bit him. There was blood on his teeth. He maybe had one arm in his mouth. The man had to be strong and he had to be calm throughout the entire attack. That takes someone incredibly well trained."

Vienna fell silent. The other women avoided Stella's gaze. She took another drink of her icy margarita. Morza, one of the Dobermans, rose and padded over to Stella to drop down beside her. He had always been her favorite of the three.

"Hey, baby. Are you missing Bailey too?" Stella continued to meet Vienna's eyes. She was going somewhere with this. "I'm listening."

"It was dark. You were running toward them. The attacker only had seconds and yet he got in four stab wounds, Stella. That would ensure that you would have to take Bailey down the mountain to the vet as quickly as possible in order to keep him from bleeding out. An ambulance would transport Sonny."

Stella frowned. "I know all this, I was there, remember?"

"Honey," Zahra said, gentle for her. "Think about how calm this attacker would have to be. How strong. How many men do you know like that?"

"How many men know anatomy?" Vienna persisted.

Stella shrugged. "Most of the men in this area hunt for meat to carry their families through the winter. They're incredibly strong because they climb and they pack out their kills. They know anatomy because they cut up that meat and package it. You aren't eliminating suspects."

"Who do you know that could remain that calm during an attack by a ferocious dog weighing in at sixty-five pounds? Bailey's all muscle. The attacker would have had to deliberately shove his arm into Bailey's mouth and then stab him repeatedly knowing you were running toward them. He got Bailey down and calmly backed off, most likely watching you attending to your dog while the sheriff came to help. Who do you know who is that strong, and that absolutely cool under fire?"

She blinked. Her stomach dropped. Sam. They were talking about Sam. She looked at each of their faces. Vienna. Zahra. Shabina. Harlow. Raine. Raine was the only one who looked unconvinced. In fact, she looked as if the others were so far off base, she thought they were nuts. Clearly, she had argued against their reasoning.

Stella shook her head slowly. She didn't understand how any of them could think the serial killer could possibly be Sam. He wasn't like that. He might kill if he had to, but he wouldn't kill indiscriminately. "The serial killer isn't Sam. Don't you think I would know? I'm sleeping with him, for heaven's sake."

No one said anything. Stella sighed and tried again. "For one thing, Vienna, he was with you on Whitney when the two climbers were thrown over the edge."

"He wasn't though. We split up."

Stella glared at her, not because she thought Sam was guilty but because that had put Vienna in danger. "You promised the two of you would stick together. Do you have any idea how much danger you were in? You could have been killed."

"I decided the killer was looking for a couple, not one single woman or one single man. We were in more danger together," Vienna argued. "We had clearly missed the intended targets and didn't know why, so we split up to cover more ground. In the end, it didn't matter. We were too late. So, no, I wasn't with him."

"Nevertheless, Sam isn't the serial killer. He was attacked first. Remember? I was there. I dove into the water. I saw someone in a diving suit trying to drown him. That diver hit me in the face and then kicked me in the chest. Do you think I'm making that up in order to protect him?"

She did her best to keep the belligerence out of her voice. She had to remind herself these were her friends and they had real concerns. They wanted her to be safe. From their perspective, Sam might be a logical choice. They didn't know him the way she did. He could be intimidating at times, she could acknowledge that. There were all kinds of rumors about him. Even Denver, his closest friend, had warned her about him. Raine had told her to be cautious about the relationship.

"No one thinks you would lie to protect Sam, Stella," Vienna said. "But the fact is, he could have had help. He could have set up that attack on himself easily. He barely had a scrape on his head. Certainly not enough to lose consciousness."

"He told me he hadn't lost consciousness," Stella admitted. "It isn't him. For one thing, he wouldn't have to break into the house, he knows the code to get in, and someone tried to break in after the attack on Sonny. And I'd see bite marks on his body from Bailey. I do actually see him naked. More than any of that, I know him. It isn't him."

"You'd better be certain, Stella," Harlow said. "People you love can be monsters."

"My father is a serial killer, Harlow," Stella pointed out quietly. "I think I know very well how people we love can be monsters. I also know that killers can have sudden episodes of enormous strength. I know that the hunters in this area are strong. They know anatomy. Climbers are strong and they are very calm in moments of extreme crisis. We have many climbers in the area that are hunters as well. I can tell you positively, without reservation, the serial killer isn't Sam."

"And you've seen his arms since the attack on Bailey?" Vienna persisted. "I'm sorry to push so hard, Stella," she added when Stella made a face, "but we love you and we have to be absolutely certain you're safe."

Stella took another sip of her margarita and then nodded her head slowly, deliberately giving them her eyes darkened with sexual "memories." "I *have* seen both arms, legs, as well as his *entire* very gorgeous body. Numerous times, I might add. There wasn't a single bite mark that I didn't put there myself. He doesn't like to wear clothes to bed and he likes to wake me up in very interesting ways. The thing about Sam is, he's very good at anything he does. Have you noticed that? He's focused. Very, very focused."

"Stop," Harlow said and pressed both hands over her ears.

"No, you need to know how focused he gets, so you understand that I've learned that same focus from him. He inspects every square inch of me with his tongue. I can't tell you how that feels. How he does this delicious little butterfly move that makes me want to scream and he isn't even to the good parts yet . . ."

"*Stella,*" Shabina wailed. "Give us a break."

"Just making certain you know I inspect him thoroughly and he's super big in . . . er . . . *that* department, so I spend a bit of time there. The dog didn't do any damage there and I'd be *quite* upset if he had. I would have reported that immediately."

"That comes under the heading of TMI," Raine said. "Even I have to object."

Zahra threw her pillow, hitting Stella square in the face. "I don't want to look at that man and wonder about his package. Don't say another word."

Stella was having too much fun. Her friends were either looking horrified or laughing, or doing both at the same time.

"I want you to know how it is totally impossible for the killer to be Sam when I've examined his body with the same absolute focus and attention he puts into mine. No scratches from Bailey's claws, but there are a few from me in the throes of—"

A hail of pillows came her way as the other women threw them, pelting her fast with every throw pillow Shabina had in the room they could get their hands on. Stella nearly dropped her margarita on the carpet. She barely managed to get it onto the end table, she was laughing so hard and fending off the pillow attack.

"I'll never get those images out of my head," Harlow said. "Ugh. Thanks a lot."

"I could have been way more descriptive, but Sam is very private," Stella said. "And you know, he probably has the room bugged or something, given that he was a secret agent." She whispered the last two words.

Instantly the women sobered and looked at one another and then around the room. Raine reached for one of the wayward pillows and buried her face in it.

"He was a secret agent?" Zahra repeated. "Like James Bond?"

"He couldn't really bug my house. My security is too good," Shabina said. Her eyebrows drew together. "Raine? Could someone really hack my security?"

Raine tried to look very serious. "I suppose James Bond could." She burst out laughing. "You all are so easy."

Vienna scowled at her. "We are talking about ruthless killers, Raine. And we're helpless women alone in a huge house on a dark and stormy night."

They all looked at the windows. The wind was blowing, but there was no rain. In fact, the moon and stars were out.

"Out of curiosity, how many of you are armed?" Shabina asked.

Stella raised her hand. Shabina, Raine, Harlow and Vienna all raised their hands.

Zahra raised her eyebrows. "Really? I'm the only one without a gun?"

"You have some kind of weapon on you," Stella said. "I know you, Zahra."

"Nothing so crude as a gun."

"So, it isn't stormy and we're not so helpless," Raine concluded.

They all began laughing again. Vienna shrugged and poured herself another drink from the pitcher on the low coffee table. "I got the part about it being dark right."

"Guns are crude?" Stella echoed. "Since when?"

"They're heavy. When you're walking on the trail, with those horrid backpacks you insist I carry, they just add more weight. I have become a minimalist," Zahra declared.

Another round of laughter went up. With great dignity, Zahra rose, skirted around Stella and the dogs, and filled her glass with the contents of the pitcher.

"I don't understand why you're all laughing. Do you even know what a minimalist is?" Zahra asked, her nose in the air. She made her way back to her spot, collecting pillows as she went. "These are really nice, Shabina, where did you get them? You always find the nicest things for your house."

"Babe," Harlow objected. "You can't be buying pillows for your house if you're a minimalist."

Zahra sipped her drink and scowled at Harlow over the top of it. "Of course I can. I'm a minimalist when it comes to gear. Each of you has enough gear to open a sports store. Stella, have you ever thrown out one piece of climbing gear no matter how old it is?"

Stella opened her mouth, closed it and then shook her head.

"Don't turn the spotlight on me. I'm not the one saying guns are crude and heavy. What sort of weapon did you bring?"

Zahra gave one of her mysterious smiles. She could easily have posed for an art painting with that beautiful smile that gave nothing away. "An ancient weapon that requires skills but can be quite deadly in the right hands."

"You had to practice to be able to use it?" Shabina asked.

"As in you actually lifted one of your beautifully manicured nails in order to learn?" Vienna sounded doubtful.

"She didn't say she could actually wield said weapon," Raine pointed out. "Only that she had it on her."

"Oh, ye of little faith." Zahra gave a haughty little indignant sniff. "I'm fairly accurate and I enjoy the challenge, much better than if I was trying to shoot someone." She lifted her arm and shot back her oversized sweater to show the rows of small beads on the bracelet on her wrist. The beads were small and highly polished, looked to be black onyx, or a stone such as that.

"Can you really use that as a weapon?" Stella asked.

Zahra touched the beads and then pulled down her sweater. "Yes. I'm getting better every single day. It took a while to get comfortable with it on my wrist, but I wear it every day and practice with it. I've been doing so since I lost Elara. It gave me something to do while I debated whether to get another dog."

"You're getting another dog," they all said simultaneously.

Zahra rolled her eyes again. "I suppose I am. I just don't know when. I keep thinking I'll make inquiries, but then I don't. I don't want to put expectations on a new puppy. That wouldn't be fair to the little girl. I want the same breed, so right off the bat, I think it might be hard for both of us. I mean, how do you get the same mix?"

"The Pyrenean Shepherds have different looks, Zahra," Raine

said. "I researched them thoroughly. Different colors and coats. And there are rescues that have mixes. They won't be exactly the same, but you don't really want the puppy to be the same."

The women all nodded in agreement.

"You all researched?" Zahra asked.

"Of course. We were going to get you one for your birthday. We tried rescue places, but they didn't have any available."

"You're going to make me cry. That's so sweet." Zahra did look like she might cry. "It would be nice to have a little companion, although that running was a pain. I'd have to teach it to want to walk at a mild pace."

The laughter was genuine at the thought of that particular very energetic breed walking when it could run. Zahra was well aware of the breed's need for exercise and she really didn't mind at all, as much as she liked to complain.

"How in the world did you ever get into playing poker for a living, Vienna?" Zahra asked. "I tried to practice not showing any expression on my face when I was coming over here and I knew we'd be talking to Stella about Sam, but the more I practiced, the worse it got. If I was playing a high-stakes poker game with a bunch of mean men who wanted to see me fail, I'd be sweating bullets."

Vienna shrugged. "I needed money and I was good at cards. I didn't really know about counting cards so much as I don't forget cards. I don't forget much of anything I see, so playing cards is easy enough as long as I get the right cards. Sometimes it isn't always about skill. I also study people. That helped too. And my opponents tend to underestimate me. The most difficult part was getting started. Getting enough money to buy into the game." She gave them a little half smile. "Then once you start winning, it's all about figuring out how to keep your winnings. Everyone's out to take it from you."

"Do you enjoy it?" Raine asked.

Vienna nodded. "Very much. I'm careful though. I've seen too many people get addicted to gambling. It isn't winning money that's thrilling for me, although it's always a rush. It's taking down the bullies. I guess when you were the one that got pushed around all the time, you get so you can spot the ones who enjoy doing the pushing. I can see them a mile way."

"Like Bale," Shabina said.

Vienna nodded. "Exactly like Bale. He's a bully. He has to run the show. His friends had better fall into line, and so had everyone else. If they don't, he makes fun of them and mocks them until they do what he wants. He'll keep going at them until he gets his way. I've watched him do it, even to his best friends. They rarely stand up to him. Sean comes the closest, and when he does, he disappears for days on end into the forest, probably waiting until he thinks Bale is over his little snit."

"I can imagine the ones in Vegas are even worse than Bale," Stella ventured.

"I don't know about worse," Vienna said thoughtfully, "but certainly more entitled. They have money, way too much money, and they each think they're the best at cards. They don't want some woman to come along and take their reputation away. It's humiliating to them. I mean, they smile and play it off nice, but you can see those tempers smoldering below the surface. I wire the money to my accounts before I ever leave the hotel and then have security walk me to my car. Even then, I had two incidents where someone tried to run me off the road on my way home. They weren't playing either."

"Vienna." Harlow breathed her name. "I hope you went to the police. Did you at least have the money to hire bodyguards after that? You lived in Vegas. Is that why you ended up here? Are you hiding out?"

Vienna laughed. "Nothing so dramatic, Harlow. I came up here every chance I had because it brought me peace when I never felt like I had any. There's something about the Sierras that slows everything down for me and puts it in perspective. I can see what true beauty is and what really matters, and the money isn't important. Putting the slap-down on the bullies isn't important. Taking the breath of fresh air and watching the sun come up over the lake makes the world right for me. When I got the chance, I moved up here permanently."

"Are you close with your mother?" Shabina asked.

"There was a time I was. We were best friends. I thought we'd always be close. She met someone and she's very happy, or so she says. I hope she is. I pay her rent and send her extra money for utilities and groceries. She writes and sends postcards she designs, inviting me to come see her and her lover. But when I do visit her, she's so nervous, I'm uncomfortable and have the feeling she doesn't want me there. I never stay more than a few minutes and she doesn't try to get me to stay."

"Is her lover there when you visit?"

"Never." Vienna looked down at her drink. "That's my fault really, not my mom's. She never talked about my father. In fact, when I asked about him, she refused to talk about him. I have no idea who he is. It's weird, like I was born into this void. No grandparents or siblings. There were no photographs or family history. Mom never talked about her past at all. It was always just the two of us."

Vienna rarely talked about her past, so all of them stayed silent. Stella wished Bailey was there. He was very fond of Vienna and he would have sensed her mood and gone to her to comfort her. She sipped at her drink and waited.

Vienna looked up at them. They hadn't turned on lights so it was only the low flames from the fireplace throwing those dancing colors onto the walls that lit up the room enough to see her expression of regret.

"I was so childish when Mom announced she'd fallen in love. I want her to be happy. For heaven's sake, I'm a grown woman. I don't want her alone or living her life out with me and my cat. It was just that I fought so hard for her to stay alive and then suddenly, out of the blue, she tells me she's fallen in love. She met a woman named Ellen at the infusion center. She was a volunteer there. They became friends."

Zahra frowned. "Did you know she preferred women?"

Vienna shook her head. "She never dated. Not once. Not men or women. Not throughout my childhood or when I was an adult. She never discussed her sexuality with me. I thought I knew everything about her. I didn't think we had secrets from each other, but it seems my entire life was built on secrets."

She gave them a shaky smile and took another drink of her icy margarita. "Thank heavens for midnight margaritas. This is a great way to spend the night."

Zahra raised her glass first. The others followed suit and they drank solemnly.

"You've never met Ellen?" Stella asked, to prompt Vienna to keep talking.

Vienna shook her head. "No. Mom and I had a terrible fight when she told me. Like I said, it was my fault. I reacted like a jealous teenager, not wanting my mommy to date. I'm embarrassed to think about how truly selfish and childish I acted. I'd been going to nursing school full-time and playing a few high-stakes games to keep the money coming in to pay the bills. I was exhausted and someone had tried to run me off the road. That was the night she chose to disclose how happy she was. I was at my lowest point. Scared. I wanted comfort and to talk things over with her. I was even considering putting off nursing school in order to pay off the medical bills faster so I wasn't burning the candle at both ends."

"Oh no," Harlow whispered.

Vienna nodded. "It still doesn't excuse my reaction. I dragged myself through the door and she was all over me, hugging and practically jumping up and down she was so excited. She didn't notice what a mess I was or that I'd been crying. She just blurted out her news. I remember staring at her. Just standing in the entryway of our apartment staring at her with my jacket still on. I couldn't talk. I couldn't get one word out. I really, really wish it had remained that way, because when I did talk, the things I said were horrible."

Silence fell again so only the crackling of the fire remained. One of Shabina's dogs, Sharif, padded over to the bank of windows and pressed his nose to the glass.

"That's always my signal to close the blinds," Shabina said. "He's bossy that way. At least he allows me to have them open if there's a storm. He knows I like to watch storms." She used the remote to bring down the privacy screens, covering all the windows simultaneously.

"Doesn't your name mean 'eye of the storm'?" Stella asked.

"Yes, although my father says I am the storm." Shabina sank back down and rested her back against the sofa. Sharif curled up beside her.

Vienna frowned. "Of all of us, Shabina, you're probably the sweetest. Why in the world would your father think that?"

"Excuse me," Zahra said, her dark brows drawing together. "I believe I'm the sweetest."

Laughter broke out immediately, and Zahra endured it with great dignity. She poured herself the last of the margaritas from the pitcher. "All of you are not my friends right now. And I'm eating the rest of the chocolate bars, so don't touch them."

Stella stood up. "I'll make a fresh pitcher of margaritas. It won't take long."

"There's lots of different cookies in the kitchen," Shabina called after her. "Throw some on another platter since Zahra isn't sharing."

"Only because the lot of you refuse to acknowledge I'm sweet." Zahra sat back down and took another bar. She waited until Stella was back and had topped everyone off with a fresh drink. "How bad did it get between you and your mom, Vienna?"

Vienna frowned over the exquisite stemware. "I hurled insults at her until she finally hurled them back. But then she said something to the effect of she wasted her entire life in hiding, a sword hanging over her head for what? I wasn't even her own blood. I know she said that. I *know* it. She stopped abruptly, turning white. She even put her hand over her mouth. I asked her what she meant and she said I was mistaken. That she hadn't said that. Maybe I wished she had. Too bad for me, I was just going to have to deal. She was the one who got very ugly after that, saying really nasty things. I believe she did so on purpose in order to keep me from going back to that little piece of the fight that actually held the truth about my past."

Stella found herself a little shocked by Vienna's story. She sounded hurt, and Stella could understand why. Vienna had grown up close to Mitzi, her mother, just the two of them. She'd worked hard to help her mother survive and was happy to do so. It had to have felt like betrayal even if Vienna was an adult. It had always been the two of them, and suddenly bringing in a third party without any warning would have blindsided her.

They should have worked it out by now. Why hadn't they? It made no sense that they hadn't. Too many years had slipped by. Vienna's mother had had cancer once already. Vienna was a nurse. She knew how quickly one could lose loved ones in accidents or to illness. She knew how often cancer returned.

"Have you tried to talk to your mother since that night about what was said, Vienna?" Stella asked, her voice as gentle as she could make it.

Vienna nodded. "I think that's why she gets uncomfortable when she does see me. She's so terrified I'll bring it up. She doesn't want to answer any questions. I tell myself I won't ask, but then, do I want to take a chance on losing her and never knowing where I came from if she really isn't my mother?" She made a face. "Even saying that out loud in front of my closest friends sounds ridiculous. Of course, she's my mother. We're so much alike. Maybe not in looks, but in every other way. I don't want anyone else to be my mother."

"No one else is," Raine said. "She raised you. She was there for you every step of the way. That makes her your mother whether or not she gave birth to you. I'm with Stella on this, Vienna, you need to find a way to resolve it. Maybe invite the two of them here for a special dinner at Shabina's with all of us. That way the conversation won't turn to anything that personal. We could all help with dinner."

"Actually, that's not a bad idea, Vienna," Stella said. "Do you think they'd come? We could gift them with a room at the hotel in town."

Vienna was silent, struggling not to cry. "All of you are the absolute best. I'll consider it, but I might want to wait until after we catch this serial killer. I don't want Stella to suddenly see him lurking in the hotel hallway while my mother is there."

Stella nodded. "Now that you mention that, it might be a better plan to wait."

# CHAPTER SEVENTEEN

*Mommy, Daddy's doing the bad thing again.*

The early morning sun tried to shine through drifting clouds. Dirt, rock and overgrown yellow and brown grass covered with mostly small debris that had drifted on the wind lay on the ground. Twigs. Leaves. Pine needles. The trail wasn't well used or well marked, but still, as Stella observed it through the narrow lens, something about it seemed familiar.

Two people walked along that path of uneven dirt and overgrown grass. She caught glimpses of shadows on the ground. Two men, both tall with what could have been backpacks, making them appear misshapen.

She felt the mood of each of them because they were both broadcasting so strongly. Both were excited. Both anticipating. They were talking, laughing. Friendly. Knew each other. She strained to listen. To hear what they were saying. At least catch the sound of their voices. She knew they were laughing and talking yet she couldn't make out the words. Laughter? Could she identify them through laughter? There was a strange thudding in her ears interfering with her ability to hear. Her own heartbeat pounded like a drum so loud she was afraid the two men might hear her.

While both seemed to share the same emotions for the day's climb, one felt more. One felt pure elation, a smug rush of sly glee, of absolute power. Instinctively she knew the killer was anticipating taking his time with this "accident." He not only knew his victim but also was friends with him. This was new. She did her best to stay calm and tried to adjust the lens of the camera in an effort to open it wider. It didn't work, only frustrated her that she couldn't ferret out additional clues on the shadows of the men or see more than the ground they covered at the fast pace the two set.

The lens began to close, that narrow opening shuttering, leaving her staring at a black screen.

STELLA SAT UP, heart pounding, scrubbing her hands down her face over and over, trying to wipe away the child's fear and face the nightmare as a grown-up. "I know them," she whispered and looked up, confident Sam would be there.

They'd gone to bed together, his arms around her, but when she had her nightmares, he always did the same thing—he gave her space. Instinctively, he seemed to know she needed it. He sat right across the room from her, directly in her line of vision, so all she had to do was look up and she'd find him. Just knowing he was there settled the terrible twisting knots in her stomach and allowed her to breathe when her lungs felt raw and burning.

Sam looked back at her, his dark eyes on her. She could see the love there and it warmed her. Sometimes it shocked her. They didn't say words like *love* between them. They were new. Two years might not be new, and they'd been together that long even if they never acknowledged it, but their feelings for each other had definitely been growing during that time.

She attempted a smile. It was shaky, but it was there. "He definitely has escalated his timetable, hasn't he? He wasn't very satisfied with his last kill to act so fast. One day? I don't know if I can keep doing this. Maybe we should talk to the FBI."

"You're exhausted, Stella." Sam's voice was gentle. "You're not getting much sleep, and after the attack on Bailey, you sleep for an hour or two and wake up. You and I both know the FBI can't catch him because there isn't any evidence. He's not leaving anything behind. The most we have on him that even says he exists are the broken fingers. Even the ME would say that's thin. There's an explanation for every broken bone."

"I know." Stella got out of bed and went to him, breaking pattern. She couldn't help it. "Sam." She crawled into his lap, putting her arms around his neck, allowing him to comfort her. "I know both of them. I know I do. There was something about them that was so familiar to me but I just couldn't pin it down."

She buried her face against his chest. He felt invincible. His heartbeat strong. His chest like iron. His arms surrounding her, a secure fortress. She just wanted to stay there for a little while and hide. Be safe. Not have to think about losing this round to the serial killer. Not have to think that she might uncover a friend and know that all along he'd been a vicious murderer, capable of walking with someone he knew, knowing he was going to kill him.

Sam's palm shaped the back of her head and then stroked caresses down her hair. "It's all right to grieve for him, sweetheart. For the loss of a friend. Whoever he is, he was lost to us the moment he went down this path. He isn't that same person anymore and we can't think of him that way. That means, Stella, we already lost a friend."

"I don't want to lose two of them." She lifted her head and looked into his eyes. "I've failed so many times now. I can't fail this time. I know the victim. There was something about the voices. The laughter. I can't say what it was. The lens didn't stay open long enough, but I know I should be able to identify both of them. And the place they were going to climb."

She frowned, biting down on her lower lip, trying to remember.

"You need to do what you always do, sweetheart. Draw it. The details come to you. Once you draw it, you can see if anything rings a bell. I'll look at it as well and then you run it by your posse. They all climb."

Stella slid rather reluctantly off his lap. He was always warm, and the loss of his heat made her shiver. Or maybe it was just the idea of knowing the serial killer was spiraling out of control. "He seemed so gleeful, Sam. So smug. I hated knowing that he was talking and laughing with a friend of his and all the while he was plotting to kill him. He was taking pleasure in knowing that."

She slipped back into bed and retrieved her sketchpad, journal and pencils from the safe built into the wall. "He isn't here tonight. No one is watching us. Or at least I can't feel him."

"I can't either. I did nose around a bit up along the side of the ridge above the bend in the lake, almost directly across from us. I figured if anyone really wanted a vantage point and they knew the property, that would be the most likely place to build a camp. They could stay there indefinitely with the right supplies, rain, shine or even snow, and be somewhat protected."

"Great. I thought you'd already discovered his hiding place after Bailey was attacked."

"That was too easy. I considered how intelligent this killer is and factored that in along with the idea that he was obsessed with you."

Stella shuddered. "I'd rather not think about him being fixated on me, Sam."

"I know it sucks, but when you considered the timing of your first nightmare, it really was around the time we started cementing our relationship. It is possible the killer saw us together and didn't like the way we were looking at each other. Or the way I was looking at you, at least. Sometimes I don't hide my feelings for you as well as I should."

She had pulled the covers over her legs, but at his last statement, she fisted the blankets and blinked at him. "Man." There was a lump in her throat she was afraid she might choke on.

"Woman." His voice was so velvet soft it caressed her skin.

"You don't look at me openly like you're wild about me. You hide your feelings very well. It's me that gets a little crazy when I'm drinking. I . . . say things."

His smile started slow and her stomach did a little somersault. Then the smile actually lit up his eyes and she melted inside. He did that to her so easily now.

"I do recall there was one night when I poured you and your friends into the 4Runner and drove you home. You did say I was gorgeous. And *hot* is another word you used, I believe."

"Did I say it in the bar?"

He nodded. "Several times. Straddling my lap. You kissed me twice. That was about the time I decided you'd had enough and I was taking you home. I could only take so much. Don't get me wrong, sweetheart, I was enjoying every second of it, but things were getting out of control."

She closed her eyes. "I was really hoping all the things I

*thought* about doing to you, I didn't actually *try* doing to you." She opened her eyes. "I did, didn't I?"

"I just picked you up and hauled your ass to the rig. Believe me, sweetheart, the only one suffering that night was me."

"And then you nearly got killed the next morning." She frowned and stroked her fingers over the sketchpad. "Do you remember what happened the weekend before? What we were doing? The nightmares started earlier. If the catalyst really was seeing you and me getting together, then we had to have been showing signs of that earlier in the week, Sam."

Her stomach muscles knotted. She didn't want her memory to be the same as the one he might name. She had kept this one sacred moment close to her, something special, when she had so few. She didn't want to think a serial killer had started murdering because he may have witnessed that "private" intimacy between them.

His expression softened. Sam was hard edges. Hard angles and planes. When he looked at her with that particular look, the one he didn't give to anyone else, she knew he was hers and he made her feel safe and wanted.

"Stella, we've been together for over two years. We go into town together all the time. We buy supplies for the resort. We stand close when we're looking at your list that is written in some kind of gibberish no one can possibly understand but you. I've got my hand on your shoulder or around your waist. You've got your hand on my arm when we're walking. We're comfortable with each other. We eat together every meal in town unless you're meeting one of your posse, and half the time I'm sitting at the table three feet from you looking out for you. Everyone knows how I feel about you. Everyone. I make it clear."

She nodded because everything he said was true. They did go

into town together. Sometime over the last couple of years that had just evolved. It still didn't explain what would have been different enough to trigger someone into becoming a serial killer. But she was afraid she knew. She hoped not, but she was afraid it was their first kiss—the kiss she had initiated.

"How do you make it clear that you feel something for me? No one can read your expression, Sam." She put it off one more time, struggling to make the killer have other reasons to stalk her.

"Men can read me loud and clear when it comes to you, Stella. There's a big *stay away* sign. Haven't you noticed the lack of males asking you out?"

"I put off vibes that say I'm not interested in dating."

"Did that stop them three years ago?"

She frowned. "Maybe not. I don't know. But if you were giving males the warning to stay away in some mysterious bro code that I missed completely for two years, why didn't the obsessed serial killer start his murder spree back then?"

"Because you were still closed off, sweetheart. You were slowly letting me in, but no one could see it but me. At first he thought we worked together and had to spend a lot of time together. Then we were friends. You have a lot of friends, and quite a few are males. You didn't seem to treat me much different than you did the others. At first. I suppose our relationship changed over time so slowly that he got used to it, just like you did."

Her frown deepened. "I don't understand."

"A lot of careful planning went into those two years. Looking over your shoulder to read your list, for instance. I'm taller, so I had to bend down. That required putting my hand on your shoulder to steady myself."

She narrowed her eyes at him. "You never lose your balance. Not in any situation."

For the first time ever, he actually grinned at her, and her heart reacted by nearly skipping a beat.

"No, I don't typically lose my balance, but I suppose it could happen."

"You were getting me used to you touching me."

He raised an eyebrow without a hint of remorse. "It worked. What do they say? All is fair in love and war. Courting you was a little of both."

She sat in the middle of her bed, back to the headboard, and contemplated the difference Sam had made in her life. She was no longer shaking and crying. No longer rocking back and forth. He was a rock to lean on, yet he didn't take over and fix things for her. He waited to talk things out when she was ready. And he'd taken his time, had the patience to "court" her differently, to gently insert himself into her life and make himself part of it, indispensable. She was both flattered and amused.

"You're a little bit scary."

He nodded. "The kind of man your best friends warn you about."

She laughed. "They certainly did." The smile faded. "If you were consistent, Sam, and we're going with the theory that the killer is obsessed with me, then something I did had to have triggered him, right?" *Don't let it be our first kiss. At least give me that.*

"It could have been a combination of things, Stella. Don't look for blame, that's a slippery road."

"I'm actually not. I'm trying to remember what I might have done differently, how I might have acted toward you right before the nightmares started. That would give us an idea of who was around then."

She already knew, but she wanted it to be something else, not that precise moment in time when she had been so certain she had made a complete and utter fool of herself. She had hoped no one saw her and Sam didn't remember, but of course he did. She'd done her best not to think about it, when she'd thought about it every night until the nightmares started.

"You were on the street with Bailey and me, trying to decide whether to go shopping right then or have lunch with Raine. We didn't have a lot of time because we had to get back and meet with the inspector. You hadn't seen Raine in over a week. No one had, and you were worried about her. I told you I'd get the chores done and take care of Bailey, to just text Raine to meet you at Shabina's café. You did and she immediately said she could meet you. You threw your arms around me and kissed me. Right there on the street in front of everyone."

She felt a fiery red creep up her skin from her neck to her face. "I did not." But she had. She remembered that kiss very vividly. It had started out very chaste. A thank-you. She meant to just kind of brush her lips against his. But then she tasted him. It should have stopped right there. He should have stiffened up or pushed her away.

Sam wasn't the kind of man who invited women to drape themselves all over him. At least if he was, she didn't know about it. His arm had come around her like an iron bar, locking her to him, and one hand bunched in her hair and then . . . well . . . she just was lost. There was nothing but feeling and fire, and she forgot where she was. She melted into him. He had to steady her, putting his hands on her hips, holding her away from him while she blinked up at him like a complete idiot, wondering what had just happened. Then she nearly went right to the sidewalk because her legs turned to jelly. Seriously, it had been that ridiculously bad. She closed the door on her behavior.

"I'm fairly certain, Sam, you kissed me."

"Anyone watching us would have seen that you initiated the action, *Satine*. I may have taken advantage of the situation, but you definitely initiated."

"Do you think anyone really paid any attention?"

His eyebrow lifted. "Sweetheart. Really? We were right in the middle of town, out in the open. You're royalty. You're out on the street, everyone is looking. Then you almost walked out into the middle of traffic and I had to stop you. You nearly made me laugh. That probably got a little reaction out of anyone watching. I walked you to the café just to make sure you made it because you were in a daze."

"I was not." She had been.

"Woman."

"He saw me kiss you."

"Most likely."

"You knew all along."

"I considered the possibility when he kept watching you. He either knew who you were, or he was obsessed with you. If he knew who you were and that you would know he was a killer, he would expect you to contact the authorities. You didn't. He didn't try to kill you. I don't believe he knows who you really are, so that means he either isn't the killer and is a stalker, or he's one and the same man."

Stella watched him closely. She loved his mind, the way he put things together but let her think things through herself. That was important to her. She didn't want anyone solving her issues, she'd been doing that for herself too long. Still, it was nice to be able to lean on him once in a while, to know he was there and that he would be a sounding board. She liked that he used her as one as well.

"I just don't believe in coincidence, that there were two different men doing these things, one a serial killer and the other a stalker, especially since they popped up at exactly the same time. It makes sense they're the same person," Sam said.

She tried to absorb that without flinching or taking on blame. What this man did was on him, not her. She wasn't responsible for what her father had done. Her foster mother had given that gift to her through her love and counseling, refusing to allow Stella to take on that burden. She hadn't allowed her to continue believing she had broken up her family and pushed her mother to suicide. She wouldn't throw that wisdom away, not now when she had to hold tight to it in order to try to save a life and prevent a killer from murdering again when he seemed to be unstoppable. But it was hard not to think that the killer was ripping away the kinds of memories she cherished and wanted to hold to her.

"I don't believe in that kind of coincidence either, Sam." How could they possibly link him to the "accidents"?

OVER THE NEXT few nights, Stella carefully recorded the details from her nightmares. She sketched the early morning sunlight spilling across sparse grass growing over rocky ground. The grass was mostly yellow and brown and had fallen over rather than having been trampled. The rocks embedded in the dirt made the path uneven, the trail faint, as if few people walked it. Still, the trail was there, no more than a foot or so wide. Now that the lens had opened a bit, it was easier to see. Leaves and debris, such as twigs and even small branches, covered the ground, making the borders of the path harder to see, but with the wider view, Stella was able to discern the twists and turns as the trail seemed to lead endlessly to nowhere.

Clearly, this wasn't a favorite climbing area for locals or tourists. October was getting late in the season for climbing, especially bouldering, but beautiful days weren't wasted. Often, since Stella was so busy during the fishing and tourist seasons, after she closed the resort, she would try to get in as much bouldering as possible before the weather changed. It wasn't surprising that these two climbers were enjoying the clear, although brisk, October weather.

Stella studied the third night's sketches, laying them out across the bed for Sam to look at with her. He liked to climb as well. That was what had originally drawn him to the area, as it had so many others. Climbers came from all over the world to try their expertise on the various boulders. Fortunately, there were all kinds of climbs, for everyone from beginners to experts.

"This is the best I could get, Sam," she said, chewing worriedly on her lower lip. "Three nights and mostly I've seen the trail going in. This is the bottom of the rock. Granite. Big surprise there. I sketched as much detail along the bottom part of the rock as I could see. There's this gnarly overhang here. I swear I've seen it before. See how the colors go from a red to an almost deeper shade of purple? That isn't just a shadow. I thought it was at first, but I don't think it is. The lines in the granite swirl here."

Sam nudged her over with his hip and settled next to her, picking up the drawing to study it. "This isn't a place I've been climbing. It has to be remote. I've looked at the trail going in several times and no one has been on it other than perhaps one, maybe two people in months. You can tell by the grass and debris. If I were to make a guess, I'd have to say it was probably the same person making the trek back there. Maybe both of them."

"I know I've been there at least once," Stella said. "I rarely forget anything, especially somewhere I've bouldered."

"It's possible you weren't bouldering," Sam pointed out. "If there are two of them, they might be trad climbing. Or sports climbing. Look at the shadows. They're carrying rope."

Stella didn't like climbing with rope. That was a well-known fact among her friends. She could do it, but she didn't like it. She preferred to solve the problems bouldering presented. She was a solitary climber. The risks were her own. "This particular place is very remote, Sam. If someone is working it, my guess is it's someone's long-term project. He's been working on it for weeks, maybe longer, but that's just a guess."

She pressed her hand to her forehead. "This is so frustrating."

Sam caught her wrist and pulled her hand down, keeping possession of it. "You're driving yourself crazy, Stella. You have to let this go for a little while. You've done everything you can do for now. Tomorrow night, you'll get a bigger glimpse of the rock and that will hopefully jog your memory. If not, then when we show all these drawings to the others, one of them will recognize the place. Always, on the fifth night, you get a much clearer vision."

"He's been killing the very next day. He doesn't wait one or two nights like the other killers. He's too eager."

Sam's thumb slid up and down over the back of her hand in a little caress as he pressed her palm over his heart. "The moment we know the location, we can drive out there. What's more natural than you practicing rope climbing? Especially where we know no one else is around? The killer is interrupted and we find out who he is."

Something in his voice made her heart stutter and then accelerate. There was no real inflection. His tone was soft, gentle even, so Sam. She turned her head, her eyes meeting his.

"Sam."

"What is it, sweetheart?"

He brought her hand to his mouth and scraped his teeth over the pads of her fingers, igniting a million fiery nerve endings, nearly distracting her. She took a deep breath.

"Once we know who he is, we have to talk to Griffen."

His gaze didn't shift from hers. He looked at her steadily, his teeth biting down. Her stomach turned over and her sex clenched.

"What exactly are we going to say to Griffen, Stella? What proof do we have? There's no way to convict him."

"Sam, you can't go after him."

He didn't say anything, he just looked at her.

She shook her head. "No. Absolutely not. You can't."

"Sweetheart, what other choice is there? We can't let him keep killing people. Once we know who he is, anyone he kills after that is on us. The cops can't arrest him without proof. You know that. They need enough for a conviction. They don't have anything on him and they aren't going to get it. He's too intelligent. They would have to wait for him to kill. Then he'd have to make mistakes during his kills."

"You can't."

"It's what I do."

"Not anymore. You aren't in that life. You came here to find a different life and you've found it, Sam. It would be different if it was self-defense, but it isn't. And don't you dare set yourself up so he comes after you. I mean it."

"He can't live, Stella." Same steady tone. Gentle. Patient. He didn't look away from her, not even for a moment.

She framed his face with her hands. "Honey, you have to listen to me. We can't be judge, jury and executioner. We don't have that kind of authority."

"I do."

"Not anymore."

"I have it. I've chosen not to use it. We can't let him continue."

"What then? You go to jail?"

"Please, Stella. I can arrange an 'accident' just as well as this guy."

"I'm not sacrificing you for him or for anyone else. We have to think of another way," Stella insisted, and leaned into him to brush kisses over his mouth to prevent him from arguing with her.

She had no idea what it would do to him to have to kill a friend. He'd gotten out of that business. Maybe he was slower than he had been. He might hesitate. Even if he did kill the serial killer and the body disappeared, or his death was deemed an accident, what would that do to Sam? He had finally come to terms with his past. He didn't need to start all over again. And whatever agency he'd worked for might see this as a sign that he wanted to come back. Or they could blackmail him into going back.

"Stella." Her name came out a mixture between a growl and a groan. "Sweetheart, let's get dressed and go for a walk. This is the third night in a row he hasn't been outside watching the place. Let's take advantage, unless it's too cold for you."

She knew Sam was restless at night and prowled around the property even more than the security guards did. "Sounds good to me."

They both pulled on warm clothes, boots and gloves and went out into the cold. The temperature had dropped even lower than she'd expected. She gave a little gasp and he laughed.

"I'll take Bailey out when we get back. You're sure you'll be warm enough?"

"Yes." The sky was clear, no clouds, allowing the stars and half moon to shine overhead. She let him take her hand in his. It still felt a little strange to her to be holding hands with him, but she couldn't help but like it. His hand was quite a bit larger than hers and his fingers enveloped hers.

"Did you feel better about your relationship with your father after talking to him, Sam?" Stella had held the question back for some time and then was upset with herself for blurting it out. "I'm not asking out of idle curiosity. I wouldn't push you for answers. It's just that the holidays are coming up. In spite of the fact that he did ask me and that has nothing to do with it, as you know, Shabina and I put on dinners for the others who are in town. I just assumed you would be spending the holidays with me . . ."

He tightened his fingers around hers. "You assumed correctly," he said decisively.

"He is your only family. If you wanted to invite him, he's welcome. I'd just have to know ahead of time. Don't invite him if it would make you uncomfortable to have him there. The point of all of us getting together is to have a good time. We can drink too much if we want, or indulge in too many of Shabina's amazing pies or desserts. You know what we're like."

"I do. Denver and I take all the dogs for walks while you ladies get a little crazy on us."

She laughed. "That's right. I can't see your father taking the dogs for walks. He did say he has a lady friend. It's possible she makes amazing holiday meals."

"I hope she plans on indulging his every whim. He was used to it from my mother."

"He never remarried?"

"No," Sam said, and pulled her closer to him as they walked around the shore of the lake. The breeze was light, teasing at their clothes. "That did surprise me. I always thought he'd at least move in with a woman, but he didn't."

"Did you ask him why he didn't divorce your mother?" Stella dared to ask. "That would have been my first question. I don't understand why men who cheat bother to get married in the first place. And when they do, why they just don't man up and leave." In a way, she was trying to tell him that was what she expected from him.

Sam brought her hand in close to his chest as they fell into step together. "I asked him why he just didn't let her go, let her get on with her life."

"Did he have any kind of an answer?"

Sam shook his head slowly. "At first he tried to weasel his way out of answering, blaming his decision on the church and holy vows. I pointed out he was breaking his vows constantly so they really didn't mean shit to him. In the end, he admitted Mom ran his house the way he wanted it. She kept him comfortable. She also prevented any of the women he slept with from getting any 'big' ideas about trying to become the next Mrs. Rossi."

Stella refrained from calling his father a really ugly name, but it was difficult. She stayed silent, thinking that was the best way to stay out of trouble. As far as she was concerned, Marco Rossi was a first-class dick.

"I think he thought because I was older now, I'd understand. I didn't. I don't. I never will. And not just because she was my mother. He's a selfish bastard and should never have married in the first place. He married her because her family was one of the ruling families and it was like marrying royalty. I thought he loved her. He claimed he did in his own way. He said he loved her more than he has ever loved any woman. He also said that was part of the reason he wouldn't divorce her. That and her family would never understand."

Sam rubbed the bridge of his nose with one gloved finger as

they continued to walk around the lake. The water lapped gently at the shore. "He did admit to having many regrets. He said he wished he'd stayed home for her birthday. He didn't because he'd already agreed to meet several of his friends at the strip club and he didn't want to look weak. He'd forgotten the date. He said he should have just called them and canceled."

"That's so sad, that his ego wouldn't allow him to back down, even though he wanted to."

"I actually said that same thing to him and he pointed out that it was a different time then. Men and women had different roles. Even children did. He was brought up in a harsher environment than he brought me up in. I suppose he's right."

"Still, it's obvious that he doesn't have much respect for women, does he?" Stella asked.

"I'm grateful he's never had a daughter. If he had, he would have treated her like a commodity," Sam said. "I might have had to arrange to do him in myself. I would never have tolerated him treating my little sister like that."

"That man with him, his bodyguard or whatever he is, Lucio Vitale, he doesn't seem as if he has much respect for women either. Or he doesn't think they have brains."

"His entire family was wiped out. It's a long story, not a pleasant one. I imagine he's very bitter and relentless in his need for vengeance. He's a man to stay away from. I'm not surprised to see him with my father, although I'm a little shocked that Marco trusts him."

Stella blinked up at him. "Do you think he would hurt your father?"

"If it ever came out that Marco had a hand in the killing of his family, damn straight he would kill him without batting an eye. He'd do it slow and ugly too, savoring every moment of his torture. His family died hard. First his father. Then his older brothers. He took care of his mother and sisters financially by fighting bare-knuckle in the death matches."

Stella frowned up at him. "What is that?" A little shiver went down her spine because she had a terrible feeling she knew. "That's not like those Hollywood films where they fight to the death, is it?" She tried to sound sarcastic so it wouldn't be real.

"That's exactly what it is."

"I didn't think those were real. He's still alive so he must have won."

"He won, but they took his money to pay his father's debt every match. That left his mother and sisters without a roof and no food. He had to do other things to get money for those things, and still, life wasn't good for any of them."

They walked in silence, listening to the familiar sounds of the night creatures and the whisper of the wind ruffling the surface of the water. Bats wheeled and dipped, catching insects as they flew in the moonbeams above the water's edge.

"You just never know how complicated a person's life is, do you, Sam?" Stella asked. "Ever since the nightmares have started, I've been finding out all sorts of things about my friends, from Denver to Vienna, things I hadn't known before." She tilted her face up to his. "Things about you. I guess everyone has things in their past they prefer stay there. I feel for him now, for Vitale, and I don't want to. I think he's too much like your father. I also think he's the man who broke Raine's heart. I don't know that, but if he did, he's indirectly responsible for her father's death and her being thrown out of her family."

"I hope not," Sam said. "Raine strikes me as the vengeful type. If they both are, that could be a very bad combination. Especially if they both are sitting at our holiday dinner table."

"Since the talk didn't go so well, I guess I won't have to worry about that," Stella said, feeling somewhat relieved.

"Actually, it went better than I expected. I had checked into his medical history before I went to see him. He does have a heart condition. I also put a couple of top-notch investigators on him to dig up as much as they could in an afternoon. It does look as if he's considering retiring. He's moved the bulk of his money, all legitimately his, into his offshore accounts. It looks as if he's been having meetings with the man he would have take over for him."

"You believe he is retiring?"

"He's taking the steps toward it. Careful ones," Sam acknowledged, turning them around, taking them back in the direction of the house. "He was looking into real estate here and he really has met a woman he seems to like. This one is closer to his age and doesn't seem to be interested in his money, although it's too soon to tell. It appears he was telling the truth about those things."

"You're taking a wait-and-see policy with him, aren't you?" Stella guessed.

"I advised him to hire a very good security firm and gave him the name of one. I have friends I know who are excellent bodyguards. It's up to him whether or not he listens. Raine's father should have hired guards. Just because you retire doesn't mean you're out of the game. You still have a lot of knowledge. The feds can still decide to come after you. It isn't like in the old days where there are shoot-outs all the time, but that doesn't mean criminal activity isn't taking place. It's just conducted behind the scenes and the families look very legitimate and stay as low-key as possible. No one wants to draw attention to themselves. So, killing an old man who is living up in the Sierras by putting a bullet in his head would be stupid. Arranging an accident would be easy."

He opened the door for her and allowed her inside. Before she got very far, his palm curled around the nape of her neck and he pulled her to him, his eyes dark with heat. Her heart immediately accelerated. His mouth descended slowly, in a way that always said she had the choice to stop him, but only made her burn hotter for him.

Then he was kissing her and everything disappeared but Sam. He could make her boneless in seconds, her body melting into his, her mind fading so there was only feeling, this sensation of free-falling, of fire in her veins and that ball of need building in her stomach and in her sex. He lifted his head and gently kissed both eyes and then the corners of her mouth and her chin, giving her time to find the strength to stand on her own again.

"You must be overheated with all these clothes on. Take them off and wait for me in bed. I'll just be a minute taking Bailey out."

That gruffness in his normally gentle voice was the only thing that told her he was as affected by their kiss as she was. That and his hard body pressed so tightly against hers. A little dazed, she nodded up at him.

# CHAPTER EIGHTEEN

*Mommy, Daddy's doing the bad thing again.*

Stella could see the climbing shoes and gear, ropes and even the edge of a backpack where it lay against a smaller rock. The shoes moved and the base of the boulder came into view. There was an overhang right at the bottom of the granite that seemed to be hollow for a long distance. She immediately knew she had climbed it—or tried to. The reason her memory was so vague was because she'd only gone there once. The boulder had been far too difficult—and high—for her skill set.

She tried to push her memories away and concentrate on what she was seeing. She needed to catalogue every detail, to make certain she got this right. Colors swept up the rock. Reds and dark grays, light yellows and golds, this rock had all the colors of granite with the early morning sun beating down on it. She even caught glimpses of a deep purple in the cracks as the two men paced across the ground, looking upward.

The boulder was very high. When one of them turned slightly and the lens followed that sweep, she caught sight of a second boulder, almost as tall with a jagged top. Both were wide and long. They looked as if they would be a climber's dream—and nightmare. Neither would be an easy climb, but few boulderers would pass up the chance to work out the problem of ascending to the top in total triumph. Apparently, that was exactly what the victim had been doing—working on his project for some time.

Stella studied what she could see of the base of the boulder. The overhang was extremely severe. A climber would have to be a spider, going upside down and finding a route to take him up and over the ledge to get to what appeared to be a smooth surface. There were cracks and outcroppings, if you just had the patience to find them. The granite wasn't smooth at all, but had little fingerholds and tiny places the toes of climbing shoes could find to lever one's body up.

The shadows thrown by the two boulders in the early morning hours indicated these two boulders would be considered "high balls." She thought they could be at least thirty or forty feet, if not higher. She didn't want to think that the climber was considering climbing without rope on his own. It was done. There were a lot of climbers who free-climbed. She didn't like heights and just the thought freaked her out. Now, knowing that the killer intended to murder his friend made climbing the heights and depending on someone else all the worse.

She could see only portions of the rock as the two men began to prepare for the climb. One was climbing, the other belaying from below. Her heart began to pound. Again, there was that feeling of absolute triumph emanating from the killer. The air felt heavy and oppressive to her, a sinister, menacing shroud the killer created with his twisted glee. He was there with a friend. His friend trusted him enough to put his life in his hands, and all the while he plotted to kill him and make it look like an accident.

Stella was uncertain how he was going to manage that and not have suspicion fall on him.

She took in every single detail she could of the boulder and the gear before the lens closed and she found herself once more staring at a black screen.

STELLA SAT UP slowly, not even fighting her way out of the nightmare. The moment she lifted her lashes, she was staring into Sam's eyes. She knew he would be there, sitting across from her in the chair, his gaze steady on her face. Calm. Her anchor. She definitely was falling in love with him. Just seeing him righted her world.

"I got more details. I've been there. I know I even tried to climb it once. It was beyond my ability. I never would have gone there alone, so it was with one of my friends. I don't understand how the killer plans on making this look like an accident without everyone knowing he was involved."

Her gaze clung to Sam's. Even though she was getting so much better at handling the nightmares, she needed that first connection with him, and he never failed her. He was always right there. She glanced at the large crate where Bailey was curled up, his gaze trained on her alertly. He was as devoted as ever. The terrible attack hadn't in any way diminished their relationship. She had so much to be thankful for. These two and her friends.

"We're going to get him this time, Sam. I just know it."

He nodded. "You've got one more night. Whatever he plans to do, you'll see tomorrow night. You always do. By that time, we'll have the location. We'll go out there and do some climbing ourselves. It will be natural enough for you to want to climb. The days are beautiful and you really don't like heights. It sounds like the perfect rock to practice on."

A little shudder went through her as she reached down to unlock the safe. "He's here tonight. I can feel him."

"He is. Whatever prevented him from coming the last three nights is evidently over. Or he just took a break."

Stella looked at Bailey again. "I would prefer that you didn't go out without me. I know you like to prowl around at night, but you've always had Bailey with you. He might have stabbed Bailey on purpose so you didn't have him to alert you."

She twisted her fingers together tightly in her lap, hoping he wouldn't notice. She had no idea how she thought she'd get away with that, because Sam noticed everything. His gaze dropped to her linked fingers, and his hard features softened immediately.

"Woman."

"Man." She whispered the response automatically, the lump in her throat threatening to choke her. His eyes had darkened. Heated.

"Do you remember what I did for a living before I came here?"

She shook her head slowly. "I'm not the kind of woman to pry. I never actually asked you. I know you're not a 'ghost.' Other than that I only know you worked for the government and you were very good at what you did."

His eyes got even darker and a whisper of a smile turned sexy. "You know what I did."

"Okay, maybe I do know. Sort of."

"I'm still alive for a reason, Stella. I walk out your door alone at night, that man watching will not be able to find me with or without his night-vision glasses. I can creep up on him. I know where his camp is. I told you it's straight across the lake where the bend is. He's cunning like an animal and he'll run the minute he can't find me, but he won't be able to sneak up on me. I'm the wild card, Stella. He doesn't know me. He can't figure out who I am or where I came from. He can do all the research in the world and he won't find records of me anywhere."

She sighed. "I still don't like it, Sam."

The lines around his eyes crinkled. "That's because you're sweet, Stella. And fierce."

"I can hit what I'm aiming at," she pointed out. "When I shoot, Sam, I know what I'm doing, and I wouldn't hesitate to protect you." She wouldn't.

"I'm well aware. And thankful. I wouldn't want you to own a weapon you couldn't use."

"The point being, I should be of equal help to you. It shouldn't just be you always looking out for me. I'm not a damsel-in-distress kind of woman." She tried not to sound belligerent, but she wasn't a woman who needed to be taken care of. She was self-sufficient. She'd turned the business around. She'd had the good sense to hire Sam, and over the last two years, she maybe had leaned on him a little more than she should have, but she could stand on her own two feet and, if necessary, take care of him and Bailey.

That shadow of a smile became a flash of his white teeth. "I think it's safe to say we've always been a partnership, Stella. We look out for each other. This is a strange situation. If you recall, at the beginning of it, you were the one diving into a freezing lake to save me."

That was true. There was some satisfaction in knowing she'd done that . . . *except* . . . "You did have your knife out and I think you might have managed to kill him right then if I hadn't interfered," she conceded.

"Maybe. Maybe not. I did actually hit my head. I wasn't expecting a serial killer to drag me underwater. I was definitely disoriented. Tell me what else you found out tonight."

"I could tell the two know each other very well. They've been friends a long time. That just makes the crime more hideous to me. I didn't get the feeling from the serial killer that he had a personal grudge against his friend either. This feels more like a power trip. A kind of rush, like he's doing it because he can. He's smarter, so much more intelligent, and no one will ever figure it out. He believes he can stop whenever he wants to stop and then start again when he decides to play his game."

Sam made a small sound that might have been a curse under his breath. "It's a game to him? Does it feel that way to you, Stella? I know you're able to get emotions from both the victim and the killer."

"This is the most he's ever broadcast. Before, he's been somewhat reserved until almost the last moment. He almost felt like a predator hunting and then there would be a rush of euphoria. This feels as though he's in a continual high, that constant rush. He likes knowing he'll spend hours with his victim and can kill him at any time."

"Twice I was sent to hunt a predator within a unit, one in the Marines and one in the Army, four years apart. The men would go out for training or a small engagement with the enemy. One wouldn't return. They would find a soldier murdered when they went looking for him. The commander began to suspect they had a serial killer within their ranks, but no matter what traps they set, they couldn't find him. I was sent for. Of course, no one knew who I was. Most of the time they never saw me. I conducted an investigation behind the scenes, so to speak."

Stella waited, her eyes on his. Sam rarely talked about his past, or any of the assignments he'd had. She found it fascinating to think that he would be sent to investigate within the ranks of the military and yet no one would even know he was there.

"I take it you found both of them."

He nodded. "I did. They were not turned over for trial." His gaze continued to hold hers steadily. "That was part of my job. I was to remove them permanently."

"Have you had to hunt very many serial killers?"

"It depends on whether or not you call terrorists or presidents of drug cartels serial killers. Everyone has a reason for what they choose to do, but if I was sent after them, you can believe they killed a lot of innocent people."

She wanted to go to him and put her arms around him. Just as she had been pulled back into her past with this horror, so had he. He'd been stoic about it. Matter-of-fact. But there was a reason Sam had ended up in the Sierras in the little town of Knightly. Like all of them, he'd been seeking peace. He wanted away from his job, and although it didn't show on his face, because it never did, she felt the underlying sadness in him that he thought he would have to be the one to hunt the killer.

"We'll figure out who this man is, Sam, and we'll get the proof we need and turn him over to Griffen." She poured determination into her voice.

"It isn't easy to get proof against this kind of killer, Stella. That's why men with my skills exist. That's why I'm sent in."

"That's why you *were* sent in. Now, someone else does that work. Not you. You're out of it. You're here to start a new life, just like I am. Just like Raine and Vienna and everyone else. Sam, you can't think the way you used to."

A slow smile heated his eyes, instantly sending her stomach tumbling into a series of loops and somersaults. He was seriously sexy without even trying.

"Sweetheart, I can't just shut down that way of thinking. It's who I am."

"You're going to have to try harder." She gave him her sternest look, the one she gave Bailey when she really meant what she said.

"Start drawing, Stella. I'll go for my walk and then take Bailey out. The look, by the way, is cute. Bailey thinks so too." Sam stood up, stretching lazily.

She scowled at him, a fierce, black scowl meant to intimidate. "My stern look is not cute. Bailey *always* minds me when I give him that look. I suggest you do as well if you know what's good for you."

His mouth twitched. The corners of his eyes crinkled. They weren't laugh lines, more like sun lines, but she thought they should have been laugh lines. They always would be to her. She would never get tired of looking at him.

"I'm tempted to see what would happen to me if I disobeyed. I think your hair is crackling, *Satine*."

His smile came close to melting her insides. She pressed her hand to her stomach and deliberately narrowed her gaze at him, liking the easy way they could tease each other even under the dire circumstances.

"I don't think you want to risk it," she warned.

He walked over to the side of the bed in that fluid way he had and bent his head to hers. Slow. Taking his time. She turned her face up to his, giving him her mouth. One large hand framed the side of her face, his thumb sliding in a caress over her cheek as his head continued to descend.

Her heart stuttered. Her sex clenched. Lashes fell to shutter her sight. The moment his lips claimed hers, sparks erupted over her skin. Goose bumps broke out. His arms came around her and he shifted her against his chest. She slid her arms up so she could link her fingers behind his neck.

When Sam kissed her, there was no room for anything else in her mind. No one else. Nothing else. Only him. Only the feeling he gave her. He could be tender or wild, and it didn't matter how they came together—they detonated, lit up the world around them, and all the while she felt safe and *home*. She felt like she belonged.

Sam lifted his head, his lips following the bone structure of her jaw and then drifting down the column of her throat. "You're so beautiful, Stella."

She shook her head. "Thank you, Sam. I've never thought of myself that way until you came along."

He tucked hair behind her ear. "Trust me, you are. I'll be back in a bit. I don't want you worried about me. I'm locking you in, but you can check the locks from your phone," he reminded.

"I need a tracking device on you," she pointed out. "Then I'd know for certain you were okay out there."

He laughed softly. "He's going to take off the minute he can't find me outside. You wait and see. I predict inside of five minutes. He's going to panic and he'll run." The pad of his thumb moved back and forth over her chin in a small caress.

"All right, Sam." What could she do but concede and let him go off by himself?

"Don't look so glum, sweetheart. He'll be gone and I'll be back in one piece. Tomorrow, the girls are coming over for lunch and you can show all your sketches to them. One of them went with you climbing to this place. They knew the way, so they're bound to remember it. While they're with you, I'll go into town and get us groceries and more treats for Bailey. We went a little crazy spoiling him."

She made a little face. "You mean I did. I hate that he has to be so quiet in his crate when he wants to be with us. I do sneak him out to lie right with me when I'm in the other room. If he has a large bone to chew on, then he won't lick his sutures."

"He's wearing the cone of shame."

"He detests that thing. I take it off of him when he's not alone," she admitted, avoiding Sam's eyes. She didn't want him to think she was weak. It was just that Bailey gave her his big pleading eyes and she couldn't stand it. She caved immediately, but only if she was right there, watching his every move.

Sam shook his head. "You're so tough, Stella."

She tilted her chin at him and narrowed her eyes as he stepped back and headed toward the bedroom door. "I am. Have you ever seen me dealing with those complaining fishermen?"

"All the time, *Satine*. It's a thing to behold." There was admiration in his voice as well as laughter. His dark eyes laughed at her—or with her. Because she couldn't help laughing too. She could be incredibly tough when she had to be, but not with Bailey. And she probably would never be very tough with Sam either.

She shook out her colored pencils and began to sketch as many details as she could remember before switching to the journal. Her gaze jumped to the clock. Sam was right. Within six minutes, she no longer felt the presence of the watcher.

STELLA COULD BAKE when she wanted to, but she honestly hadn't thought about cooking or baking lately. Her mind had been consumed with trying to figure out who the serial killer was and how to catch and convict him. Having her friends come to her home meant feeding them. She'd forgotten that. Before she could panic, Sam had pulled several blocks of cheese from the refrigerator and unearthed a couple of boxes of crackers from the pantry.

Sam never minded helping in the kitchen. In fact, he did more of the cooking than she did, especially now. He made certain she ate. They cut up cheese together and put crackers on the tray for the women. Sam found the fruit he'd recently purchased, so at least that was fresh.

When the five women arrived, Stella wasn't in such a panic. She and Sam had already walked Bailey and returned him to his crate by the time her friends were out of the car and had gone into the living room. All of the women were used to making themselves at home in one another's houses. Shabina and Harlow had already gotten the lemonade from the refrigerator and put the tray on the low coffee table. Raine set the cheese-and-cracker tray on the floor and sat down next to it, beside the other two women.

Vienna yawned. "I'm sorry, I'm just still so tired. I've been at the hospital two nights in a row in surgery with these terrible car accidents. The victims were airlifted in from off the mountain. I couldn't believe it. Both were single-car accidents. Dr. Teller was brilliant. I don't know how he managed to save the kid's arm, but he did, and then the mother's life. We lost the father. That was the first night. The second night, it was a young couple. Dr. Teller again pulled off a miracle. I thought for sure he'd have to amputate the woman's leg, but he saved it, as well as both their lives. It turned out to be a long but good night. I slept all night the following night and then had to pull a shift last night, although it was quiet. I still feel like I need to sleep for the next decade."

"Vienna, you should have opted out," Stella said. "The rest of us could have figured this out." Vienna looked tired, something that was rare for her. "Why don't you go lie down in one of the guest rooms?"

"I'm good right here. I'll stretch out on the couch, and if I start snoring, just dump water on me, okay? Snoring is so obnoxious."

The women laughed but exchanged worried looks as Vienna really did lie down on the couch, something she wouldn't ordinarily do. She often worked in the ER, but she was the hospital's top surgical nurse, and when it was an emergency, it was Vienna who was called in. No matter what, she always answered the call.

"I'll leave you ladies to it. I've got work to do." Sam leaned over and gave Stella a kiss on top of her head before sauntering out the door.

Zahra stood at the window, watching him walk away from the house with his easy, fluid stride. "He really is pretty, Stella," she said.

Stella burst out laughing. "Get away from there. You aren't allowed to flirt with him or drool over him. If you do, I'm putting ice in my water and crunching it every time I'm anywhere near you."

Zahra hastened away from the window. "It was only an observation. No one should drink cold water, let alone put ice in it." She gave a little shudder. "Hot water with lemon only." She snatched up cheese, put it on a cracker and popped it in her mouth. "Crunching ice is pure torture." She threw herself on the floor beside the others and sat, tailor-fashion.

Stella spread the sketches out on the floor of the living room. "I've been here before, so that means one of you took me out there. The climb was definitely way above my ability. Does anyone recognize the way in or the boulders just from what little I've drawn?"

She did her best to keep her heart from accelerating out of control. She was counting on them to help her find this elusive set of boulders. She'd lived there a long time, and yet she didn't know where this place was.

Zahra scowled down at the sketches. "I've never seen that place, Stella, and I go bouldering with you all the time."

Actually, that wasn't quite the truth. Zahra preferred trad climbing. Give her a harness, a few friends, someone to lead climb and someone else to clean up, and she was happy. Bouldering was definitely *not* her preferred climb, but she did it when Stella wanted company, just like she hiked or backpacked when Stella wanted company.

Raine looked the sketches over carefully and shook her head. "Sorry, hon, I don't recognize them."

Shabina leaned over Raine's shoulder, examining the drawings closely. "Me either. It wasn't me who took you out there."

That left only Harlow and Vienna. Harlow was already shaking her head. Vienna stayed on the couch but held her hand out for the sketches. She moved through the drawings quickly and nodded, stretching her arm out again, eyes closed.

"I took you out there three years ago. Very few locals know of it. The boulders are called Twin Devils. When you're up on top of either one of the boulders, you can see forever. You have to take the old Hot Springs Road, the one no one uses anymore. Keep going and approximately seven miles past the hot springs there's a turnoff. It isn't marked. There's just a dirt road, probably mostly grown over by now. It's on the left side. Nothing marks it. No fences, nothing at all. That's why no one ever goes out there. It's mostly forgotten and when people try to find it, they get lost. The road is flat right there, so it looks like you're turning into a meadow. You have to look really carefully or you'll miss it."

"Why isn't the road marked?" Raine asked.

Vienna cleared her throat, a faint grin coming and then disappearing. "I was told the property is privately owned, a pretty big acreage, but the owners don't live up here and there's no house or cabin. They never come around. They inherited from great-grandparents or something like that and it's been in the family forever. Since no one goes out there, the land just gets wilder and wilder. Lots of wild animals. Bear. Mountain lion. Rattlesnakes."

"Why don't they sell?" Harlow asked.

Vienna sighed. "Some sort of feud going on, if any of this is to be believed."

"No one ever goes out there?" Zahra said. "Are there No Trespassing signs up?"

"There used to be. There hasn't been for years. At least the last time I went out there I didn't see any signs."

"*Vienna*. You knew it was private property and you still trespassed?" Shabina said. "Who knew you were such a bad girl?"

"All of you knew."

"And you took me out there too," Stella pointed out. "If we'd been caught, I would have had to plead innocence."

Vienna waved her hand in the air, eyes closed. "I would have lied my ass off and said you knew everything. If I'm going down, so are you. We may as well have fun in jail together."

Stella burst out laughing. "I suppose."

"We'd bail you out," Zahra promised.

"Thanks." Stella blew her a kiss. "Are the boulders on a map somewhere?"

"If they are, I don't know about it. A climbing buddy of mine showed it to me. He was head of Search and Rescue before me, but he left Knightly, saying he needed to go somewhere else, where he could broaden his dating field."

"Sheesh, Vienna. What did he think was wrong with you?" Harlow asked. "You were right there in front of him."

"I said no."

"That would be the reason he left, then," Raine said. "I'll Google Earth the boulders and see if I can find them, Stella. The more directions we get for you, the better. Do you have a plan?"

"Yes. It's solid. We don't want the killer to know we're onto him. Sam and I will go out to the boulders as if we're going to spend the day climbing, and we'll outlast him."

"Sam can pull it off," Raine said. "But you don't exactly have a poker face, Stella. The killer will know something's off, especially if it's someone you know."

"Maybe we should all go out there," Zahra suggested.

"Not on your life," Stella objected instantly. "If you think I'd give it away, the more of us there, the more likely one of us will trip up. No, we'll stick with the plan. Sam and I will go. It makes sense that he'd take me out to the middle of nowhere to practice belaying with him when I don't want anyone to witness my freak-outs. This is the right time of year for me to climb since I just closed the resort."

"Will you be able to keep from warning the victim, since he's a friend?" Harlow asked.

Stella pushed a hand through her hair. "I don't know. I just hope we can find the place. I want to find out how the killer intends to get away with the murder, making it look like an accident. That piece should come to me tonight. Sam and I will get up first thing and go out there. I'll text all of you tomorrow and let you know what happens and who we believe it is."

She looked around the room at her friends. "You really are the best. I don't know what I'd ever do without all of you."

STELLA SAT UP in the middle of the night, heart pounding, eyes meeting Sam's. "He's belaying him. All friendly. The victim has been working this project for months. The killer lets him fall and then removes all trace of being there. He secures a top rope so it appears as if the victim was working on his project alone and fell. He hummed while he wiped footprints from the dirt and collected gear."

Her stomach lurched while she told Sam. "I couldn't exactly hear the humming, more like it was a sound buried in the wind and I knew what he was doing. He was meticulous with every detail. I even saw him casually break the victim's finger. Just his hand reached into the lens of the camera and grasped the victim's finger. It was sickening to hear the crunch."

"Did you see any part of the killer?"

"I only saw his shadow on the rock. He spent so much time working to stage the scene, to make certain it looked as if his victim had been there completely alone. He knew no one was going to come out there to disturb him." She tried to keep the bitterness from her voice. "He felt so much elation, Sam. This triumph. Feelings of superiority and even euphoria. He isn't going to stop. He likes it too much."

"Unfortunately, that was the kind of thing I witnessed when I was investigating the deaths of the soldiers being killed. Once I was certain I had the killer in my sights and I started shadowing him, I could pick up those little nuances as he stalked his victim. The flushed face. The elevated breathing. Sometimes he'd stalk the victim over and over just to prolong that euphoria, the feeling of power, of holding life and death in his hands."

She leveled her gaze on him. "You had to take lives, Sam. Did you ever get that feeling?"

He frowned. "In the beginning, I always felt a little sick. I never hesitated, but there was always revulsion in the pit of my stomach. Eventually that went away and I was numb. At night, when I was alone, I wouldn't be numb, but then that went away too." He lifted his lashes and looked into her eyes. Steadily. "I decided it was time to get out, *Satine*. I wasn't taking any chances. I served my country and I did my best to serve with honor. I took chances that maybe I shouldn't have because I was a dumb kid who felt I had to pay for the sins of my father and the blood running through my veins."

"I felt that way for a long time. I think we're very much alike."

"I think we're not, sweetheart. I think you're someone very special."

"Sam. To me, you're an unexpected gift. You don't even know. I felt responsible for my mother and the breakup of our family. I learned not to ever talk to anyone about what was going on in my life. It just became such a habit that I found it hard to let anyone in." She sent him a small smile. "You snuck in when I wasn't looking."

He gave her an answering smile. "That was the idea." The smile faded. "Maybe we both had the same codes drilled into us and that's why we were able to understand each other's need for privacy. I was raised in secrecy as well. My profession only added to the need to maintain that code."

"The mystery adds to your allure. My friends perv on you," she told him, to lighten the moment.

One eyebrow lifted. "The same friends who tried to convince you I was a serial killer?"

"Well . . . yes. With the exception of Raine. She didn't believe it for a minute. I'm convinced Raine may have information she hasn't disclosed to anyone else, or she just has a sixth sense about people. She's different and always has been. She knows what it's like to love and lose her family. She always talks about them, Sam. Her mother, father and brothers. Her childhood. She had a happy childhood. I had no idea they considered her dead to them."

"I've heard of that punishment," Sam said. "It seems extreme, especially as she was never told that her father was in the mob. I find it odd that her mother would go along with what is obviously her brothers' punishment . . . Unless—" He broke off abruptly.

"What?"

He shook his head. "I don't know Raine very well. She's always quiet. Almost always stays in the background observing everyone, but she's very intelligent."

"That's an understatement, Sam. She's off-the-charts smart. Cool under fire. She can handle herself in any situation."

"Would she set herself up as a target to draw out her father's killer? Get her family to cut her off in order to protect them?"

"What do you mean?"

"Would she talk her brothers and mother into publicly disowning her? Whoever had her father killed would think her family blamed her and they wouldn't look twice at a little slip of a girl living up in the Sierras alone. She doesn't go near her family. If they are monitoring her brothers, her brothers aren't making inquiries into their father's death. They've accepted it as the price one pays for being in the business."

Stella's breath caught in her lungs. That was exactly something Raine might do. She was very probably patiently unraveling the trail leading to who was behind her father's killing. "If that's what she's done, she would find a way to talk to her mother and brothers without risk. Not in person, but through her computer," Stella conceded.

"I think your friends fit with you, sweetheart, because they know about keeping secrets and about love and loss, just the way you do."

"We do," she corrected.


STELLA STARED AT the familiar truck and then slowly turned her gaze to Sam. "He's going to kill Denver. Sam. He's going to kill Denver. *Our* Denver." She could barely conceive of anyone doing such a thing. "He's part of our family. Yours and mine. We have to hurry. What if we're already too late?"

She shoved open the door to her 4Runner and all but hurtled herself out, her heart pounding, her mouth dry. Who would want to kill Denver? Of everyone in the community, with the exception of Vienna, he was the most helpful. He was the sweetest. He was needed as the resident anesthesiologist. He was on the Search and Rescue team. He helped the elderly get through the winter by sharing the meat he hunted and the fish he'd caught. Even vegetables from his large garden were canned by many of the community members. He was always willing to help with repairs at their homes, going with Sam when they were told of an elderly person's home with a leaky roof or sagging floor. The two men often cut and split firewood and brought it to those who could no longer get it for themselves.

Sam caught her wrist and hauled her back onto the seat. "Stop, Stella. Take a deep breath. You aren't going to be any good to him flying off the handle that way. If you can't play your part, you'll have to stay here and I'll go alone. The killer can't know we're onto him. Denver believes he's out here with a friend to work on a project. They have to believe we came to work on *your* fears. The killer has no reason to think we're onto him. None. Unless you give us away, he'll believe it's sheer coincidence we chose today to come. And it makes sense. It's a beautiful day."

Stella forced air into her lungs. "It's just that it's Denver. He's family. He's practically an icon in the community." She looked past Denver's rig to the SUV parked in front of his. Her breath hissed out. "I should have known. Should have guessed." Maybe a small part of her had. "Jason Briggs. He's the one who issued the warning to Shabina to stay out of the forest." She looked at Sam's expressionless mask. "Why? Was that supposed to cast suspicion on his friends? Or was he tempted to go after Shabina?"

"I don't know, but we have to get moving. Let's get the gear and start walking. We want to make certain we're right behind them."

"You're right," Stella agreed, taking another deep breath to calm herself. "I don't want Denver on that rock before we get there. There can't be any accidents, especially as we walk up. He may change his plan midstream, like he did out at the lake because we interrupted him. We have to have a natural way to keep Denver safe."

They hiked the distance fast, the climbing gear in their backpacks along with water bottles and food as if they planned to spend the day. Stella hoped they wouldn't have to, but just in case, they were prepared to outlast the killer.

It was a beautiful day, the sun shining, throwing beams across the boulders as they approached. They heard the low laughter of the two men carried on the slight breeze. Sam moved slightly in front of her, his larger body partially blocking the two climbers' vision of her as they turned to face them.

Jason's smile faded, a scowl marring his good looks as he put his hands on his hips and turned fully to glare at them.

Denver's smile widened in greeting. "Sam. Stella. What are you doing all the way out here? Don't tell me Stella's going to climb this thing?"

Stella couldn't help herself, she launched herself into Denver's arms. He caught her in a hug. "You're going to brave this boulder?"

"It's not a boulder," she objected against his shoulder, not wanting to lift her head and look at Jason, afraid she'd shoot daggers at him.

"What are you doing here?" Jason demanded.

"Stella doesn't like heights," Sam said easily. "I'm going to belay her while she practices getting comfortable out here where no one is around. What are you doing here?"

Sam sounded cheery. Easygoing. As if nothing was wrong and he talked to serial killers every single day.

"I've been working on this project for months," Jason admitted. "I've been telling Denver about it and how slow it's been going for a while now. He offered to come out with me and belay me today. It will be so much easier without having to use a top rope."

Stella heard Jason as if from far away. She'd already taken a step away from Denver so she could look into Jason's face. She wanted to see his expression when he answered Sam. She did her best to process Jason's statement. To make it fit with the facts.

This couldn't be *his* project. It had to be *Denver's* project. Jason had to be the one to volunteer to belay Denver. None of this was making any sense. She looked up at the boulder and then again at Jason's face. Then to Sam. As always, his features were set in an expressionless mask. No help there at all.

Had she heard right? Again, she tried to twist Jason's statement around to fit with what she was certain were the facts, but no matter how many times she replayed the audio, it came out the same. This was Jason's project and Denver had volunteered to belay him. Which meant . . .

She turned back to her beloved friend, heart sinking, lashes lifting, and her eyes met his.

# CHAPTER NINETEEN

*Mommy, Daddy's doing the bad thing again.*

The camera lens focused on a dark room. The room appeared to be rectangular. Stella did her best within the narrow vision she had to take in as many details as she could, but it was dark. The only light came from what appeared to be a penlight that was being flashed around the room, and that was even shielded, as if the person holding the light feared it would be seen. She caught a quick glimpse of the edge of a crash pad. Just the tip, but she was certain it was a crash pad. The lens was already closing down. Just as it was, she saw the light flash across the pair of hiking boots in the corner. The lens snapped closed.

STELLA SAT UP, fighting her way out from under the covers, kicking at them, scissoring her legs in desperation to get blankets and sheets off, her breath coming in painful gasps. She leapt up, trying to get out from under the remnants of the nightmare, uncaring that she'd gone to bed in practically nothing and it was very cold this time of year. Sam was a furnace at night and he took any clothes off her anyway.

"Sweetheart."

Sam was in the chair across from the bed like always when she had her nightmares, but she didn't even look at him. Truthfully, she didn't even see him. She didn't notice the freezing floor under the bare soles of her feet, or that Bailey scrambled to a standing position in his crate. She just ran from the room, heart thundering wildly in her ears. The back of the house was dark and she hadn't thought to bring a light. She stood in front of the back door leading to her mudroom—the same room someone had tried to break into the night Bailey had been attacked.

"Stella. Talk to me." Sam came up behind her.

She stood in front of the door shivering, but not because of the cold. She was numb—unable to feel anything in that moment. She just stared at the closed door. She didn't want to turn on the overhead lights. If she did, and the killer was watching, he would know she was onto him. She bit her lip. She still couldn't bring herself to say his name. To let herself think it was him. Her friend. One of her best friends. Why? Why would he start killing? It didn't even make sense.

She put her hand on the doorknob and started to twist it open. Sam placed his palm above her head and leaned, preventing the heavy door from moving.

"Talk to me, Stella."

"You knew it was him, didn't you?" She was afraid it came out an accusation.

"I had no way of knowing, but I became suspicious when Bailey was stabbed four times so viciously and not killed. It took nerves to do what the attacker did. Nerves. Strength. Knowledge of anatomy. And then, it was a small thing, but Denver had suddenly taken an internship with the ME. He claimed he was restless. And because of your nightmares, Vienna pointed out the strange coincidence of the broken fingers to the sheriff and the ME. Denver lost interest after that. I think he wanted to be the one to point it out and get the glory. It nagged at me. He was already into so many things, so why go there? And then to just kind of drop it."

"You didn't say anything," she persisted.

"I had no real proof and I didn't want the killer to be Denver. I don't have many friends, Stella. Denver matters to me. So, no, I didn't know, but he had all the right abilities and he was in the right place at the right times."

He sighed again. "And then there were the times the watcher wasn't present. Vienna was exhausted the other day. She mentioned that there was an accident two nights in a row and the third night she'd just slept. I realized that if she was in surgery, they would need an anesthesiologist, and that meant Denver. If he was at the hospital, he couldn't be here. I checked. He was there. I checked back on the other days in town when you said no one had been watching, and again, out here, and he was at the hospital every single time."

"He came to the vet's the night Bailey was attacked."

"He came late, and none of us saw the condition of his arm," Sam pointed out.

"You never said anything to me." She held herself away from him, whispering, and this time it was an accusation. "Why not, Sam?"

"Yesterday, when we went out to the Twin Devils and Jason and Denver were climbing together, you thought at first that Jason was the killer, didn't you?" he countered, stepping closer. Not answering her. Sam. Her heart hurt for him. For both of them.

Stella could feel him radiating heat against her back. She nodded but didn't look at him. She kept her eyes on the door to the mudroom. Kept looking at Sam's hand, fingers splayed wide, holding the door closed. Pandora's box. If she opened it . . .

"Yes," she whispered. "Then Jason started talking about how he had been working on the project for months and Denver offered to belay him, and I looked at Denver. Into his eyes. I knew. He went out there to kill Jason. He was going to kill him and make it look as though Jason had gone out there to work his project alone with just a fixed rope. We got there and he didn't have his chance."

Sam very gently wrapped his palm around the nape of her neck. "You didn't want to talk to me about it last night."

He had left early in the evening for several hours, and when he came back, he hadn't said a word and she hadn't asked him any questions. She was terrified of what he might have done, but now, after her nightmare, she knew Denver was still alive.

"You were quiet all the way home, and every time I tried, you just shook your head. I had to give you your space to grieve, Stella."

His voice was so gentle. Too gentle. Too compassionate. She couldn't take it right then. She couldn't fall apart more than she already had. Sam was too important. Her Sam. She had to think clearly, carefully go over every move she made before she made it. She took a deep breath and turned to face him, deliberately turning her back to the mudroom door and pressing her weight against it.

She couldn't run through her house in a panic and Sam couldn't go into that room with her or see her sketches or talk about her nightmare. Not this one. He would take matters into his own hands, she knew he would. He would feel it was his responsibility to bring justice to Denver. He had already indicated he thought he should. But it was Denver, and he loved Denver whether he could say it out loud or not. She knew he was grieving just as she was.

"This is so terrible for both of us. For *all* of us. We're going to have to tell the others, Sam. I still don't know how we're going to tell them, but we have to. Jason could still be in danger."

"I talked him out of going there again for a little while," Sam assured her. "But that isn't going to save another climber from Denver retaliating. We have to talk about it, Stella, and we don't have time to wait. I need to know what spooked you tonight."

"It was a nightmare."

"I'm well aware it was a nightmare, sweetheart. I see you have them all the time."

"No." She looked away from him, unable to meet his eyes when she was lying. "It was just an ordinary nightmare, not a serial killer nightmare."

There was a long silence. She could feel his gaze on her face and she couldn't help squirming under the intensity. His fingers were very gentle as he cupped her chin and forced her head up until she found herself looking at him.

"I think we both are going to have to confess, sweetheart, because you are possibly the worst liar on the face of the planet and I don't like keeping anything from you, especially things you won't like."

She knew instantly what he'd done. "You went to see Denver."

"He's in the wind. We have to talk to Griffen, Stella. We have to put everyone on alert. If we don't, anyone he hurts, you know that's on us."

"I agree." She didn't want Sam hunting Denver. She took his hand and tugged, trying to get him to head back toward the bedroom.

Sam didn't budge. "What don't you want me to see in the mudroom?"

She sighed. "Let's go talk in the bedroom. I just panicked."

"Sweetheart. Don't make me resort to throwing around the L word and freak you out. Just tell me."

"He knew. Yesterday at the boulders, when I realized it wasn't Denver's project and I looked at him, there must have been something in the way I looked at him that made him realize I knew what he was planning. The nightmare showed a mudroom. Gear. But the last thing was hiking boots. I swear, Sam, they're my old hiking boots. I leave them in the corner of the mudroom. He's coming after me."

"Why didn't you want me to know?" He stroked his hand down her hair.

"I don't want you to hunt him. He's your friend. I didn't want that for you anyway, but it seems so much worse now. I knew if you thought he was coming after me, that nothing would stop you from hunting him."

His hands framed her face, one thumb stroking a caress down her skin. "Nothing was ever going to stop me, Stella. He has to be stopped. But you're right. The fact that he would try to kill you makes him even more of a priority. We have to warn all of your friends and the sheriff."

"Denver could live off the land indefinitely. He could be anywhere. He hunts, fishes, he knows every cave and old hunting cabin on properties most people have forgotten," Stella said.

"He could very well be staying on this property, in the fishing camp, some of the older cabins," Sam ventured. "The ones we had designated to fix up. Denver certainly knows about them. He went with me several times when I was working on the floors. He even helped me with the sinks and electricity."

"I don't want Sonny or Patrick anywhere near those cabins," Stella said hastily.

"If Denver had taken off, that would be one thing," Sam said, "but the fact that you had that nightmare, and you know he's coming after you, means he's sticking around here. He really is obsessed with you, Stella." There was a note of worry in his voice.

"He doesn't know about me, though," she whispered. "He still has no idea that I was that little girl who saw serial killers in my dreams. If we alert him, we take the chance of him getting away. Do we trust Griffen and his boss, Paul Rafferty, to not go immediately to the FBI with this? We can't, but we have to tell them something so they warn everyone."

Sam followed her down the hall to the bedroom. "Have to get those privacy screens up on the windows. We special ordered them and I paid a fortune to ensure they got here fast."

"You did?"

"I think in terms of snipers, *Satine.*"

She slipped back into bed and reached for her sketchpad and journal. She definitely didn't have the feeling Denver was watching. If he was out there, he wasn't close. He had a healthy respect for Sam and wasn't taking any chances.

"Since Denver doesn't know about your abilities, we can set a trap for him. In the meantime, I will be hunting him. I'm not going to lie to you about that, sweetheart. I want your girls to know. Shabina can't be running around in the forest for a while."

"They're going to be so upset."

"I know they will," Sam agreed. "I'm going to ask for a meeting with Griffen and Paul first thing in the morning. I'm not going to say anything about your nightmares, but I am going to say that we've been worried about Denver and he's said things that have led us to believe he's unstable and possibly committing these crimes."

Stella sighed. She knew there was no getting around talking with law enforcement. It had to be done. They had no proof, but Griffen would vouch for them with his boss. The ME had already expressed her concern to the sheriff once. Perhaps Sam was right and talking about her nightmares would just muddy the waters.

"What can they do? They can't accuse Denver, there's no proof of any crime."

"The sheriff's office can put a missing person's report out on Denver and spin it any way they see fit, that he's mentally unstable and not to approach him, but let law enforcement know immediately. Something along those lines."

Stella was already sketching the details the lens of the camera had shown her. The glimpse of the mudroom and what contents she could make out. She drew each item she saw with meticulous care, including corners of the cabinet, the flooring and her hiking boots.

"I hate this for you, Stella," Sam said softly. He reached down and wiped just under her eye as a tear dropped on the sketchpad.

"It's just as bad for you, Sam," she whispered, aching for all of them.

THERE WAS A stunned silence. Stella was the only one standing in Shabina's beautiful great room with its high ceiling and gorgeous stone fireplace.

Vienna's hand went to her throat protectively. "That can't be, Stella. There has to be a mistake. You've made a terrible mistake. Denver is . . ."

"Family," Harlow finished for her. "One of us. Part of us."

"He saves lives," Vienna added. "Do you know how many lives

he's saved? I've seen him fight for people. Risk his own life over and over to save a complete stranger. No, you're wrong, you have to be wrong."

Silence fell on the room again. A kind of hopeless despair as each of them tried to process what Stella had told them.

"You're certain he's going to try to kill you next?" Raine asked eventually.

"I haven't seen the victim," Stella admitted. "But it's definitely my mudroom. Those were my hiking boots. He could be after Sam. Maybe both of us. That seems more likely. I'll know more tonight. Sam went to meet with Griffen and Paul Rafferty."

"Have you talked to Jason to make certain Denver doesn't circle around and go after him again?" Shabina asked. "If Denver is ill enough to want to kill you and Sam, then he would have no problem carrying out his original plan to kill Jason."

"Sam warned him. I don't know what he said, but yes, he should know to be cautious, although most people in Knightly are going to have a difficult time believing anything is wrong with Denver," Stella said.

"Are you absolutely positive, Stella?" Zahra asked.

"Unfortunately, there's no question. He's in hiding. He hasn't left the area, and he's definitely hunting me. Or Sam and me." She looked down at her hands. "I don't know why. We spent the day out at the boulders with them. Sam did most of the talking with Denver. I was on the rock. I couldn't talk."

"How did Denver know you were aware he was going to kill Jason?" Raine asked in her quiet way. She sat beside Vienna, keeping one hand on her friend's knee in sympathy.

"When Jason said he had been working on the project for months and Denver had offered to belay him, I kept trying to turn it around, but that didn't work. I remember this horrible chill went down my spine and I looked up at Denver. I must have looked at him with accusing eyes. With knowledge. He looked back at me. He was smiling. The smile faded and I saw him. The killer. He saw me. It was just for a moment and then he was Denver again. I turned to Sam and buried my face in his chest and he wrapped his arms around me, and I just stayed that way until I could get control."

"He must wonder how you knew," Raine mused.

"A while back, Denver told me Sam was a ghost. We were at the Grill before all this happened and Denver told me his father and uncle had died and he'd inherited a lot of money. He also told me Sam was a ghost and not to get involved with him because it was too dangerous. He thinks Sam knows everything. Denver would come to my property all the time and watch us. Or me. I'm not certain which. Maybe Sam. He said men like Sam aren't seen. He was very intrigued by him. Sam thought Denver was fixated on me, but I'm beginning to be afraid he was fixated on Sam. Not in a sexual way, but in the way of pitting his skills against Sam's."

She turned to face Raine. "He was really the only friend Sam let close to him, and that was mainly because Denver pushed the friendship. You know how Denver is. He just would invite himself along or persist in inviting you. He did that with Sam. Showed him the fishing spots. The best hunting areas. Would go help when Sam had too much work. Denver would talk. Sam rarely talked, but he was a good listener and he liked Denver."

"Everyone likes Denver," Harlow said.

"What exactly did he say to you about Sam being a ghost?" Raine asked. "Can you remember his wording? You asked me about it, but I don't recall what you told me Denver said."

"He'd been drinking pretty heavily. He never drinks very

much. I'd been drinking too. That's when he started telling me about his father and uncle and how they were dead. He'd had a really ugly childhood. He never talked about his past so I felt really privileged that he opened up about it to me. I could also tell he was a little bitter. Then he said something about Sam and me having a relationship. That we never danced more than one dance and Sam had his hands all over me. I was kind of upset that I'd been drinking so much I didn't get the full benefit of feeling Sam's hands all over me, so I texted him and asked."

"You texted Sam and asked him if he had his hands all over you?" Harlow echoed, laughter bubbling up in spite of the seriousness of the conversation.

"I told you I had too much to drink," Stella defended.

"Keep going," Raine insisted.

"Yes, but start with what Sam said," Zahra suggested.

Stella wasn't sharing that. "That is not pertinent."

"I'll bet it's not," Zahra muttered.

"I reminded Denver that he was Sam's friend and he said no one was really friends with a ghost and that was what Sam was."

Raine's eyebrows drew together. "He actually said no one was really friends with a ghost and that was what Sam was? You're certain?" There was speculation in her voice.

Stella nodded. "Yes, because I said Sam was real flesh and blood. That he worked his ass off at the resort and on Search and Rescue, that Denver was the one who told me he did. Then he started talking about the military again."

"Wait." Raine stopped her. "Again? He'd been talking about the military?"

"Earlier, when he was talking about his life, he said even though his family was wealthy, he didn't touch their money. He put himself through school by going into the military. That was how he became an anesthesiologist. He was an officer in the Army and became a doctor. He said men like Sam were necessary and were called in when all else failed."

Stella went over to the side table Shabina had set up with water bottles and the kettle with hot water, mainly for Zahra, and the baked goods. She took a bottle of cold water and drank from it, needing the break.

"Stella, I know this is difficult," Raine said. "I wouldn't keep harping on this conversation if I didn't think it was important. Can you tell me anything else he said regarding Sam being a ghost?"

Stella frowned, trying to remember. "Something about sometimes seeing them like shadows, hunting like wolves, but alone, always silent. I remember that because it stuck with me. Sam does kind of stay in the shadows and he is very quiet. He's difficult to spot, so that resonated with me. Denver said you didn't see ghosts most of the time, you just felt them. They got you out of a bad situation. I thought that was a good thing and said so."

Her other friends were staring at her wide-eyed, as if what Denver said about Sam was gospel. She hoped Raine had a reason, a direction she was taking this.

"I need to know what he said about his family. You said he was upset, Stella. Tell me what he said."

Stella detested going over Denver's past with everyone in detail. In a way, as silly as it sounded, it felt like a betrayal. He'd never shared his secrets before and she had felt honored that he had, even though they both had been drinking.

"I wouldn't ask you if it didn't matter," Raine said. "It isn't idle curiosity. If I understand Denver's state of mind, it's possible I can figure out what his endgame is."

Stella was well aware of how Raine's mind worked. She fit

pieces of puzzles together very fast. The others were all watching her closely. Even the dogs seemed to be on alert. She took another drink of water to steady herself.

"He said lawyers had called him with news a week or so earlier that his father and his uncle Vern had shot each other and bled out before anyone could get to them, and he was still processing. Denver said it was so stupid, but inevitable. He tried to act like it didn't matter or affect him, but his hands were shaking pretty badly. His mother died while he was in the military so he said he inherited the entire estate. The implication was that his inheritance was large."

"Give me a few minutes," Raine said, and opened her computer, typing fast.

Vienna stood up, wrapping her arms around herself. "I don't even know what to think. Denver is about the nicest human being on the face of the earth. I can't imagine him flinging random strangers off Mount Whitney or drowning James Marley." She rubbed her hands up and down her arms. "No matter how hard I try to make myself believe he could have done those things, I just can't."

"I'm the same way," Stella said. "With the exception of that one moment when I looked into his eyes. I saw someone else. He looked back at me and it wasn't my Denver. Our Denver. It was someone else altogether. I don't know how to explain it."

"If Denver came from all that money, why would he need to be here?" Zahra asked.

Harlow raised an eyebrow. "Just because a person comes from money doesn't mean bad things can't happen in their families, Zahra, you know that. Didn't you hear what Stella said? He didn't want them to pay for his medical training. He joined the military in order to be able to become a doctor."

"Denver had a horrific background," Raine said. "I'm in his medical records. His father and uncle should have been prosecuted a million times over. Another interesting fact is the uncle was suspected of torturing and killing three young women on three separate occasions, but he ended up having an ironclad alibi in each case. The reason he was suspected was because his nephew reported he saw his uncle drag one of the women into his vehicle. The second time his nephew reported he saw his uncle with the missing woman in a warehouse and she was tied up. The third time he claimed the uncle had another missing woman in a basement of an abandoned building."

"Did the cops begin to think Denver was the one killing the women?" Shabina asked.

"At the time he was too young. But they stopped believing him. Get this, Denver had his finger broken multiple times and reset when he was just a child, corresponding to when he told the police about the young women he saw with his uncle," Raine reported.

"How many women were killed?" Stella asked.

"I'm doing a search," Raine said. "If I were to come to a conclusion, I would say the father and uncle were both killing, trading off, to give each other alibis. They had Denver watch, maybe forced him to participate, from the time he was a little child. They were monsters."

Stella turned away from the others and walked over to the window. She wanted to go home and just close herself in her house with Bailey and Sam and pretend none of this was happening. She thought her childhood had been monstrous. Denver had truly lived through a destructive, hideous childhood, and now there was no way out for him.

"He came here for peace, so they couldn't get to him," she whispered. "He didn't ever want to be like them."

"The police were suspicious of his father and uncle many times in various disappearances of women over the years," Raine said, "but they never could get enough proof to build a case." She closed her computer. "What else did Denver say about Sam being a ghost, Stella?"

Stella clenched her teeth for a moment, biting back a retort that Sam wasn't a ghost. He was a flesh-and-blood man with feelings. Denver had been his friend as well.

"He said ghosts were used for other tasks outside the military and they usually didn't last long, they died young. He said if they did break free, they were hunted down because they were too big of a security risk, they knew too much and the government wanted them dead."

"Which would imply that Sam, because he's alive, is too good to get caught even by any other ghost hunting him," Raine said.

"I guess so," Stella agreed, not knowing how that helped them at all.

"You need to repeat this entire conversation to Sam."

MOMMY, DADDY'S DOING *the bad thing again.*

Glass shattered in the windowpane, bursting inward, and then, as a gloved hand appeared, smashing fast and efficiently, the shards fell like rain onto the floor of the mudroom. He knew exactly where the door lock was and had it open in seconds, uncaring of the blaring alarm. Reaching back outside, onto the porch, Denver dragged his hostage into the mudroom and shoved her so hard she fell onto the floor. Unable to catch herself with her hands tied behind her back, Vienna's face hit the corner of the built-in cabinet and she gave a little cry.

Denver crouched down beside her, sweeping her hair aside to examine her cheek. He seemed gentle with her, but he didn't get her up. Instead, he put the edge of his knife to her throat and waited. She was the bait to lure Stella into the mudroom, otherwise there was no way Stella was going to come in. He'd already texted Stella, and sure enough, she opened the door very slowly, looking frightened, putting her head in to observe first. He didn't say anything, just touched the razor-sharp blade to Vienna's throat and let a line of ruby-red drops of blood appear. Stella stepped inside just as he'd instructed, despite Vienna's cries of warning.

"Denver, what are you doing? Honey, you have to stop." Stella put one hand out to plead with him.

Denver didn't look at her face. He didn't wait. He was on her in seconds, sweeping her legs out from under her, taking her down beside Vienna, his knife already stabbing. Over and over, twisting and raking. Twenty, thirty times. Not once did he look at her face or the trails of blood. The pools. He blocked the sound of her screams. He didn't feel the familiar elation or the rush of euphoria. He just kept stabbing on automatic.

One minute. Two. Three was all he had. Then he was up. He lifted Vienna's head up by her hair and slashed across her throat with the knife, cutting deep, dropping her casually as he went on out, leaving the mudroom walls splattered with red and the floor pooled with it. The lens of the camera closed abruptly, everything going to black.

Four nightmares later, it was very clear to Stella that Denver was hunting her, not Sam.

Stella leaned back against Sam's chest, looking out over the lake, watching the sun come up. They stood together on the private pier, the various shades of gold and crimson pouring across the surface of the water. There was little wind to ruffle the water. It appeared like glass, with the various shades of colors sparkling like gemstones. No matter what time of year, the view of the lake never failed to move her.

Sam's arms felt like her own place of safety, yet he hadn't been there when Denver had managed to get into the mudroom. They might know what Denver planned and how he planned to do it, thanks to her nightmares, but they were no closer to finding him. The sheriff's office had put out a missing persons report on him, stating there was concern for his mental health and not to approach but to call the sheriff's office if he was spotted. No one had seen him.

Sam had gone to every one of Denver's favorite hunting and fishing camps, every cave he had talked about, but he hadn't found tracks. Denver was too familiar with the forest, the private properties where most owners only came up at certain times of the year. He could be anywhere.

There was such beauty and a sense of calm and peace just looking out over the lake, watching the sun rise. Standing with Sam's arms around her allowed Stella to breathe when she felt as if she'd been unable to draw in air for hours.

Sam nuzzled the top of her head with his chin. "You feeling better, sweetheart?"

She'd cried for hours—or it had seemed as if she had. Until there were no tears left. Her eyes and face felt swollen, but the cool morning air was helping to make her feel refreshed again. Sam had made the suggestion that they walk out onto the private pier and watch the sun come up. He hadn't flinched away from her red, splotchy face. He'd held her hand and helped her over the rocks as they made their way to the private dock and out to the end of it.

She'd sketched every detail of the nightmare, journaled it and then told him everything she could think of, all the while sobbing for their lost friend who wanted to kill her and Vienna. Sam was Sam, and he just let her grieve. Then he'd held her while he studied the sketches, read her journal and listened to her account, asking her a question every now and then in between handing her tissues. After, he told her to get dressed in warm clothes, that they'd watch the sun come up over the lake and drink coffee. She wasn't about to turn that offer down.

"I'm going to take you into town, Stella. You and Bailey both. I want you to stay with Shabina until I come for you. I've asked her to have all of you stay there, Raine, Harlow, Zahra and Vienna as well."

She turned her head to look over her shoulder at him. He was back to inscrutable. "Why Shabina's?"

"She has the best security. I know you'll be safe there," Sam said. "And just in case, to err on the side of caution, I've asked a few of my friends to help out. They'll be outside on her grounds, patrolling. No one will get in or out. That means they won't be bribed by Shabina's baked goods or seduced by any of your friends' charms. They're professionals."

"Oh my God, Sam, you know where he is, don't you?" She stepped away from him, forcing him to drop his arms so she could turn around and face him. "You do. You know where he is. You plan on killing him."

Sam didn't respond. He kept his gaze steady on hers.

Stella shook her head. "You can't. Sam, you can't. Call Griffen. Let Griffen arrest him."

"For what? You aren't thinking straight. Griffen can't arrest him. Denver hasn't done anything they can prove."

"Then we should go together. Talk him into a confession. Get it on tape or something. I don't care. You can't kill him. I want you to stay with me. If you do this, how can you stay here? You'll come to regret it and you'll want to move on."

"Why would I regret it? Sweetheart, listen to me," Sam said gently. "I know you're thinking in terms of protecting me, but think in terms of Denver being family. Being ours. What do you think Raine was trying to tell you? Denver knew he was deteriorating. He didn't want to be his father or uncle. *You* were always his last resort, Stella. He knew, ultimately, if he went after you, I would hunt him down and I would end him."

Stella shook her head, unable to speak past the terrible lump in her throat. "Sam, no."

"You said it yourself, there was no feeling of triumph, of power, when he was stabbing you in your nightmare. It was different from all the other times. He could barely look at you or Vienna. He killed both of you because in his sick mind it was the only way for him to get me to end this for him."

"You don't know that," she whispered.

"I do know he can't kill himself, but he's willing to pit his skills against mine. It's his game and he's made the rules. I have to know all of you are safe. He believes he can lure Vienna to him, but he can't. I've made certain of that. The moment you told me about the nightmare, I texted one of my friends and he collected Vienna and took her to Shabina's. He did remove her cell phone before he left her there." He sent her a faint grin. "Apparently, she was spitting mad. That girl has a bad temper."

"Where did all these friends come from all of a sudden?" Stella asked suspiciously, but it was really more to buy time. He'd never seemed to bother with friends, other than Denver.

"When I first became suspicious of Denver, I called a few of my friends who owed me favors and asked them to get out here fast if they could. I was fortunate in that they were between assignments and they came. They've just been waiting for me to give them the word on what they needed to do. Keeping Denver from getting to Vienna or any of your friends is number two on my priority list. Keeping him from getting to you is number one on that list."

"Keeping him from getting to you is number one on *my* list, Sam," Stella murmured. "I know you and Raine both think this is some well-thought-out plan by Denver to pit you against him, and that just makes it worse. He has a side to him that thinks he's intellectually superior. You know he does. All of us know it. That night at the Grill when he'd had too much to drink, when he was warning me about you being a ghost, he had that note in his voice."

"Meaning?"

"He was an officer, Sam. He came from a background of money. Whether or not he turned his back on that money, he still was raised with it. He was a doctor. He was always in a position of authority. Everyone looked up to him. He might be quiet and seem unassuming, but he was looked up to. He was used to a certain amount of deference, and he would have gotten it in the service just as he did here."

Sam didn't interrupt her. He never did. He waited to hear her out. He always did. Stella couldn't hide her fears for him. "Denver wasn't a very sexual man, Sam. He didn't date a lot of women. He would ask someone out now and again, but not really pursue them. But he liked being considered really good at everything. He was falsely modest about it. The first one to volunteer for the most dangerous climbs when it came to the rescues, because he could do them. He shared the meat he could with the elderly. The fish. Everything he did, he was good at. Everyone in town liked him and sang his praises. He was a big deal in Knightly. And then you came along."

Stella's gaze moved over Sam's beloved face. She didn't know which of them was right, but no matter who it was, Denver wasn't going to go peacefully. She did know that much.

"He was an officer and he thought his men looked up to him and yet he couldn't get them out of a tough situation. Along comes a single man—someone they referred to as a ghost, someone with no rank or real education, in his eyes. His men admired that man because he single-handedly saved them. How do you think Denver would really feel no matter what lip service he would pay?"

Sam nodded slowly. "That's a good question, Stella."

"And here, when he's the center of attention, no matter how low-key he is, how do you think he really feels, Sam, when you're good at everything you do, and you might very well be one of the ghosts who stole his thunder back in the day? You drifted into his town, a dirtbag, one of the ones who just comes to climb and then moves on, but you didn't move on. You stayed and you're good at everything, and even though you're low-key, everyone takes notice. Even Bale and his crew back down around you."

He leaned down and brushed a kiss over her trembling lips. "I see where you're going, sweetheart, and in the end, it doesn't matter what kind of trap Denver is setting. It only matters that I find him. I've got my friend Rafe waiting in your rig to take you and Bailey to Shabina's. The other women will all be there. I'm walking you back to the house, you're going to pack a bag and I'll walk you to the 4Runner."

"Sam." She wondered if he'd already thought of every one of her points. Probably.

"We're not arguing about this. You've done your part, you have to let me do mine."

Stella wanted to argue, but she didn't see any other solution, and she wasn't the type of woman to argue for argument's sake. She couldn't help Sam, and what he was doing was his field of expertise. He obviously had a plan and she didn't. She could only hope he was as good as he seemed to be.

# CHAPTER TWENTY

Denver stood up slowly in the middle of his camp. It was impossible to find him. He had avoided every single place he had ever been. He didn't go near a hunting, fishing or empty cabin. He'd covered his rig with branches. The paint was special, impossible to see the way it blended into the leaves and brush even from the air, especially when concealed the way he'd done. He hadn't used a campfire or anything that might draw attention to his position. His clothes blended into the brush around him. Still . . . his gut told him he wasn't alone.

He put his hand on the hunting knife in the scabbard at his side. He was more than good with a knife. Very carefully, and very slowly, so as not to draw attention to himself when he was hidden in the circle of brush, he looked around. He had excellent vision. Far better than most people, and also good hearing. The insects were still droning on and on. There had been no break in their incessant noise. Squirrels ran up a tree, fighting with one another, trying to get a few last nuts for storage for winter. Birds flitted from tree to tree. Life went on in the forest even as the needles and leaves fell to the ground in preparation for the coming season.

A frisson of awareness went down his spine. A chill. He'd never had that before. Was it actually fear? He didn't feel fear. He felt . . . excitement. He'd entered a game. This was his game. He didn't feel fear. Still his legs shook. There was a tremor in his hands. He didn't even know why. If all around him the lizards slid through the rotting vegetation and the insects droned without breaking even for a split second, then nothing was stalking him. Why did he feel as though he had a target centered right between his shoulder blades? Or between his eyes? Or over his heart? Each spot itched for a moment and then that itch moved to his throat. He was going crazy. He refused to accept that diagnosis.

Swearing under his breath, he caught up his two large water bottles and moved to the small entrance of his camp. He had only to wait a couple of hours before he put his plan into action. Right now, he needed to get fresh water. It was the only thing he hadn't managed to get enough of, but he'd set up camp near the top of the tall waterfall running over rocks. The water fell a good forty feet to a churning pool below. He could purify the water easily.

Denver stepped out of the tight circle of brush he'd created using actual plants, and made his way along the deer trail to the falls. It wasn't far to go and he was careful to walk lightly, not brushing leaves or snapping off twigs to show his passing along the way. The sound of the water rushing over the rocks was loud as he approached the waterfall, drowning out his ability to hear anyone sneaking up on him. He had to rely on his warning system and his gut.

Just like the deer he hunted, before he stepped out of the heavy brush he stopped again and sniffed the air, head up, doing his best to catch the scent of any enemy hunting him. The insects and birds continued their chatter. The wind touched his face and there was nothing to indicate an adversary was close, yet his hands had gone cold. Clammy even. His heart accelerated until it was pounding, making his mouth dry.

Denver stood at the mouth of the deer trail, peering out into the open like a wild animal, frozen with genuine fear for the first time in his life. He didn't know why. There was nothing there. It was broad daylight. The sun was shining on the water. Birds were actually singing. He tried to draw in air, but his lungs had seized, and terror clawed at his gut until he was light-headed and feeling faint.

He stood there for several minutes, fighting for control. No myth was going to beat him. He wouldn't allow that to happen. This was his game. His rules. He wouldn't lose. He was superior. He repeated his mantra, the words that had saved him so many times in his life. After a few more minutes he managed to take several deep breaths, pushing the fear and dread away and gaining back control.

Holding out his hand, he waited until it wasn't shaking before he smiled, showing his perfect, white teeth. "If you're out there, Sam, looking for me, you don't scare me. You can't possibly find me. The forest is too big and I'm too good at what I do. I'll take away the one thing in this world that matters to you and we'll see how good you are when you're thrown off your game."

He didn't whisper. There was no need. None. He was alone and he knew he was. He was absolutely certain of it. He had left no tracks. He had outsmarted anyone trying to figure out where he would go. The Inyo National Forest was far too large for anyone to find him. He had skills beyond even the rangers who had worked there for several years. He'd quietly gone about studying the area through hunting, fishing and his search-and-rescue efforts. He'd hiked and camped and climbed. He was familiar with most of the trails. He had waited for this time and prepared for it.

How Stella ever realized his intent, he would never know. That was the most shocking, and exhilarating and depressing, moment of his life, when he stared into her eyes and realized she knew. Someone *saw* him. The real man. All of him. That moment was one he took out over and over and examined from every angle. How had she known? What had tipped her off? He savored that recognition even as he despised it.

Had it been Sam? Had he realized what Denver was and told Stella? No, she'd been so happy to see him. That greeting had been genuine. Something he'd said or Jason had said had been the catalyst, but that would mean she knew about the others, and that just didn't make sense. Had she been hunting him since the fiasco at the lake when he'd nearly killed Sam? He would probably never know.

Once more filled with confidence, he waded into the fast-moving water. Anchored by the rocks, he took one look at the view, just the way he always did before he filled his two bottles. Standing right on top of the powerful waterfall, high above the trees and the creatures making their home there, he always felt invincible.

He'd been drawn to this spot for a reason. It was his place of power. His center. He felt the wind on his face, felt it tug playfully at his clothing while it swirled in eddies over the water running toward the rocks just before it disappeared over the edge to make the long drop.

He had the bottles around his neck on a cord. He unscrewed the lid to the first bottle and bent to dip it into the fast-running water off the opposite side of the rock where it would normally drop into space to descend. The bottle filled quickly and he straightened to screw on the lid tight and unscrew the other lid.

The wind seemed to pick up, blowing harder, pushing against him, tugging at his shirt and retreating only to rush back, teasing at the hairs on his neck. As he bent once more to fill the water bottle, the wind whispered to him, a low, familiar voice. One that was always gentle. Never raised. *The ghost found you.*

Then he was falling. Headfirst. Tumbling. Out of control. His body hitting something hard over and over. The pain was excruciating. Freezing water soaked him as he hit jagged rocks sticking out of the cliff on his way down, his back, his legs, his head, his shoulders. He knew bones broke, smashed, as he struck those rocks, and then he landed hard on the jagged mass of rocks sticking up in the river. The current pulled at him immediately. He had landed on his side, driving his ribs into his lung. He felt the burst of his lung collapsing and then it was nearly impossible to breathe. But after hitting on his side, his body had been flung to a second mass of rocks by the force of the water, and one pierced his back low, just as surely as a dagger would have.

Denver lay gasping for air on the top of the rocks, desperately trying to see without turning his head. That way lay even more pain. If he moved from the rock, the current would surely get him, but he couldn't stay there, he would die. His back was broken in several places. He had a head injury. His left arm was broken. Both legs. His ribs were caved in and one lung was collapsed. That wasn't the worst of it. He had somehow, when he landed, punctured his kidney. He was bleeding and it was severe.

He needed medical attention immediately. He was a doctor and he knew for certain he didn't have long, not with his injuries. He had to stay right there, with the rock in his body, because if he lifted himself off it, he would bleed out very fast. The rushing water was trying to force him off the rock, and each push at his body was pure agony.

He looked up at the sky. The sun was bright and he had to squint. A shadow fell across him and his heart leapt. Someone was there. On the bank not more than a foot or so away. They could help. He forced his head to turn a scant inch in spite of the pain. He blinked to clear his blurry vision.

Sam was crouched there, looking at him dispassionately, as if Denver was nothing, less than an insect crawling on the ground. There was no expression on his face. All along, even though he'd told Stella Sam was a ghost, Denver hadn't believed it.

"Ghost," he croaked, or tried to. He could barely breathe, let alone talk.

"You got a few things wrong, Denver, when you were warning Stella away from me. The government doesn't hunt down and kill us. We're too valuable to them. They like us around so we can do jobs for them when they need them done. Did you really think I wouldn't recognize a sociopath? Stupid move making a decision to go after my woman."

He couldn't possibly know. No one knew. "How?" He coughed up blood. That wasn't a good sign, and every movement hurt.

Sam stood up. "It doesn't matter."

"She'll know you did this," he choked out.

"I don't lie to her. In any case, the world is going to know you for what you are. You left behind a detailed account of your superiority—encrypted, of course—on your computer. The world and all your friends need to know how you planned in such detail to be a far better killer than your father and uncle, and you had set the stage so carefully, unlike them."

Horrified, Denver tried to protest. He would never make such a mistake. Only bubbles of blood and spittle came out of his mouth and trickled down his chin. Shadows slid over him and he looked up at the sky and could only see the blurred images of circling birds, high overhead. Terror mixed with agony.

He coughed again and more blood spewed out. He blinked. Sam wasn't there. His heart nearly exploded. He despised Sam, but the man couldn't leave him there to die alone. Had he even been there? Had his mind played tricks on him? No one could have known what he'd planned. He'd been so careful. Taken years to perfect his plans. Found the perfect cover. Everything was going dark and the cough grew worse. He couldn't get any air and he was choking. Where was Sam?

STELLA SAT ON the end of the pier staring out over the icy, sapphire-colored water, waiting for the sun to rise just as she had every morning for the past week. Seven days Sam had been gone, doing only heaven knew what as payment for favors owed to someone she didn't want to think about. The promise of snow was in the early morning air. It wasn't that far off now. She'd handled snow alone many times over the years and she could do it again. She just needed to know Sam was safe. Unfortunately, when he was in the field somewhere, he couldn't text her and her messages didn't go to the phone he carried with him—for her safety, not his. At least that was what he'd told her before he left.

The mountain rivers feeding Sunrise Lake were already dumping water into the lake fed by the storms in the mountains. The wind tugged at the few stubborn leaves remaining on the trees overlooking the pier, determined to drag them onto the planks with the rest of the golden and red vegetation.

Waves lapped at the shore and rocks as well as the pier supports, creating a kind of song. She'd always loved listening to the early morning insects, birds and frogs as they called to one another, along with the sound of the water in the background. It always brought peace to her chaotic mind.

She hadn't slept very well in the last week without Sam, and sitting on the pier, watching the sun come up, helped lessen the strain of fearing for him. Bailey curled close to her, the way he always had, as if nothing had happened to him and he hadn't endured stab wounds and stitches just a few short weeks earlier.

A hand gripped her shoulder without warning and she nearly threw herself off the pier, but the arm locking around her waist prevented her from going off the edge. She recognized Sam's touch. Bailey didn't look up but he wagged his short tail.

Not daring to breathe, she turned her head to look over her shoulder at the man crouching behind her. *Sam*, she tried to say, but no actual sound came out.

He looked the way he always did—tough, angles and planes, arctic-cold eyes that warmed for her and that bluish jaw that she found terribly attractive. She blinked rapidly to keep tears from her eyes. She cleared her throat several times to remove the large lump threatening to choke her. "You're back."

"I'm back, *Satine*."

"It was a long week."

"It was."

He sat down, sliding his long legs around her, giving her his chest to rest against. Dropping his chin on her shoulder, he locked his arms around her waist. "We don't need any more excitement around here for a long time, woman."

She kept her gaze on the lake. The sun was beginning to rise, spilling colors over the water. Today, due to the mist from the breath of snow, the colors were shades of blues and lavenders and purples. It happened rarely, but when it did, the phenomenon was beyond beautiful. Stella had captured the misty rise of the sun on film, but she'd never been able to paint it the way it really looked because the painting didn't seem real enough.

"As it turned out, *man*, *I* was not the reason for the excitement. That was you. In any case, talk has died down in Knightly. I stopped going into town because I didn't want to talk about serial killers anymore. I think everyone who knew Denver feels that way." She kept her gaze on the sun rising slowly into the sky. The higher it went, the wider the blues and purples spread across the lake's surface. "Are you going to have to leave again?"

He nuzzled her hair off her neck with his chin and then kissed her right over her pulse. "No, it was a one-time payback. I asked my former handler for a pretty big favor and in return he asked me to take care of a little problem for him. It took a little longer than I expected, but it's over and I won't have to go back for any reason."

She dropped one of her hands over his. "It wasn't a little job, or one of his other men would have taken care of it already."

"That's true, Stella, but it's over now, and I'm not going back."

She was silent, watching the colors expand over the surface of the lake. "You don't get to trade your life for mine, Sam. Essentially, that was what you were doing. By trading a favor like that, you knew what they were going to ask of you. It was already dangerous enough hunting Denver."

Sam rubbed his chin on top of her head, the silk of her hair catching in his seven-day growth. "Sweetheart, I'd trade my life for yours every time. Every single time, Stella, so we're going to keep the drama around here to a minimum."

She loved Sam. She had to take him the way he was. She

tipped her head back and gave him a half smile. "You're the one with the father wanting to come to holiday dinner and bring his new girlfriend. Dinner is at Shabina's. She said they could come if you gave the okay. He said three, because he needs his own bodyguard. Shabina's security wasn't enough for him. That's considered drama, isn't it?"

He heaved an exaggerated sigh. "That's considered being a male diva. Believe me, Stella, if he moves here, you haven't seen anything."

"Maybe having him come to dinner will be a good thing since Denver won't be with us this year. He can help get us through this first year," she ventured.

"Oh, he'll definitely provide the entertainment. He'll boss everyone and make certain everyone's attention is entirely centered on him. And his new lady? Once he gets wind of Shabina's cooking, he might toss his new woman over on the spot and propose."

Stella laughed, happy with the sun rising over her lake and her friends once again planning a dinner with or without Sam's father. She thought dinner with his father sounded like a lot of fun though.